Guardians of the Time Stream

Book One

The Blue Lotus Society

By

Michelle L. Levigne

www.YeOldeDragonBooks.com

Ye Olde Dragon Books
P.O. Box 30802
Middleburg Hts., OH 44130

www.YeOldeDragonBooks.com

2OldeDragons@gmail.com

Copyright © 2014 by Michelle L. Levigne

ISBN 13: 978-1-961129-12-2

Published in the United States of America
Publication Date: September 15, 2023

Cover Art © Copyright 2023 Ye Olde Dragon Books

Chapter One

1877
Washington, DC

When did "quiet" become "too quiet"?

"Some company would be nice. Would it be too much trouble, Charles," Ess Fremont murmured, squinting at the door on the far side of the pool of moonlight, "to come take your shift early for a change?"

She adjusted her position, perched in the "V" of the warehouse rafters, and turned to look down the length of the building, at the other doors. This dratted warehouse had far too many doors for her peace of mind. The moonlight through the skylight cargo entrance made her guard duties trickier, because she had to keep adjusting her vision from dark to light.

As warehouses went, Ess considered this one of the better, cleaner ones to have made her acquaintance. Other than the crates chained to the floor to protect the artifacts shipped from Egypt, it nearly echoed with emptiness. That made her job easier — who could sneak up on the pile of crates through all that moonlight? The warehouse was relatively clean, recently built to house the flood of exhibits coming to fill the newest buildings of the Smithsonian Institution. Even taking that into consideration, the rafters where she perched on watch were exceptional. Ess considered herself a connoisseur of rafters in her four-year career among the Pinkertons.

She glanced down at the crates on the flagstone floor of the warehouse, then sat back into the semi-comfortable cradle tucked up against the roof. A blur of white among the shadows caught her gaze. She silently growled at herself and tugged her jacket sleeve down over her shirt cuff. Why had she worn a white shirt under her jacket for a nighttime job? Then again, when she walked into that clothier shop to buy a suit for her non-existent younger brother, she couldn't say to make the shirt dark blue or even black. The upper crust sort of woman she pretended to be for this job wouldn't want anything but a white shirt of the best linen. She hadn't known she would take watch in a warehouse before the team arrived in Washington, otherwise she would have brought her own boy clothes, more suitable to nighttime work.

This exhibition of Egyptian artifacts would be on display for two weeks, after a major opening celebration attended by three-quarters of Washington's society. After tomorrow night's opening, this assignment would be a cakewalk. Every night, Ess would be on alternating guard with four other Pinkertons — she, the only woman. Guard duty was easy. She relished silent watch, perched high above the stone floor, compared to what awaited her tomorrow night. The grand opening party might be the worst part of the duty, but she would not just endure, she would triumph. However, if Allistair Fitch, the smug, too-smart-for-his-own-good dandy leading the team, gave her a dress she couldn't breathe in, she swore she would make sure *he* wore it before the team left for Chicago. The man had positively glowed with anticipation, when he returned from the meeting with the leaders of the agency, and gave them the roles they would play. Ess would be dressed to the nines, tasked to speak with authority and expertise on the history and culture of Ancient Egypt. She needed to impress and distract the intelligentsia, political powerbrokers, and fashionable upper crust of the nation. The rest of her team would study the attendees and make sure the exhibition hall was as secure as the city's police force and the Smithsonian's own security team promised it would be.

Ess shivered, wondering how long the heads of the Pinkerton Agency knew about her family's heritage, rooted deep in archeological studies. She knew Horace, her mentor, hadn't told them she had been raised reading hieroglyphics and cuneiform before she could read English. It only made sense that they would choose her to pose as a scholar and historical expert, because it wouldn't be a pose. But *who* had told them she could handle the job in the first place?

That question, like so many others, was best left to be asked once the traveling exhibition, sponsored by the British Museum and the Cairo Museum, had reached its final stop in San Francisco and agents of the British throne and the British Museum resumed custody of the crates of artifacts. That was just the way it was done among the Pinkertons, Horace had warned her when he recruited her. *Do your job, don't ask questions, girl, and ignore the mush-for-brains who think women don't have brains or the guts to fire a gun. When you get your bonus pay for a job well done and the big guns praise you, then you can ask your questions. But not before then.*

For now, Ess happily perched high above the floor, where she had a good view of the many crates, the doors, and the skylight where airships regularly let down their cargo in enormous nets. The crates were wrapped in chains to the point of vanishing under all that iron, chained together, and padlocked to enormous iron staples thrust into the stone floor.

A dark shadow seeped into the foggy white moonlight that spilled over the pile of crates. Ess rested her hand on the lovely little derringer tucked inside her jacket, which her grandfather had taught her to shoot. Bracing on the beam over her head, she slid onto her knees to lean forward and get a better look up through the enormous iron-reinforced glass skylight. When airships had become popular and economical for transporting cargo, every warehouse had invested in the skylights on enormous hinges to swing open and allow cargo to enter from the air.

Ask why no one thought to move the crates from directly under the skylight since the airship dropped them there this afternoon. Ess reached for her little bound notebook and fountain pen, to write the thought down. Keeping an eye on that shadow moving with glacial speed, she jotted the idea.

From the corner of her eye, she caught flashes of phosphorescence as the ink reacted to the open air. It was lovely to be able to write notes in the dark, but not quite so lovely when she worried about being seen in that dark, betrayed by her pen and ink. At least it wouldn't glow in the dark once it dried. Too bad her grandparents had vanished on that research trip before her grandmother had perfected the reactivation spray, to let her read what she had written while she was still in the dark.

A metallic sound, like a handful of pinkie-size ball bearings rolling down a flight of stairs, interrupted her thoughts. Ess held still, breathing as softly as she could, trying to locate the origin of the sound. Rats wouldn't make that kind of noise, would they?

Automaton rats would, that delightfully nasty part of her mind replied. That inner voice always sounded like her older brother, Ulysses.

No, automaton rats would still scratch and scurry and move in serpentine paths across the floor. They wouldn't go in straight lines, which was what those larger, heavier, definitely solid metallic taps were doing.

Ess shuddered and wished she hadn't thought *serpentine.* Snakes were just as good at climbing as rats. Now her advantageous perch in the rafters didn't feel so safe. It didn't matter that most thieves never thought to look up. Animals could smell fear, or in her case, loathing, and follow the scent.

Those aren't animals.

Those shapes moving from shadow into moonlight were round, like a ball a young man would kick in college games, with protrusions that looked like small ladies' hatboxes on top, and six appendages sticking out from perhaps halfway between the equatorial line and the top. There was a distinctive brassy gleam when they passed through the moonlight spilling down through the first cargo skylight a good thirty feet from her perch. Four of them, Ess saw now. The tapping sound matched perfectly with the rise and fall of those appendages as they walked across the stone paving of the warehouse, quickly and neatly and in perfectly straight lines.

Automatons, yes. But no automatons she had ever seen. As they tap-scurried through the angled spill of moonlight almost directly under her perch, she saw no keys to wind them up, so how did they move? How did they keep moving? There wasn't room inside those bodies for any kind of steam production, so they weren't steam-powered. She stared, trying to analyze. All other emotions fled under the weight of fascination.

Curiosity killed the cat — or at least, the slow, careless cat, Granny Matilda said with a chuckle in her memory.

Ess leaned out from her perch to watch the automatons walk away from her. One of the four stopped, and the round box on top lifted up on a rod of some kind and pivoted around. She never put a fingertip or strand of hair or thread of clothing outside of the sheltering darkness, yet obviously, those things sensed her movement. She could have sworn it was looking at her, though she could see no eyes.

It tap-tapped away from the path the other three took straight to the pile of crates and settled down directly under her perch in the rafters. Ess fought not to move, not even to turn her head and look all around herself. Even if she had no idea what that thing was, no proof it was just her imagination insisting it watched her like a cat, she wasn't going to give a single hint that she was ready to flee.

Before the Pinkerton Agency recruited and trained her, Ess made it a habit to find at least three escape routes in any situation. Even friendly ones. Sometimes frothy social situations were the most dangerous of all. She had tested the rafters before sundown, making sure they were close enough she could leap from one to another if necessary. Say, if someone shot at her, or came climbing after her. She knew where the rafters were closer together or dangerously far apart. She knew the places she could jump down onto the heavy iron shelves lined with planks to hold crates. She knew where the ladders were, to get down to the ground.

No brass ball with invisible eyes and a pillbox head was going to trick *her* into revealing her escape routes before she needed them.

Anthropomorphism, my dear, Grandfather Ernest scolded in her memory. *Sometimes it can be very helpful, and sometimes it can be deadly. Try not to let it become a habit. In the final analysis, animals do not think or react like people. We merely apply human motivations and characteristics to them to help us establish patterns and justification for what we see. The same holds true for machines of all kinds. Especially the ones mistakenly tricked out to look human.*

What would her grandfather say about the brass ball sitting on the stone floor, watching her, waiting for her to make the next move?

It wasn't a bomb, was it? Even though it made no sense to waste an expensive automaton to deliver a bomb, no law stated criminals had to use common sense. After all, if they were selfish and evil enough to try to steal Egyptian artifacts on loan from Britain and Egypt, then they were probably also wasteful. If they were like the villains in the penny dreadfuls some of her fellow Pinkertons liked to read, then they were the nasty kind who enjoyed using bombs in the act of robbery.

It's not a bomb. It's a distraction. Ess muffled an indrawn breath of air that threatened to become a hiss of fury and frustration.

While she tried to have a staring contest with the thing's non-existent eyes, the other three automatons had reached the pile of crates. Their legs split and bent on the ends, turning into pincers and claws that worked with amazing efficiency to pull aside chains and lever up the lids of the crates. A hissing pierced the air, and she froze at the sight of smoke wafting up from the big padlock that held all the smaller chain-and-padlock combinations together. She had missed whatever produced that sound and the smoke, but a good guess was a strong acid of some kind. Just how had the automatons delivered that acid?

The rafter she was on passed slightly to the left above the pile of crates. At the very least, she could try to get a closer look. Resisting the urge to stick her tongue out at the automaton watching her, she feinted backwards, as if to head toward the wall, moving along the rafters. The automaton popped up on its legs and tap-tapped toward the wall. Ess swallowed down a bark of exultation and reached for the angled bar of the rafter in front of her. Sitting so long made her legs stiff and achy. She fought down the discomfort with all the strength of mind she had inherited from both grandparents.

It took all her self-control not to look back as the tap-tapping of the guard automaton stopped. Could it possibly have *sensed* she wasn't making a break for the nearest exit?

Now she heard it coming after her.

No, the tapping had stopped. Had she confused it?

How could she confuse something that wasn't alive, and therefore couldn't have a mind to confuse?

Ess swung up into another "V" perch in the rafter beams. She was almost directly over the pile of crates. Moonlight angling down from the skylight spilled over her, cool despite the piercing brilliance. She smelled the distinctive hot sting of acid in the air, and saw one automaton with an extended leg, the tip of it over the keyhole in the lock. So the leg was a conduit for the acid, but how did it carry the acid without endangering its brass legs? Maybe porcelain, a glaze, even a glass lining in the leg?

Her rafter vibrated...with the same rhythm of the automaton's movements. Ess looked back and swallowed down a yelp as she saw the automaton walking along the *side* of the main beam. Why didn't it fall off?

Logic told her those legs had sharp tips that dug into the wood and the metal legs were strong enough to hold it in place.

Definitely, she didn't want that thing catching up with her and striking her. Or even shooting her with acid from a storage compartment in its belly.

Ess glanced around and thought a silent prayer of thanks that she had mapped out the rafters earlier today. She looked down. The other three automatons were still at work, pulling aside chains. She turned to check over her shoulder and saw the fourth, coming after her with an unhurried pace that made it seem that much more threatening. Then she leaped sideways, pushing off with all the strength in her aching legs.

Even before her hands caught at the beam of the next line of rafters, she turned her body, preparing to swing upwards and settle into the "V" perch to sit for a few moments. She glanced back.

Ess faltered as she saw the automaton shoot out a thin black cable that hit the rafter beam three feet away from her with a sharp *thud-squelch* sound. It had a hooked tip that sank into the wood. A whirring sound came from the automaton, pulling the cable tight, and then it pushed off from the other rafter and swung out, heading straight for her.

She scrambled down the rafter beam, and before the automaton landed, leaped for the next one in line. It shot out another cable. Ess flinched at the sound of the sharp hook embedding in the wood. Her rebellious imagination showed her the consequences if that hook hit flesh.

The next beam down was too far away to jump to, so she climbed along the beam until she was in nearly perfect darkness. The moonlight coming from the skylight seemed like a solid silver-white wall, so far away. Ess shivered with the sudden certainty that the light was dangerous. Whatever those automatons were, whatever it was they wanted, they were working *in* the moonlight. She could only hope they were more like their human creators than animals, and they couldn't see in the dark. Then again, they didn't seem to have eyes, and navigated just fine without them. Proof: the one that had seen her, despite her hiding place in the dark, and tracked her so ably now.

The beam vibrated with that thudding rhythm, growing stronger every second. The automaton was catching up with her. Ess let instinct rule and leaped, back to the beam she had left only a few seconds ago. She kept going, to the original beam she had been perched on when this nightmare started, then on to the next. She doubled back, heading toward the moonlight spilling down through the skylight. The other three automatons had stopped working. They sat in a neat, utterly still row in front of two open crates, with their pillbox heads withdrawn into their bodies.

"Charles," Ess muttered as she felt the thud in the beam that meant the automaton had landed somewhere behind her in the darkness. "Where are you? You're late."

If she could have spared the breath, she would have laughed. Her inborn sense of time was accurate within a minute or two, and it seemed to clang through her body now with the realization that Charles, who was supposed to trade places with her, was late. Yet he was one of the most punctual men she had ever known.

Maybe he was truly *late*? As in, deceased, dead, murdered by other automatons roaming the darkness outside the warehouse?

A crystalline chime filtered through the air, coming from directly overhead. Ess looked back along the beam and saw a dark blot of movement. The automaton was coming after her. The most maddening part of all this was that it didn't change its pace at all, moving with almost leisurely steadiness. It reminded her of those nasty boys she had dealt with when she first fled her boarding school, disguised as a boy. They were the same in far too many dingy back alleys and shadowy stables. The kind of nasty boys who thought because they were bigger and stronger, they would always win, and therefore it was beneath their dignity to hurry. They just kept coming, and coming, sometimes smirking as she and the others who had been their targets tried to escape the barn or the dead-end alley strewn with garbage.

At least the automatons didn't have faces, so they couldn't smirk.

They didn't have faces, she reminded herself, as she swung around the central anchor beams of the rafter and into the strongest shaft of moonlight. If they didn't have faces and they didn't have eyes, they couldn't, shouldn't be able to see her.

However, her grandmother had theorized that where fish could feel movements in the water, perhaps there were creatures of the air—flying creatures, like bats and gliding squirrels—that could feel vibrations in the air, even if no sound was audible. Perhaps light itself had some kind of mass, however delicate, and moving through light set off some reaction that animals could feel.

The three automatons on the floor popped up to stand on their legs again and their pillbox heads protruded from their round bodies.

Apparently the automatons could feel movement in the light.

Ess suppressed a snarl of frustration and aimed herself at the darkness on the far side of the rafter beam. A ladder waited there, nailed to the wall. It led to the top shelf of the long line of iron and wooden shelving filling the warehouse. She would get to that top shelf and run as fast as she could and scream at the top of her voice to bring help. Surely the other agents in her team could shoot the brass automatons and shred their inner workings so they stopped following her.

Cables shot up and out of the three automatons, hitting the beam with hard, high-pitched thuds that she felt as she scrambled away from them. Ess couldn't help it—she looked back and watched them rise up in the air with purring sounds, the cables vanishing inside their bodies.

The automaton chasing her continued on its path, walking along the side of the beam. She thought for a moment it would collide with one of its identical brothers and perhaps they would both fall to the floor.

She was disappointed.

The four brass automatons walked in perfect synchronization, parallel with the floor, two on each side of the beam. She swallowed hard and headed for the darkness and that ladder she needed more than breath right now.

Where was Charles? It galled her to wish for her teammates to rescue her. Horace Winslow, her mentor and recruiter, would have been amused and probably have something suitably earthy to say, to comfort and tease her for failing to convince men everywhere that women were their superiors in all things. Ess wished she were sitting in the back room of the Pinkerton Philadelphia office right that moment, studying case reports and drinking sour beer and arguing with him—usually over her assertions that women and men were equals, that women's intellectual superiority made up for physical discrepancies.

If Horace were here, he would take one look at the automatons tap-

tapping their way along the beam behind her, curse just enough to make the air smell like brimstone, and then open fire with every weapon within reach. Considering Horace knew how to store an arsenal on his person without anyone being the wiser, that was saying a lot.

Her beloved derringer wasn't doing her much good, tucked safely inside her jacket, was it? Then again, she knew her limits when it came to shooting in the dark, and the range of her gun. All she would have done would be to make the automatons angry. Could they get angry? Such speculations did her little good now, because she didn't dare sit still long enough to pull out her gun and try to aim.

A flicker of movement in the corner of her eye had Ess pausing and turning to look. She muffled a Horace-like burst of curses as an automaton swung out onto the beam to her left. Instinct had her look right. A second automaton swung out onto the beam to her right.

They doubled their pace, bracketing her now.

Her heart tripled its pace and Ess swung out along the beam, picturing the monkeys she had watched clambering in the trees when she had been a child, visiting a South American jungle with her grandparents. Her grandmother had taught her many disciplines of the mind, including mimicking the movements of animals, to aid her in different tasks.

Both automatons shot out cables and swung back onto the beam in front of her.

Two in front of her now. Two behind.

All four stopped the moment she stopped. Ess settled into the "V" of a rafter beam. It wasn't much protection, but at least she had something between her and them.

What were her chances of grabbing one of them, pulling that cable out, wrapping it around the beam and making the infuriating sphere spool out the cable to let her drop to the floor of the warehouse -- before the other automatons jumped on her and shot her with acid from their legs?

The closest automaton raised one leg.

Could the wretched, unnatural things hear her very thoughts?

A hissing sound preceded a white cloud that emanated from the tip of one leg. Ess flung up her arm to shield her face.

Chapter Two

The hissing stopped... and she felt nothing. Heard nothing. Smelled... something chalky, not hot and acidic.

A sudden wave of dizziness made her close her eyes.

That didn't help.

She dug her fingers into the wood and turned her head, seeking clean air. Whatever that brass thing had shot at her, it was probably a sleeping drug of some kind.

Please, Granny, let it work, she thought, and dredged up the disciplines her grandmother had taught her.

Matilda Fremont had firmly believed and taught that the human mind was stronger than any physical substance that might attack the body. With discipline and training, people could slow their bleeding when they were shot, muffle pain from the wound, and speed up the rate of natural healing, including fighting off infections.

Ess concentrated on the image of little blobby creatures moving through the river of her blood, catching the invading drug in fine nets and dredging it from the river before it could take root in her flesh. Her heart leaped unevenly at an image of losing consciousness, then her balance, and falling from the rafters. The floor was very hard stone.

The dizziness dissipated, and she dared to open her eyes.

The two automatons sat perpendicular to her, all six legs on each planted on the vertical sides of the rafter beam. Perfectly still. No ticking or whirring sounds came from them, no indication of clockworks. Their eyeless pillboxes were partially retracted into their bodies. Moving slowly, ready for another spray of the chalky substance, she looked down the beam in the other direction. The two automatons there copied the same pose.

So we just sit and wait until someone falls off?

Ess hoped she would find this situation amusing in the future.

Another crystalline chime sang through the air. Two automatons, one from each pair, popped their pillbox heads out, making Ess flinch and gasp. They climbed up the vertical beams of the rafters and tap-tapped along the roof, hanging upside down, heading for the skylight. She kept watch, as much as she could while keeping the two quiescent automatons in sight. Ess shivered. The moonlight had faded by at least three-quarters of its intensity. How long had those things been chasing her around the warehouse rafters? Or had the clouds moved in for that predicted rainstorm?

The two automatons prodded at the skylight latch. Ess flinched and rose up from her perch in the "V" when they grabbed onto the control cables for the lock and rode them down to the ground, pulling the skylight open.

The two automatons still with her raised one leg each, pointing them at her. A definite threat. So, she reasoned, she could watch, turn her head to look around, but she couldn't move any other part of her body?

Fine. She had a very good, unimpeded view from her perch here. So what was going to happen next?

A soft, three-note whistle warbled through the warehouse, from the far door. She choked on a totally irrational giggle. The distinct hiss-clop of very large feet trying to walk noiselessly in heavy boots came through the waiting quiet.

Charles was late. Fortunately, not fatally late.

However, he was walking right into trouble.

"What in the Sam—Odessa?" Charles hissed, appearing in the doorway. "Where are you, girl? Are you hurt?" The snick-click of his Colt cocking rang loud through the warehouse.

"Run!" she shouted. "I'm trapped." She stared down a leg now pointed at her face and braced for another cloud of sleeping gas. Or maybe the acid this time. The automatons didn't have visible ears, either, but they seemed to understand exactly what she was doing when she shouted.

"What are those things?" Charles stepped out into the moonlight, staring up at her.

She was touched that he was worried about her. Glad he assumed she was hurt and hadn't fallen asleep on the job. But the man was an idiot. What part of "run" didn't he understand?

"Get out, now! Look behind you!" She dared to point. No reaction from the automatons.

The automatons on the floor moved at triple the speed she had seen before. Their tap-tapping sound turned into a rattle as they skimmed across the floor, heading right for Charles. He let out a shout and backed up, pulling his other pistol and letting go with both barrels.

He missed.

Charles was a crack shot.

The automatons became dark brass blurs as they circled him, dodging bullets and moving in faster, until they leaped, hitting him square in the chest and taking him down. He hollered a string of curses.

A string that cut off two seconds later with choking. Ess heard that hissing sound and prayed it was the chalky sleeping gas and not the acid. Charles turned onto his side, curling into a fetal ball as he gasped for air, then abruptly went limp.

The two automatons went back to the controls for the skylight, leaving him lying there. Ess prayed he was sleeping, not dead. She closed her eyes and fought down her overactive imagination, which painted a picture of Charles inhaling acid and drowning in his own blood.

That purring sound resumed. Ess dragged her gaze up, until it caught on four black cables and men riding them, coming through the skylight. The moonlight shifted, vanished, replaced by a cold, blue-tinted light that cast hard-edged black shadows. Where did such light come from? No oil lamp or reflector had ever created such light. Ess leaned forward, trying to see up through the skylight. Another gust of the chalky gas hit her in the face.

It tasted different. Almost fruity. Rotten fruity. Like those exotic, long yellow fruits her grandmother made her try on that trip to Egypt.

"I—will—not—" She wiped her face and leaned back, bracing against the upright of the rafter. The dizziness faded, but it left behind a heavy, churning sensation in her belly.

She couldn't see anything beyond the men coming down on the cables, with the same whirring sound the automatons made when they went up and down. She guessed an airship hovered over the warehouse. The captain had obviously waited until the moon went behind the clouds before he approached.

These people were either desperate, or insane. Nobody flew dirigibles down the streets of cities at night. Even a city as sprawling as Washington, with so much open space and so few buildings taller than ten stories. It was too dangerous, too many obstructions to run into in the darkness. Especially if there was any kind of industry or an academic community. People were constantly stringing all sorts of wires through the air, between buildings, or sending up enormous poles, lightning rods, playing with electricity and different alloys of metal. Plus there were the lunatics who passionately believed the surge in industrialization was a sign of the end of the world. Some of her jobs since joining the Pinkertons had included infiltrating groups of fearful, violent people who set themselves up as defenders of humanity. They declared themselves the judges of what level of technology was permitted, and the longer their battle, the fewer warnings they gave their targets. In large cities, people constantly climbed the highest buildings to shoot at airships to take them down.

"Well, what do we have here?" a man said, his voice deep and amused.

Ess gritted her teeth at the laughter thickening his voice. The men gathered around Charles. One bent down and rolled him onto his back, and they searched him.

"Not good." A second man spoke. "A detective."

"No, that's very good," the first man said. "These people sponsoring the exhibition are finally taking the danger seriously."

"Pinkertons are the best of the best," a third responded. "They'll make our job harder."

"The mobis found something. If we're lucky, that's the last of it."

"Since when are we ever lucky?" the second man said. "How are his vitals?"

"He's sleeping soundly and should be awakening in another hour or two, with nothing worse than a headache," the first said. "And some rather odd memories."

The other men snorted. Ess grudgingly admitted that if she weren't sitting up here in the rafters, feeling she might lose the remnants of her dinner, she would have found the thought of Charles' awakening confusion amusing.

"Where are the other two?" the second man said.

"Taking care of any other problems out there. Where one Pinkerton is, others are sure to follow. Let us take what we came for, and leave before we have to confuse more people."

The men left Charles and hurried over to the crates the automatons had separated from the others. Mobis, the men had called them. Ess wondered what the name had come from.

They were worried about leaving before anyone else showed up. Could she do something to slow them down, until the rest of her team arrived? She glanced at the automatons. Mobis. Judging from the different smells, they could change the kind of gas they used on her. Probably there was something inside them that increased the strength or even the effect of the substance whenever there was failure. How long could she keep resisting them before something succeeded in knocking her unconscious?

Would she remain unconscious as she hit the floor, and never feel the blow that might kill her?

Ess had endured too much in the years since her grandparents vanished on their second expedition to South America, leaving her imprisoned in a boarding school she had fled for the sake of her sanity. She wasn't going to allow mechanical devices to end her life now in such an ignominious manner. Especially with so many unanswered questions.

"Excuse me?" She kicked both legs, and was both pleased and chilled to find the mobis didn't react to that particular motion. Meaning they could judge what was a threatening movement. What sort of clockwork mechanisms were they, to be so perceptive?

Could they have people's souls trapped inside their metal bodies, or human brains directing their actions?

Her grandfather had speculated about such developments, if the advancement of science and technology continued its breakneck pace. But he had said such intelligent machines were many generations in the future.

"Hello?" Ess kicked her legs again, when only one man of the four looked around. His three companions continued digging in the crates belonging to the exhibition. "Up here."

"Found the other two mobis," the man said, gesturing for his companions to look. "They caught a flying boy."

Ess muffled a chuckle.

"Come down, boy."

"They'll just shoot me again if I move. I would prefer not to stink like rotten bananas," she added, remembering what the fruit was called.

"What's that?" The first speaker stepped away from a crate. He had something long in his hand, and slid the item inside his dark jacket before walking over to stand underneath Ess. "They gassed you?" He pulled something from his jacket pocket and put his hand to his mouth. "I think we need to talk." A high-pitched sound made her think he had a whistle.

The two automatons hummed and plummeted downward on their long cables. Ess pulled her legs up, hauling herself up into the rafters by just her arms. She swung away toward the darkness and that ladder she wanted to reach, so desperately, she could taste it.

"Halt, boy!"

Ess swallowed down a string of curses and tried to move faster. A hard thud vibrated through the rafter beam under her feet and a yelp exploded from her. A dark shape rose up from the floor, accompanied by that purring hum and she almost lost her grip as she saw one of the men shoot up toward the rafter in front of her. For two seconds she considered trying to pull the sharp hook free. The mechanism pulling him upward moved so swiftly, the man was already there, hauling himself up to perch in front of her before she could succumb to temptation. Or was it desperation?

"Well, and what's so special about you that level one and level two don't give you the sleepies, eh?" he said.

Ess hated his arrogant pose, one foot jammed in the "V" of the rafter vertical, one hand holding onto the board, and his other leg and arm hanging out in empty air. At least she couldn't see his expression, though his voice certainly sounded smug.

"You're just a skinny boy. Were you just taking shelter here, or were you working with the detective down there?"

She glared at him. She hated his tone of voice, even though her harmless, youthful appearance was exactly what made her so valuable and useful to the Pinkertons. She could fight with the best, unafraid to punch and kick like any boy raised in the unfriendly streets, and two hours later, with the help of curling tongs and a demure dress, pass herself off as a lady of quality. Dressed in boy clothes, she could convince anyone she was a boy. Forgettable. Nearly invisible. No threat to anyone. If the criminals she spied on noticed her, the worst they would do was threaten her to forget what she saw and heard.

But it still irked her to have this man talk to her as if she were an idiot. Shouldn't he be worried that she had been shot twice with their foul-smelling gas, and she hadn't fallen asleep like Charles?

"What's wrong, boy? There's something special about you, if you're unaffected. Who do you belong to?" He tugged on the cable hanging from his waist and moved along the rafter, swinging his other leg over to step into the next opening in the rafter beams.

This close, Ess could see the crisscross of dark straps around his waist and chest, almost blending with his dark clothes; a knit jersey, dungarees and short boots. Some kind of harness, she supposed. The swing of the cable gave her an idea.

"Pinkertons," she said, and swung her legs out, holding tight to the vertical beam.

The man dodged, but not fast enough. Both of her feet hit him high in the chest, knocking his breath out with a satisfying *oof*. Even more satisfying, he tumbled backward, over the other side of the beam. He fell a dozen feet before the shortened cable stopped him. Tangled.

Ess kept going, down the rafter toward the wall and that ladder hidden in the shadows. She strained her ears for the purring of those cable mechanisms. The man behind her laughed as he struggled up onto the beam. Ess spat, wanting to curse. She could like him, under other circumstances.

That purring hum came from in front of her and Ess faltered. Where was it? That blue-white light cast such odd shadows, and then cut off with such sharp lines. She muffled a sob of relief as she stepped into shadows. Just a few more feet and that ladder would be within her grasp. Once she was down on the ground, no one would be able to catch her.

"Men can be so blind, don't you agree?" a woman said from the darkness in front of her, her voice smooth and alto-low.

Ess lost her footing and scrabbled at the rafter beam. Rough wood scraped at her cheek. The nauseous ball in her gut expanded and threatened to send tentacles up her throat. She smelled sulfur, and heard a hiss. Light exploded in her eyes, softening a moment later into a flame on the end of a match. It illuminated a woman with dark hair caught up in a long braid. She stood at the top of that ladder nailed to the wall. She held the match out toward Ess, with her other hand hooked around the top rung of the ladder.

The light didn't go out in a few seconds, like other matches.

"I'm guessing you're partnered with the man down on the floor," the woman continued. "Clever, disguising a woman as a boy. People only see what they expect to see. Or they're trained to see." She tipped her head to one side and narrowed her eyes, looking Ess up and down a few times. "Our inside man says the Pinkertons have an upper crust lady archeologist hosting the gala opening tomorrow night. I'm guessing that's supposed to be you." She sighed. "Or rather, that *was* supposed to be you. Very sorry."

"Are you going to kill me?" Ess pressed one hand over her heart when it sped up, pressing with almost painful intensity against her breastbone. Did she dare draw her derringer? Would she have time?

"Hardly. Someone immune to the first two levels of tranquilizer gas has quite a lot to offer." Her gaze flickered up to land beyond Ess's shoulder. "We're just going to introduce you to Zeus."

"What's—" Ess flinched as a thin, hard cord wrapped around her waist. She turned to find the man she had knocked off the rafter, perched only a few feet behind her now.

Distractions. Avoid distractions.

"This is Zeus," the man said, smiling crookedly at her. "Stings a little."

He brought up a pistol, but the barrel was solid with several different colors of wire wrapped around it. Sparks spun around inside the barrel, revealing it was some dark glass. The sparks shot out, filling Ess's eyes. She felt her legs fold, just before blackness picked her up and spun her around.

At least the nausea was gone.

Then everything was gone.

~~~~~

"Athena." The thoughtful note in Dr. Sylvia's voice raised the hairs on the back of Athena Latymer's neck.

The ship's doctor for the airship, *Golden Nile*, couldn't possibly have found anything so early in her examination of the girl-disguised-as-a-boy... unless it was a very large, significant something.

Athena stood up slowly from the bench that circled the perimeter of the narrow room and crossed the waiting area outside of the sickbay. She had listened to that sense of warning she considered a gift from God and had stayed here to wait for the results of the examination instead of going to the conference room where she did most of her work. The artifacts the mobis had detected in the exhibition's crates needed testing, to verify they were indeed parts of the Great Machine. The sooner she tested them, the sooner the airship could move on, away from Washington, in pursuit of other artifacts scattered throughout the country. This ridiculous passion for all things Egyptian had spread from Britain to the United States in the wake of the renewed, peaceful negotiations after the war. Athena could almost have hoped that the bitter feelings the government harbored for Britain and Queen Victoria, because of her support of the South during the Civil War, could have remained strong. It made life so much simpler. The resources of the Originators were stretched thin as it was, testing artifacts in Britain and Egypt, but now the area of search had doubled.

Those concerns had to wait until she resolved the mystery of this girl who resisted the tranquilizer gases.

"Look at this." Dr. Sylvia beckoned, and Athena stepped up to the examination table. One of four built into the metal deck of the airship.

The older woman's long, dexterous fingers tugged up the tightly braided and pinned hair at the nape of the mystery girl's neck. It had been covered by a cap until she fell, stunned by the Zeus gun, then stopped short, caught by Theo's safety cable. The sudden jerk of arrested freefall had knocked the cap loose, despite the pins holding it tightly in place.

The hair pushed aside now revealed a faded blue and green tattoo.

"No," Athena whispered, even as a light, cool feeling spread through her chest. She blinked away tears, looking at the blue lotus tattoo. "Her ankle. She should have another on the ball of her right ankle."
~~~~~

Simon, Sylvia's nephew and apprentice healer, hurried to peel off the girl's battered boots and thick socks, revealing narrow, calloused feet, still pretty with their high arches, but showing signs of hard use. On the bulge of bone on the outside of her right ankle, another blue lotus.

"Vivian's girl, you think?" Sylvia whispered.

"Who else could it be?" Athena's thoughts raced. "There's no way the Revisionists could know we would come here, before the tour even started. How could they plant someone to work among the Pinkertons to guard the artifacts?"

"I make it a point never to underestimate people who would try to erase the very existence of the Savior," Theo said from the doorway, where he had kept watch ever since he carried the girl into the sickbay. "But would they go so far to try to fool us into thinking Vivian and Edward's daughter is still alive?"

"We have to test her," she said, staring down at the unconscious girl. That pale face, lightly smudged with dirt—did it look like Vivian and Edward, or even Matilda? "Merciful God in heaven, if You have answered our prayers, we thank You."

"And if You haven't," Theo said, his voice turning hard, "have mercy on our souls for what we will have to do to protect all of eternity."

Chapter Three

Ess woke slowly, troubled by the sensation of being watched. It clashed with the stillness in the air that told her she was alone in a small, enclosed place.

The last time she woke up with that prickling along her skin when someone focused all his attention on her, she had been in the Watertown jail, and Horace had been on the other side of the bars.

No Horace sat on the other side of the walls surrounding her now. Ess lay on her back, limbs neatly arranged, on a real mattress. She twitched the fingers of the hand pressed between her hip and the wall, vibrating with the hum of machinery, and cautiously stroked the cloth she lay on. Fine cotton sheet and wool blanket. They smelled of chamomile soap. Ess took a deep breath and flinched, feeling an ache around her ribs.

Right where that black cable had wrapped around her.

Just before the man shot her with that odd gun full of sparks.

Another deep breath, more ache, but she couldn't help it, as all her memories snapped back into place in her mind.

She had been in the rafters of the warehouse, above a stone-paved floor.

Logic said the man had caught her in his cable before he shot her to keep her from hitting the floor. From the ache, she had fallen far enough to be bruised from the sudden stop.

"No thanks for small favors," she whispered.

The sound of her voice bouncing back at her in the enclosed space told her more details. She lay in a bunk, with either the ceiling of the cell or the top bunk a few feet above her. A snail-slow shifting of her other arm revealed open space beyond the bunk. A room of some kind.

That steady, almost subliminal humming in the thin wood of the wall told her she was most likely in the airship that had disgorged the automatons and the dark-dressed men on those cables. The engines of trains and steamships had different patterns and rhythms. Trains rumbled over uneven tracks, and steamships had to contend with waves, no matter how calm the day. Ess had never been in an airship, but other Pinkertons had told her about traveling in them, so she could guess at the smoothness of flight, except when storms churned the air in the heights.

So, if she was in the airship, the next question was why those people who invaded the warehouse had brought her here. Why hadn't they just left her on the floor like with Charles? Thanks for not letting her crash to the stone pavement to die in a shattered heap, by the way. Was he here on this airship, too? And if so, why hadn't their captors imprisoned them together?

Unless they brought her up here alone? Logic said they wanted to find out why the gas knocked out Charles but not her.

Ess wanted to know what those sparks were in the Zeus gun. She could guess the sparks were lightning, just as Zeus was the Greek god of lightning. Such a weapon would make her job much easier, and safer. There had been no sound when the man shot her. At least, no sound she heard. Much nicer and tidier than a gun with the loud bang and stink of gunpowder. She imagined how much safer her prowling jobs for the Pinkertons would be if she could silently knock her enemies unconscious and go on her way, rather than hiding in cramped places, sometimes even on top of wardrobes or the rafters of buildings or filthy alleys for hours at a time, until they went away and she could sneak out.

Other than the bruises around her ribs and the dryness in her mouth, she felt fine. When her captors knew she was awake, they would question her and she could try to get information from them. Would they be the kindly or foolishly arrogant kind of people whom she could talk into giving her some freedom or information that would let her plan her escape? Or would they be the intelligent, suspicious, cautious kind who wouldn't leave her alone for a moment, and tell her nothing?

That brought her back to the theory that they wanted to find out why she hadn't been vulnerable to the two gasses. Ess fought down a shudder, remembering when she was eight and wandered into her grandmother's laboratory without permission, to see her dimpled, smiling Granny performing a vivisection on a rat that had been subjected to various jolts of electricity and yet refused to die. Her grandmother hadn't been smiling, hadn't seemed to particularly enjoy tormenting the rat that struggled against the restraints. But it hadn't bothered her, either. What sort of tests could or would these people perform to find out why she was immune?

Better get it over with. The longer it takes, the farther we could be from Washington. It's a given I won't make the opening gala for the exhibition.

At least Horace wouldn't know she had failed this assignment. He had died last January, after rescuing his granddaughter who had fallen through rotten ice.

Taking another deep breath, Ess opened her eyes and rolled onto her side, putting her back to the wall.

A dimly lit room with a copper basin bolted to the wall, a matching covered pitcher sitting in a rack next to it, floor-to-ceiling cabinet doors on the wall parallel with her bunk, and what looked like a hemp mat on the floor. She lay in the bottom bunk of two. Her boots sat on the deep bench underneath the basin-and-pitcher arrangement, on the short wall of the room. The opposite short wall was the door. Efficient sleeping quarters, but claustrophobic.

metal walls and wooden floors, like her prison room. The heavier the vessel, the more steam and fuel required to keep it airborne and moving forward.

So her captors were wealthy and powerful.

Powerful enough to take whatever they wanted, served by automatons that her grandmother had only dreamed of in those long-ago days of blissful innocence and wonder.

What did they want with her?

If they knew she was a girl, were they slavers, taking advantage of having her in their power, and plotting even now to break her will and sell her to some exotic foreigner for nefarious ends? Ess had read some of the reports that Pinkerton agents along the frontier sent in, tales of woman kidnapped by Indian tribes or Spaniards or even the Orientals along the western coast. Usually such women had blue eyes and blonde hair, taken specifically for their coloring that was so exotic in other lands. With her moss-colored eyes and dark hair, she wasn't exotic in the least. That didn't discount the theory of slavery.

She had run away from the boarding school where her grandparents left her, just because those people intended to mold her into a delicate flower intended for a politically or socially astute marriage. Another form of slavery, and more insidious than simply being sold as a concubine or sexual toy, because it required the numbing of her mind and soul.

Ess would escape this place, too. She was sure of it. Even if she hadn't the faintest idea right that moment how she would accomplish it.

First step was to put her boots back on.

The door clicked open the moment she finished tying her laces and took her foot down from the bench where she had rested it. She had few options, so she sat down again on the edge of the bunk and waited.

A woman with large, dark eyes and a sharp-boned face, framed in a ronet of dark braids, paused in the open doorway. After a few seconds of dy, Ess felt sure she was the same woman who had appeared out of the ness to distract her so the man could come up behind her with the Zeus She wore a man's leather vest with extra pockets down the front, e white shirt, and long, loose blue trousers, and carried a book bound red leather, open in her hands. The book had writing in red ink on t-hand page, while the right-hand page was blank. The woman Ess up and down for several seconds, and a soft smile grew as the ts of silence extended.

am Athena Latymer. As for who you are... well, we shall certainly t soon. Are you hungry? Or have you read too many penny ls, so you're certain we'll drug you?"

s read challenge and humor in her eyes and voice.

Haven't you already proved —" she emphasized that word, since na had used it, "— that I'm immune to your concoctions? Wouldn't it waste to try to drug me again?"

"Most certainly, but just because an action is wasteful doesn't mean it is illogical, or that people who take such steps are illogical. What would you like to eat?"

"Bread and butter." Ess fought the urge to press a hand against her belly. The mention of hunger and eating revived the nausea that had dug spurs into her belly after the second, banana-smelling gas hit her. "Tea, heavy on milk and honey. Please," she added, hearing an echo of her grandmother's admonition that everyone deserved to be treated politely, no matter who or what they were.

"Hmm, choices that are soft on the stomach. That's a telling reaction." She pulled a short pencil from behind her ear, where it had been hidden in the soft abundance of her dark hair, and made a notation on the blank page.

"Is all that about me—about what happened last night?" Ess amended, stunned at what she had blurted without thinking.

"This is a day-book, noting everything that has transpired on this mission thus far." Athena nodded. "Although, I must admit, you have filled up quite a handful of pages since we bumped into you. Tonight," she added. "Only four hours ago." She gestured at the pitcher, then at the closest cabinet door as she spoke. "There are fresh clothes, as well as linens and soap powder, so you can freshen up as you feel led. Having been awakened in strange surroundings one time too many, I told them to leave you be. Better to be a little filthy than to wonder what was done to you while you slept."

"What was done to me? Besides taking off my hat and shoes?"

"And your gun? And proving your femininity?" That smile grew again, turning just crooked enough it hinted at slyness, but with such warmth sparkling in her dark eyes, it was impossible for Ess to decide if the woman was playing cat-and-mouse with her, or inviting her to enjoy a joke that she didn't quite comprehend yet.

"How were you watching me?" she said, to keep from blurting a doz questions jammed up at the base of her tongue.

"Ah. Interesting. We weren't exactly watching you -- not visually same sensor mechanisms that allowed the mobis to surround you warehouse allowed us to monitor you. Your modesty is quite safe, if what concerns you. No peepholes or sliding panels or one-way trans panels in the *Golden Nile*. That is the name of our valiant airship." patted the doorframe next to her. "I'm sure with time, with adventures, she shall take on a personality of her own, like other renown. Perhaps, if all works out well, you shall come to love her as

"That sounds like you plan on me staying here a long time. I ha I have work to do."

Chapter Four

"Hmm, yes. It speaks well of you that you would work with the Pinkertons, and that they would permit you to dress as a boy and take such an uncomfortable, dangerous assignment."

"Keeping watch in the rafters at night for six hours isn't that dangerous."

"If the Revisionists had gotten to the warehouse instead of us, it would have become very dangerous. They wouldn't have hesitated to use every weapon at their disposal to bring you down from the rafters, without taking any precautions to catch you and keep you from harm."

Ess swallowed hard, thinking of that long fall, the ache in her ribs where the cable had wrapped tight to keep her safe. What chilled her more, though, was hearing the capitalized "R" in "Revisionists." As if it was a name or designation. Like the Resurrectionists. Those rebel Southerners refused to admit the South had lost the war and were devoted to bringing down what they called the "illegal" government. Failing that, they intended to divide the United States neatly along the Mason-Dixon line and build high walls to keep the North securely in the north. Other goals Ess found even more repulsive included reclaiming all the slaves who had been freed, and enslaving all Negroes who had been born free.

Most certainly, she wouldn't like learning just who, exactly, the Revisionists were. Especially in relation to Athena and her comrades. What exactly were they trying to revise?

"What do you want from me? What were you looking for in the exhibition's crates?" she hurried to add.

"All in good time. After we figure out who exactly you are."

"How are you going to do that, when you haven't even asked my name?"

"You'll prove yourself. Names are secondary, compared to who you are in relation to us." Athena stepped back, over the threshold. "Your meal will arrive shortly, and something to keep you amused while we attend to some important chores of our own."

~~~~~

Amused? Ess ran her fingers over the satin-smooth finish of the pewter flute that came on her meal tray. She trembled at suspicions that jammed so tightly together in her brain, she couldn't examine them one at a time. She hated feeling like she had walked into a class she had never attended before, required to pass a test on subjects she had never studied. This was worse
~~~~~

than the most illogical situation she had faced in Miss Van Hastings' boarding school. More serious than the threat of being sold into a politically astute marriage at age fourteen for the venomous headmistress's profit.

Chills ran through her gut again, as she turned the flute over, the soft golden-rose glow of the ceiling light gleaming warmly across the surface. She had owned a flute exactly like this when she was a child. Before her grandparents vanished in South America. Before Miss Van Hastings decided to remake her into an accomplished young lady, took away her science texts, her books of Indian lore and campaign strategies and her flute, and filled her schedule with dancing, dressmaking, flower arranging, and the language of the fan. They tried to squash her brain into a tiny box.

That had been the first of many mistakes. At nearly the same time Ess found the letter from her grandparents' lawyers, notifying the headmistress that they were "missing, presumed dead," and the rough draft of a response letter claiming she was too distraught to take visits from the lawyers, she discovered that the headmistress's older brother was using the extensive estate of the boarding school as a gathering place and storage facility for a group of Resurrectionists. When Ess discovered that the headmistress had forged her signature and was keeping the lawyers from contacting her with the excuse that she had become "quite delicate" at finding herself an orphan, the sum of the deceptions had galvanized her into action.

Ess discovered the Van Hastings siblings' plans to confiscate all her grandparents' property. She used several of her grandmother's inventions to copy documents as proof and sent everything to the Secret Service. Then she wrote to her lawyers, informing them of the deception perpetrated by the Van Hastings, and her plans to venture to South America to seek the truth of her grandparents' fate. Ernest and Matilda Fremont, dead? Highly unlikely. The current unrest in South America made it illogical for her to head there as soon as she was free, so she set out to find her older brother, Ulysses, who had vanished more than a year before the ill-fated archeological expedition. Once she had found him, then they could find and rescue their grandparents.

To Ess's delight and satisfaction, the Secret Service had acted on all the proof she sent them. She hid in the attics of the school and witnessed the raid that netted most of the Resurrectionists. Her grandparents would have been pleased by her sense of responsibility and patriotism. Disguised as a boy, she headed west and north, in search of Uly. She had thoroughly enjoyed her life of adventure, including working as a waterboy on a massive construction project for an airship docking tower, then worked as a messenger for the Secret Service, joined the circus, and even met President Lincoln during his third term in office. She met Horace Winslow shortly before her seventeenth birthday, and he recruited her for the Pinkertons.

Since joining the Pinkertons nearly four years ago, Ess had delayed stepping back into her former life. While she had admired, respected and even liked her grandparents' lawyers, she hesitated contacting them because she knew they would feel duty-bound to take custody of her as her legal guardians until she turned twenty-one. While there were so many questions about her grandparents' lives and their secrets that the lawyers could answer, Ess hesitated to become Miss Odessa Fremont, the scholarly Fremonts' granddaughter. For a few more years, while she continued to search for Uly, she was content to use her Pinkerton connections to find those answers, and simply be Ess Fremont, Pinkerton agent.

Holding the flute now in her hand, she trembled slightly and felt crushed under the weight of all those questions and the regrets that came with her hesitation. Endicott, Lewis, and MacDonald would give her life back to her, but at what cost? Could they have replaced the flute Miss Van Hastings had taken from her? Several teachers had admonished her that "young ladies of quality do not indulge in vulgar activities that require blowing and raising their arms. Red cheeks puffed out are not comely or attractive in the least."

Ess had learned there were many different definitions of "quality" in the world, and many kinds of qualities, to be worn like costumes when the occasion demanded, and then discarded as soon as possible.

So now she held in her hands a flute amazingly, disconcertingly, like the one her grandparents had given her when her fingers were barely long enough to span the holes. Why or how did these people on the *Golden Nile* have this particular flute? More important: why did they give it to her?

Common sense said they wanted her to play it. But why, and what?

"No," she whispered, just to hear a voice in the silence that rang with memories and emotions she could barely understand, surging from inside the hot, prickly knot that filled her chest.

Did these people want her to play that one particular song? The signal? The call for help and identification? The one she was never to play unless she found herself lost, separated from family and friends, and in need of answers and shelter and allies?

Ess had neglected the song in those first months after fleeing the boarding school. After all, she didn't have her flute. Then, when she could borrow a flute, she only tried a few times. Somewhere in the struggle to escape, she had lost her child's faith and the belief that the signal song would eventually bring help and friends. People who could find her grandparents and bring them back to her.

She had given up on the song and hadn't been ashamed of that lapse, though she still sometimes felt a flicker of shame that her daily prayers had fallen to perhaps twice a week. Such thoughts about spiritual matters usually only came when she was in the company of those who prayed over meals, or during long, lonely night watch duties. Like last night.

A snort escaped her. Last night she had several long, one-sided conversations with God. Were her present circumstances in answer to her words? Had she somehow irritated God, or perhaps He had finally gotten around to answering?

Should she play the signal song? Part of her shouted no, with a force that ached in her chest. Where had these people, this Athena Latymer, been all these years? If they were friends of her grandparents, shouldn't they have known what happened to them? Shouldn't they have come looking for her sooner? Shouldn't they have been looking for her grandparents all this time?

She had done just fine on her own. What did she need them for, anyway?

A grin shattered her furious musing, when it occurred to her that maybe these people needed *her*.

Whoever they were. Whatever their self-avowed mission. Something having to do with the Egyptian artifacts.

Bottom line: until she made a few moves in their game, she wasn't going to get anywhere. Starting with escaping this comfortable little prison cell.

"All right," she muttered, and slid the meal tray from the mattress to the little bench built into the wall. Settling back against the long wall of the bunk, she made herself comfortable, closed her eyes, and dredged the notes of the signal song from her memory.

She played slowly, letting her irritation and years of feeling abandoned come through the grudging notes. Let them think she had lost her skill, if they chose. Ess closed her eyes against the hot sting of tears, when her fingers moved almost under their own volition. Her nose threatened to clog with the pressure of tears that rebelled against her iron control, so she had to pause regularly to breathe through her mouth. She played the signal song to the end. Then started a second time.

After the third measure, like a ghostly echo, she heard the countermelody. Ess choked and nearly fumbled the flute. She continued playing, but altered the song, just as her grandfather had taught her, to signal that she heard the person who accompanied her.

The other flute, on the other side of the wall, took over the melody and changed the tempo. Ess squeezed her eyes tight shut as she wracked her brains for what that change in tempo was supposed to mean. It had been a game, when she was six, learning all the messages that could be passed along through a simple song, just by changing the key, the tempo, switching the melody back and forth, or repeating the refrain and the bridge out of proper sequence.

A third flute joined in and she nearly dropped hers. The opening measures of *The Battle Hymn of the Republic* filtered through the melody, causing notes to clash.

"Uly?" Ess didn't care that her voice cracked, revealing the tears she fought to hold in. She half-turned to get up on her knees on the bunk and pounded on the wall with one fist. "Uly, is that you?"

"No, Ulysses isn't on the *Golden Nile*," Athena said, appearing so silently in the cabin, Ess turned too fast and slid a little on the wool blanket. "Welcome back to the Originators, Odessa Fremont."

"How can I come back, when I never belonged in the first place?" she snapped, swallowing down a dozen other, less civilized or mature retorts. They were far preferable, however, to breaking down in tears and begging like a child to know where her brother was, and how these people knew him.

When Ulysses, six years her senior, had vanished under mysterious circumstances, Ess had harbored the belief, the hope, that their grandparents knew where her brother had gone, and the South America expedition was actually a rescue attempt.

"You have always belonged." Athena slid out the short bench, revealing it sat on runners that extended from the wall. "Your great-great-great-grandparents established our organization with my great-great-grandparents."

"Uly told you how he would destroy my flute practices and drive me into fits, by interjecting songs into the melody?"

"Only the *Battle Hymn*, yes." She sat down and clasped her hands in her lap, looking totally at ease. "I know he will be delighted when we get word to him that we have finally found you."

"Finally. Meaning you've been looking for me?" Ess smothered the urge to snort and explain in blue language just how intensely she didn't want to believe her.

The funny thing was, she did believe Athena: the Originators, whoever they were, had been looking for her. The fact they knew the signal song, and they knew the joke, the game that had existed between her and her brother, all came together as incontrovertible evidence.

That didn't mean, however, she had to be happy about the timing, sit down obediently, and let others tell her what to do from now on. Ess had been on her own too long for that. Even under the orders of the Pinkertons and with Horace guiding her, she had been her own person, responsible for her actions, defending her honor, obtaining whatever she needed to do her job to the best of her ability. If she died in the course of an investigation, it would be her own fault.

"You must have had a good idea who I was before you gave me the flute," she said now.

"It was the final test. Your tattoos were convincing enough for most of us." Athena reached up and touched the nape of her own neck and gestured at her feet by way of explanation.

"But not you?" Ess responded, barely managing to keep from saying, "What tattoos?"

She had honestly forgotten the existence of the marks. More evidence, she supposed. Her grandparents had explained the tattoos were another safeguard, along with the signal song, when a friend of theirs came one rainy weekend and put them on her neck and right ankle. Ess thought about her boots and her hat, both removed. That was some kind of evidence, she supposed, that these people knew what to look for, to identify her.

"I am responsible for the security and safety, and the continued existence of the Originators, along with our disguise organization, the Blue Lotus Society," Athena said with a shrug. "It is my duty to be skeptical, to expect the Revisionists to try to infiltrate us. They can copy your markings, put them on one of their dupes who might have enough physical resemblance to pass as a member of your family, but they can't teach anyone the signal song or how to respond to the various sequences. No one but Ulysses Fremont, Odessa Fremont, and I know about the trick with the notes of the *Battle Hymn*."

She reached inside her vest and drew out a flute similar to Ess's, but longer, thicker, with a golden patina instead of pewter. It had markings etched into the metal. Ess could only make out the Eye of Ra clearly before the older woman slid the flute back into its pocket in her vest.

"What made you decide to test me instead of leaving me with Charles?"

"Your immunity to the tranquilizer gas. Your entire family line is remarkably resistant to many noxious compounds. It could be because there's always someone experimenting with poisons and tonics and such, and exposure creates resistance."

"So if you knocked me out with the first whiff, and I hit the floor and broke every bone in my body. you would have just left me there with Charles and gone on your way?"

"Most likely." A smile quirked up one corner of her mouth. "You quite pushed the mobis to the limit of their coding, fleeing them like that. Fortunately, we trained them to give chase and to learn from the reactions of prey animals."

"Mobis are those round automatons? How could they chase me when they don't have eyes? What mechanisms let them follow me? How do they keep moving, when there is no key to wind them, and no room for steam engines? Who—"

"Enough." Athena held up one hand, palm facing her. "All lessons will come in their proper time. First, we need to catch up with what you have been doing since you fled that horrid nest of lying vipers disguised as a school."

Ess stared, astonished by the vehemence in the woman's voice and face. Athena shared her estimation of Miss Van Hastings and her staff. Then Ess laughed. As she hadn't laughed in years. Not even with Horace, in the exhaustion that came after a dangerous, hard-to-crack case, released by smooth whiskey and satisfaction.

~~~~~

Athena wondered what amused the Fremont girl more: that their
~~~~~

organization had been looking for her since she fled that mind-numbing boarding school, and she never knew it, or that she had been nearly invisible to them, never knowing she hid from her allies. It pleased her that Ess was amused, rather than infuriated or frustrated. That said good things about how well she would fit in among the Originators, which was her heritage, while remaining her own person. With no old grudges to overcome. Athena admired the fact that she left not a single clue to her identity or her current living quarters on her person.

The girl had decided to trust her enough to divulge the Pinkertons' assignment here in Washington. Even then, it was clear she only shared information to obtain information. She outlined the plan. The Egyptian artifacts were to be guarded along its journey among the larger, most advanced cities of the United States. The traveling exhibition was a gift from the British Museum and Her Majesty's government to show there were no hard feelings after the war, on both sides. Queen Victoria had sent help in the form of scientists, military advisers, and airships to assist the South, because a United States no longer united would allow Great Britain to remain the most powerful nation in the world. On their part, the Northern forces had confiscated every airship and seagoing vessel, every crumb of food, every electrical cell and ounce of brass, and imprisoned every stranger with a British accent as a suspected enemy spy. There were bound to be hard feelings on both sides. Her Majesty sent the Prince of Wales as her representative at President Lincoln's third inaugural festivities, and in return the President had gifted the heir to the throne with a clockwork menagerie. That had started the reparations.

With the upsurge in interest in Egyptology after the cessation of hostilities, and the restored safety of travel by both air and water, the British Museum had taken advantage of the situation to proffer the next olive branch of peace and cooperation. In exchange for several teams of archeologists from the States' pride and joy, the Consortium of Natural History to join the Museum's efforts in Egypt with their proprietary digging-and-sensing machines, the Museum sent their favorite artifacts to the States to stir further generations of enthusiasts and dreamers. They had arrived just yesterday, brought across the ocean in the *Prince Albert*, Her Majesty's flagship of the Royal Aeronautical Fleet. The artifacts were kept in their crates for safekeeping and would not be put on display until this afternoon, in time to open the doors for the gala festivities. Pinkertons would be on guard. Ess was chosen for her ability to go from inconspicuous boy to lady of the gentry with the power of gracious intimidation. She would be in the center of the exhibition, displaying her knowledge of all things Egyptian, while her teammates would roam the perimeter, keeping the artifacts under constant guard.

"It seems to me, from what your bully boys said in the warehouse, you're either in league with the crooks who have been pilfering private

Egyptian collections around the world or you're in competition for the same artifacts. In fact, it seems to me you did retrieve some, got to the prize ahead of your enemies. The Revisionists, you called them?" Ess crossed her arms and leaned back from the long table in the main conference room of the *Golden Nile*. She and Athena had been talking over a second and far more satisfying breakfast, now that Ess's stomach had completely recovered from the effects of the tranquilizer gas. "What exactly are you looking for? And why?"

"A necessary question, and justified."

Athena cradled her half-empty teacup in both hands and gazed down into the golden depths, at her reflection. She knew Ess waited for an answer, but she delayed by drizzling honey into the lukewarm liquid, then filled the cup with cream, until she couldn't see anything but caramel swirls among the white.

"There is a... a machine. Powerful. Integral to the war between us and the Revisionists. It was disassembled long ago, and hidden among the tombs and treasures of Ancient Egypt. Now that Egypt's secrets and treasures have become the passion of the modern world, archeologists have uncovered secrets better left buried. We are in a race against time, traveling all over the world, searching every crate, every train car, every cargo hold. We must find all the pieces, because if the Revisionists find enough of the machine, they could conceivably recreate the missing pieces and activate it." She shuddered, imagining what the Revisionists could do if they could turn the Great Machine back on. Just because the first generation had failed in their first attempt to subvert the time stream and make even God bow to their desires, that didn't mean their heirs would fail in the second.

"What does it do?" Ess scowled when Athena just shook her head. "Well, the threat is eliminated from this shipment, at least. Since you're telling me this, I assume you want me in on the hunt?"

"It is your legacy."

"Maybe." A twinkle in her eyes kept the snorted word from being a nasty challenge.

Athena found she liked this young woman more with every sentence, every minute spent in her company. She quite looked forward to seeing Ulysses Fremont's reaction when they told him his "baby sister" had been found and was quite capable of getting into as much trouble as he had ever done. With far more style.

Not yet, however. Uly was on assignment, and even if Athena had the slightest idea where to find him or how, the less he was distracted, the better for everyone. Since the Originators had scooped him up and erased his tracks, giving him a new identity and life to keep the breath in his body, he had proven useful. But he would never be the survivor, the thinker, the analyzer that Ess had already proven herself to be.

Clever girl, to hide in the rafters and have the skill to move about them like a monkey, to know when to fight, when to flee, and when to sit and listen until the odds were in her favor.

Speaking of odds... Athena wondered if Ess played poker. She suspected her new protégé didn't, just because she was the sort who wanted to make sure everything affecting her was under her control. That didn't mean she couldn't be taught to play it, to use it, even if she didn't like it.

"Your grandparents were quite the experts in ancient cultures."

"Such experts, they couldn't keep their focus on the modern one, and couldn't identify enemies until they had a gun pointed in their faces," Ess said, her tone and the life in her eyes going flat.

"Granted. What did they teach you about Egypt, about the hieroglyphs and the pantheon, the Book of the Dead and the architecture of the tombs? As well as their counterparts in South America?"

"Why?"

"Once we make sure we have examined all the artifacts that have been shipped from Egypt, we need to double our efforts at the site. Nothing can leave Egypt without us examining it, making sure the machine's parts do not pass out of our hands. And we must do what your grandparents apparently could not accomplish when they went to South America."

"Me? On an archeological dig?" Ess leaned back, turning just enough to hook her arm over the back of her chair. A casual pose, but one that clearly let her turn toward the half-open door.

Athena marked that preparation for flight and found it hard not to smile. Yes, definitely, she liked Odessa Fremont. Her parents and grandparents would be proud, if they could see her now.

"I don't think so," the girl said with a crooked grin.

"Neither do I. I'm thinking you will be part of the team tracking tomb robbers and smugglers and watching dilettantes to keep them from getting themselves killed. Idiots always seem to have the most incredible talent for finding by accident what the rest of us have been killing ourselves to locate."

"True." A spark of laughter lit her eyes again. "But what do you think I'm going to do for you in the meantime?"

"You have to go back to work." Athena pointed down through the floor of the *Golden Nile*.

"Uh huh. And why would any of them trust me now? It's going on nine in the morning."

Inherited Edward's time sense, Athena noted. She had removed the clock from the wall of the conference room before bringing Ess in here, and while she had a pocket watch tucked into the hip pocket of her vest, there was no possible way the girl could have seen it.

"I've been missing a long time," Ess said. "Unless you put things back in place exactly as they were, and put back the pieces you took from the crates, nobody is going to believe me when I claim I was knocked out and kidnapped, and then just let go, and can't lead my partners right to the people and the place where I was held."

"True." Athena heard the muffled thud of boots on the hemp matting of the passageway. "Right on time. Vulcan, come in." She watched Ess as the Society's chief artificer stepped into the room.

"So... she's named for her ability to make things," Ess said, studying the dusky-skinned woman with her iron-gray hair cropped short, goggles tipped back above her forehead, and swathed in a long, scorched duster, smeared with multiple stains from years of experiments. "Why not Hephaestus?"

"People expect a big, sweaty man in a loincloth when they hear it, that's why," Vulcan said with a wink for the girl. She held out the tray with the replicas of the artifacts the extraction team had stolen last night. "The 'eh?' factor has always worked in my favor. Especially in tight situations."

"Those aren't the originals, are they?" She got up from her chair and leaned across the table to study the bits and pieces laid out on the tray.

"Of course not. How can you tell?" She shoved the tray closer to Ess for inspection, after a momentary glance at Athena.

"I can't. But it seemed from the little Mrs. Latymer here—"

"Miss," Athena corrected. "And please use my Christian name. We are all allies here, whether you're ready to believe us or not."

"All right. From what little Athena has said, you're not going to give up what took a lot of effort to retrieve, and you got your name because you're good at making things. Like forgeries." She glanced over the pieces and whistled, a low, drawling note.

"What can you tell us about these pieces?"

"Besides them being from different eras? Expensive bits of trash. Faience bracelet. Copper ankh. Amber scarab collar. Pretty bit of enameling, looks to be fourth dynasty." Ess narrowed her eyes. "These don't look like pieces of any machine I've ever heard of."

Chapter Five

"That's because the pieces are hidden inside the items. We had to destroy them to retrieve what we needed. It's only right that we replace what we took, so no one suffers."

"Forgery." There seemed to be no judgment in either direction in Ess's voice or face. "Let me see if I have this right. Without being sure I won't turn you in, you want me to go back to the Pinkertons and the museum muckety-mucks, hand them these forgeries, tell them I was grabbed by the thieves and I escaped after getting the stolen items back."

"Close."

"Girl has an attitude. Just like Matilda. Still amazes me that you didn't pick it up, considering all the time you spent with her," Vulcan said, tugging the tray of artifacts back to her side of the table.

"Time you spent with her?" Ess echoed.

"Your grandmother was my mentor. Just as I plan to be yours," Athena added, carefully watching the girl for her reaction. "We will be going to the museum with you. I believe your story will be more believable if we tell them that yes, you were kidnapped by the thieves. Always tell as much truth as you can, in every situation. The trick is learning what details to leave out, so people draw their own erroneous conclusions, but in such a way that it serves you. You were kidnapped by the thieves when, in the struggle, your hat came off and your hair came loose, and they learned you were a girl." She approved of the thoughtful mask that gave no indication whether or not the girl liked the story. "The Blue Lotus Society and I are stateside representatives of the World Consortium of Preservationists, an actual, legitimate organization, recognized by every civilized government on the planet, dedicated to protecting ancient artifacts from thieves, both the private collectors and those who would profit from private collectors."

"Tomb robbers and smugglers." Ess nodded.

"Exactly. Our story, which is mostly true, is that last night we had established a perimeter around the warehouse because we could see that the Pinkertons and the museum's people had a more-than-adequate guard established inside. That is another lesson—always subtly flatter the other side, even if they fall flat on their faces. We became concerned when we heard your associate calling to you and realized there was trouble inside. We arrived in time to witness you being knocked unconscious and tossed into a basket being drawn up into an airship. We gave chase in the *Golden Nile*, and managed to catch up a short time after you regained consciousness and were fighting for your freedom. The thieves never had a chance to stow their prizes, so you were able to retrieve what was stolen. We have spent all this time making sure you were unharmed, that the thieves did escape without leaving a trail, and then returning to your teammates."

"Just how much of that was the truth?" One corner of Ess's mouth quirked up, exactly as Athena remembered her grandfather had done, when something struck him as ironic as well as amusing. "How'd you think of all that? Or have you been working on the scheme since you knocked me out?"

"Somewhere in between."

"Still not sure why you want me to go back there, why you'd put in so much effort to protect my job."

"The Revisionists made no effort to get at the artifacts last night. Tonight is their best chance. You and I will be next to the display cases."

"When these Revisionists snag-and-grab, we'll be in place." Ess rolled the idea over in her head. "Sounds like a plan."

"Oh, no, they won't snag-and-grab. Because if we give them a chance to look, they'll realize what they want isn't in this particular shipment." Athena laughed when the young woman just frowned at her. "How can they know? Is that what you're wondering?"

"Like this," Vulcan said, reaching into one of the enormous pockets of the duster. She pulled out a rod of crystal, twisted in a double helix and as long as her palm. With a gentle rap, she hit the corner of the table.

Athena held her breath, hearing the pure note of the crystal, feeling it in her sinus bones and that spot between her ears and behind her eyes. Instead of closing her eyes as she usually did when the crystal sang, she watched Ess.

The girl's eyes widened. She looked at her fingertips, rubbing both thumbs over the ends of the other four fingers on each hand, then pressed her index fingers to her cheekbones, right over the sinuses.

"Uh huh," Vulcan said, with a satisfied smirk thrown at Athena. "Just like her granny. Sensitive."

"To what?" Ess demanded, her voice a little rough with surprise.

"This is what is hidden inside each artifact. Just like we do, the Revisionists have... I suppose the simplest explanation would be the equivalent of a tuning fork. They tap it against the artifact, and no matter how tightly packed inside, how deeply buried by clay and metal and other materials, the crystal will sing and reveal its presence."

"So it's like a puzzle." She considered for a moment. "Makes sense. So we go walking around the exhibition, pretending to be scholarly, genteel ladies who get other people to move the dirt on our archeological digs. Then we listen for the crystal to sing, to tell us who the Revisionists are and they're on the move."

"There won't be any crystal to sing," Athena corrected. "But yes, succinctly put. Are you in?"

"I'm not going to get the rest of the answers unless I play along, am I?"

"Smart," Vulcan said, chuckling. "Just like her granny. With a good dollop of her granddad thrown in, of course."

"If you're my grandparents' friends, why did I never meet you? And why weren't you there when they vanished?"

Athena noted Ess didn't ask why her grandparents' friends didn't swoop in to save her from the boarding school before she made her escape. Was that refusal to ask going to be a problem later, a sign of a grudge or refusal to trust, or just a sign of the girl's common sense?

"The simple answer," Athena said, instead of offering explanations that would only lead to more questions, as Ess was so much like her grandparents, "is that we are spread very thin across this planet. Those of us who are settled in one place, as your grandparents were, rarely see other Originators for months, even years at a time. The mobile force—" she spread her hands to indicate the airship, "—has the illusion of a large circle of associates, because we are constantly stopping to share information and news, to confer over leads, to commiserate over losses, to deliver Vulcan's newest inventions, and to wear masks, when necessary."

"Do tell," Ess murmured. A slow smile lit her face as if a bonfire flared to life inside her. "If you're taking me to the hotel, you need to get me a dress. I never show my face in the light of day unless I'm painted and cinched and tottering on heels only a man would consider sensible."

She blushed when both Athena and Vulcan burst out laughing. Athena was delighted to see that bit of self-consciousness. She had feared her mentor's granddaughter had become hardened, callous, and cynical in the years since she had struck out on her own.

They moved to the costume shop, as those who lived on the *Golden Nile* called the supplying room, to pick out an appropriate outfit for the reunion with the Pinkerton men. Athena filled her in on the rest of the story. The same storms that caused the landslide and flooding that cut off the elder Fremonts' expedition from contact with the civilized world had also kept the Originators' mobile force from making their regular visit. Several emergencies with other expeditions and outposts had prevented them from returning as quickly as they wished. Ess's grandparents had been declared missing, presumed dead, and the news had reached the States, before Athena's team had reached the expedition's abandoned compound.

"We weren't concerned for you because, after all, your grandmother trusted the headmistress at the academy to tend to your needs. We never guessed that once your grandparents were out of the picture, their instructions for your education would be thrown into the fire." Athena stepped back to get an overall impression of the outfit Ess had tried on first.

No, this one was too mature, too old for her. She thought that just as Ess had managed to pass herself off as a boy in his early teens, the best tactic would be to take advantage of her youth and sell her as someone very young, fragile, and defenseless.

"I hope you like lavender," she said, gesturing for the young woman to remove the maroon hat with jet beads and veiling.

"Does it matter?" Ess shook her head as if the hat had been an impossible weight and she enjoyed the freedom from it. "The question is if lavender likes me."

"You've never enjoyed dressing up, have you?" Sylvia said from the doorway.

Athena wondered how long the older woman had been there, listening to them talk, watching Ess handle the costumes, her reactions to the wigs and theatrical-quality makeup, false beards, shoes designed to add extra inches to height, harnesses to create stoops, and other paraphernalia.

"I had great fun creating my disguise when I first ran for my life and sanity." Ess shrugged and reached behind herself to untie the lacing at the neck to release the dress. "I worked hard on it, and imagined all the times I could walk right under Headmistress Van Hastings' nose, even talk to her, and she wouldn't recognize me."

"Did you test your disguise that way?" The platinum-haired woman settled onto the nearest bench, placed next to the door.

"That would be arrogant and foolish. But everyone accepted me as a boy. Even when I was thrown into a holding tank full of drunks."

Athena fought not to react. She thought she had succeeded, when Ess cast a brief glance her way, most likely testing her. She used the break in the conversation to introduce Sylvia, as the *Golden Nile's* resident doctor. It amused her a little, how Ess's eyes widened and she cocked her head to the side just a little, visibly surprised at the idea of a woman doctor of her age. Yes, women served as doctors now, but even ten years ago, most still took their skills to the frontier, where people in desperate need of medical care didn't look askance at such odd creatures. Sylvia's age implied she had been practicing as a physician for decades, which was true. Somehow, Athena thought the granddaughter and heir of Matilda Fremont wouldn't let social conventions guide her assessment of people's abilities and worth.

"As I was saying about that despicable Van Hastings woman," Athena said, pleased when Ess picked up the lavender-sprigged pale green dress Sylvia indicated.

"Oh, please, she hasn't arisen from the muck and mire, has she?" Sylvia groaned. She tipped her head back a moment later, laughing delightedly, when Ess froze in the act of stepping into the dress, apprehension widening her eyes. "Don't worry, child, she has been put in her place. Do go on, Athena. Tell her how she finally met her proper end."

"As near as we can tell now, we made contact, seeking information on you, a good three weeks before you, as you put it, fled for your life and sanity. Miss Van Hastings, however, chose to protect you from the inferior influence of your grandparents' former associates."

"She also wanted sole access to all that lovely money the lawyers would dole out for your care until you reached twenty-one," Sylvia said in a stage whisper.

"So when you asked for me, they told you I wasn't available? Or I had gone somewhere else?" Ess asked. "Indisposed, just like they told my lawyers?"

"She claimed she had never heard of you." Athena shuddered, remembering the frustration of those days. "She had a solid foundation of lies established through years of manipulation and practice. We were just starting to realize she was a conniving liar when you vanished." Athena chuckled and settled down on the bench next to Sylvia, waiting as Ess pulled on the elbow-length lace gloves with the lavender embroidery to match the print on the dress. "She who lives for money shall be tripped up by that same money. Or crushed by it."

"Oh, please," Ess said, turning around and curtseying, with her index finger delicately placed against a nonexistent dimple in her cheek, "please tell me one of her money bags landed on her head?"

"She did suffer some physical ailments, thanks to the horrid stress of the scandal," Sylvia said, nodding and smiling serenely.

"I learned the richest parents yanked their darlings out of her clutches. That scandal? Or the Secret Service raid that uncovered the Resurrectionists using the premises? Or the fuss Mr. Endicott raised, after he visited and faced them with their lies?"

"All of the above. Miss Van Hastings nearly collapsed of apoplexy, or at least the effort to convince people she was delicate and overwrought and much-abused by her traitor brother. Her reputation is in tatters, and she is no longer trusted to mold genteel young ladies into the perfect future leaders of society."

"Meaning a woman who turns off her brain and lets her husband tell her what to think and feel, who never acts unless it profits him." Ess's mouth moved as if she wanted to spit.

"Odessa..." Sylvia's eyes narrowed, but Athena saw malicious delight sparkling in them. "Am I wrong, or are you the little bird who brought the Secret Service in at the perfect time to catch those Resurrectionists?"

"Where did you hear that?" She settled down on the bench set into the opposite wall and folded her hands neatly in her lap.

Athena noted that unconscious conformity to the dictates of the costume. She was pleased that Ess acted to match whatever she wore. Indeed, there had been a boyish swagger and abruptness to all her movements when she had worn those trousers, suspenders, jacket and boots. Now that she was clad elegantly, down to lace and silk underpinnings, her movements had turned slow, almost languid, and a gentle sway had replaced the swagger.

"The newspapers. We thought some of it was rubbish, idle speculation.

Tell us how it really was," Athena said.

"How it really was?" Ess closed her eyes and tipped her head back, as if she had to think and gather her thoughts.

Athena suspected her mind worked so quickly, a long pause for her under normal circumstances would still seem like a flicker in time to others.

"Frightening, in some ways. Insidious. All the lies that weren't detectable as lies because of so much truth mixed in. Yes, the school had the highest academic standards and was connected with captains of industry and great minds of science. Their granddaughters and nieces were students. But was any girl encouraged to go into engineering and medicine? We were taught just enough that we could ask intelligent questions at society functions, where great businessmen, inventors and military minds would be present. Yes, the school had won honors in equestrian competitions, but those trophies and ribbons never told you that hardly anyone rode their horses faster than a leisurely walk around the park. More ribbons were won for the appearance of the *horses* than for how well the girls rode." She shuddered and wrapped her arms around herself momentarily.

"We were promised we would be educated and trained to contribute to the grand and glorious future of our country. Well, that was true, but only as decorations, clapping softly when the awards were handed out, or speaking words of encouragement behind closed doors. Or producing sons who would bring honor to their fathers' families with their achievements. We wouldn't be allowed to do anything that we would get credit for. After all, even our wombs didn't belong to us, but to the men who bought us in marriage."

"It's nothing new, child," Sylvia said. "That attitude has existed since time immemorial. It just seems more monstrous when other women encourage the belief that women can't do anything, can't think for themselves, shouldn't dream, shouldn't even know how to defend themselves. As if men would implode and vanish if they didn't have someone to defend and order around."

"I've seen all kinds of women out in the world, in all levels of society, and there aren't many women who actually *need* men for their survival. The really strong ones somehow manage to make men think they're in charge, while behind the scenes they're manipulated like paper dolls," Ess said. "Van Hastings and her underlings took away my archeology and biology texts, and claimed that Grandfather didn't really want me to study them, even though he bought them for me. They wouldn't let me study any languages other than French. Certainly not hieroglyphs and Latin and Greek. I was only allowed to study painting and needlepoint. My only choices were to be ornamental, or else invisible and silent. When they finally deigned to tell me that Granny and Grandfather were gone, just vanished, like Uly..." She took a deep breath, and for a moment that glitter in her eyes looked wet.

"I refused to believe. Especially when those horrid people seemed so happy. As if they thought Granny and Grandfather were bad influences on me, and now that they were out of the way, I could finally be raised properly." She shuddered. "So I poked and prodded and spied and used Granny's copy paper to gather evidence of all their plans and sketched maps of the Resurrectionist tunnels under the school, and I let our lawyers and the Secret Service know what was going on. Even that odious woman couldn't lie her way out of trouble when everything collapsed around her."

"One solid dose of truth made all the other false walls fall in a chain reaction. You performed admirably. Your grandparents would be pleased and proud." Sylvia nodded for punctuation. "I daresay you did profit from your time in that school, if just in the social niceties."

"Learning mannerisms for a part that I can remove like a particularly uncomfortable pair of boots is very different from making them part of my mind and soul." Ess stood up and turned around, showing off the dress. "Is this more what you had in mind?"

Athena debated pushing for details of how Ess had discovered the activities of the Resurrectionists and gathered enough evidence to bring in the Secret Service. When she understood the girl better, she would ask. It would be an amusing tale, suitable for Matilda Fremont's granddaughter.

~~~~~

The part Ess and Athena were to play in a short while did not pair up well with the basket she watched the *Golden Nile* lower at exhilarating speed, to let several of the Society's agents disembark ahead of them. Four of the ten were the men who had invaded the warehouse last night. Their leader, Theo, was the man who had shot her. He saluted her when they met up in the bay of the airship, and he had just enough time to introduce himself and say he was a friend of her brother. Ess made a mental note to ask him later—and promised herself that "later" would be soon—about Ulysses, and what he had been doing since he vanished. So many questions hadn't been answered yet, such as the source of that strange, strong blue light last night. Athena had said it was part of a future lesson when she asked, and changed the subject. Ess watched the men drop, holding onto the inside of the willow and metal basket, and promised herself, next time there would be no more changing subjects and waiting until later. Next time, she would ride in that basket. For now, however, she and Athena, dressed as they were, waited for the *Golden Nile* to tie up at one of the airship towers that ringed the city, so they could debark in a ladylike manner down one of the enclosed ramps.

"Ladylike" seemed to be the order of the day. Porters in stiff uniforms gleaming with brass buttons waited at the end of the ramp, when they disembarked the airship half an hour later, to offer their arms for the five-inch step down onto the dock proper. Ess found it rather ironic no one was there to escort the ladies along the twenty-foot, swaying ramp from the
~~~~~

airship, with rope netting strung along both sides as high as her shoulders. She threw herself into the part she was to play, traumatized by the ordeal she had undergone. At least, until she and Athena were in closed quarters with her fellow Pinkertons. Those who weren't at the warehouse right that moment, gathering details, analyzing what had happened during the robbery last night. She wondered if anyone had climbed up into the rafters where she had perched and tried to follow the path she had taken. The dust on the beams had to make noticeable marks everywhere she put a foot or hand or sat momentarily.

Allistair Fitch was the head of the team. Other than his smug delight in making her wear the most excruciatingly confining clothes for her part as the snobbish intellectual, Ess respected him. She hoped he was observant enough to look at the outfit Athena and Sylvia had put together for her and realize that ladylike appearance and movements didn't require being cinched in like she wore an Iron Maiden. The outfit she had worn yesterday to meet the curator of the museum had kept her so tightly bound that she had needed a longshoreman's pike to help herself take a deep breath. Didn't the idiot man and the dressmaker he hired understand that corsets were supposed to be comfortable, not torture devices that reshaped the body into unnatural formations?

The brass cage of the lift taking them to the base of the airship docking tower hummed with the energy of the steam engine crouching in the foundations of the building. Ess lightly rested her gloved fingers on the main support bar, filled with the control cables, and wondered if it was her imagination that something felt unbalanced about the engine. So much of her mechanical education had been shunted aside for the duration of her grandparents' expedition. Her short apprenticeship with Gus, the head engineer of the circus she had joined for a few months, had only wetted her appetite to learn more. A throb of anticipation shot through her, similar to the energy vibrating in the lift as they approached the ground floor. Would Athena take up that delayed education with her? Learning about steam engines and airships and electricity, and all the incredible machines that could be powered by the energy from the sky, had been her dream since she was a little girl. Now there were all the mysteries and wonders of the *Golden Nile* for her to explore. At least, by implication. Hadn't Athena said the Blue Lotus Society and the Originators were her heritage?

Chapter Six

In the lobby, another porter hurried up in his long uniform coat, this time with gleaming ebony buttons, most likely to signify his higher rank. He bowed and asked for their destination. Ess let Athena do all the talking while she surveyed the lobby. Now that she knew about the Revisionists, what little she had been told about them, she had to expect their agents to be everywhere. Not that she had any idea what they would look like.

Her gaze landed on a familiar face, and Ess's chest tightened in something like panic when she couldn't put a name or circumstances to the face. Where had she seen that man with the chipmunk cheeks and silver-streaked muttonchop whiskers? His gaze locked with hers for a moment and passed right over. Ess breathed a little easier, and almost laughed when she remembered where he had done the exact same thing to her before.

The day before, to be exact.

"Mr. Bloomingard from the museum is directly ahead of us," she whispered as the porter signaled that their cab was at the door. "I'm scholarly Evangeline Peabody now, if he recognizes me."

"What luck," Athena whispered back, and caught hold of her wrist to squeeze it. "I have an appointment with him this afternoon."

"For what?"

"Society business, of course. The consortium is here to assist in the protection and proper treatment of the artifacts, after all." A tiny bubble of laughter escaped Athena as they continued across the lobby to the massive front doors, each wide enough for three people to pass through at a time. "You didn't believe me, did you?"

"I believed it was a cover —"

"The best cover story, my dear protégé, is always the truth. Mr. Bloomingard from the Smithsonian Institution, I presume?" she said, holding out her gloved hand to the man, who had turned back to give Ess a second, prolonged, frowning look.

"Yes, ma'am. I don't believe I've had the pleasure of being introduced?" He bowed over Athena's hand, and glanced again at Ess.

"We haven't, but my associate, Miss Peabody, has informed me she had the pleasure of meeting you yesterday."

"Miss Peabody?" Bloomingard's eyes widened and he hurried to bow again, tipping his bowler hat. "Yes, of course, Miss Peabody. You're quite all right now?"

"Yes, thank you, very well." Ess wondered what exactly he had heard about last night's events. "I had a bit of a scare, but—"

"Athena Forsythe Latymer," Athena said, holding out her hand again to Bloomingard. "Of the World Consortium of Preservationists."

"Miss Latymer." His eyes widened. "Madame, it is a distinct honor and pleasure to make your acquaintance outside of official business. My morning business has concluded, and I was on my way back to my office. Would you do me the honor of allowing me to help you two ladies on your way? Would you happen to be going to the museum, perhaps to take a tour before our appointment?"

"That is our ultimate destination, but first we need to repair to the hotel where Miss Peabody needs to speak with her associates."

"Ah, yes. Of course. I had heard..." He shook his head slightly, lips pursing, clearly indicating to Ess that he was bursting with what he had heard, but chose not to speak.

Honestly, the delicacy of men who insist that women are delicate and need protecting. It could drive me to drink!

"Yes, I suppose there are some unfounded rumors going around the city," Athena said, lowering her voice. She rested two fingers on Bloomingard's bent arm, and he leaned in closer. "Could you be so kind as to tell us what those rumors are, so we may plan a defense against them? After the traumatic experience of last night, Miss Peabody needs as much assistance as you can render, to protect her nerves as well as her reputation."

Ess bowed her head, glad of the wide-brimmed hat Dr. Sylvia had chosen for her. It cast her face into shadows in the bright gaslights of the lobby, and let her appear demure and delicate, even if she was actually fighting not to burst out laughing. Her nerves were in incredible shape this morning, and now that she knew she hadn't been in any danger, even when the mobis tried to knock her unconscious, last night had been the best fun she had enjoyed in quite a while.

"I'm not sure Miss Peabody—"

"Please," Ess said, tipping her head up again and fluttering her eyelashes. "I am quite well, and I am of sturdier stuff than I might appear. I would not be entrusted with the rigors of this assignment, helping to curate the exhibition, if I were not. The best defense, sir, is to know all the lies so that we might counteract them." She offered what she hoped was a shy smile and a tiny bow of her head. "It is providence, I do believe, that we encountered you on our way. Please do say you will assist us? I should be ever so grateful."

"Miss Peabody. Miss Latymer." Bloomingard swept his hat off and bowed low to them. "How could I resist the opportunity to assist such gracious ladies?" Replacing his hat at a slightly more jaunty angle than before, he offered them both an arm.

It was a good thing there were doormen waiting to push open the heavy bronze and glass panels, Ess decided. Bloomingard would look mighty ridiculous, freeing himself of their hands, resting in the angle of his elbows, to open the door just a moment after offering his arms to them.

On the short cab ride, he filled them in on the rumors going around about the events in the warehouse the night before. The story could have been told in half the time it took, but he assured them every other sentence that the story had not gone beyond the warehouse staff, the Institution, and the police. Ess kept her head bowed and her hands folded sedately in her lap, when she wanted to tip her head back and laugh long and loud. If the police knew about the robbery, then the newspapers knew, and that meant half the city had likely known since before sunrise, including many busybody politicians who would turn it to their advantage, come election time. Even if not a word made it into print.

"Please, Miss Peabody, do be assured that no one believes you were in league with the brigands. Your own associate swears that you shouted for him to run, that it was a trap, and you were under some duress." Bloomingard frowned. "I am curious, however. What were you doing at the warehouse at all? Isn't it the duty of your associates to stand guard, while you are concerned with the academic aspects?"

"I was inspecting the layout of the warehouse, and ensuring that the locks and chains securing the crates were still in place. I believe the, as you said, brigands who broke in distracted the regular watchman, so that I was alone just long enough for them to overpower me. They took me to use as a hostage in their flight, but when no one challenged them... well, we can't expect to understand the reasoning of people of such low character, can we?" Ess fluttered her eyelashes again, until Bloomingard's frown faded.

She would never understand how otherwise sensible men could fall prey to fluttery eyelashes and tears and false protests of helplessness. Still, just because she couldn't understand that weakness in men didn't mean she wouldn't use it whenever possible.

"They were extremely foolish," Athena added. "Their first mistake was in forcing Miss Peabody to go with them all the way to their lair, when they should have released her as soon as they were safely escaped from the warehouse. Their second mistake..." She offered him a secretive, thin smile, and a delicate shrug. "Let us leave that for when we reach the safety and security of your museum, shall we?"

Mr. Bloomingard was disappointed, but too enchanted by Athena to protest. Then they reached the hotel where the Pinkerton team had their headquarters. He promised to make sure "all details" would be "in order" when they joined him at the museum later in the day, helped them out of the cab, and stayed standing on the curb, watching over them, as they climbed the steps of the hotel.

"So the Society really is... real," Ess mused.

"Have you read the macabre Mr. Poe?" Athena regally nodded her thanks as the hotel doorman tipped his hat and pulled the thick oak panel open for them. "One of his stories is about an incriminating letter that was stolen, and though the thief's quarters were searched several times, no one ever found it because it was sitting out in full view. The philosophy is called hiding in plain sight. The Revisionists have overlooked us many times, because they disdain to advertise the expertise they have gained during our... contest, shall we say?" She chuckled softly as they paused at the top of the steps into the lobby and looked around. "I must admit, I find no small satisfaction in earning quite a good living off our activities that both hide and support our quest."

"It opens doors and solves problems, doesn't it?"

"It does indeed."

Athena and Ess strolled into the lobby, just starting to fill with patrons arriving for the early lunch seating in the hotel dining room. Ess spotted Charles coming in another door, with a thick wad of newspapers tucked under his arm. She winced at this evidence the newspapers most definitely knew about last night's robbery. When Charles' gaze landed on her, he winked and pressed his free hand against his trouser leg as he twitched his fingers, using their abbreviated sign language to flash her a few quick questions.

Ess responded with her hand against her hair, pretending to check her pins and the set of her hat. *New friend. HQ. Assemble.*

"Very clever," Athena murmured, as they crossed the lobby heading for the grand staircase. It curved upwards in the center of the hotel, six people wide, its intricate inlaid wood patterns gleaming despite the regular traffic. "You need to be a little more casual about breaking eye contact. Still, if I hadn't been looking for your associate, and if I hadn't seen him last night, I wouldn't have noticed."

Ess couldn't respond, because they reached the stairs and several people started the long walk upwards ahead of and behind them. Charles reached the stairs several people behind them. Ess felt his gaze on her, the entire journey up two circuits of the staircase, to the third floor.

No one else stepped off onto the landing, and Charles caught up with them, walking only a few steps behind, as they found the hallway leading to the suite taken by the Pinkerton group.

"Ladies." Charles moved past them, his long legs somehow making his rapid pace look like a casual stroll. He glanced back the way they had come, then his calm mask cracked. "Blast it all, Odessa, do you know how many morgues this filthy city has?"

"Fitch had you checking all of them for me?" Ess tried to shrug, as if she didn't care. A chill flashed through her at the realization that if the Resurrectionists had struck last night, she might indeed be lying on a slab in some cold, dank room right that moment. "I thought he had more confidence in me."

"He does. Scares the rest of us, that he'd be that worried. Ma'am." He tipped his hat to Athena and reached blindly behind himself for the doorknob of the suite's parlor. He didn't wait for an introduction, but pushed the door open and stepped through, holding it wide for them. "Nice dress, by the way."

"Doesn't turn my skin green?" She fluttered her eyelashes at him, and he barked laughter.

The other three men at the round parlor table looked up sharply. For just two seconds, the expression on Allistair's narrow, aristocratic face was pure joy and shock. Then it settled back into the grimness that made him such a drudgery to deal with. Mostly, Ess admitted in that moment, because he made so few mistakes, no one could argue with him.

"Gentlemen, may I present Miss Athena Latymer, of the World Consortium of Preservationists, one of the parties involved in the security of the exhibition that we weren't told about." Ess stepped aside to pull up a chair for Athena. "Her people pulled my bacon from the fire last night."

"Ma'am," Allistair said, gesturing with a flick of his hand.

Roger and Briscoe hurried to take the chair from Ess and pull up another, so she and Athena could sit together. Roger winked at her. Briscoe raised a skeptical eyebrow, but his perpetually scowling mouth threatened to curve upward for a few seconds. Ess felt a little breathless at this sign that indeed, her teammates had been worried, and might even be pleased she had returned unscathed. She made the introductions before sitting down, and finished by handing Allistair the box of forgeries. He gave her a long, unblinking look before opening the pasteboard container. The pieces were nestled in a layer of cottonwool, with all the delicate care such supposedly rare, ancient artifacts deserved.

"Which one was gassed last night? Mr. Charles, yes?" Athena said. When he raised his hand, she tugged a green glass bottle just a little larger than her thumb from her handbag and offered it to him. "Odessa was vilely sick from the dose of sleeping gas the thieves used on her. Our ship's physician prescribed this to purge the blood and ward off any headaches. She sent this along, in case you were still feeling the aftereffects."

"Thank you kindly, Ma'am." Charles' face lit up. "Feels like there's a pony taking a kick at the back of my head, regular as clockwork."

"Yes. Thank you very much." Allistair finally took his seat, the last to do so, as usual. He faced Athena, but his gaze kept sliding back to Ess. "Is this everything stolen from the crates?"

"Everything I could find when I woke up," Ess responded.

"I don't suppose you have the thieves waiting at the delivery door out back?"

"Very sorry, Mr. Fitch," Athena said. "In the darkness and the maze of buildings down at the docks, it was enough of a challenge for my associates to extract Miss Fremont and the artifacts. There was quite literally no one for them to apprehend, when all was said and done."

"Well, Odessa and the artifacts have been returned, both undamaged. That's the important thing. And maybe we'll have some clue of what to look for in the future. Odessa, feel up to making your report?"

One of those knots at the base of her neck relaxed under Allistair's cool tone and even cooler gaze. Everything was back to normal. When he asked if she was feeling up to making her report, he wasn't giving her an option. That was fine. The sooner she told the simple, as-close-to-the-truth-as-possible tale she and Athena had put together, the better. Every time she told it, she would be more secure and settled in the sparse details. The fewer details she offered, the better. The smaller the lie, the easier to defend it.

The tranquilizer gas was a big help in the story. She didn't have to explain why the thieves had taken her if she was unconscious. Athena suggested that in the struggle, her hat had come off and the thieves knew she was female and therefore might have thought about using her as a hostage. Allistair might have argued with the theory if Ess had come up with it, but he gravely thanked Athena.

Lunch arrived while they were still talking, going over several floor plans of the museum, comparing what Athena's people knew to what the Pinkerton group had learned. Allistair wasn't happy to learn that the museum had held back the useful, perhaps even vital news of the participation of the Consortium. When he suggested that it might be prudent for him to accompany Athena to her meeting with Mr. Bloomingard and other museum officials, she welcomed him.

"Odessa, dear, it's going to be a very long evening, and I'm sure you haven't quite recovered from last night's adventure," Athena said, standing. She nodded graciously when the four men leaped to their feet. Charles nearly knocked over his coffee cup. "Since your team leader will be with me, why don't you spend the afternoon resting? He can fill you in on what we decide. Which, of course, Mr. Bloomingard would be foolish not to accept."

The other three men chuckled. Allistair seemed to be focused on Ess and her reaction.

"A nap in my own bed sounds... incredibly good," Ess said.

"Make sure you do that," Allistair said. "No dressing up as a boy and going back down to the docks to find the bullies who snagged you. With your luck, you'll get a black eye and have to put on makeup like plaster to cover it up."

Ess fought the urge to stick her tongue out at him. She didn't know what it was about Allistair Fitch that made the juvenile in her come out, full force. The urge grew so strong that she finally gave in, as Allistair pulled the door closed behind him and Athena, a short while later.

Roger barked laughter, while Briscoe cuffed the back of her head.

Chapter Seven

"Leave her be." Charles pushed out a chair from the table, gesturing for Ess to sit. "Even with that medicine they sent over, I bet her head's still swimming and throbbing."

"Maybe," Ess said, settling down with the three men again. "I suppose you want the rest of the story?"

"Horace trained us all. There's always more to the story than the capture and the retrieval. What's with the archeologists?"

Ess hooked her thumb across the room to the sideboard, where the whiskey bottles and squat glasses waited. This was part of the ritual that Horace had instilled in all of them. Except Allistair. He had been trained at a different Pinkerton office. Horace always had them sit down around a table, usually late at night, everyone with his glass of whiskey, and they talked. Everyone shared every thought that had been in their heads during the case and the clean-up. No matter how obscure the thought, and even if it had nothing at all to do with the criminals they were tracking or the stolen goods or people they were trying to retrieve. Ess knew it was far too early in the afternoon for drinking, but the ritual was important.

If all went as Athena expected, this might be one of the last uninterrupted, relaxed social times she spent with her teammates. So she told as much truth as she could about the Blue Lotus Society and the Consortium, and what she had seen of the airship, the *Golden Nile*. That drew most of the questions from the three men. They didn't ask her to arrange a tour for them, and she was grateful. She was still getting used to the idea that she had an inborn right to be on board the airship. The chance to travel by air, and to explore all the wonders of science and technology that Athena hinted were kept aboard the airship... that weighed strongly against the ache as she considered leaving her team. Leave the place she had earned among the Pinkertons. Yet if she couldn't answer all their questions, she might lose some friends anyway.

Was the exchange worth it? Athena had barely skimmed the surface of all the things Ess wanted to know, and hinted that there were many questions she would not answer until the young woman had committed herself irrevocably to the Blue Lotus. Not by choice, but because she would have no other choice.

That irked Ess, so she understood why some men dove repeatedly to the bottom of a bottle, just for a few stolen moments of oblivion, of not thinking, of forgetting. Until oblivion drank them down. She wouldn't do that, but she understood the temptation.

~~~~~

Museums, in Ess's estimation, were fancy-dressed graveyards. All the fragments of ancient civilizations were depressing because they always seemed to be broken, and hinted at a greatness and beauty that might never return. The little placards, neatly mounted on the railing that kept museum visitors from touching the items, never had enough information. They only hinted at the wonders and treasures of history. What good were fragments when the whole vast picture couldn't be re-assembled from them?

"Someday," she said, meeting Athena in the entryway of the vaulted room where the Egyptian artifacts were on display, "there will be enormous displays to answer all the questions anybody could think of. They will talk and move, and respond to all the questions people might ask. And not get bored or snooty," she added, seeing one of the sour-faced museum guides peering into the exhibition room.

If people looked like they were sucking half-ripe limes all day long, from working around dead things, she would re-think the resurrected dream of going into archeological pursuits like her grandparents.

"Hmm, yes, that would be fascinating," Athena said.

She had that look in her eyes as if she knew a great deal she wouldn't share. Ess had seen it far too much already for her taste. For all she knew, among all the wonders of the *Golden Nile*, they probably were able to record images and sounds for display at a later time.

"Museums would probably draw many more visitors, if they offered such things," she continued. "Archeology would certainly garner more respect."

"I don't care about that, I just want to be able to get answers when I think of questions."

"Speaking of questions, I don't think your Mr. Fitch quite trusts me." Athena hooked her arm through Ess's and started on a wide circuit of the room.

"No, he looks dyspeptic all the time."

That startled a chuckle from Athena. She patted Ess's hand, caught in the crook of her arm, and kept walking.

Other than her companion's witty comments about various fancy-dressed museum patrons, or highly educational commentary on the various Egyptian artifacts, Ess considered the entire evening an uncomfortable waste of her time. She hated corsets, for one thing. Just because corsets were designed to be comfortable for all-day wear and promote proper posture, that didn't mean she *was* happy to carry an extra twenty pounds of weight in cloth and whalebone. Men were lucky, she mused for what had to be the millionth time. True, they had to wear ridiculous collars and the ever-changing fashions for beards and moustaches were ridiculous. Yet by and large, their unthinking freedom of movement and dress made them rich in
~~~~~

ways many of them probably didn't even realize. Athena had intervened, making changes in the outfit Allistair decreed Ess had to wear as Evangeline Peabody, scholar. Her new clothes were almost bearable, even while they accomplished their purpose of impressing everyone she met.

If only the Revisionists had made some token appearance. After all the work they had done to prepare, Ess almost felt unjustly treated when the evening passed without a bump or distraction.

No one made any effort to reach over the velvet barrier ropes or wooden railings or lift the lids of the brass and glass display cases. No one created a fuss, effectively distracting the armed guards who were visible everywhere in the exhibition room. No appearance of the Revisionists. No attempt to test and steal the artifacts.

The only highlight of the evening came when Mr. Bloomingard announced that a tenth crate of artifacts had been delivered late to the museum, sent separately from a private collector who had been resisting the British Museum's importuning for months. The man nearly glowed as he hurried into the exhibition room and spoke in a low voice, announcing the "happy accident" to Athena and Ess.

"Would you like to be present when I open the crate, Miss Latymer? Miss Peabody?" He bowed and offered his bent arms to both of them.

Ess wanted to go. Badly. She glanced across the room to Allistair, currently engaged in conversation with a little man who was as wide as he was tall, with an amazing shock of white hair and a monocle. He didn't look up, but she knew she had to stay in the exhibition room. Her duty was here. Even though there was nothing to steal.

"Perhaps tomorrow, before the museum opens again? If you would permit me to watch as you set the pieces out on display?" she said, tipping her head to one side in what she hoped was a beseeching manner. Ess had grown quite tired of fluttering her eyelashes and demurely glancing away to charm the rich and powerful of the nation's capital. She swore her eyelids would cramp if she fluttered her lashes one more time.

"Quite right, Miss Peabody," Athena said, as she slid her hand into the crook of Bloomingard's elbow. "Your duty is here. I shall be sure to give you a full report on the wonders our dear host is so kind to share with me." She patted his hand, and the man actually blushed.

Charles stepped up to take Athena's place at her side almost before the two of them had stepped out through the arched entryway. Briscoe took his place after Ess told him what had happened, and he walked over to report to Allistair. Their leader joined them as Ess pretended to give Briscoe a tour of the pieces. It was easy to call up memories of what Athena had told her earlier, almost down to the same inflection of voice and gesture.

Perhaps too easy. Dangerously easy.

"I didn't know you were a mimic," Allistair said, as the three of them moved on from a mummy case belonging to a minor priest of Horus.

"When I get tired, I do it," she offered. His observation drove away the weariness that made the gaslights seem a little too bright.

"Useful," he said with a grunt. "Just don't let anyone think you're mocking them."

For a moment, she was angry. As if she would dare mock Athena?

A shimmering sensation ran across her skin in that moment, halting her as she focused all her attention on it. At first she thought someone had opened a door or window, and a blessed trickle of cooler air had slipped into the room. The air was starting to feel positively thick with the scents of pomade and cologne, brandy-soaked cigars, and lavender toilet water, and warmly stale.

In that same moment, as the shimmering slipped under her clothes, Ess remembered where she had felt and heard that sensation before.

The crystal of the mysterious machine.

Logic said Athena had brought the crystal rod to identify hidden pieces of the machine, and she had struck it while Mr. Bloomingard's back was turned. Crystal hidden inside the new artifacts had reacted.

Ess glanced around the room, looking for anyone who might be reacting in turn to the silent chiming of the crystal. Athena had said not many people could feel the crystal resonance, so it made sense that only someone hunting crystal here tonight would react. No one seemed to be stopping and studying the occupants, as she was doing. No one else's companions were starting to frown at her, as Allistair and Briscoe did now.

"I'm sorry. I thought I heard... have you ever had those moments, when you hear something and you are sure you heard it before, but you can't identify where?" To her relief, both men lost those is-Odessa-losing-her-mind frowns, and they nodded. "All I can think is that I heard something before I quite lost consciousness last night," she offered. "A familiar voice."

"Then the thieves have come in search of what you took back." Allistair offered her a tight smile, and stalked away.

Ess pretended not to watch, as he walked past Roger, signaling him with the barest flick of his hand against the seam of his trousers.

"This evening isn't ending any too soon," Briscoe said. Then, louder, "Miss Peabody, please don't take it as an insult, but I fear you grow weary. Shall I find you a chair?" He tipped his head toward the archway. Ess followed his glance, straight at a large wingback, presently unoccupied.

"No insult at all, Mr. Williams. Thank you." She let him lead her over to the chair and bow her into it.

He immediately hurried from the room, probably to meet up with Allistair and Roger, who had both vanished. If she were in charge of this operation, Ess thought she would remove their visible presence and then sneak back in through the doors hidden behind those monstrous Renaissance tapestries that clashed horribly with what the museum's decorators mistakenly thought of as Egyptian décor.

Ess settled demurely and made a show of checking her tiny handbag for a handkerchief, which she used to dab at nonexistent sweat on her forehead and down her neck. If anyone in the room had heard about her alleged kidnapping the night before, let them think she was weary and not paying attention to her surroundings. Meanwhile, she would take advantage of this perch that gave her an excellent view of the entire exhibition room, and take a rest from her ridiculous high-heeled boots. Ess swore a man had dictated that women needed high heels that raised them up at a foot-aching angle. Probably to make it harder for a woman to flee an unwanted suitor.

"Or perhaps make it hard for her to chase a man she terrified," she mused aloud.

The grandfather clock in the main hallway chimed eleven just a few heartbeats later, signaling the end of the exhibition. The clock was four minutes slow, she noted. Ess sighed in relief, and sighed again when it seemed everyone in the room looked at her. Of course they did, when she was sitting next to the doorway. Silently cursing the multitude of rules of etiquette, she stood and stepped aside, so she wouldn't have to make farewells with every person leaving the room.

Athena returned, her timing perfect, to interrupt the farewells of a particularly obsequious man with rum on his breath. He claimed the Egyptians believed in reincarnation, and three times this evening he had tried to corner Ess, claiming he recognized her as his bride, Nefertiti. Ess knew better than to get into an argument with him and test his knowledge of Egyptian history, such as asking the name of the pharaoh who was married to the famous queen.

"Did you feel it?" Athena whispered, as the two of them stepped aside, away from the stream of exiting museum patrons.

"You must have found quite a few, or very large pieces, for me to feel it all the way out here."

"It's a solid box, all the seams sealed with gold and inlaid with lapis. It looks impossible to open without destroying it." She sighed and nodded, smiling, at a group of men in clerical collars who tipped their hats to them.

"You're going to destroy it anyway."

"Not if we can match the resonance properly. The box won't open so much as the concealing panels will fall away. Then it's a simple matter of warming the gold to join the seams again."

"Simple? How big is this box?" Ess repressed a low whistle when Athena held her hands apart, indicating a rectangular shape at least a foot long and half as wide, and perhaps six or seven inches tall. "Many pieces of crystal inside?"

"If we're lucky, one solid block of it."

"What does it do? No. Forget I asked." She tried to smile, but her head was hurting and a sense of frustration rose up in her throat. "You're not going to tell me that, are you?"

"In time. Some knowledge has to be learned in bits and pieces, rather than dropped on you in one enormous lump."

"Grandfather did that to me and to Uly all the time. He would hand us books as big as our heads and tell us to read them from cover to cover, and if we didn't understand anything, to make notes and come to him with our questions at the end."

"That sounds like him. How did that work as an educational method?" Athena tipped her head to one side, indicating they should step further into the shadows of the main foyer.

"He was always highly disappointed if we had any questions for him. Usually, after we had read long enough, we were able to figure out the pieces we didn't understand. I found it highly annoying, until I went to school and the teachers only doled out useless, disconnected fragments of information that made no sense until many weeks later, when we had enough to put together a small part of the picture." Ess caught her breath at a sudden, sharp pain in no identifiable place. "Is there a chance they are still alive? Somewhere?"

"Knowing Matilda and Ernest, it is a sure thing, nothing whatsoever having to do with chance."

~~~~

Ess smelled rotten bananas, faint in the air that still reeked of pomade and bitterly strong cigars and musk and violets. Naturally, she was entirely alone in the exhibition room, waiting for Mr. Bloomingard and two guards to come cart away the displays and lock them up for the night. If only Mr. Morse could come up with a telegraphic device that didn't require wires. Something with an independent power source, to let her communicate on the move with the rest of the team.

It was disheartening, to say the least, to realize in that split second that the Revisionists had the same tranquilizer gas as the Blue Lotus.

Immediately, she thought of the cube of crystal Athena had described to her. Ess considered how strong the subliminal chiming had been. If she could sense it, untrained as she was, and know it came from a large quantity of crystal, then someone of the Revisionists who was nearby would know that detail for certain. They would ignore the small pieces of the exhibition sitting out on display now, only going after large pieces. There weren't many such on display. That footstool, an urn, a set of canopic jars sitting on top of their ossuary box. How soon until the thieves left the exhibition area and searched the back rooms, where the new pieces had been left?

"Miss Peabody." Mr. Bloomingard paused in the doorway and looked around the room. "I believe tonight's grand gala was an unqualified success. If—" He frowned, pausing. Two guards came up behind him, pushing heavy wheeled carts. "Do you smell something... odd?"

"Yes, I do. We need to exit immediately." Ess tugged a handkerchief
~~~~

from her tiny handbag. As if that scrap of lace would do any good against the smell or the effects of the gas now spilling into the room? Was she hallucinating, or did yellow-tinted mist creep across the floor from that vent? "That's the same smell that knocked me unconscious last night."

Mr. Bloomingard, for all his fastidiousness, wasn't an idiot. He signaled for the guards to follow him, and then he followed Ess as she hurried into the back room. That box hiding the chunk of crystal was her goal. She would think about a cover story later.

The guard bringing up the rear let out a gargling sound and dropped to his knees. The other guard looked back, then turned, reaching for him.

"No, don't. He'll be all right." Yes, those were billows of yellow-tinted mist, spilling through the air as if sentient and chasing them.

The second guard fell.

"Mr. Bloomingard, come!" she snapped, picking up her skirts with both hands. Despite her ridiculous heels, she was nearly three yards ahead of him when she reached the door marked "No Admittance. Staff Only." Fortunately, it wasn't locked. Ess slammed through it and he caught up with her in those few seconds of pause, pulling it closed behind them.

Then the foolish man stopped, fumbling through his pocket, to pull out a ring of keys.

"Locks won't keep the mist out!" She yanked on his arm. The silly man had to stay awake long enough to tell her where the new shipment was, so she wouldn't have to tear the back rooms apart to find the crystal.

"Yes, but they'll keep those thieves out," he nearly growled.

Maybe he wasn't quite so foolish after all. He snapped the key in the lock and grabbed a ladderback chair to jam under the doorknob before hurrying down the hall.

"The new artifacts—"

"Of course." He gave her a grim smile. "Third door on the left. We have to hide as many pieces as we can before the gas reaches us."

Definitely not foolish at all.

He locked the door of the room and gave the wide windows on the opposite wall a disparaging glance. Ess guessed they allowed the room to be flooded with natural light for a large portion of the day, since they faced south. Much better for the delicate work of the museum caretakers than gaslight or lanterns.

She found the crate Athena had mentioned, the contents carefully lined up on layers of wool padding spread across one table. The box of crystal was easy enough to spot.

"Put the important pieces in your pockets," she said, "and rearrange things so it doesn't look like any were removed. If they think we were knocked unconscious before we could do anything, they won't search us."

Please, Father God, don't let them search us.

Bloomingard nodded, his expression tight-lipped with determination.

He didn't fuss, didn't hesitate, scooping up chains and figurines, wrapping some of them in the lengths of wool and putting them in his pockets. She busied herself, hiding the more valuable pieces down her bodice and in her hair and the fussy shoulders of her dress. Then she rearranged the items that were left, and kept the box in the corner of her eye as she worked. How in the world was she going to hide that? Could she get out one of those windows? At least she didn't have the hoops that were in vogue just a few years ago. She did have a bustle, though.

Enough of a bustle, to lift out her skirts... perhaps she could hide something underneath them without anyone suspecting?

It would require lying down in such a way that she would look like she had collapsed naturally, and yet hide the box.

"They're here." Mr. Bloomingard pressed a length of wool padding against his mouth and nose and backed away from the door, heading for the far wall. He held out twice as much for her, and Ess silently apologized for the mocking thoughts she had harbored toward him. "Miss Peabody, perhaps if you hide under a table, they won't realize a woman is in the room, and they won't search you and take liberties with your person."

"Mr. Bloomingard, you are a gentleman of the highest order." She coughed as a thicker, stronger gust of rotten banana odor caught up with her. Just because she had proven immune before didn't mean the smell didn't nauseate her. When his back was turned, she snatched up the box and went to her knees, twisting and sliding under a table that seemed to provide the most shadows.

"Miss Peabody, if — if — when — oh, dear..."

A rustling of cloth and a dragging sound told her he had succumbed to the tranquilizer gas. He dropped facing away from her, and she was strangely grateful for that. Not just because she still had to tuck the box up under her skirts, necessitating lifting her petticoats in a quite indecent manner.

"Thank you, Father God, that I am a woman. I will never again complain about the idiocy of having to wear enough cloth to sail a schooner," she whispered, as she tucked the box against one thigh, the other thigh lying over it. Ess prayed if anyone found her, she would look as if she had tried to hide from the gas under here, and lay naturally.

Chapter Eight

How long would it take for Athena and members of the Society to smell that distinctive stink and know their foes were here? Ess winced at the thought of the members of her team coming in, smelling the gas, and realizing too late what it was. She did smile a little at the thought of Allistair's discomfort, realizing he was about to suffer what she had. Not that he had shown any disbelief when she made her report, but she always suspected he took everything she said with several grains of salt. More than once, she had caught him making notes that contained her name. As if he constantly recorded her every movement and word and expression for analysis later. Convenient, the ability to read upside down, but it gave her more fuel for irritation with him. If he was nauseated from the gas, she would feel properly avenged for all the recent frustration he had caused her.

A sharp rap on the door startled her. She held still, concentrating on lying limp and breathing as shallowly as possible. A harsh thud followed the rap. Then the door rattled in its heavy iron hinges. She caught her breath when a burning smell pushed aside the rotten fruit odor. Had they set the museum on fire?

The door banged and rattled again. Her heart tripled its pace as she opened one eye. Through the legs of the table between her and the doorway, and the crates stored underneath the table, she could see the closed door. A red glow surrounded the lock. That explained the burning, but how were they doing it? Saying a quick prayer that the smoke wouldn't reach and affect her on the floor, Ess lay down, made sure she was arranged convincingly, and closed her eyes. This time, though, she draped one arm across her face, so she could open one eye and see what was going on around her without being caught at it. She hoped.

What she wouldn't give for that Zeus gun right that moment. Then again, it was always wise to know the limits and possibilities of a weapon before using it. What if it only let her shoot lightning two or three times? What if there were four, five or more people trying to get into the room? No, better to play on the expectations of the thieves: they used tranquilizer gas, they didn't know she was a Fremont and therefore somewhat immune, so they expected her to be unconscious and helpless.

The lock fell to the floor with a shower of sparks and a dull thud on the polished wooden floor. The metal had to be very hot, making it somewhat soft. Ess winced, and made a mental note not to go near the door for a while, if she could help it.

The door banged open, shoved hard. Feet stomped into the room. No caution over being heard. Why would they worry, with all possible witnesses rendered unconscious? She counted six pairs of trouser-clad legs that came through the doorway. Last was a woman in a long gown in a distinctive shade of reddish-purple. It reminded Ess of the blue work shirt of a man she had shot just a few months ago, after the shirt soaked up the blood. A good guess was that this woman had been at the opening gala. She had probably felt the response of the crystal when Athena tested it, which explained why they came here after the exhibition was supposed to have shut down.

There has to be a better way of testing artifacts for crystal without alerting our enemies, she mused. She nearly laughed at the realization that she had definitely sided with Athena and the Society. When had that happened? She always made it a practice to take several days to decide on a major change in her life. Granny had always maintained that people who insisted on quick decisions over important matters usually pushed for a decision to keep others from discovering the negatives, and the reasons to say no.

Later, she told herself. *Think about joining the Blue Lotus after you survive this evening. Survive first, decide tomorrow.*

Ess closed her eyes when the first set of trousers and boots moved around the end of the table. She listened to the other feet follow, no one speaking, and cursed herself for choosing a hiding spot so close to Mr. Bloomingard. If they bent down to examine him, they would undoubtedly see her.

"Bates." The woman spoke. "Test these pieces. Be quick about it."

"Here's that irritating little man who wouldn't let you get a sneak peek," a man said, his voice coming from above Mr. Bloomingard. There was a scuffling sound. Ess cautiously opened her eye, just in time to see him withdrawing his booted foot from Mr. Bloomingard's side. "Is he wearing a corset?"

"What did you do, Carruthers?" The woman sounded bored.

"Kicked the stupid —" He finished with several guttural syllables in a language Ess didn't understand. They sounded incredibly nasty. "He's got something in his pockets."

"Not so stupid, then, trying to protect some trinkets. More presence of mind than you have shown lately." She sighed. "Well? Search him."

Ess held her breath, silently insisting she was invisible, praying the shadows under the table were indeed as thick as she had estimated, and the people working on Mr. Bloomingard kept their backs to her. She nearly inhaled when she heard two men grunt, then a sound like a full sack being dragged across the floor. The footsteps went away. When she estimated they were on the other side of the table, she dared to open one eye. Of course, they had taken Mr. Bloomingard to where the light from the lanterns was better. From the thuds and grunts and sounds of cloth sliding on cloth, they were undressing him. Poor man.

Another set of running footsteps came from far off, sliding as they approached the doorway. Another young male voice gabbled in that language of gutturals. He sounded afraid. The woman snapped orders, again in that language. Ess tried to remember some of the words, to repeat them to Athena.

She would have to learn the enemy's language, wouldn't she?

Then they fled. But not soon enough, she was cheered to note. The sound of gunfire erupted only a few breaths later, accompanied by the sounds of more running feet, then shouts. This time, thankfully, all in English. She stayed still, waiting, in case those people decided to stage their last stand in the artifact preparation room. How long was the tranquilizer gas supposed to be effective? She was starting to feel cramped, and the floor was cold. The pressure of the box under her thighs was cutting off circulation, and that prickly feeling crept up both legs. That wouldn't be convenient if she had to run.

Blast it all, she was just going to have to pretend she got a smaller dose of the gas than Bloomingard. Ess had to move, just in case she needed her legs to run soon.

More footsteps, skidding a little as they slowed and dashed into the room. An unfamiliar male voice cursed. The footsteps came around the table and stopped at the end where the Revisionists had been searching Bloomingard. Another man cursed and the feet clattered on the tile, coming straight toward her.

"Odessa?"

Strong, long-fingered hands grasped her upper arms and turned her over, pulling her out. She nearly let out a yelp, feeling the box slip out from between her legs. She resisted enough to wrap her left leg more firmly around the box to drag it with her, and for effect let out a moan.

"Careful now," that same voice said, and suddenly became recognizable as it lost that note of fear.

Allistair? Could he have been *worried* about her?

Ess knew better than to play wilting and delicate. She let out a long moan and opened her eyes, and reached up to press one hand against the back of her head. Hadn't Charles said he felt like a pony was kicking his head, as an after-effect of the gas?

"I'm all right," she said, needing desperately to sit up under her own power. Not that it wasn't nice resting back against Allistair's chest, but he didn't like her and she didn't like him. Once he got over his worry for her as a fellow-agent, he would be upset. She simply did not need whatever coldness he would heap on her in retribution.

"The he—heck you are," he corrected, but he helped her sit up. "Why isn't he waking?" he asked as he slowly got to his feet.

"Mr. Bloomingard got more of the gas than I did," Ess said, and silently ordered Allistair to go check over the museum official instead of helping her to her feet. "He might be out longer than me."

"What were they doing to him?" Roger asked, as several men in museum guard uniforms came into the room, escorting Mr. Pettigrew and Mrs. Montcreif, the head trustees of this particular building belonging to the Smithsonian Institution.

"Searching him. He thought if we hid some of the new artifacts in our clothes, and the thieves got in here, maybe we could save some." Ess made her voice rough, rather than pitiful and weak. None of her fellow Pinkertons would believe it, anyway.

"Good man," Mr. Pettigrew said.

"Miss Peabody, this is inexcusable. To have a scholar of your stature treated in such a way," Mrs. Montcreif began in her high, warbly voice.

"I have endured far worse in the name of preserving history, ma'am," Ess said. It was hard to keep a straight face when, from the corner of her eye, she caught Allistair rolling his eyes. "In fact, I took the chance of hiding some artifacts and... well, I would appreciate some privacy to retrieve them." She pressed a hand over her bodice.

Mr. Pettigrew's eyes got wider than coffee cups and he blushed. Mrs. Montcrief's mouth dropped open, wide enough Ess could tell she had false teeth, because they shifted and would have popped out if the woman hadn't clamped her hand over her mouth. Then a moment later the woman giggled. A few guards chuckled.

"May I be of assistance?" Athena said. The guards parted like the waters of the Red Sea, revealing her standing in the doorway, framed by Theo and Herman, two of the men from the night before. Had it only been the night before?

"Please." Ess deliberately fumbled, leveraging herself upright, to waste time while Roger and Briscoe took care of carrying Mr. Bloomingard out.

Allistair came back to offer Ess his hand, and she had to take it, but she kept her knees bent, making sure the edges of her skirts stayed over the box. Charles picked up the discarded vest and coat the Revisionists had pulled off Mr. Bloomingard. On the way out, Allistair picked up several pieces of artifacts the Revisionists had dropped after removing them from Mr. Bloomingard's clothes, and put them on the wool padding on the table. The thud of the door closing was a welcome relief.

"Well, it's a very old-fashioned technique, and not very imaginative," Athena said with a soft sigh of laughter, as Ess reached into her low-cut neckline and plucked out three rosy quartz carvings of sacred cats, and pulled a long ebony stylus from the heavy roll of hair at the base of her neck. "Is that everything?"

"Unfortunately, no. Allistair obviously described me as being more... generous... in certain areas, when he obtained the dress. I have several necklaces caught down my back. And I emphasize caught. Help?" She turned, gesturing for Athena to undo the fastenings at the back of her dress.

Athena stepped closer and stopped short when Ess moved back just enough to reveal the box tucked under the edges of her skirts. Her eyes widened for a moment, then she tipped her head to one side, her smile sly.

"Clever girl," she murmured as she got to work retrieving the artifacts from where they were trapped between Ess's dress and corset. "Just as sneaky as your brother, with his speedy reaction time."

"Do you know where he is?"

"I'm not the one charged with keeping his head on his shoulders, but I have sent word to let him know you've been found. It could take some time, as he was sent on a retrieval mission."

"So he's been worried about me?" A warm sensation lit in her chest at the thought of Uly suffering some of what she had felt toward him all these years since he vanished.

"Admittedly, he has grown up some in the last few years." Athena let out a huff of satisfaction and reached past Ess to lay a carnelian necklace on the wool padding. "Enough to think beyond his escapades and adventures. It took a while to impress on him that if the Society wasn't able to locate you, that maybe you weren't safe. Then he took it into his head that you had been kidnapped by the Revisionists and they were torturing you to learn all your grandparents' knowledge. We had to resort to stringent measures to calm him, so he wouldn't jeopardize our operations by breaking into enemy strongholds to find you. There. Is that the last of them?"

She put a small pectoral collar on the table. Ess estimated it had probably been made for a royal child, or even for one of the cat statues that were included in tombs to protect the spirits of the dead on their long journey to the Underworld.

"The last of them." She cast a glance over the artifacts Allistair had put on the table, which the Revisionists had dropped. "It looks like everything got left behind. What stringent measures did you use on Uly?"

Athena fussed with closing up the back of her dress, then attempted to tuck some of her hair back into the sedate chignon. Ess repeated her question, a little louder, drawing a sigh from the woman.

"We have retained quite a lot of knowledge from the ancestors, despite the need to protect the time stream..." Another sigh. Athena grasped Ess's shoulders and turned her so they were eye-to-eye. "You fought the effects of the gas last night with the mental disciplines your grandmother taught you, yes?" She waited until Ess nodded. "There are higher levels of such mental disciplines. At the highest levels, we are able to impose our will on those... let us say, those lacking in discipline."

"That describes Uly." She tried to smile. "What do you mean by imposing your will?"

"We made him forget you, for a time. Now, what shall we do about sneaking this lovely little treasure out of here, and blaming it on the

Revisionists?" Athena continued, when Ess stared, barely able to breathe as the implications of that simple sentence crashed through her mind.

Athena bent and picked up the box. She put it on the table, compared it with her handbag, then Ess's, then attempted draping her lacy black shawl over it. She emptied her handbag, which was certainly twice the size of most women's handbags, likely for such needs as now, and put the contents into clever slit pockets in the sides of her skirts. The sight of pockets in an evening gown was startling and amusing enough to help Ess jar her mind back into the present moment. She took a couple deep breaths, and that got rid of the swimming sensation in her head.

"You made him forget," she whispered, trying out the concept. Yes, she supposed there was more to the mental disciplines her grandmother had taught her. Imposing the power of one's will on the mind of another could be the logical conclusion to mastery of such disciplines. Many years in the future, after long practice.

"Odessa, we can't delay in here for much longer," Athena said, resting a hand on her shoulder.

"I suppose if I play sick and upset, or maybe just weak after a second dose of that gas, no one would wonder if you had your arm around me, supporting me out of here. We could press the box between us, and in the darkness of a cab, no one would notice."

"Good girl. I can see I shall have a lot to report to Matilda when we find her and Ernest."

"You will find them? What exactly were they doing when they vanished? It wasn't just an archeological expedition, was it?"

"Later. You have much to learn before we discuss what your grandparents specialized in." She slid the box inside her handbag and let out a soft grunt of satisfaction when it fit. However, she couldn't close it.

"How much later? How much time?"

"That is the crux of it." Athena shook her head and swung the shawl around her shoulders, then gestured for Ess to hold out her arm.

She doesn't trust me, Ess decided, as the woman threaded first her handbag, then Ess's evening bag up her arm, effectively blocking most of the gold and enamel shining through the opening of the handbag. Athena then wrapped her arm, and the shawl, around Ess's shoulders.

The bulk of the two bags between them made for awkward walking, but Ess slumped and walked crooked, leaning into Athena's support. When they left the room, Mr. Bloomingard was fully awake and looking rather green, perched on one of the long benches that lined the halls in this part of the museum.

Allistair insisted on sending Charles with them back to the hotel, since he had the most experience with the aftereffects of the gas. Theo and Herman had left while Athena helped Ess remove the hidden artifacts, and were presumably on their way back to the *Golden Nile.* Ess pleaded a headache to keep from answering questions from Charles about the gas attack, and silently seethed.

In the hotel, Ess had a small parlor room next to the suite the men shared, mostly for propriety's sake. Still, she had teased Charles and Briscoe several times that she had insisted on a separate room because they both snored enough to wake the dead. Now, her separate room gave her some privacy to speak with Athena, though chances were good Charles was even at that moment leaning against the door. Solely out of concern for her, of course.

"You have saved us an inordinate amount of scheming and maneuvering," Athena said, settling down at the little table in front of the narrow window in the parlor half of the room. She held her handbag on her lap, and both hands resting on it, the very picture of protectiveness. "I do believe we need to send some younger members of the Society out on their own, to live by their wits for a few years. If we could guarantee they would turn out as clever and resourceful as you, of course."

"Flattery." Ess settled on the edge of her bed, when what she longed to do was kick off her tight shoes and peel out of the dress. She couldn't afford to relax. Not yet.

"Of course, that means the *Golden Nile* can go on ahead of schedule and deposit our findings."

Ess noticed Athena did not say where the deposit would be made. Meaning the woman didn't trust her with that much information, even if it wouldn't mean anything to her.

"I do want to come back to check in with you regularly," Athena continued. "Would you write down the exhibition schedule, so we can arrange rendezvous points and dates?"

She slid off the bed and walked over to the little writing desk perched on the far side of the table, for paper and ink. Ess silently scolded herself not to snivel. What made her think Athena would invite her to come with them? Just because she knew Ess's grandparents and claimed she was born a member of the Originators, that obviously didn't mean Ess was expected to immediately uproot her entire life and throw her lot in with them.

Not that I really wanted to. I like my life, my work. I made a promise to Horace, when I signed on.

Ess forcefully shoved that pitiful voice into the back of her mind, and recalled the schedule of the exhibition, along with the hotels where the team would be staying, and the names of the museum officials who were their contacts. She was proud of the straight, bold strokes of the pen, not a single blot or wiggle revealing the turmoil in her belly.

"San Francisco. Very good. We have a stronghold a short distance down the coast." Athena gently blew on the drying ink and glanced over the list again. "What difficulty will you have, ending your association with the Pinkerton Agency, if necessary?"

"What do you mean, 'if necessary'?" Ess slowly sank into the other chair at the little table. Now her head really did ache.

"It might be very helpful to us to have someone among the Pinkertons, with all their access to information, connections to law enforcement and authorities across the country. You might find, however, when you learn more of your heritage, that you would prefer working somewhere else." Athena took a deep breath and leaned back against the chair. "If, that is, you wish to join our mission at all."

"I thought it was a given. Born to it, no choice in the matter."

"Those of us who grow up knowing all the dreadful secrets and our mission, yes, that is how we view it. But you, though you were born to it, were raised... hmm, not in ignorance, but shielded, shall we say? After all, your parents died for the cause. Your grandparents wanted you and your brother to have the right to choose. How could the leadership refuse? Ess?" Athena reached across the table to clasp her hand.

"My... parents... died..." She swallowed hard, fighting a churning lump that was either a howl of fury or a totally humiliating need to spew. "Did the Revisionists—"

"No. They were archeologists, through and through. Investigating one of the Incan pyramids. There were booby-traps, much like the pharaohs are reported to have, to punish those who violate their tombs. The Incans, however, seemed to have far more bloody and brutal imaginations, when it came to punishment." Athena shuddered, and her hand holding Ess's tightened.

"Did you know my parents?"

"Your mother was a student of Matilda's, just like I was. Vivian was like a sister to me, in many ways."

"Then why don't I remember you?" Ess managed to keep her voice down, so Charles couldn't hear, if he were still at the door. She couldn't keep the growl out of it. "Or did you take those memories away?"

"Odessa..." Athena slowly withdrew her hand. "I do swear on the Blue Lotus, our most solemn oath, I will teach you your heritage and answer your questions when we meet again. In San Francisco. Now is not the time."

"Will it ever be?" She held her clenched fists in her lap, when she wanted to slam them on the table, just to release some of the aching fury surging up in the back of her throat with an acid taste. "Why did Uly vanish like he did?"

Chapter Nine

"To save his life." Athena waited, her gaze locked with Ess's. When the younger woman didn't speak, she continued. "Your grandparents were training him, revealing the activities and goals of our organization. He wasn't mature enough to see it as anything more than a grand adventure. He made mistakes. Attracted the wrong kind of attention. We made him vanish, changed his identity, took him to the far side of the world until he was forgotten." Her mouth twitched in a brief, flat smile. "We can do that. We have had generations of practice in hiding who and what we are. Unfortunately, his actions brought suspicions down on your whole family. That is part of why your grandparents went on that expedition and dropped you in that horrid boarding school, rather than taking you with them."

"I wondered," Ess admitted. "After all our foreign travels, why leave me behind when I was finally old enough to be of some help?"

"Splitting up your family, taking uncharacteristic steps. All part of the plan, to throw enemies off their trail. Think about it. Anyone who knew Matilda and Ernest Fremont would never in a thousand years expect them to leave their granddaughter in a stultifying place like that. It saved your life. And theirs."

"Are they alive?"

"Time will tell."

"That's always the answer, isn't it? What does the Great Machine do?" Ess hurried on, before Athena could answer. "The bottom line, despite everything you've told me, is that you don't trust me. Isn't it?"

"We must know each other far better before we can trust each other. Some in the leadership would argue that I have trusted you far too much. That I endanger the cause by leaving you to run free, leaving you with these far too clever and observant agents. However, I have always listened to my... well, in the vernacular, I listen to my gut. My sense of people. I think you can be trusted. Once you have been further educated. But the time is not right."

"Time. Time. Time!" Ess pulled the force of her blow, so her fists only hit the edge of the table, not too loudly, but enough to make the inkwell and pen jump and send one tiny splotch of ink onto the blotter.

"Some among us," Athena said, a weary smile lighting her face, "use that word as a particularly effective curse."

"I suppose that's something I'll learn later. Much later." She leaned back, feeling hollow and spent. Now she understood what Charles had meant, about the pony kicking his head.

"According to your Mr. Fitch, there is a possibility of new artifacts joining the exhibition along the way, as private collectors loan their treasures at each stop. You will need to test them. I will send you one of the crystal rods before the *Golden Nile* leaves dock."

"You can't expect me to steal anything that has crystal in it."

"No. If you can send us a sketch of the artifact so we can make a copy to replace it, and tell us who has it, so we can retrieve it after you are long gone, that would be the best plan. A telegram to our offices in San Francisco should be sufficient to alert us." She reached across the table and picked up the pen, dipped it once, delicately, in the inkwell, and quickly stroked out the address. "Leave the sketch at the hotel where you stay for a representative of the Society to retrieve, and the team who comes after you will take care of crafting a replacement and retrieving the crystal."

"You don't even know if I can draw worth a lick."

"Oh, but I do." Athena stood, and reached out to briefly brush Ess's cheek with her fingertips. "I have some of your early sketches among my mementos of your parents. You never met me, but I sent you birthday presents, and Vivian taught you to call me Auntie Eena." She sighed and stepped back, when Ess could only stare at her, trying to digest this new bit of information. "Good night, Odessa." She tucked her handbag close under her arm, wrapped her shawl around herself, and turned to the door.

"'Night," she murmured. Athena pulled the door closed behind herself. The silence rang in her room before she bent to laboriously untie her torturous shoes.

~~~~~

In the morning, a parcel waited for Ess at the hotel front desk. Several vials of the tonic, in case the Pinkertons encountered more of the tranquilizer gas. The double helix crystal rod. Two books bound in dark blue leather. Both had an Egyptian lotus inscribed on the covers, front and back. One was blank, and accompanied by an inkwell filled with blue ink and a marble pen carved to look like the reed pens used by Ancient Egyptian scholars. The other book was printed in a fine, clear, square font. The frontispiece claimed it was a history of the Blue Lotus Society.

The next page, written in hieratic, pronounced a curse on those who would read the secrets enclosed in the book without the permission of the Blue Lotus Society. Ess shuddered, even as she smiled at the bit of whimsy displayed by whoever had assembled the book. The smile faded when she flipped through the pages, and discovered that she understood perhaps a tenth of the symbols that served as a decorative frame for the information printed on the pages.

"Those Egyptians sure had an odd alphabet," Roger commented, looking over her shoulder. He stepped around her, to settle at the table in their suite for the morning conference over breakfast.
~~~~~

"Very odd. My grandparents were archeologists, and published a number of well-received books on Ancient Egypt, their alphabets and gods." Ess flipped the book closed, but the images stayed in front of her mind's eye for a few moments more.

She had only read four pages so far, but each one had a message that added to what was written in English. Or so she theorized. She would need to brush up on her hieratic. Perhaps after what happened last night and the part she played with Mr. Bloomingard to protect the new artifacts, the museum would loan her a book?

There was far more to the Blue Lotus Society than simply promoting education on Ancient Egyptian civilization and the preservation of its artifacts. Despite the anger still quietly seething deep inside, Ess knew for a certainty now that she would be part of it.

Slowly. Cautiously. Most importantly: on her terms.

~~~~~

There were times when Athena wondered at the wisdom of her predecessors, not only to name themselves after the blue lotus, but to bring the original blue lotus of the ancestors from its safe hiding place of centuries. Besides taking the risk that the Revisionists remembered what the blue lotus was, what it did, and thereby advertise the Society's objective, there was the larger risk of the lotus being stolen.

This, however, was not one of those times.

A soft blue radiance, like the morning after a day of rain in a hot, dry summer, filled the conference room aboard the *Golden Nile*. It washed over the table and nearly three dozen pieces of crystal, including the handful most recently retrieved from their centuries of hiding. It passed through the grain of the wood and Athena's clothes, and soaked into her flesh.

The light was a tangible, solid thing, like honey that slowly coated and penetrated everything. When the source was put away for safekeeping again, the light would remain for hours, ebbing like a gentle spring tide.

The source sat, not in, but nearly two inches above her cupped hands. The blue lotus opened and closed its petals in soft ripples that created the pulses of blue light. It looked like something made of the purest lead crystal, clear, all the details, the textures and veins of a living flower perfectly delineated. There were times, after Athena had worked with the lotus for perhaps half a day, when she thought she could smell the particular perfume of the lotus, green with life, sweet and fresh.

As the ripples of light moved out from the petals, the fragments of crystal floated up from the long conference table, taking on the blue tinge of the lotus, growing stronger and deeper, until they gave off their own light. Athena flinched, then smiled at her own foolishness, when five pieces, including the large cube Ess had protected, rotated slowly in the air and moved toward each other. A soft sigh escaped her when first one, then another, then finally all of them made contact with soft, crystalline chimes
~~~~~

that added to the subliminal song in her blood.

The chimes grew until they formed a chord. However, not a complete chord. She felt the emptiness where several notes belonged but couldn't identify the specific ones. Several of her colleagues theorized that the notes themselves corresponded to the functions of the various pieces of crystal within the Great Machine.

The joined lump of crystal pieces spun toward Athena. She kept her eyes open, refusing to blink, though they watered as the light grew brighter and other colors in the spectrum joined the pulsations, faster, until the lump seemed to be a smooth, light-streaked oval of brilliance. Chimes shimmered out of the lotus, up and down the scale, until the song coming from the new lump also changed, and the two matched. Then the spinning slowed and the lights faded, and the blue began its slow fade. The lump settled down on the conference table, sending ripples through the stream of blue radiance still coating everything, as if settling down in a shallow stream.

Athena took a few unsteady, euphoric steps over to the table and blinked her watering eyes until she could see clearly. The individual pieces of crystal that had joined with the cube were still distinct, and yet with no seam line where they had attached to each other. The sharp edges of the cube had softened, even dimpled in a few places. As if, perhaps, it prepared for where other pieces of crystal would attach to it.

"Blessed God, creator of all that is and was and ever shall be, in this world and all the permutations thereof... we thank You for this gift," she breathed. "Please, is it presumptuous to think this is a sign, a promise of further success soon? A sign that Odessa is a necessary part of our mission?"

She settled down in her usual chair at the middle point in the table, and sighed softly as the light and power emanating from the blue lotus faded enough for it to land in her hand again. Athena continued to pray, asking for protection and guidance for those on the other side of the world, hunting down more artifacts that disguised the fragments of the Great Machine. She gave thanks for the safety of those who had gone into danger recently and asked that blindness and confusion fall upon the Revisionists, to defeat them in the ongoing battle started by their ancestors.

All the time Athena prayed, she kept her eyes open, unwilling to miss even a few seconds of the radiance. She understood a little why Moses veiled his face after speaking with the Lord. The fading of the glory that soaked into his flesh would have been discouraging, even damaging to the faith of the Israelites. Yet at the same time, she wondered how he could have justified depriving them of the sight, of experiencing a tiny glimpse, a muted reflection, of God's glory.

Finally, knowing she had a long list of errands and details that needed attending to, Athena put the blue lotus in its specially designed, padded case and slide aside the plate in the decking under the table, to put it back in its hiding place. She had helped design the *Golden Nile*, and had created nearly a dozen pockets and bolt holes to hide people and treasures. Only three other people knew about this specific hiding place. Like her, they were descendants of the women who had disassembled the Great Machine and scattered the pieces to prevent it being used. And misused. They were the only ones who could take the blue lotus into their hands and sing it to life, and ask it to assemble the pieces of the Great Machine.

Odessa Fremont was a descendant, through both her mother and paternal grandmother. Athena longed for the day when the young woman had been trained and had proven herself loyal to the Originators. On that day, she would teach her about the blue lotus, and the fragments of knowledge that had come down from the ancestors.

"Who knows?" she whispered, as she slid the panel closed and adjusted the chairs back into their normal configuration. "Perhaps she is the one who will take the final step, and open the portal. Once the lotus finds the portal, of course." Athena sighed, smiling at her flight of fancy, and stepped over to the door that opened the conference room to the main corridor through the *Golden Nile*.

The other members of the council waited in the corridor, reading through reports or working on their latest projects. Theo had a heavy leather satchel-box that he carried slung against one hip at all times when he was on board, with the pieces of what would be a larger, more powerful Zeus gun. He worked on it whenever he had to wait for anything or anyone. As Athena paused in the doorway and looked over those waiting there, Theo put the longer, rainbow-streaked glass barrel back into the box. He met her gaze and nodded once before standing. His movement caught the attention of the others, and they all turned to look at the open doorway and stood.

"Success?" Sylvia said, the first one to reach the door. She flipped closed the spring-locked folder that kept her various medical reports and projects neatly compacted and organized.

In answer, Athena stepped back and gestured at the conference table. Most of the glow had faded from the individual bits and pieces and rods and sheets of crystal they had freed of the disguising robe of clay or wood, gold leaf, enamel and other materials the ancestors had used. However, the lump that Ess had protected still glowed with enough blue to elicit soft sighs of wonder from the council.

"What do you think something that big does?" Abernathy asked, as he settled down into his usual chair opposite Athena's spot.

"Let us hope it grants us the power of invisibility," Cedric Towslee offered, his clipped British accent a little stronger than usual. As far as Athena could tell, that meant he was excited. The young aristocrat had the "bored, unflappable noble" role nailed down to perfection. He glanced around the room as he took his seat two to the left of Abernathy, with his trademark good-natured smirk. "That is our ultimate goal, is it not? Go about our business without the world ever guessing who we are and where we came from? Since we cannot erase the Revisionists from the face of the planet without a lot of fuss and questions, invisibility is our best weapon."

"Succinctly put. Thank you." Athena took her seat, allowing herself only a moment of regret, once again, that Cedric was so much younger than her. If she were a decade younger, or he a decade older... then again, she had never had any use or tolerance for romantic fluttering. Even with Fordyce, she had always felt slightly uncomfortable with the way her pulse quickened in his presence, and how at the oddest times she wished he would kiss her.

Romance and finding a spouse had always seemed a waste of time, even knowing how happy her friends had been when they found a life partner. With her few surviving yearmates watching their children reach adulthood, or some of them even becoming grandparents, she had started to wonder, and wish. Having someone to curl up with in the cool of her quarters at night, to talk with and share her deepest fears and dreams, to understand what hurt her when her position as leader of the *Golden Nile* demanded she show no doubts or hesitation... she longed for that. If Fordyce hadn't vanished on that chancy expedition to Antarctica, if he hadn't taken so many similar ventures for the cause over the years... maybe?

Cedric was so much like him, it made her heart ache at the most unexpected times.

Perhaps he and Odessa would be good together, that voice in her conscience offered.

It sounded like her voice, most of the time. Sometimes it didn't, and she wondered if the pressures of her duties and the secrets she carried, even among the highest echelons of the Originators, caused her mind to splinter, just enough to make it easier to survive. Perhaps she was already going insane. After all, despite the evidence of the lotus, the avowed history of the ancestors couldn't possibly be real. Yet because she was always such a rational, organized, controlled person, even she couldn't tell if she was truly insane. At least, not yet.

As the other members of the council settled into their places and the routine that made their duties just a little easier, Athena gladly sat back and listened and took notes and didn't participate. She might be the ultimate authority on board the *Golden Nile*, and responsible for the success and failure of its missions, but she preferred to think of herself as a coordinator or facilitator, not the leader, the one who made the decisions. Besides, using the lotus to test and assemble the fragments of the Great Machine was always draining. The others understood.

Better to be silent and thoughtful and considered wise and cautious, her great-grandfather had always cautioned, *than to open your mouth and reveal you weren't paying a bit of attention. People like to think they've made an enormous contribution, even if you never actually use anything they give you.*

~~~~~
~~~~~

The *Cygnet* was an experimental aircraft to be used for stealth. Athena had chafed at the long detour she had been asked to take, to oversee the final stages of testing the craft, and then report to the Originators leadership in Sanctuary, south of San Francisco. Especially now when she wanted to follow Ess and keep in contact with the girl, to oversee her re-education. Fortunately, most of the leadership didn't know her team was part of the Blue Lotus Society and had built the *Golden Nile*. For security, the Originators had divided into small units generations ago, only the highest ranks able to contact all the arms of their organization. The ability to fly rather than being limited to steamboat or train gave her more time to attend to tasks she considered more important.

However, the time had come, and indeed was running out, to attend to the team designing and building the *Cygnet*. The whole concept of the workshop building the craft rubbed her the wrong way and made her edgy. Her idea of stealth involved heavy forests, cliffs, ravines, and canyons to hide among. How could anything be considered high-security, out on the plains of western Illinois and eastern Iowa, where someone on the ground could see for seemingly miles?

The presence of the long, four-story-tall building was impossible to miss, no matter how far away someone moved. Everyone in the surrounding five towns had to be talking about the people building the odd airship with long wings like a bird and a sail rudder bigger than some sailboats.

She wished she had fought harder to have the research and development station closer to a metropolitan area. Especially now, when she could see the location despite the darkness of the night and the distance between it and the *Golden Nile*.

The fire that raged in the middle of the night made it visible from miles away. Captain Astrid woke Athena at two in the morning, when the *Golden Nile* should have been an hour away from the station, and asked her to come up to the bridge of the airship. In this part of the country, only the largest cities had streets lit by gas lamps. There should have been no concentration of lights large enough to be seen from their altitude and distance, but a golden-red splotch lay low on the horizon ahead of them.

Athena listened to the gut instinct that Matilda Fremont had trained to razor sharpness and gave the order to double the *Golden Nile*'s speed. The instantaneous response and smoothness with which the airship obeyed indicated the captain had anticipated the order.

"I'll take care of the rest, Captain." Athena turned from the glow that grew bigger, just in a few seconds. She flipped the cover off the speaker tube and pulled up on the handle that let her hold the cup mouthpiece close to her mouth. "Attention. Maybe I have your attention, please?"

A faint echo of her voice spilled through the communication tubes in the core of the ship, augmented by the crystal that made so much of the

Society's technology possible.

"May I have your attention? This is an emergency. Landing crew, prepare to deal with an attack. The *Cygnet*'s ground facilities seem to be on fire. Appropriate teams, prepare to deal with fire, attack, and resulting injuries."

Athena hurried off the bridge and back to her quarters. She had very little time to change into something more appropriate for a rescue.

Even though the schedule said they should have been an hour away from the *Cygnet*'s facilities by now, she felt sure the airship was much closer. Captain Astrid preferred to fly at night because air traffic diminished after dark. She also enjoyed taking risks to see how much more speed she could coax out of the *Golden Nile*'s boiler. Athena had never found reason to restrain the talented woman. It was a matter of frivolous pride to always arrive at least fifteen or twenty minutes sooner than anticipated.

So maybe that put them less than half an hour away from the *Cygnet* building? That was a good thing. Maybe, besides a chance to rescue some possessions as well as people, the enemy would still be close at hand and could be captured as well.

"We're high enough to try the sail-wings," Heinrich announced less than ten minutes later, as Athena stepped into the lower level bay area, where the rescue party assembled. He hooked his thumb over his shoulder at a stack of constructs — feather-fine metal woven into the shape of bat wings, lined with silk to catch the air and not only halt descent but allow the wearer some maneuverability. Flight was impossible without an engine of some kind to provide impetus, but Heinrich's years of tinkering had convinced him to give up flight in favor of floating and gliding.

"Do it," Athena said with so little hesitation, the big inventor took a step back, blinking a few times.

Then he grinned, revealing the little boy with the big imagination inside his hulking frame, and whistled for his assistants. She watched as they gathered around, while she stepped around the seams in the floor of the bay, where icy air gusted through every once in a while, and joined Sylvia at the cabinets holding the medical supplies.

"How long will it take him to realize you made the decision to let them participate in the next rescue weeks ago?" the airship's physician asked.

"Probably after we start the cleanup. Please, blessed Savior, we will not have to clean Heinrich and his followers off the ground."

Sylvia muttered an "amen," and continued packing medical supplies.

Chapter Ten

Athena's presence acted as a magnet. As various members of the rescue teams reported to the bay area, they went to her first with suggestions and ideas or just to let her know they were ready. Then they settled into their assigned spots around the perimeter of the massive room, sitting or standing, depending on the equipment they had packed, every one of them taking the precaution of attaching themselves to the safety straps.

Only once in the *Golden Nile*'s operation had the bay doors opened without warning, and only because a saboteur had managed to set the control room on fire and sever the cables that controlled the mechanism. Four people had fallen, but no one had died, thanks to the quick thinking of the basket team. Two jumped into the basket with enough force to send it over the edge, out the gaping hole, while the third member of the team released the ratchet mechanism that let them control the fall of the basket. It had immediately gone into freefall, pulled down faster than the four victims by the weight of the two people in the basket. With ropes and hooks, they had caught the four falling crewmembers and pulled them in, and the one remaining in the bay had hit the emergency stop mechanism. Everyone in the basket had suffered broken bones from the sudden stop, but no one had died. That was the important detail.

Since that day, extra precautions had been instituted. Especially in emergency rescue situations.

"Smell it?" Theo said, coming in and attaching himself to the wall next to Athena.

She started to say no, then realized yes, she could smell the burning. There was an odd, noxious odor, unlike anything she had ever smelled before. She would have said it was kerosene, but this was as close to kerosene as a wax daisy was to a rose still on the stem.

"What is that?" She glanced down at her feet, and was startled to see light filter through the thin material under the gridwork that formed the floor of the bay. How close were they to the fire, if the light from it reached them now?

"They're experimenting with making solid fuel for the engines of the *Cygnet*. Easier to store, and if sealed properly, less likely to burst into flame from a chance spark or extreme heat. I'm guessing they failed. Maybe there was an explosion that set the whole place on fire."

"Solid fuel? Like paraffin?"

"But with oil. Imagine taking the liquid element out of fuel, so a block as big as your fist provides the power of a fifty-gallon tank of lamp oil." He shuddered dramatically, then grinned when Athena cringed, imagining the explosive power of such a thing. "Exactly."

"So it could be an accident down there, and not an attack."

"I hope so," was the last thing he said before the call came that the bay doors were about to open.

Athena shuddered again, knowing all the implications of those three words. If the Revisionists had found this building and had set fire to the solid fuel stores, they were in even more danger. How could they continue to operate if the Revisionists found them despite the layers of disguises? Thanks to steam power and airships and faster transportation, the world had grown far too small, and it was harder than ever to hide from a truly determined hunter.

Still, if the fire below them had been caused by an accident, that meant the world wasn't quite as small as she feared, and the enemy hadn't caught their trail just yet.

Athena found the whole situation depressing. Maybe it was just the lateness of the hour, or her concern because the latest report on Ess's activities was late in catching up with her. Maybe.

She didn't think so.

Heinrich and his crew unfastened their safety ropes and took the five steps to the short sides of the opening in the bay floor. Their faces were nearly hidden behind their goggles and breathing gear, to protect them from the fumes that filtered into the bay thick enough now to be seen. Athena imagined they all had that eager, child-hellbent-on-mischief expression that Heinrich wore when he worked on his inventions. She raised a hand to get their attention and then pressed her closed fist against her heart in silent salute. Heinrich returned the salute, then spread his artificial wings with a snap-click loud enough to be heard despite the roar of the wind in the bay and the fainter roar of the fire below the *Golden Nile*. His team mirrored his actions. He jumped up and out, and vanished before Athena could see if the wings caught the air. One after another, in perfect synchronization, the team leaped into the air until all eight were gone.

She tried to remember what she had learned years ago about the differences in air thickness and speed of descent, depending on humidity and temperature. She hoped the heat rising from the fire below worked in their favor. Testing the artificial wings from cliffs two hundred feet high, with safety harnesses and nets any circus trapeze artist would envy, waiting to catch them in case of an accident, was a very different situation from jumping from the bay of an airship at more than five hundred feet up, in the dead of night, over a blazing inferno.

"Lord God of us all, please, protect them. Give them angel wings if their mortal wings refuse to work," she said, and made no effort to keep her voice quiet. Athena could barely hear herself speak as it was.

Almost before she finished praying, the lower bells rang, meaning the airship had come down far enough to use the basket to lower the rest of the teams to the ground. The stink from the burning buildings grew thicker in the air, making her cough. The blue-tinged gray smoke had black streaks in it. Athena unclipped her safety harness and walked around the bay to the basket waiting for her.

"I don't like it," Polly said, climbing over the side of the ten-foot-by-six-foot open weave basket. The female head of the Society's Marines always said that whenever Athena joined a rescue mission. She knew better than to try to stop her from participating.

"Consider that if I am as valuable to our efforts and God's service as so many of you believe, my presence guarantees safety for everyone else." Athena nearly had to shout now with the roar of the wind yanking on their faces and clothes, and the bellowing growl of the fire below and behind them. "The Lord will not let me die."

"You hope!" the battle-scarred woman said, baring her teeth in a grin.

Athena climbed into the basket and looped her arm through the bracing rope. They had the same argument every time. It suddenly struck her that she knew Polly's real name years ago, but someone had slapped her with the nickname of Hippolyta, for the Amazon queen, and the name had stuck, to the exclusion of all else. Suddenly, that made her feel very old.

Warriors wearing helmets and goggles, packs of supplies strapped to their backs, with Zeus guns in their hands, clipped their belts to the safety straps on the outside of the basket and shoved the toes of their boots into the holes provided for them at the base of the basket. Four warriors on the long sides, two on the short. The basket crew shouted the countdown from ten. On the other side of the bay opening was another basket with the same arrangement -- six inside and twelve on the perimeter. On eight, the baskets lifted off the bay floor, held up by a complicated arrangement of massive pulleys. The warriors moved their bodies like children on a swing, pivoting the baskets out over empty space. On four, the control ropes lowered them until the tops of the baskets were even with the bay floor. On one, the latch holding the control ropes for both baskets opened and freefall struck.

Athena hated freefall. She closed her mouth and refused to close her eyes. The falling feeling was worse when she couldn't see what was going on. She counted to five.

On five, just like all the other times, the basket caught, coming to the end of the slack in the cable, but not so hard that the people inside and hanging on the outside of the basket were jolted loose. Athena exhaled, relieved when she felt the slight resistance. They were still falling, but there was an illusion of control. She counted again, and watched the ground come racing up toward them out of the darkness.

The *Golden Nile* was far enough away from the edge of the fire, Athena only felt a pulsating, almost solid wall of warmth, not the inferno that those on the front lines experienced. She saw a winged figure framed against the flames, folding up the wings against its back, and prayed that was Heinrich, safely down on the ground. He would stay up in the air until all his team had landed, so if he was down, they all were down and were dealing with any enemies they had spotted from the air.

At ten, the basket jerked just slightly, meaning the second level of pulleys to control the descent had come into play. They caught on the cable, creating resistance and slowing their fall. Athena glanced at Polly. They stood close enough they touched from thigh to shoulder. The rescue team leader cocked an eyebrow at her, amusement and excitement in her eyes, but said nothing.

In perfect synchronization, the warriors on the outside of the basket let go, falling backwards, diving head-down. Four seconds later, their parachutes bloomed, looking like bloody roses against the flames off to their left. Athena counted down the sequence to landing, telling herself she wanted to catch the basket crew once, just once, making a mistake. Just two seconds off in counting, that was all she asked.

The basket thudded and bounced twice in landing as she was about to silently say "one" in her head. She swayed into Polly, who swayed into the person on her other side. Athena let go of the support rope as everyone but her and Polly caught hold of the basket rim and swung their legs over the side, running toward the fire almost before their feet touched the ground. Polly followed two seconds later, after looking around to assess the situation. As if she hadn't been studying it on the way down.

The silence, other than the roar of the fire, made this seem just a bit eerie. Athena readied her Zeus gun and sat on the basket rim, looking around before swinging her legs over. She said a silent prayer of thanks that she was still fit enough to complete such maneuvers.

Why was she thinking of her age so much recently? Other than having Odessa Fremont constantly in her thoughts, of course. Seeing the young woman, carrying her mother's and grandmother's features and bits of their personalities, had impressed on Athena how much time had accumulated behind her, and made her wonder how much still lay ahead of her.

It's always a matter of time, one way or another, she mused. For once, she didn't laugh at the double meanings in the simple four-letter word.

Then one of Heinrich's winged followers raced up to her with the first report on the situation, and she had no more time to wax philosophical.

Theo, it turned out, was half-right. The fire was indeed fed by the different varieties of solid fuel the scientists here had created, and the fire *had* started by accident. However, only accidental because the Revisionists who had attacked had not set the fire. It was a result of the battle, and only at the end, when the enemy fled. An unlucky bullet had shattered the barrel of a Zeus gun, causing a shower of sparks, which had caught in a pile of debris from a collection barrel that had been upended in the struggle.

Because of the nature of the work being done here, keeping the ground clear of any and all flammable substances was a priority. The Revisionists had pulled out the wheeled barrels of collected debris as barriers to slow down the security team chasing them. Those sparks had lived long enough in the dry twigs and lint balls and wood shavings to be blown against the side of a tent that held one failed attempt at solid fuel. It was highly unstable, and released fumes so pungent they made anyone who breathed them instantly sick. They were being stored in the tent to provide maximum ventilation until a way of disposing of the experiment could be decided on that wouldn't blow a crater in the ground.

No one was dead — one good result. Four enemy attackers had been captured, and were already being bundled up to the *Golden Nile* under guard, in the other lift basket, by the time Athena got that report.

Unfortunately, in the first explosion that spewed liquid fire across the compound, several people on both sides had been badly burned. The experimental fuel was extremely difficult to smother. Another reason why it was considered a failure.

"We need the lotus," Sylvia said, when she finished the preliminary report on the injuries for Athena.

"The only question is if I bring it down here to them, or if we can take them up to it," she responded.

"Right now, speed is more important. They're all in so much pain, moving them won't make it any worse."

Athena rode up in the basket with the most badly burned, the ones splashed with liquid fire. Something shriveled inside her with every moan, with the shudders that constantly wracked the bodies of the sufferers. Fury had kindled deep inside her by the time the basket reached the *Golden Nile* and the bay crew reached out to haul it in and secure it for offloading Sylvia's patients. Athena rarely wept, but she wept now for these people, the ones she knew and the ones she didn't.

Who infuriated her more? The Revisionists, who insisted on inflicting their determination of what was "good for all mankind" on the world? Or her own predecessors, who had mistakenly believed that dismantling the Great Machine and taking technology out of the hands of the rebels would prevent disaster centuries in the future? Fortunately, some of those predecessors had argued against the need to destroy all records, anything that would reveal future events to those who would be the guardians of Earth's time stream. Athena had copies of some of those books. In one of them, an event referred to as the "gun control debate" had been discussed. Someone, whether trying to be funny, or simply to state the obvious in a way that would remain in people's minds, remarked that, "When guns are outlawed, only outlaws will have guns." If peace-loving people put aside their guns, they would have no defense against the criminals and brutes and those who felt justified in taking whatever they wanted by force. To protect lives and what people had created with hard work and honest effort, a method of defense had to be not only workable, but visible. Someone had to act, rather than just waiting to react to the next attack or disaster. That was what the Society did now, after generations of insisting on merely monitoring the events of the world.

Athena still couldn't decide if the proliferation of technology was a sign of interference in the time stream by the Revisionists, or a natural result from changes made centuries ago. It didn't matter. What mattered now was finding the Revisionists, stopping them from acting, and ensuring that they could not find any more pieces of the Great Machine than they had found already. No matter what it took.

~~~~~~~~

As Athena carried the blue lotus from the conference room to Sylvia's domain, in her mind she heard the scolding, the criticism from some of the Elders. What was the greater crime she was about to commit? Allowing those who could not make the lotus come to life to actually see it? Using it for such "mundane" tasks as healing the fatally injured and easing the suffering of the burned warriors? "Wasting" the energy of the blue lotus to heal some who might die anyway?

Sometimes when she was weary and aching from head to toe from using the lotus, Athena heard a quiet voice in her mind, insisting that the naysayers among the Elders were simply jealous. She brought light from the lotus when they could not, by a simple "accident" of birth. She could request help from it, guidance in the form of images from the ancient memories stored in the lotus when the Great Machine had been in one piece and functioning. She could touch it without being burned by the energy that flared from it. They could not.

"Thank the good Lord," Sylvia said, as Athena stepped into sickbay and the lotus flared a deep blue that drove away the shadows, reacting to the atmosphere thick with pain.

"Who first?" Athena tried to ignore the wide-eyed wonder, the pleading expressions, the fear and pain that warped familiar faces into gross caricatures of human beings.

What she meant was, "Who is worst off?" but she knew better than to say that aloud.

Athena felt the attention of all the sufferers in the room focus on her as she followed Sylvia to a bunk that had been closed off with curtains. The air was thick with steam from a pot that simmered next to the wounded man's pillow, spilling soothing herbals into the air and filling it with healing moisture. Athena choked on a whimper of horror and fought not to gag as Sylvia pulled back layers of gauze soaked with ointment, and she saw the ruined half of a face, red and black char, and the shoulder that had been burned down to the bone.

"Make me an instrument of Your grace, oh my Lord and Savior," she
~~~~~~~~

whispered, and held the lotus over the suffering man's chest as she bowed her head and gratefully closed her eyes. Even through her closed eyes, the intensity of the blue radiance that spilled from the lotus as it worked seeped into every corner of her being.

And so it began.

The morning passed in a blur of images and sensations. The power of her will guided and yet was subservient to the power of the lotus. The process had been described to her by her teacher as a weaving together of her body's processes with the energy stored in the crystal of the lotus. It used her healthy body as a pattern and imposed that pattern of wholeness and regeneration on the damaged body, which by necessity was in some ways woven together with Athena's. It shielded her from the worst of the pain, the burned aching that flowed with every beat of her heart, the stiffness in her lungs where smoke had poisoned the tissues, the charred sensation that reached down to the bone. It shielded her, but not completely, and Athena had to consciously fight every moment not to give in to the suffering that tried to overwhelm her like an oncoming storm tide. It would be too easy to drop the lotus and flee, to seek clean, cool air and the sheltering quiet and darkness of her quarters.

Three warriors were dead by noon, when Sylvia told her, multiple times before it sunk in, that there was no one else in need of healing.

"Put it away, and then put yourself away," the *Golden Nile*'s physician ordered, raising her voice, when Athena tried to ask about the wounded she had worked on.

Despite Sylvia's best efforts to get her to go to her quarters and rest after the long effort of healing, Athena stayed in sickbay until she could get the names and conditions of everyone. The ones who had gone back to their quarters with minimal scorching on their skin and pots of salve to smear on at regular intervals. The ones who were still finding it difficult to breathe but improving as the minutes turned into hours. The few who had to remain in sickbay were asleep in the long tubs of a concoction Sylvia and her fellow healers had created. The base was gelatin from hooves, hides and cartilage, infused with blood-purifying herbals and lanolin, and a healthy dose of sedatives. The theory was to have patients sleep their way to health.

Athena planned to do the same, after one final stop on her way to her quarters. After all, she was responsible for every soul aboard the *Golden Nile*.

She knew there was nothing she could do, but she went to the morgue anyway. The words caught in her throat—the apology she wanted to make, the ritual words of thanks and blessing and freeing them from their sworn duty, to send their spirits on to their reward. She paused in the doorway of the long, narrow room, letting the chill of the air soak into her skin. It was a welcome relief after experiencing the heat and stinging of the fire over and over with every new sufferer she helped. In a burst of weary fancy, she wondered if the souls of the departed lingered to watch over their bodies, and they appreciated the cool relief as well.

"Thank you," she finally said. "May the good Lord welcome you home, with rejoicing, and may He say, 'Well done, good and faithful servant,' as you enter His presence."

It was all she could say, physically and emotionally. It would never even begin to pay the debt.

As she curled up in her bunk in her quarters a short time later, skin and hair still damp from a vigorous scrubbing, the anger that had planted seeds during the horrific morning sent up its first malignant, skeletal white shoots from deep in her soul. She was too tired to do more than know the new heat came from anger. Then she slept, and a longing for vengeance on the Revisionists whispered in her dreams.

Chapter Eleven

The first report on Odessa Fremont's exhibitions came the day the *Golden Nile* docked to conduct funeral services for the warriors killed in the fire. Athena put aside the thick packet of papers and photographs, comforted by the plain yellow sealing wax on the envelope that contained all the disparate elements. If the sealing wax had been green or purple, she would have worried, perhaps would have hurried to her quarters to read everything through. Of course, then her mind would have been full of whatever trouble Ess had gotten into instead of the funeral services. Indeed, the report did keep bobbing to the surface of her thoughts as Reverend Whitlach conducted the memorial services and Sister Devona led the singing, but not as a distraction. She looked forward to finding out that nothing much had happened to Ess. No attacks by the Revisionists. No problems with thieves, trying to collect pieces for the idle rich who considered themselves above the law and rationalized that because they had money, they could have anything they wanted. Learning the young woman was applying herself to her studies and keeping out of trouble would be boring but refreshing.

Sister Devona, as always, turned the time of mourning into a time of reflection, and then celebration. The dead had gone on to their reward, each one greeted at the gates of Paradise with the words Athena hoped one day to hear: *Well done, good and faithful servant.* For them, the war was over.

Athena didn't quite subscribe to the pleasant imagery of the dead who had gone before them being able to look down from on high and watch the activities of their descendants and philosophical heirs. Still, it was comforting, sometimes amusing, to imagine her predecessors shouting out encouragement or criticism, depending on how well she had carried out her duties. Several teachers who had since died were the sort who could never be satisfied, no matter how well she learned her lessons or performed her duties. Athena imagined them standing just inside the gates, tapping their feet, impatiently waiting until Christ welcomed them, then clearing their throats and stepping up. "Begging Your pardon, Lord, but if You will recall the incident when the Revisionists were operating a fraudulent archeological dig in Sumatra, if Athena had acted sooner..."

The same people who had frustrated her to tears and an urge to give up and go home and devote herself to support activities now made her want to smile. So Athena easily stood with the others and joined in the long afternoon of singing one camp meeting song and Negro spiritual after another, looking forward to the end of time and their great reward.

In some ways, funerals and memorial services were better than weddings and christenings, because Sister Devona knew how, with song, to take them from the lowest of low points and bring them all out on a high note, singing and smiling.

Athena felt a song vibrating softly in her throat, waiting to burst out, as she climbed the steps to the top of the elevated docks, and stepped back on board the *Golden Nile*. Very few of those who boarded with her were in any mood to talk, and she was grateful. She nodded to those she passed and skimmed down the passageways to her quarters at long last. Then she sighed in anticipation, as she stepped through the door and saw the thick envelope with the yellow seal, signaling no priority ranking to the information inside.

The first exhibition after Washington had been Chicago, followed by St. Louis. Florence Hightower was head of the station house in St. Louis. She and her daughters and nephews ran a livery stable, with a side business of shuttling people from one side of the river to the other with ferries and rowboats. Florence needed a somewhat wry sense of humor to deal with her busy, sometimes aggravating life at her particular post, and Athena knew whatever she had to say about Ess and the Pinkertons protecting the artifacts, it would be amusing. The more boring the duty, the wittier Florence grew. Sometimes even acerbic.

Something is wrong with that girl, but I cannot put my finger on it. Other than a suspicion that she has an attitude like her grandmother. I loved Matilda. You know that. All the girls under her tutelage loved her. But sometimes you wanted to back the woman against the wall with a pistol under her chin until she gave someone else's viewpoint a chance.

Fortunately, Ess isn't like her brother. And you know my children all think Ulysses hung the sun in the sky. Thank the good Lord, my girls have too much sense to believe anything when he flutters those long lashes and gives them soulful looks, and my boys prefer to get into their own trouble, rather than follow him into his.

Athena sighed and put down the letter to unfasten her shoes and her skirt. This was going to be a long letter. It was easy to see Florence was in a talkative mood, and had no one to air her thoughts with.

Our associates along the way have been checking on her. If the train stops at a side rail for an hour to let another train pass, one of us manages to get onto the train or at least look through the windows from a high angle. She's one of those people who brood, if she doesn't have her nose in a book. You gave her the special book, did you not? The one to test her memory and understanding and her ability to learn? Because I have not moved in close enough yet to see what's printed on the binding, but it looks like ours. At one stop, our man at that station reported she sat alone on the train, with a book in her lap, and several more spread on the seats next to and facing her, and looked perturbed that she had to stop and pull out a penknife to sharpen her pencil.

Athena glossed through the next two pages, full of the reports of the people who had checked on Ess along the way: porters, ticket station workers, hotel workers. At every stop of the exhibition journey, someone affiliated with the Originators came to watch her, guard her, and assess her actions and character. Athena wondered what Ess's reaction would be when she realized just how little privacy she had since she stepped under the watchful eye of the Originators. For all she knew, the young woman had inherited her father's sensitivity, and she knew she was being watched. Perhaps that sense of no privacy, of being watched at all times, affected and influenced her actions? Perhaps that was the "something wrong" that Florence couldn't identify yet? Ess was uneasy, and it affected how she reacted to and interacted with the people around her.

When our watchers played the signal song outside her window at the side rail, and then outside her hotel room window, she never responded.

Athena frowned. That was a problem, definitely. Ess knew they wanted to keep in contact with her. Maybe she hadn't had her flute nearby when the signals came? Or perhaps she didn't feel free to play the response notes, because someone was in the room with her?

I had my youngest boy sneak into her room and leave her a flute, in case she lost hers, but there it was, sitting out in full view, on top of her pile of books. He was some perturbed, because he could not figure the language the books were written in.

A smile flicked across Athena's lips. She could hear Florence chuckling over that remark as she wrote it. While the many nephews under her care were good, honest, reliable, creative boys, they had a dislike for books of any kind. They enjoyed ciphers and playing with coded messages, and their dearest hopes seemed to consist of being horseback messengers with enemies chasing them down, guns blazing, and creating a new, unbreakable code. It had to irritate the boy that such "easy tricks" as books could defy his comprehension. Maybe when it finally occurred to him that there were languages in the world besides English, that assembled words differently, and even alphabets that didn't use the same letters, he might just apply himself to "silly old book learning," as one of the many nephews had expressed the last time Athena visited the Hightower household.

> *We have tried twice since then to make contact, making sure she was
> alone and had her flute ready. No response whatsoever. And here be
> something that worries me: I sent my oldest, Isabella, into the hotel,
> dressed as a junior housekeeper. She has quite a future as a pickpocket or
> a magician, if I do say so myself. No more than ten minutes and she had
> the main housekeeper's big old key ring and was on her way to Odessa's
> room. Isabella reported she did indeed find the Society book for new
> recruits, sitting out in plain sight on the lamp table. It did not look like
> it had seen much wear. No creases in the binding. She thought there
> might even have been dust on it. That made little sense to her.*

Nor did it make sense to Athena. Especially after the previous report
from some watchers along Ess's journey, when they clearly reported the
young woman was constantly studying. Unless...

It was an old trick, but one Matilda Fremont had taught her students.
Carefully placed threads or hairs or bits of lint or even dust, to give
indication that the room had been searched, items moved or examined,
while the occupant was out of the room. Athena smiled and hoped Isabella,
who had quite a future as a logical thinker and analyst for the Society, had
thought of that particular tactic and had not fallen into the trap.

> *Bella thinks either our Miss Fremont is brushing up on her
> understanding of all the different Egyptian alphabets before she works
> on the messages printed in the margins, or she is one of those people who
> are very careful of their possessions. You know the ones. We had a few
> when we were training under Matilda. They sewed covers for their books
> and were careful of the bindings, so you could swear they had never been
> read. Did not occur to my Bella until later that maybe the dust was a
> trap. Hindsight is not always clear, especially when trying to remember
> what you did not really see, if that makes sense. Maybe the book's cover
> might have been touched up with dye, to make it look new?*

"Ah, now that's a new trick I didn't think of. But does that mean you
know we're watching over your shoulder, Miss Odessa?" Athena
murmured. She turned onto her side in her bunk and slid the page of the
letter to the bottom of the stack. But slowly, to make the suspense last, while
she waited to find out what else Florence had to say about Ess.

One of her favorite presents from Fordyce had been a stack of tabloids
featuring Sir Arthur Conan Doyle's stories of the adventures of Mr. Sherlock
Holmes. Athena loved mysteries and puzzles inside stories, but felt sure
that real life was far more mysterious and fascinating than anything the
most talented author could create.

The next page was filled with reports from the two nephews and three nieces who took turns following Ess and her associates as they moved about the city, establishing contact with the local police and the museum authorities, and prepared for the opening night of the exhibition. Ess availed herself of the local library, a matter of pride for the scholars in the area. She also borrowed books from the museum curator, who was proud to say he had several books on Egyptology that weren't available anywhere else in the United States. She also checked with several book stores in the city, requesting titles or suggestions for other books on anything having to do with Ancient Egyptian writing.

Athena agreed with Florence's theory that Ess was rebuilding her neglected education in all things Ancient Egyptian. Her education had been interrupted at the worst possible time by the necessary trip Matilda and Ernest took to Peru. All the years of study, the foundations her grandparents had built for her, had left her poised at the point in her education when everything would have come together to make total sense. Ernest had confided in Athena that he expected his clever Odessa to make new discoveries in Egyptian languages and writings, once she was allowed to take the bit in her teeth. That had never happened because of those fools at the boarding school. Athena still felt her gut tighten when she thought about those books that detestable Van Hastings woman had taken away from Ess. She was very lucky Ess had only revealed her activities to the Secret Service, instead of tearing down the school around her.

But no... Athena sat up and swung her legs over the side of her bunk and cradled the pages in her hands, unseeing, as a new revelation spun through her mind. No, Odessa Fremont wasn't like her impulsive, flamboyant brother at all. She was clever and patient. She was willing to wait and plan and work slowly, to reach her goal, evidenced by how thoroughly she had escaped and erased her trail. Couldn't the same be said of revenge for whatever harm others caused her? She wouldn't strike back immediately, but wait for the proper moment. She would study her enemies and learn about them, establish a foundation before doing anything.

Which was what she did now, studying before she read and translated the messages embedded into the decorative borders of every page of the Blue Lotus Society book.

It was quite a logical, sensible, laudable strategy. Athena silently applauded Ess. Yet at the same time, she was sure something was very wrong in doing exactly that.

"She doesn't trust us, does she?" she murmured aloud to help her grasp the theory rumbling in a semi-nebulous cloud in her mind.

The question now was whether Ess had been dissembling, when she seemed so cooperative and eager to learn, back in Washington...or something had happened after the *Golden Nile* flew away, to make her doubt and question, and drag her heels now.

Athena finished reading the letter, pleased to note that Florence had included the original notes from the watchers assigned to Ess's hotel up until an hour before the messenger packet was sent. Only a day had passed since then. The exhibition had been running for three days, with no odd events, no attempts to steal artifacts, no indication that any Revisionists had followed the crates of artifacts to the next city.

That was no guarantee, however, that the Revisionists wouldn't be waiting in Kansas City. No high society folk in St. Louis had loaned their private artifacts to the exhibition, but two families with pretensions of archeological expertise had foolishly announced in Kansas and Missouri papers their decision to "assist the British Museum in the education of our citizens about the mysterious, fabulous, ancient civilization of Egypt." After stories had appeared in those same papers about burglaries targeting Egyptian artifacts, that announcement was equivalent to stepping into a shooting gallery with targets on chest and back, begging someone to shoot.

Whether the Revisionists would be there or not, Athena made up her mind that she would be. It was high time she attempted to learn what churned through Odessa Fremont's clever mind.

~~~~~

A knock came on Athena's door at nearly ten that evening. She had been waiting for the *Golden Nile* to leave the dock and head north for Kansas City, but the airship had yet to do anything more than stoke the great engines. The maintenance crew had been all over the ship, inside and out, from the moment they reached the docks, making regular repairs, and even touching up the paint since they had the time. There was nothing left to do, unless of course specially ordered supplies hadn't been loaded yet. If that had happened, someone would tell her. So what caused the delay?

"Yes, who is it?" she said, barely stopping herself from snapping. Knowing she was letting her personal feelings intrude and make her impatient just aggravated the tension tightening her jaw. Her footsteps were rapid and sharp as she crossed to the doorway, and it took conscious effort not to yank the door open. What was wrong with the fool in the hallway that he couldn't answer? Couldn't he hear her over the growing rumble of the engines?

"Thought you'd be ready to chew though the door by now." Captain Astrid stepped back and gestured for Athena to precede her down the passageway.

"If you had a good excuse and you had the time, you would have told me," she responded.

"There's always something, leaving the dock." The scar tissue covering the right side of Astrid's face hid most emotions, and she had learned long ago to put the untouched side of her face into shadows. Especially when playing poker or dealing with strangers. She did it now to Athena as they walked down the passageway to the common area in the core of the ship.
~~~~~

"You're enjoying this too much," Athena accused, catching the sparkle in her old friend's crystalline gray eye.

"Hmm, maybe I just like seeing you react to surprises. We were signaled a team was coming to catch up with us. Their arrival would only make us half an hour late casting lines, so I didn't bother telling you." She shrugged. Athena caught the twitching of her lips.

"The team is only arriving now? Nearly two hours late," she added, tugging her pocket watch out, and pressing the stud to flip the cover open. "I stand corrected. One hour and forty-eight minutes."

"That's nearly two hours, by my books," Astrid said, her tone just a little too even and calm.

"I repeat: you're enjoying this too much." She reached to push open the door into the common room, but the captain beat her to it. "This had better be good."

"Define 'good,'" a gravelly male voice barked from the other side of the eight-sided room.

Athena rarely experienced shock so great she couldn't speak or even move. She was aware she stood there in the doorway, staring at the gaggle of travel-stained, grimy, bearded men, most of whom were eating as if they had been starved for the last year. All except for their leader, a bull elephant of a man who could go for a month on nothing but coffee and still have "reserves" to spare.

Staring was quite logical in this situation. It wasn't often that a man came back from the dead. Once was a miracle. Twice was suspicious, as her father had said in one of his expansive moods. Three times was making a habit of something that tested all propriety and God's patience.

If anyone could make a habit of coming back from the dead and get nothing but a sigh and a "Boys will be boys" response from the Almighty, that man was Fordyce Chamberlain.

"Oh, I know the definition of 'good.'" Athena managed to get tongue and brain and feet moving. She stepped out of the doorway and felt as if the floor moved underneath her as she gingerly crossed the room.

Everyone else sat, but of course Fordyce couldn't do that. He had to stand at the head of the table, one hand full of bread folded around enough meat and cheese and pickles to choke an elephant, the other hand holding a bowl of soup. He grinned now at her and lifted the bowl to his mouth, guzzling it down while she approached.

Funny, but the floor wavered under her feet. Or had the *Golden Nile* finally cast the mooring lines and moved away from the docks? Yes, she thought, after a moment of testing the vibrations. It was just the airship's normal vibrations when embarking.

"The problem is finding a definition for you," she finished, waiting until Fordyce had put down the bowl, just in case he laughed at her sauciness. The last time she had made him laugh while eating, the results had been... regrettable.

More regrettable was that since she had last eaten with Fordyce Chamberlain, five of their friends had died in the war with the Revisionists. Three couples had married, and nine children had been born.

"Lads, I can see right now, we wasted the last six years, fighting our way back from Antarctica," Fordyce announced, after only a bark of laughter. He took a big bite from his bread-and-meat combination. Not by any stretch of the imagination could it be called a sandwich, because that word indicated some sense of decorum. Chewing, he waited until the men around him at the long table slowed their eating and most of them looked up, finally noticing Athena and Captain Astrid in the room. "Our dear Miss Latymer has already discovered the secret to controlling time. Younger than the last time I saw you," he added, bowing.

"Obviously," Athena shot back, her face scorching hot, "you haven't had anyone to practice flattering while you were away." She swore she could feel every gray hair on her head, and the gaze of every man focused on those hairs, as if they glowed with a light of their own.

Younger than the last time, indeed!

"You're the only one I'd ever want to." Fordyce snatched up a napkin and wiped his mouth, then down his chest. "Give us a hug, darling?"

Later, Athena couldn't really say why she complied, why she didn't even hesitate. Maybe it was still the shock. Maybe she needed to prove to herself he was real and not a dream coming to taunt her years after she had made her peace with God for letting Fordyce die. She crossed the last few feet between them, rested her hands on his broad chest, and leaned in to kiss his cheek. Of course, he wouldn't settle for that, and she was glad. Her heart tripled its pace as he wrapped his arms tight around her and picked her up off the floor, turning them around twice before settling her on her own feet. He didn't let go until he had kissed both her cheeks.

The men who didn't have their hands or mouths full of food let out cheers or applauded and Athena had to force herself to turn and look for Captain Astrid. The airship's captain gave her a nod and a pleased smile and showed no sign of leaving. Then again, what good would it do, when the common room was full of these big, dirty, starving men, shoveling food down like they had been reduced to hard tack or boiling their own boots for food for the entire time the Antarctica mission had been missing?

"Who do I blame for your return from the dead?" she asked, turning to look down the table at the semi-familiar faces. Her face hadn't cooled. If anything, it felt warmer, when Fordyce wrapped his arm around her waist and kept her at his side. At least he put down his food.

"That would be me, ma'am," Ulysses Fremont said, standing up from a chair two seats down on Fordyce's right.

"Thank you." She pressed a hand over her heart. "You have the gratitude of the Society." A broken chuckle escaped her, as she thought of how she could repay him, just as soon as they had some privacy. "If anyone could have found this scapegrace and his fellow ruffians, I should have known it would be you."

"Thank you, ma'am." His grin made Uly look ten years younger.

"Gratitude?" Fordyce said. "Can it be you're actually glad to see me?"

"I'll be even more glad when you've had a bath and changed your clothes. If these filthy rags can even be called clothes." She made as if to slap his jacket. Standing this close to him, she could see that he had indeed lost several stone of weight.

"I've never known you to be in such a soft mood toward me, my love."

"Ford—" She tried to step back, but he held her tight against him. It wouldn't do her any good to stomp on his foot. She had tried that before.

"So since you're so glad to see me—what do you say, lads?—I'm going to take my chances and ask you again to marry me."

"Again?" Athena pressed hard with both fists against that chest that was still as broad, despite the weight lost through hardship. "When, you big buffoon, have you ever *asked* me?"

"Why, plenty—" He gaped when she shoved free.

"Never. You have yet to gather up the courage to ask me. You sidle up to the subject and you drop hints, and then when you don't get the answer you want to a question you never asked, you stomp off to drink with your rascal friends and complain that you don't understand women. Truer words, I might add, have never been spoken!" Athena stepped back, fists in her hips, face hot, and fighting not to laugh.

At the back of her mind, she played with the idea of accepting his backhanded proposal. In front of witnesses. Wouldn't that serve him right?

Maybe, just maybe, he wouldn't hare off on his death-defying missions and vanish for years at a time, making her worry and wonder and consider knocking him senseless when he did return. Or he might take her with him, the next time he felt it necessary to travel past the boundaries of civilization to prove that mythology had a basis in fact.

Fordyce stepped back and scratched the thick thatch of hair, still blue-black despite all the dust ground into it. He looked at his men, some of whom sat back, arms crossed over their chests, grinning and ignoring their food. Consternation crinkled his face. It happened rarely, but Athena loved it when she managed to embarrass him. He was such a fumbling dear when it finally got through his thick, obsessive mind that he had made a mistake.

"Sorry, love. I've just been thinking about this for the last couple years. I had it planned a little better than this." He shrugged, looked around the room, offered one of his rumbling little chuckles. "Actually, I planned to catch up with you in the library at the Sanctuary, sweep you off your feet, carry you out to the garden and ask you. And if you said no, I'd hold you over the waterfall until you said yes," he added with another shrug.

"Well, I shall consider myself duly warned, not to let you anywhere near me when I am at the library in the Sanctuary." Athena's glance swept the table full of men, most of whom seemed to finally be slowing down in their eating. "Gentlemen, welcome home. When you've had a chance to wash up and rest, I would appreciate a written report, but even more, a chance to speak with you. Mr. Fremont?"

"Ma'am?" Uly made as if he would step around the table to join her when she stepped away.

"When you're finished, please join me in the conference room. Both of you," she added, turning to include Fordyce. "After you've both had a chance to wash and change your clothes."

"Together?" Fordyce sounded like a little boy deprived of a treat he thought he had earned.

"Separately, of course." She choked, fighting down laughter, when his face lit up. "Gentlemen."

Most of them scrambled up from their chairs to bow or at least nod to her as she left the room, with Captain Astrid right behind her.

"I don't know if I should hug you or write up a reprimand," she muttered, as they headed down the passageway again.

"Worth it, just to see your face. The man really does love you, you know."

"As much as he can love anyone."

"Athena..." She sighed as they came to a cross passageway and she turned to go another way. "We lose too many good people. So what if you're not children anymore, with a long life to share and drive each other insane?"

"The problem is that we're both so set in our ways..." Athena stopped and put her back to the wall, after glancing down both passageways, to make sure they truly were alone. "We're both unable to say no when the leadership gives us work to do. I'd go with him in a heartbeat, but with my duties as guardian for the lotus... what can I do?"

"Maybe it's time to stop asking that question. Do what your heart tells you." Astrid took a few backward steps down the passageway. "Maybe he's finally learned to put you ahead of the leadership, too. What about Odessa?"

"What about her?"

"She's born to be a guardian for the lotus, just like her mother and grandmother. Train her to take over for you, then you and Ford can run off together and be young fools in love for a while."

"Fools in love, yes, but not young anymore, are we?" She managed a smile and wrapped her arms around herself against a chill from deep inside.

Chapter Twelve

Uly Fremont came through the door of the conference room first, before Athena had finished spreading out the reports and maps and photographs provided by Florence and her team in St. Louis. She was both disappointed and relieved to have the young man appear first. His hair was still dripping on the ends and the point of his beard, meaning he hadn't taken enough time to dry off before dressing and coming to report. What had she given away in her simple order? Or had someone who had encountered Ess during her visit to the airship told Uly that his sister had been found, and he came here so quickly to get all the information? Athena nearly laughed at the disappointment that shot through her. Yes, she admitted, she had wanted to be the one to give him the happy news.

"Ma'am." Uly waited until she gestured with her pen at the seat facing her, which had been pulled out from the table and waiting for him. Then before sitting, he handed her a sheaf of papers, some of them wrinkled, others with ragged edges, as if they had been torn out of a book, all slightly grimy and travel-worn. "If you'd like, I can copy these over, but I've been keeping a record as we went along, so nothing would be lost."

"Oh, please, Uly, no formality. Not this late at night." She bit her lip against the urge to remind him that he used to call her Auntie Eena.

The years had molded Ulysses Fremont into the valuable warrior for the Originators that she had always hoped he would be. A confident, dedicated young man who would have made his parents and grandparents proud. He had learned discipline in the intervening years since they had snatched him out of his life and made him vanish to save him. At one time, it had been a choice between killing him to protect the Originators and their mission, or block his memory. To his credit, when she explained the damage he had done to what his grandparents had dedicated their lives to, Uly had been broken and remorseful, and he had almost eagerly accepted the option of having part of his memory blocked, to control his actions.

Even more to his credit, he gave her a verbal report of the two years he had spent searching for Fordyce and his team of explorers before he asked the question he asked every time he completed a mission.

"Ma'am, has any word come about my grandparents?" He gestured down, nearly straight at the spot where the blue lotus was hidden.

Although the ability to handle the blue lotus and make it sing and glow only passed along through the female line, Ulysses was able to sense its presence and hear its music. He knew where the lotus was hidden

"No, no fluctuations in the power reverberations. I'm sorry."

"I had hoped, maybe a rescue team had been sent to follow some trail we had missed all these years." A tiny smile quirked the corners of his mouth and he looked away.

Athena knew the question he wanted to ask. She was proud of him, the maturity he had attained through denial and discipline. Even if not quite perfected yet. At first, he had demanded answers and some action, any kind of action, to follow his grandparents wherever they had vanished. Then demands had turned to pleas, then sullen half-accusations flung at those who wouldn't or couldn't tell him what he wanted to hear.

He had grown up, but the question that followed him everywhere he went had changed: Had he grown up enough to be trustworthy and useful in making Odessa a part of the Society? If she told him the news about his missing sister, would he get in the way or help them reach her heart and mind that much quicker and more easily?

"I have a new mission for you. One made specifically for you, so I don't even need to contact the governing committee for their confirmation." She paused just long enough to catch his attention, make him look her in the eyes. "We have found Odessa."

For a long moment, Uly didn't move, didn't even seem to breathe. Then his eyes widened and he leaned back in the chair.

Athena wondered if she had expected some recriminations from him. Despite his agreement that he needed to have his memories temporarily blocked, so his distraction wouldn't interfere with his duties, Uly had been angry when his memories had been freed. He hadn't even remembered for a space of three years that he had a younger sister, and the return of those memories, as he had described it, was like having a hole chopped in his side to attach a new arm, after he had learned to go through life without one.

"Where is she? How is she?"

"You should be proud of her. She is working as a Pinkerton, protecting a traveling exhibition of Egyptian artifacts."

"Egyptian artifacts." He nodded. "I can guess that's how you found her. The Revisionists tried to take something at the same time you did?"

"Rather, Ess got in our way, defending the artifacts from our extraction crew." She approved of his calm, his self-control, enough that she rewarded him by telling him everything that had happened that night in the warehouse, and how his sister had helped protect the crystal cube the next night when the museum was attacked by the Revisionists. He laughed, and other times he gripped the edge of the table until his knuckles were white.

"Where will the exhibition be next? I can leave immediately."

"You most certainly will not." Athena brought her hand down hard on his, when he started to push himself back from the table. "You have earned several days of rest, at the very least. Doctor Sylvia will want to make sure you and all your team are in good physical condition. Besides, the *Golden*

Nile is heading to Kansas City, the next stop for the exhibition. Why wear yourself out racing across the ground when you can take a leisurely flight to get there?"

"If it were anyone else..." He shook his head, blinking hard against a sudden brightness that Athena suspected was tears. "Ess has always been more aware, I guess. More sensitive. Sometimes you'd think she could read minds. If I know her, she knows that I know she's alive. If I don't get there as soon as I can..." He shrugged, his more normal crooked smile returning. "There'll be no making it up to her."

"You think she'll be angry with you? Ulysses, she knows you're alive, and that's more than she's had for the last seven years."

"She should hate all of us. What the Society has done to our family."

"Odessa knows the situation. I left her the introductory manual. Your sister is a clever girl, and cautious. Do you honestly think, if she knew where you were tonight, she would abandon her job and go haring off across the countryside to find you?"

"No." Another shrug. "That's more what I would do."

"Your sister needs training and testing. She is years behind the education that we had planned to give her."

"I'm the one who needs training, not Ess. She's a natural."

"Perhaps. But your sister is heading for Kansas City and so are we, and I am not going to order the *Golden Nile* to reduce altitude so you can steal a horse and ride it into the ground to reach the city maybe four hours ahead of us. Is that understood?"

"Understood." Mischief lit his eyes, put color back into his face. "But I bet no matter how bad the nag, I could get better speed and beat you to Kansas City by six hours."

"Fortunately for us, I'm not a gambling woman."

"So what's my assignment, once we reach the city?"

"You will join the observation team if you promise to control yourself and not make contact with Odessa until we are sure of the situation. After she foiled the Revisionists, they could guess who and what she is. Anyone who manages to deprive them of their spoils gains their attention. Even if she appears to be a fancy-dressed, self-important, pretty girl."

"How pretty?" Uly's eyes narrowed. "Anybody who needs a black eye from her big brother?"

"Your sister is more than capable of blacking eyes and breaking teeth, while she's at it. She's a Pinkerton, after all."

"That's a little hard to swallow." He sat back in the chair, making a visible effort to relax. "In my mind, she's still a little girl."

"I think your sister was never quite a 'little girl,' with her intelligence and her... talents, shall we say?" Athena patted his hand. "As soon as we convinced her we were friends, one of her first questions was to ask about you. She was very glad to know you were safe."

Uly snorted. "As safe as anyone can be, doing what we do."

"We have a duty from God Himself to protect the time stream and to repair the damage done by our ancestors. Your family line and mine, more than anyone else, if you really think about it."

"Doesn't the Bible say that children won't be punished for their fathers' crimes?"

"True. But that doesn't negate the responsibility we have inherited. Those who have the greatest talents, the greatest gifts, also carry the heaviest responsibility. That is also in the Bible." She offered him a smile. "I'm glad to know you've been reading your Bible."

"Sometimes it's the only thing that seems sane in this insane world. What if my grandfather was right?" He leaned forward, resting his elbows on the table, and lowered his voice. "What if our ancestors changed history? How can we ever put things right? And should we?"

"That question was taken out of our hands when our ancestors destroyed records and created the laws we live by. We can only guess, and have faith, that this world, this time stream, is the one that was meant to be." She took a deep breath. "I've worked myself into too many headaches and sleepless nights, wondering if the Revisionists succeeded after all, and history has been changed irrevocably."

"Or, as Granny insisted, we're in a totally different Earth altogether from the one that made the Great Machine," he offered with a faded version of his usual cheeky smile.

"We are in the world we need to be in, and we have a duty to fulfill. If we never find out the truth until Judgment Day, so be it." She lightly tapped her flat hands on the surface of the table. "We both need our sleep more than anything, now. It is good to have you back safe, Uly."

"I'm not the little boy you decided to be responsible for." He grinned more naturally as he stood up.

"Hmm, in your opinion. In some ways, some men will never grow up, even when they're gray-haired and bouncing grandchildren on their knees." She caught his wrist when he started to turn to step away. "I must reinforce this, Ulysses Fremont. When we reach Kansas City, you will be allowed to move about freely and watch over your sister, but until we are sure of the situation, you will not make contact. You will devote yourself to looking for Revisionists, not catching up with your sister. She doesn't need to be distracted any more than you do."

"Me? Distracted?" He widened his eyes and pressed a hand flat on his chest in a nearly convincing posture of innocence.

"You are more likely to distract the rest of us. Please, Uly, obey me in this. As your mother's friend, if not as your supervisor."

"Auntie Eena," he murmured.

Fordyce stood in plain sight when Uly opened the door to leave the conference room. He leaned against the opposite wall, arms crossed, head tilted to one side, and looking rather heavy-eyed. Athena didn't doubt he had been there during her whole conversation with Uly, with his newest listening device pressed to the door. The man fancied himself the forerunner of a new breed of sleuths. The only thing that stopped him from establishing his school for master spies was that he couldn't resist haring off around the globe, proving the impossible was possible.

"Lovely boy," he said, after he had stepped into the conference room and closed the door. "Not as much respect for his elders as I like to see—"

"Since when?" She made her voice as sweet as possible, watching him saunter across the room to the long table.

"But he wouldn't be such a good, intuitive soldier if he had to keep thinking about what others would say or want or do. No, young Mr. Fremont is an original. Don't go breaking his spirit with rules and regulations and propriety, my dear."

"I'll take your advice under consideration. Oh, for heaven's sake, Ford—" Athena let out a loud sigh, fighting not to laugh, when he dropped to one knee next to her chair.

Then she couldn't think of anything, couldn't even breathe, when he caught hold of her right hand with his left, and turned over his right hand to display a ring. It was a wide band, silver or white gold, encrusted with sparkling, twinkling gemstones the same color as the lotus.

"Now do you believe me, my love?" Fordyce murmured. His smile looked closer to nervous than smug, and that convinced her.

"Where did you get that ring?" Throat and mouth went dry.

"Had it made. Nigh on two years ago."

"Yes," she said quickly, when he paused and his hand tightened around hers, making her think he was ready to leap to his feet and flee.

"Yes?" He blinked three times. "You mean—yes?"

"Yes, I believe you." She took a deep breath. "And yes, I'll marry you."

Fordyce whooped loud enough for the sound to bounce off the ceiling. He snatched her up into his arms and staggered back from the table as he adjusted his grip on her. For a moment, Athena thought he would fall, he looked that pole-axed. Then he settled down on the edge of the table and kissed her.

She couldn't help laughing at the first thought that came to her.

"Love of mine, I'm terrified to ask what you're laughing about."

"I hope you didn't drop my ring."

With a loud, exasperated sigh, he adjusted her on his lap so he didn't have to hold her with one arm under her legs. Then he slid the ring on her waiting finger.

"That wasn't what you were laughing about, I'll wager."

"No." She leaned in and kissed him, lightly, and leaned back quickly when he tried to prolong the contact. "I was thinking that we are going to be in exceedingly great trouble."

"How?" Fordyce tried to scowl, but the laughter was so strong and bright in his eyes, it strained his voice.

"If it takes years of absence to make you kiss me like that, our marriage—" A squeak escaped her as he swooped in for another kiss, just as energetic as the first. They were both laughing, breathless, many heartbeats later when he took his mouth off hers.

"Now what do you think?"

"I'm always willing to be proven wrong," she whispered. "Ford, you really did plan on asking me, that long ago?"

"Been wanting to stake my claim on you for years before that, but... never felt right. Never thought I'd be willing to slow down enough that I wouldn't drive you mad trying to corral me."

"True. What helped you decide?"

"Oh, I'd been planning it for a long time. Saw the crystals and I saw the ring in my mind's eye right away. The perfect ring. Wasn't sure about the timing. Felt sure you'd laugh in my face or I'd even find out you got tired of waiting for me and some other lucky cad stole your heart."

"Hardly." She gladly snuggled down against him, her head on his shoulder. They wouldn't be able to enjoy this moment of quiet intimacy for long. Any moment now, someone would walk in and be scandalized by the sight of Athena Latymer, not just sitting on the conference table, but sitting on the lap of a man who sat on the conference table. "What helped you step over the threshold?"

"The lad, Uly. Knew him right away. He has his father's profile and way of talking. Reminded me right away of the last adventure we went on, right before he married Vivian. Brought back a lot of memories, all of the good folks we've lost. All the time we lost. It was worth it to ask you, in front of witnesses, maybe shock you into saying yes, finally trap you where you couldn't get away."

"Did you ever think I was trapping you?"

"Never. You're too clever to trap a man. You could have had me shackled years ago, but you knew I'd make us both miserable." He sighed, deeply enough to move his entire body. "Let's promise each other something, my love. We'll pack enough living for a dozen lifetimes into however much time we have left."

"Ford, you big, blithering fool." She laughed as she pressed her palms against his cheeks. "You're talking like we're both ready to retire to rocking chairs. I have quite a bit of life left in me. I'm relying on you to make sure it's... interesting, to say the least."

"Interesting can be a good thing. And it can be considered a curse. Depends on who's doing the interesting, if you—"

"Ford, be quiet and kiss me before someone interrupts us."

~~~~~

By the time an interruption came, they had settled into chairs, so
~~~~~

Fordyce could give her a general idea of what his team had done and seen and discovered in the years they were missing in Antarctica. Athena listened and let the speaker-writer transcribe his words, lightly tracing the lead stick across the long sheet of paper on rollers. Fordyce spoke softly, which proved he was indeed exhausted. Softly enough she heard the *snick-click* of the mechanism that moved the paper up every time the arm holding the lead stick slid over to the left again. She watched his face, seeing the little details she had missed under the dust and muss of travel. Sitting close to him now, the grime gone, she saw the changes in him. A few streaks of silver in his hair, new angles and planes to his face and collarbone and shoulders. She wondered just how much "it took a while to learn to hunt the local creatures" translated into near-starvation, and how long it lasted.

Too soon, he finished what was only an outline of his tale. The details would be filled in later, when he and his men had rested and relaxed, and they could tell their stories and consult their journals.

"Now, what's this about Matilda and Ernest's girl rising to the surface?" Fordyce said, when Athena turned off the speaker-writer.

"Did you hear that at the door, or the gossip in the washroom?"

"Eh, you can't hear yourself think in the washroom. Nigh on had a mutiny, between the men who wanted to soak a good hour in the first hot water they've known in years, and the ones who wanted them out half an hour ago, so they could try it." He winked. "No, all it took was a little flattery for the cooks who fed us, a little praise for the lad and his soldiers, wondering if their families knew they had arrived safe and sound, that sort of thing. This big balloon of yours is fair on buzzing with excitement. The girl sounds like she has a good head on her shoulders. Might even give Matilda herself a run for her money, if she gets herself into a hissy."

"She might." Athena contemplated his phrasing. Maybe that explai the young woman's actions, avoiding contact with her watchers, stu but not reading much of the manual given to her. She was upse something and raring to make someone pay.

Fordyce would be sharing her burdens from now on. Wh with her concerns about Odessa Fremont and all that incredib potential, so long untrained?

He listened like he always did, with frowning conce appreciated it when he reached out halfway through the in the rafters of the warehouse, and held her hand. when she finished, and interlaced his fingers with h

"Well, we definitely are in for interesting ti him.

"What's so funny?"

"I almost feel sorry for the girl."

"Sorry for her?" Athena smiled. Ju guaranteed she would be as well. Eventually.

"Between the two of us, no matter how stubborn Matilda's granddaughter might turn out to be, she doesn't stand a chance. She's going to be a member of the Blue Lotus Society, and by gum, she'll enjoy it, too." He thumped the table with his free hand for emphasis.

"Did you hear what you just said?"

"I think so." He cocked his head as if listening, then nodded a moment later. "Yes, I definitely did. What did I miss?"

"She's *Matilda's* granddaughter."

"Ah. Of course." He pulled his mouth down in a somber expression. One that never reached his eyes. "But still, it's two against one." He brought her hand up to his lips and kissed her knuckles.

Athena laughed, and it felt glorious.

~~~~

"You? You are Evangeline Peabody?"

The red-faced man, stuffed into a uniform he might have worn twenty years ago, managed to look down his nose at Ess despite being a good head shorter than her. He wore boots with very visible extra height in the heels. She almost felt sorry for him, but she had taken an instant dislike to his white hair reeking with macassar and that ostentatious monocle. Especially the monocle. Or maybe it was the way he clutched a wooden box against his chest, perhaps eight inches by eight inches, and about fifteen inches tall. As if he thought someone would snatch it from him.

"Yes, sir. I am. Is there some problem with the exhibition you need me to address?" Ess glanced toward the main entryway of Kansas City's new museum and wished one of her associates was close to signal him.

But of course not, no one in sight. Ever since Washington, all four men had been just a little too solicitous, as if they refused to let her out of their sight. It was nearly impossible to do any of her studying to catch up on her Egyptian alphabets without one of them looking over her shoulder. Why did they decide to leave her unattended *now*? Wasn't the situation sure to turn dangerous now that the artifacts had been unloaded from the train and deposited in the museum storage room?
~~~~

Chapter Thirteen

"They told me to bring my doodad to you. Said you were some sort of expert. A slip of a girl like you? Barely out of the nursery."

"I assure you, sir, I have been out of the nursery for quite a while." Ess fought not to grit her teeth, though his Bostonian accent grew thicker with every sentence that slipped out of his mouth. "Thank you, very kindly, for the lovely compliment. I haven't been called a slip of a girl for several years now." She fluttered her eyelashes at him, tipping her head just like that featherhead in St. Louis had done, just before she flustered Briscoe out of all good sense.

What was it about fluttering eyelashes and pretending she didn't have a brain in her head that softened crusty old lions like this one? He beamed at her and blushed. Either that, or he was on the verge of apoplexy and didn't even know it.

"Now, when you said doodad, do you mean you are one of the museum's benefactors who are loaning some of your precious Egyptian artifacts to the exhibition?" Without thinking, she tugged on the chain holding the crystal rod Athena had given her, bringing it out of the waistband pocket where she kept it tucked at all times.

"Well now, I wouldn't say I was a benefactor..." He hemmed and hawed for a few moments, grinning as if she had paid him an outrageous compliment. "Eh? What's that?" He pointed at the rod.

"Oh, this is one of my tools. It allows me to check the condition of artifacts, to make sure they are sturdy enough to stand the strain of so many bodies in one place. The pressure of the airflow can sometimes threaten the cohesion of the ceramic, or the paint that might be all that truly holds it together. We wouldn't want to deprive you of your treasure by putting it on display, would we?"

"Check its condition?" He took a step back, chewing on the corner of his moustache, and glanced down at the box. "How?"

"Vibrations, sir. Like so." Ess held the bottom of the rod and tapped it on the edge of the table where she had been going over the schedule for assembling the exhibition. A faint ringing hovered in the air.

Then it was answered by the chiming of crystal. Muffled. Whatever the whiskered gentleman had in the box, it held crystal. She had so little experience in detecting crystal, but she fancied there was something odd about this sound. As if there were a great deal of crystal nearby, and yet small and frail.

She glanced at the man, but he seemed to hear nothing. Although, he did seem to be increasingly uneasy. He rubbed his hands up and down the box, almost losing his grip. It struck her as odd.

The crystal chiming turned into a chord. The chord made her think there were many, many pieces of crystal in the box, the sound growing as more pieces of crystal joined in the song.

"What good does that do?" the man said, frowning so deeply his bushy white eyebrows nearly obscured his eyes.

"Do you hear anything coming from your artifact?" She gave him the most concerned expression she could muster.

"He—umm, of course not. Should I?"

"Well, that's a very good sign. If you heard a chiming, that could mean something was broken." Ess muffled a chuckle when the man hurriedly put the tall wooden box down on the table, right on top of her paperwork, and pried the fitted lid off.

He drew out an object wrapped in multiple layers of what turned out to be a scarf. Well, at least he had the sense to pad the object. Her puzzlement grew when he unwrapped the bundle, reducing the size in half, and revealing a very plain, somewhat badly made canopic jar. Whoever had his internal organs stored in the jar, he was important enough to have a ritual burial, but obviously not important enough for decorations. Ess felt a little queasy when she wondered if all his internal organs—heart, liver, brains—had been stored in the jar, instead of separately, per ritual. Maybe this was a minor royal child's burial.

What, she wondered, had happened to the organs over the centuries? Had the various disgusting insects of Ancient Egypt destroyed the seal, crept in, and eaten the tissues, leaving nothing but insect carcasses and dust? More important, did this upper crust gentleman, now gently running his fingertips over the jar, realize what he had taken home from Egypt as a souvenir?

Quite frankly, Ess had a hard time understanding the whole fascination people had with Egypt as a whole. Pyramids made no sense to her. Even less sense was the ancients' reverence for and worship of scarabs and cats and frogs. All were useless nuisances, as far as she was concerned. Ess much preferred dogs over cats. All frogs were good for was frog legs to roast over a campfire. As for bugs, why not something not associated with rotting corpses and dung, such as ladybugs?

"One more test," she said, and gently placed the still-humming crystal rod on the lip of the jar.

The vibration went silent, but it traveled up her arm, making her bones hum, and then created an itching in the roots of her teeth.

"The lid—"

"Secure as all get out. If you'll excuse me," he added with a huff of embarrassed laughter. "It's sealed. Don't know what they used, but I'm not about to risk breaking my little beauty here to try to look inside. Feels kind of heavy. And listen." He picked up the jar in both hands and made a swirling motion with it.

The chiming grew louder, making the rod come to life in her hand. Through the chiming, Ess heard what she could only describe as a dry sloshing sound. As if the jar were filled with sand.

Or more accurately, crystal *dust*?

A trickle of cold sweat raced down her back, at the thought of the disaster that could have resulted if this gentleman, who still hadn't told her his name, had succumbed to curiosity and pried the lid off the jar. Whoever had put the crystal dust in it had wanted to make sure it wouldn't be opened and spilled and lost to wind and common traffic.

"This is an amazing treasure, to be sure," she said, after licking her lips several times, trying to find some moisture. "Do you have any others, or did you just bring this one home with you?"

"Home?" He blinked three times, then chortled. "Oh, no, missy. I've never been all the way over to Egypt, though it would be a grand adventure, wouldn't it? No, I'm a little ashamed to admit I bought it off a gent who spent several years there. He ran into some financial difficulties. Always had the impression he might have run afoul of the law and was busy paying off fines and such. This is all I bought. Thought it would be a good start to a grand collection of my own, and then..." He shrugged and carefully put the jar down on the table again. "Just been too busy, I suppose."

"Well, you have plenty of time to build up a grand collection, and yes, it is a wonderful start. It is so very generous of you, to loan your first piece to the museum for the exhibition." Her breathing grew a little easier as the last shimmer of sound from the crystal dust died out.

How odd.

She took his name, Cyrus Watkins Stephenson III, and address, and learned a little more about the gentleman who sold him the piece. Ess wondered if any of the Society's watchers had been close enough to hear the song of the crystal. She doubted her refusal to respond to their signal songs had discouraged them. If anything, she would expect them to creep closer and closer, until she could identify them. She was very certain that at least one worker at the St. Louis hotel had been a member of the Society. It amused her a little, to think of their reactions to her seeming refusal to read the book Athena had given her, to learn about the Society. As far as she could tell, no one had looked for her journal, in which she made notes on the research she had done along the way. Wearing butter-soft, scrupulously clean gloves, she had started reading the margin decorations of the book, to decipher the hidden messages. When she wasn't reading, she kept the book wrapped in a silk scarf an admirer in Chicago had given her, to keep it looking like new.

What would happen if someone from the Society heard the chiming of the crystal dust? More important, what would they ask her to do?

Ess felt sure the jar had been sealed with wax, which would be relatively easy to remove and replace. As long as no one did any tests on it, to see if the wax was the original seal, there would be no harm. She wondered what had possessed the member of the Society who hid the crystal, to put it in such a disgusting container. What had been going on, all those years ago, when the Society had taken apart the machine Athena had barely described to her? What sort of danger had existed, that they took the time and effort to hide the pieces of the machine inside Egyptian tombs?

She would worry later about what kind of machine was made of all crystalline parts.

Maybe when she sent this information to Athena, the woman would deign to show up herself, and Ess could get some more answers from her.

Finally, Mr. Stephenson left, with a jovial threat to bring his nephews and grandsons by to court her and convince her not to leave Kansas City. Ess pretended to be shy and shocked, and was grateful when he didn't pinch her cheek. Why was it, when she set out to charm people who had the potential of being a problem, the men turned avuncular and doting, while the women considered her a pretty child, and all of them decided she needed to find a husband and settle down? What was wrong with the world that a young woman couldn't find purpose and fulfillment in academic work?

Ess muffled a snort as she imagined the response of Mr. Stephenson if she told him she was actually a Pinkerton agent, and could handle several different kinds of guns, pick locks, and hold her own in fisticuffs with men and boys of her own weight class. She had learned quite a few lessons from Kate Warne, the first woman to work with the Pinkertons, and who had uncovered a plot to assassinate President-elect Lincoln. She could dress and walk and talk like a high society miss or a dance hall floozy. From Horace she had learned everything a Pinkerton had to know, although her mentor did stress her best defense was to run as fast as a thought.

The rest of the afternoon passed without incident, and no more donations to the exhibition. Ess had access to the workroom that the museum's workers used to carefully clean items brought in for assessment. Since it was a Sunday, no one was present, and she said a brief, rare prayer of thanks for that. When the other members of the team announced they found all the security precautions satisfactory and they would take a walking tour of the museum before going back to the hotel for the night, Ess knew this was her best chance. She was left alone with her paperwork and the display tables that needed to be covered with the wool padding. She finished that job quickly, while her mind struggled with the best method of opening the canopic jar without leaving any sign it had been opened.

Replacing the crystal dust with something of equal volume and weight was easily handled. The museum had a large bin of fine white sand in the back hallway, to fill the fancy brass buckets that sat next to the spittoons, for gentlemen to stub out their cigars.

Ess calculated that the fine silk lining of her day dress could donate a length of material to create an impromptu bag to hold the crystal dust, which would all fit into her handbag without creating too noticeable a lump. She could always come up with an excuse for why she had lost the dress. Easier than explaining why a large piece of material was missing from it. She would hold the handbag by the wooden panels at the top, instead of the braided silk cord, so no one would notice that it hung heavy.

How to open the jar? Even when she had her arrangements put together, laid out neatly on the table in the shadowy, echoingly quiet workroom, Ess still couldn't decide. Heat wouldn't be a good choice, because if she melted the wax, how could she replace it? She had searched for candles, but all the candles in the museum were colored. The wax sealing the jar currently seemed to be either colorless and transparent, or such a close match in color to the material of the jar that it was impossible to tell where one started and the other ended.

The frayed edge of the length of silk, once she cut it from the inside of her skirt with her knife, gave her an idea. Ess worked at the material until she had several long threads. She pulled hard on one, testing its strength. Was one strong enough to cut through the wax seal? Was it too fine a line?

Time was running out. She had to try. If she failed, then she would have to clean up her preparations and try again tomorrow.

A clamp attached to one end of the worktable allowed her to put the carefully wrapped jar into a vise to hold it securely, so she didn't have to worry about keeping it in one place while she worked on it. That let her use both hands for manipulating the silk thread to cut through the wax. Ess held her breath, afraid to even breathe on the ancient jar, and slowly worked the thread back and forth, willing it to slide through the wax. She wondered how the person who had hidden the crystal dust in the jar had managed to seal it so neatly, how he had even come up with the idea in the first place. She hoped he hadn't run afoul of whoever was responsible for guarding the ancient tombs. Did he worry about curses?

Not that Ess believed in curses, but there certainly were enough odd things happening lately, weren't there? She could almost believe.

The thread seemed to catch on something. Leaning forward and looking around the jar, Ess estimated the thread had gone in a good inch. Maybe it had gotten through the seal and was scraping against pottery? She wasn't sure about the arrangement of the lid. Hadn't she seen something in her grandfather's books, sketches of the odd jars the Egyptians used, with the lids fitting over the lip of the jar on the inside and the outside? She hoped that if this was the type of lid here, the wax hadn't gotten on the inside of the jar. She would have a devil of a time cutting through it.

That was her heart pounding, rather than approaching footsteps, wasn't it?

She raised her head and listened, and scowled when she found holding her breath just made her heart thud harder and louder.

Bending back over the jar, she worked the thread around the outside. Once she had the feel of it, the next several cuts went more smoothly, and faster. Her jaw hurt a little from clenching her teeth, but that didn't worry her in the slightest. Then the last cut through the wax met the first, and the jar lid scraped and moved, just slightly. It sounded horrendously loud because she nearly had her ear pressed to the jar from the awkward angle of reaching to get the thread in place. Ess carefully let go of one end of the thread, drew it back with the other hand, and moved back from the jar. She pulled on her clean kid gloves, and carefully lifted the lid with both hands. She had a painfully clear image of the lid suddenly going to pieces once separated from the jar.

Nothing happened. A few more drops of sweat rolled down her back to catch in the cotton padding of the edge of her corset. Ess put the lid down on the wool pad she had prepared, then looked into the jar.

At first it seemed to be nothing but white dust. Then as she moved closer, her shadow shifted out of the beam of light from the lamp over her left shoulder, and suddenly rainbows coruscated upwards from the jar. Ess inhaled softly, stunned and delighted. The sound reminded her that she was alone, with no guarantee of how long that would last.

Ess counted to twenty as she carefully spilled the crystal dust into the length of silk, to make sure it didn't stream out and across the tabletop like grease. She concentrated on wrapping up the bundle of dust and sliding it into her handbag before pouring in the replacement white sand. Fine dust rose up in the air and she was horrified to feel it tickling the inside of her nose. Now was not a good time to sneeze! What about the dust coating the jar? Could she get it off without marring the finish?

The next step, the one she couldn't be sure of in advance, was to test the thickness of the wax coating the lid of the jar. Ess breathed another prayer of thankfulness. She had been praying much more often in the last few weeks than she had done in years, which suddenly struck her as odd. The wax was nearly a quarter inch thick on the lid. She clicked the igniter on the tiny gas-fed flame on the workbench directly behind the table. It was a matter of seconds to swirl the lid around above the flame, just enough to cause the wax to glisten and start to melt.

"Covering your tracks is always the hardest part, isn't it?" Ess muttered as she visually lined up the lid with the bottom of the jar and forced herself to move slowly to bring the two halves back together. She nearly yielded to the temptation to press hard and then run her finger around the edge to smear the seal. That would not be wise.

Just in time. Those were definitely booted feet approaching. From the echoes, they were still in the first entry hall of the museum. Ess made a mental note to remark to someone that security wasn't all that secure, if anyone who came through the front door could walk down two hallways and find themselves in the workroom where all new acquisitions were inspected.

Ess flicked off the flame, moved the canopic jar over to the shelf where loaned items were to be kept, and stripped off her gloves, jamming them into her purse on top of the crystal dust bundle. She settled into a chair at the desk by the doorway and flipped over half of the stack of floor plans of the museum. She bent her head over the stack, reading, as the approaching footsteps came to a stop.

"Always studying, Odessa," Allistair said, leaning around the doorframe.

"You never know what you'll find, what just pops out at you," she said, and fought down the instinctive reaction to go on the defensive.

She wasn't sure why Allistair still made her feel like she had to prove herself. He had been complimentary a handful of times since Washington, and seemed a little easier with her on the team. He was actually good company when it was just the five of them on the train.

"You might have a good future in the analytical part of the business," he said, stepping back, and almost running into Charles.

"Come on, you two." Charles clapped his hands twice. "We're all starving. What do you say, Allistair? Can the expense account splurge and take us out to dinner tonight before we start our watch shifts, instead of eating in our suite again?"

Ess turned away and bent to pick up her handbag and her hat. Eating at a restaurant would be a pleasant change of pace from constantly eating in their suite, discussing security, and then falling into the same patterns of every other night. While she didn't mind another game of poker, or answering more questions about archeology and Egyptology, a change from the same old routine would be heavenly. However, she didn't dare go traipsing off to a restaurant with a handbag full of crystal dust in her possession. The sooner she got it secured in her room, and started the process of making contact with the Society, the better she would feel.

What good a bag full of crystal dust would do in assembling the Great Machine, Ess couldn't even begin to imagine. Unless the dust acted like graphite lubricant in ordinary machines?

She stood up and found both men looking at her. *Oh, please, no, don't make me decide.*

A yawn cracked her jaw, startling her. Her face warmed as she hurried to cover her mouth. Allistair laughed.

"I rest my case."

"On what, exactly?" she retorted.

"Our running argument," Charles said with a scowl directed at Allistair. "He insists you have the hardest job of us all, dealing with the elitists and intellectuals, and you shouldn't have a watch shift at all, that playing mental games all evening is exhausting enough."

"He's right." She muffled a chuckle behind her hand when both men stared at her. "Go on?"

"I was planning on reworking the watch schedule, to divide it among the four of us and let you have a night off," Allistair said. "The brutes insist you're capable of standing a double shift and still dealing with the opening gala tomorrow night."

"The question," she said slowly, fighting laughter, "is which one of the brutes gets to take the night off while I handle his shift."

"Ah ha. I thought so." He nodded, narrowing his eyes at Charles, who did a credible job of acting innocent. "Just for that, Odessa, you do get the night off. After we have a civilized evening out at a fine restaurant." He shrugged and turned, gesturing at the door. "I received a telegram from headquarters, commending us on the fine job we've done so far, and authorizing some luxuries."

"Very nice," Charles said. "It's high time, too. So, Odessa, where shall it be?"

"No, please." She was relieved when another yawn pressed at her jaw, and even more so when both men grinned. "The rest of you go ahead. I am quite content to have dinner in my room and spend the evening reading. Or practicing my flute," she added, as inspiration struck. "Don't let me ruin your evening of indulgence."

"You're an angel," Charles said, and lightly thumped her on the shoulder with his fist.

"Indeed. Too good to be true," Allistair murmured.

Now he was more like the leader of the team that Ess was used to. She wondered what thoughts went on behind that unreadable expression.

Chapter Fourteen

The balconies on each floor of the hotel were all part of one long unit, with wooden partitions, and the ones across the front of the building looked down over what would someday be a lovely city green, with trees and paths and a stream running through the middle of it. Ess changed into her boy clothes once dark had fallen, planning to sit on the balcony and play her flute until someone responded to the signal song. A knock on her door had her sighing loudly as she flung a shawl around her shoulders and headed for the door. She hoped no one would look down at her feet while they were talking.

It was only a redcap with a message someone had just sent up. Ess almost forgot to give him a tip. She listened for the creak of the door inching open as she told him to wait a moment and then hurried to her handbag. The bundle of crystal dust still inside made it difficult to find her few coins. She pulled the bundle out and slid it between her mattress and the rope support and hurried to give the redcap his tip. She waited until she heard his footsteps fade down the hall before locking her door again.

Who in the world would be sending her a note at this time of the night? She prayed it wasn't Mr. Stephenson, following through on his threat to introduce her to some of the "best young men in the entire territory."

The crystal song reached our ears. We will be waiting for your signal.

An odd feeling of disappointment trickled through her. Ess had hoped that someone she had met on the *Golden Nile* would be there to make contact. Athena hadn't exactly said outright that she would be contacted by people she at least knew on sight, but wouldn't it make sense, just for security's sake? Especially if she had to hand over crystal she had found? What happened to the agreed-on contact method? Wasn't she supposed to play the signal song before anyone contacted her? She swallowed her disappointment and stepped out onto the balcony, and found she didn't much feel like playing at all.

Ess stayed in the deepening shadows, watching the gaslights come on all through the center of the city. She wondered what San Francisco would be like, and the headquarters of the Originators. She had several days here in Kansas City to study at night and finally decode all the messages of the Society's book, and the few days by train to learn everything Athena had wanted her to learn. Chances were good she would have some kind of test waiting for her at the end. For all she knew, taking everything on her own terms had turned into a black mark against her.

Fine. So be it. She had made her way splendidly without any help from her grandparents' associates. Hadn't she been able to live all these years without their help? Or should it be termed interference? What made them think she needed them now? She was a grown woman with an exciting, fulfilling career full of challenges, and associates who respected her, even if they didn't quite like her, such as Allistair.

That brought her up short, with the flute poised at her lips. Ess rested her back against the wall to her room and slid down so she sat on the balcony with her knees nearly up to her ears. Ah, the glories and freedom of wearing trousers. Why in the world had she allowed thoughts of Allistair to sneak into her mind? He bothered her. He had never been solicitous of her since the day they were assigned to the team, but he had never been cruel or cold, either. Why this marked warming in the last few days?

At the beginning of the assignment, she had thought perhaps Charles and Briscoe had been a little warmer than required for teammates. However, as time went on, and after she had spent the first train trip dressed as a boy, their extra warmth and concern for her comfort and opinions faded. They treated her exactly as they treated each other. She theorized that seeing her dressed as a boy got in the way of seeing her as a woman.

Which, when all was said and done, suited her admirably.

However, Allistair had changed toward her. Slightly, but enough to notice. Either he had decided she had earned her place and his respect, or...

Here, her theorizing fell apart. Until a chill raced across her scalp and she nearly pressed her free hand to her cap to fight the sensation that her hair was rising so drastically it would push the cap right off her head.

Unless Allistair had been in the employ of Athena's adversaries this whole time? It was a brilliant strategy, of course. Place someone within the vaunted Pinkerton Agency against the time they would need an inside hand. She wondered if Allistair had worked hard to get himself appointed to this team, or if it had been merely a happy accident.

"Don't be a total fool, Odessa Fremont," she muttered, and scowled into the gaslight glow of the streets below her. She let her racing thoughts scatter where they would.

The thin notes of a flute drifted up in the cooling air, at first so softly, Ess didn't hear them. She felt them, though. That sense of something being not quite right, something she couldn't put her finger on, intruded into her thoughts, finally hooking onto her attention and dragging her back to the present moment. She sat still, the flute in her lap, and she listened.

She didn't know the tripping little tune... or did she? From long ago, so far back in her childhood she couldn't put a name to the tune or even anticipate where each new phrase of notes would go next. Yet it felt familiar.

What had happened, that the flute player was reaching out to her, instead of waiting for her to make contact? Athena told her specifically, she was to play the signal song, someone would respond, she would play the next verse of the song, depending on whether she needed to arrange a meeting or warn them away from danger or ask them to come back the same time tomorrow. Ess knew those particular songs and meanings down pat.

So why wasn't her contact following the sequence?

Angry, she raised her flute and played the challenge sequence listed in the first few pages of the Society book. She flubbed a few notes, when it occurred to her that despite waiting so long to study, she had already learned something useful. Her mind, as her grandparents had pointed out on too many occasions, was like a sponge, indiscriminately picking up and retaining everything that crossed her senses, whether she wanted to or needed to or not.

Silence from the other flute. Had she scared them away? Was she wrong, and the song came from an innocent party who had merely come out on his or her balcony for some private relaxation?

Another flute song rose up in the air. The warning song. She felt some of the tension bowing her shoulders ease up, as she recognized the song. That ease faded a moment later.

The song came from another direction. Another flute.

Ess sat still, visualizing where everything lay in her room. The bundle of crystal dust was jammed under her mattress, to muffle any possible reverberations. The problem was that under the mattress was the first place she would look for something hidden.

Her mouth was dry as she raised the flute to her lips and played the request for identification. Had she got it right? She had only read the notes on the page, had never played them.

Fool! You've been out of your depth and didn't even know it!

Both flutes played at the same time. The first one, coming from a balcony two floors below her and to her right, squeaked with the effort of volume, to drown out the other. Ess closed her eyes and concentrated on the second flute. If she had read the book Athena gave her, she would probably understand what the flute was telling her. That odd arrangement of long and short notes certainly wasn't a song. They were almost all the same notes, the long three steps below the short.

Stupid, stupid, stupid, she scolded herself, clutching the flute tightly enough she thought the metal dented under her fingertips. *Morse code!*

R – e – p – e – a – t, she played, trying to match the notes, praying she remembered Morse code well enough to communicate.

T – h – e – o, the other flute responded.

She waited for more of the word, then realized that was the name. Theo? Yes, she remembered Athena's associate. How could she forget the man who shot her with the Zeus gun?

The danger signal song played. The other flute had fallen silent.

Ess wondered if she had eaten something at dinner that slowed her brain. She should have gotten up the moment the second flute started playing. Anyone with a gun and good night vision could pick her off the balcony. Just because she sat in the shadows didn't mean she was invisible. After all, both those flute players had seen her. She got onto her hands and knees, hugging the side of the building, and crept toward the door. Why had she been so foolish as to sit in the corner of the balcony furthest from the door? Besides avoiding the light spilling from her room, what good did it do her?

There was the chance that second flute wasn't Theo, and he wasn't warning her to protect her but to send her crashing into the arms of the enemy. In that case... Ess stopped moving, and studied her bedroom through the open door. As soon as she got into that doorway, with the light from the room shining around her, anyone watching would see her. She would be a target for however many or few seconds it took to get her door closed.

If she fled, the enemy would assume she had taken the crystal dust with her.

Why had she allowed Allistair to quarter them on the third floor? Ess knew she could jump from the second floor balcony without any trouble. Then again, people could climb up just as easily, with —

A *thud-squelch* of something hard and sharp digging into the wood of the balcony cut off her thoughts. Turning, she pulled the knife from the sheath at her waist, ready to fight. Unless it was another of Athena's mobis coming to protect her. A face appeared above the railing, a pale blob in the shadows, a man in a fisherman's knit cap, bearded. She had that long to take in the features while he looked directly at her open door. The man frowned, obviously expecting to see her there. Too soon, his gaze dropped down and caught on her.

"Where's the lady?" he snapped, and pulled himself up and over the railing.

He was big and blocked most of the railing. Time slowed, as it sometimes did when Ess faced danger. He was at his most vulnerable while he straddled the balcony railing. At least, she hoped so. Ess stood and backed up to the wall of the building and the man sneered, taking her movement for fear. As he momentarily turned his back to her, to swing his other leg over the railing, she leaped, grasping the railing and swinging herself over the side to take his place.

A gasp of giddy relief escaped her when she felt the rope he had used to climb up. Wincing against the future pain in her unprotected hands, Ess twined the rope through her legs and then slid down. Above her, the man let out a curse and leaned over the balcony, glaring down at her. She was already even with the second floor balcony. A second body suddenly swung past her, on a second rope. Why hadn't she anticipated more than one attacker? That second person was an impression of angry eyes, a bald head, and a big knife slashing at her hands.

No, at her rope. Ess released the tension in the rope she held with her feet and increased her fall. The rope jerked. Her best guess was the man on the balcony was cutting at it.

The rope jerked upwards. He was trying to pull her up to him.

She dropped, hitting the pavement at the feet of two fancy-dressed men walking in a cloud of whisky. Two rough hands grabbed her by her shoulders as she stumbled backwards, and hauled her upright.

"What is it, with you and heights?" Theo growled, half-carrying her into the shelter under the hotel's overhanging façade.

She gladly let him lead, a grip on her arm, as he darted across the front of the hotel, to the wide, dark alleyway between it and the next building. From the smell of horses, she guessed the alley led behind the hotel to the stables. Behind her, she heard shouts from people on the sidewalk and the sounds of bodies falling, hitting the pavement. Did she dare hope someone had taken offense at the two men chasing her nearly landing on them, and had started a fight? Any delay would be welcome.

"At least they're not searching my room," she muttered, as she and Theo emerged into the pool of lantern light filling the stable area.

"Decoy?" Theo glanced over his shoulder at her. He didn't loosen his grip on her arm, but did slide it down to her wrist. "Smart thinking. Let's hope the Revisionists don't realize you're that smart. Through here." He didn't wait for her to respond or even obey, halfway yanking her off her feet as he darted into the third doorway.

Ess decided Theo and his team had familiarized themselves with the hotel, anticipating future need. He moved too smoothly and surely for someone navigating unfamiliar territory. In no time at all, they were headed up a flight of sturdy wooden stairs with a massive dumbwaiter system running alongside them. Definitely the staff stairs, for carting food and linens and wash water up and down for guests. She barely had the breath to laugh when she wondered, in those seconds of pounding up two flights of stairs, how soon fancy hotels like this would have indoor plumbing, as efficient as what she had experienced on board the *Golden Nile*.

"Can you shoot?" Theo asked, as he paused with his hand on the handle of the third floor door.

"Yes, but I try not to."

"Smart," he said, with a decisive nod and a twitch of his lips that might have been a smile. He reached into his coat and pulled out a Zeus gun. "This awakens the charge." He demonstrated a small metal switch, twisted sideways to move along a narrow slot, then twist sideways again to lock into position. A faint, gray-blue light appeared in the solid barrel near the hand grip. "Point, and pull this trigger, just like in an ordinary gun. It reaches its target best if you aim just a little over the mark, then draw your arm down a bit as you shoot. Something like cracking a whip."

"A whip made of lightning," she muttered, gingerly taking the gun. She felt a little better when he pulled a second gun from inside his coat, pulling the side back enough she could see the crisscross holster under the coat, where both guns had been securely strapped to his chest.

"Apt. Ready?" He turned his back on her without waiting for the answer and tugged the door open, allowing less than an inch-wide opening to look out. Apparently satisfied no one was on the floor, he pulled the door open wide enough for them to slip out.

All around them, the hotel seemed sleepy silent. Ess preferred that to the watchful, held-breath silence that meant disaster poised high above her, ready to land at break-neck speed.

Her room door was locked. That was encouraging. She had half-envisioned agents of the Revisionists breaking down her door while the two men came at her from the balcony side.

"I don't suppose you—good girl." Theo smiled when Ess produced her room key.

"My associates have had some embarrassing moments," she explained, once they were inside with the door shut. "Locked out of their own rooms when they had to run out at a moment's notice. Always wise to keep the key on you." She glanced at her balcony door, then studied the room. No sign at all that the room had been searched. "They think I had it on me when I ran."

"Ah, then you did find something, and they knew. We half-feared they decided to go after you just because we had arrived."

"The *Golden Nile* is here, then?"

"And more." He shook his head when she opened her mouth to ask what he meant by that remark. "What is 'it,' exactly?"

"Make sure we're secure."

He took care of locking her room door and the balcony door while Ess dug the swaddled bag out from her bed. She unwrapped it enough he could see the length of silk, formed into a bag, securely tied, the edges sealed with wax from her bedside candles. Theo frowned when she handed it to him and hefted it a few times.

"It's... moving."

"Dust." She sighed when he just widened his eyes, as if he couldn't visualize what she meant. She snatched up the crystal rod from the inside pocket of her jacket and rapped it smartly against the bundle in his hands. Theo's eyes widened further, and his mouth matched them.

"Where did—no, that's a waste of time. You can tell me when we get this safely aboard the *Golden Nile*."

"How, and where? If those two haven't followed us up here by now, they're going to be waiting at the most logical place for us to pass on the way to the city airdocks."

"Leave that up to me, Miss Odessa. Your sole responsibility is to not let the crystal off your person until we reach our ship." He opened her wardrobe and tugged out drawers as he spoke.

"Most people call me Ess."

"Theo. Let's see what you have that we can use—ah ha. Just the thing." He held up a messenger bag with the name of the *Kansas City Star* blazoned across it, in ink so fresh Ess could smell it. "I am constantly amazed by the good Lord's little coincidences, aren't you?"

"You think God did this?" The words left an odd taste in her mouth as soon as she had said them.

"When you have been with the Society long enough," he said, tugging at her jacket, "you will realize there is no such thing as coincidence. It is either the hand of God moving on our behalf, or the hand of the enemy, moving against us." He stepped back when she finally took over removing her jacket. "Everything, no matter how small, is part of the grand pattern of history and time."

In moments Ess slid the long strap of the messenger bag over her head so it slung across her chest with the bag resting on her hip. Theo adjusted it by knotting the thick cloth strap at her shoulder, until it hung to his satisfaction. Then he snatched up several hatpins from the fancy new hat Allistair made her wear to every opening gala. Ess muffled a chuckle. She couldn't wear the wretched, top-heavy monstrosity of beads and feathers without the pins to attach it to her hair, could she? Once the bag of dust was in the messenger bag, Theo fastened it closed with the hatpins and tossed her jacket to her. He stepped out into the hall to look and listen while she put the jacket back on and buttoned it up.

She saw the writing desk tucked into the corner and knew she had to leave some sort of message for Allistair and the others. When they returned from dinner, they would all meet to discuss the schedule for the next day.

"You can't leave that here," was all Theo said, when he came back into the room and found her scrawling a note and making a mess, spattering ink all over the hotel's fancy stationery and the blotter.

"I won't."

Invited out for the evening with our Washington friend. Will return by morning. S.

That ought to tell Allistair enough to keep him from worrying, searching for her, and scolding her in the morning. Ess slid it under Allistair's door as she and Theo headed for the staff stairs.

He took her up instead of down. When they reached the top, a staggering fifteen stories above ground, she felt a little rubbery in the knees. Ess scowled into the darkness around them, not at all enchanted by the fairyland of all the lit streets and buildings stretching out below them on all sides. Why was it that this building felt so much higher above ground than the *Golden Nile* had been, when it was three times as high?

Maybe it was the image of those two men, bursting through the stairwell door at any moment, and tossing her over the side of the building without hesitating or demanding to know where the crystal was hidden.

She looked up, half-expecting the *Golden Nile* to come sweeping down at them from the dark sky. There were very few clouds, and the stars seemed exceptionally bright. Perhaps that was because Kansas City didn't have quite as much haze in the sky from factories as larger cities did.

"We're not going up." Theo gestured for her to sit on one of the benches that seemed to have been placed there, most likely, for the staff to sit and catch some fresh air.

"You don't have a rope inside that coat, do you?" She settled down, patting the ungainly lump of the bag under her coat. The feel of the Zeus gun tucked between her belt and her stomach felt a little more reassuring every minute that passed.

Theo settled down on the bench facing her and pulled out a whistle, as thick as his thumb and as long as his index finger. He blew it, and Ess stared as a blue radiance filled the whistle, revealing it was transparent. She guessed it was crystal. She pressed her hands over her ears as a note seemed to ring inside her head.

"Huh. That's interesting," he muttered, narrowing his eyes as he stared at her.

"What?"

"Most people can't hear the whistle."

"Dogs?" she guessed, reaching for humor.

"You'll see. If you don't mention that useful little talent to Athena, I will."

"How useful?"

"If you haven't guessed by now, much of our technology is linked to the crystal. Other than providing light, we haven't figured out how to tap the energy stored in the crystal, as our ancestors did. They destroyed too many books and records when we first arrived, to protect the time stream, so we can't figure out half of it."

"What's a time stream?"

Immediately, she knew that was the wrong thing to say. His thoughtful look took on that blank look some men wore when they were struggling for self-control against some overpowering emotion. Shock, anger, grief. If Theo fought it, Ess didn't think any of them were good choices.

Chapter Fifteen

"You haven't read any of that book Athena left you."

"I've been catching up. The rest of you grew up in the traditions of the Originators, remember? I got sent off to a boarding school that would have surgically removed my brain if they could have got away with it."

Theo laughed, trying to muffle the sound with one hand pressed over his mouth.

"What's the time stream?" she asked again.

"Later. Let Athena fill in the gaps in your education. Back to what I was starting to say before. Crystal." He waved the whistle in front of her face. "The mobis are built to respond to different harmonics, resonating from the crystal. Everyone belonging to the Society carries a piece of crystal to identify them, so if something goes wrong, the mobis as a last resort can find them. And retrieve the bodies, if that becomes necessary. They aren't quite thinking machines, despite the analytical devices they're coming up with in England and Germany. We command them with the whistles."

"So you called a mobi to us."

"Somewhat."

She sighed, rather than releasing the shriek catching in her throat. "Are you punishing me because I was too busy to read that book?"

Theo sat back, his head cocked to one side as he studied her. Then that flat, mirthless smile that frightened her a little returned. "No, Odessa. You're punishing yourself."

The familiar tap-tapping of mobi legs on brick interrupted before she could retort. It climbed up the far side of the building and maneuvered over the parapet. Ess had walked around the hotel early that morning, before anyone was truly awake, to get an idea of the layout of the place. There were no stairs on that side of the building, no balconies, nothing but windows. She imagined all the tiny holes the mobi's pointed legs had dug in the brick in the side of the building to climb up to them, and then imagined an army of mobis with their pointed legs, attacking anyone who threatened her.

The mobi came to stand in front of Theo, then retracted its legs so it seemed once again a featureless brass globe with a pillbox on top. The pillbox tipped up sideways, and then with a click and a hiss, the top third of the globe tipped up as if on a hinge. She had an impression of glowing spots and tangles of wires and cogs and something that spun like a top, creating a faint, blue-tinged glow in the center of the mobi's innards. Theo reached in and brought out a brass box that flipped open to reveal what looked like a compass, but the cardinal points were crystal, they glowed white as he stared at it, and there was no arrow to point to true north.

"What does—"

"One trait," Theo said, cutting her off, and raising a hand as if he might put it over her mouth in another moment, "you share with your brother is a lack of patience."

"I consider it a refusal to let people think for me. Which, if you'll remember, is what has kept me alive." She felt suddenly as if she had been rapped right in that ticklish spot in the throat. "Did you say my—"

"Do you know what patience is, Odessa? Show me. Wait until we feel it's safe to give you answers."

"I'm not sure I'm ready to trust you. I'm definitely not ready to let you do my thinking for me." She winced, hearing her own voice sounding too much like a sulky brat.

"Yes, you're keeping yourself alive. Or so you think." Theo chuckled, and the sound was somewhat comforting. "Still I dare you to say you know what real living is. You'll find out."

Ess barely heard him, transfixed as the lights of the pseudo-compass grew brighter and seemed to move around the perimeter, gathering at one point. The effect happened three times. Theo glanced in the direction the lights seemed to be moving. Pointing? He tapped the central point of the lights, snapped the lid closed, and put the box back in the mobi. Then he reached in again and brought out some of that ubiquitous black cord, strung through a small device that looked like several pulleys and hooks hammered together.

"The Revisionists will be looking for us. We want to lead them away from the hotel, first of all." He walked over to the corner of the building the mobi had walked up, attached the device to the stonework at the top of the parapet, and hung the black cable over the side of the building as he spoke. "It would just confirm how important you are to us—do not let that notion linger too long—if the *Golden Nile* came sailing into the city and sent down soldiers to rescue you." He formed a loop in one end of the black cable with a few twists and knots, then a second loop, about three feet up from the first, then sat down on the edge.

Ess decided right then, she definitely did not care for heights. Not when there was still the chance of someone racing up from the shadows and shoving her over the edge. Still, she obeyed when Theo directed her to sit on the parapet on the other side of the device. She nudged it, having a vague, uneasy idea of what they were going to do. The device held fast to the bricks as if it had melted into them. Comforting.

He put his right foot in the bottom loop, leaving his left foot free, and grasped the cable. He waited until she followed his example with her left foot in the upper loop, then he counted down from three.

On "one," they linked arms and slid over the side of the parapet, all their weight immediately caught by their feet resting in the loops. Ess held her breath and gripped the cable as tightly as she could. It had an odd texture; smooth, almost pliable, and it seemed to hold onto her as much as she held onto it. She looked down, but only for a few seconds. Despite the controlled descent, courtesy of the device holding onto the top of the building, they were descending far too quickly for her stomach. She looked up, watching the device.

"Careful," Theo said.

She looked down again, to see an obstacle come hurtling up toward them. An extra deep windowsill. Almost a ledge to step out on. What fool put that sort of thing on a building this high? It invited suicides. Ess reached out to ward off the windowsill.

"Don't." He bumped them out from the wall with a shove of his fist. "If we hit it directly... well, you wouldn't like the reaction."

Then they landed in the shadowy alley between the buildings. Ess expected any moment now to hear running footsteps and shouts. Would the Revisionists give any warning at all before they attacked? Did they have Zeus guns? She was glad for hers, ready at hand, and hoped she wouldn't grasp the wrong end and stun herself when the time came to shoot. Theo helped her release her foot from the loop, then he pulled out his crystal whistle and blew it. This time, she definitely heard a difference in the notes he played. Maybe it wasn't so much hearing as *feeling* the changes in the resonance and vibrations in the bones of her skull.

"Come on," he said, and caught hold of her hand.

"What about the cable?" She wondered if that was a stupid question. After all, it wasn't like they could climb back up and unhook the device that held the cable to the top of the building. She didn't like losing such an ingenious device. What if the Revisionists got hold of it?

"That's what mobis are for." He cast a grin at her as they dove deeper into the thoroughfare of alleys that ran behind and between the large buildings at the center of the city. "They pick up after us."

Ess felt a bit of the tension leak out of her, as she envisioned the mobi gathering up the cable in neat coils, putting it and the anchor device back into the storage area inside its belly, and then calmly walking down the side of the building.

Theo released her when they stepped out of the last shadowy passageway and into a semi-lit street. He gestured upward, at the same moment she caught a flicker of movement. Specifically, a blur of gaslight on brass. With a humming sound, the mobi dropped down on its own retractable cable and joined them on the pavement just before it gave way to packed dirt. They were at the outskirts of the city.

"Would it be possible to build one of these big enough to carry a person?" she asked, as they crossed a rutted expanse of ground that looked like wagons and cattle came through there on a regular basis. Not a speck of vegetation was visible, and there was a faint odor of manure that she suspected could never be washed away in a year of torrential downpours. "How fast could they run on those legs?"

"It might be interesting to try, but there is the problem of structural integrity when you increase size. Spiders in nature can only get so big before their exoskeletons can't support them. The same with our mobis. Their bodies are hollow and so are their legs, except for the ones made to dispense tranquilizer gas or acid or pincers for manipulation. We build them light, and they are able to go quite a long distance before running out of energy."

"I was meaning to ask about that. They don't have keys or clockwork mechanisms to keep them going, so—"

"Clockworks, yes, but powered by electricity. Much like the Zeus guns. A sort of modified perpetual motion machine."

"Electricity?" Ess marveled at the idea. "But how do you collect it and store it, and keep the mobis from scorching themselves? They do have metal bodies, after all."

"That will be among your many lessons when you join us," he said with a smile.

They reached the other side of the beaten, open ground and stepped into a cluster of trees.

"When, not if?"

"Just like your brother. He was rather stubborn about joining us. Until he figured out he only had two choices."

"Join the Originators, or have his memories not just blocked, but erased completely?"

"No." Theo gave her a cold look. Combined with the streaks of moonlight that brushed over them as they tramped through the trees, it made her feel small and rather foolish. Probably unreasonable, she supposed. "The choice between us and the Revisionists. And believe me, he would not be happy among the Revisionists."

"How do you know?"

"I was born among them, and after I saw some of the things they did, the things they tried to do to change the time stream to suit them... I couldn't stomach it. I realized there usually are only two sides to any proposition in life, no matter what the question might be. The side of heaven or the side of hell. I wanted to be on the side of heaven."

"So the Blue Lotus Society works for God?" She thought about the Bible she had seen on Athena's desk, the short time she had been in the woman's quarters. She thought about the references to God and scripture and the history of the world as recorded in the Bible, that she had glimpsed in the Society's book.

"For the sake of our souls, yes."

"So the Revisionists work for Satan? They do horrific things, like those people were accused of doing in the Salem witch trials? And other witches and such through the ages? Eating babies and having sexual congress with animals and drinking blood?"

"Of course not." He chuckled, but it wasn't an amused sound. Ess rather thought he fought not to choke. They were in a deep enough patch of shadow, she couldn't see his expression. "The Revisionists consider themselves men of science and rational thought. They don't believe in God and heaven, nor do they believe in Satan and hell. They believe that time and reality are mere blobs of clay that can be molded and re-molded to suit their designs. What they don't understand is that changing history must indeed change the present and the future, and simple logic says it is impossible. Or at least disastrous."

"I don't understand. What sort of device could ever be made that changes history?"

"We're not sure. But here's something you need to understand: the Revisionists, or at least their ancestors, were sure they knew better. Either there is no God, or He is helpless or careless and has had nothing to do with the actions of men since Adam and Eve were thrust from the Garden of Eden. They felt they had the right, even the duty, to try to change the course of history."

"I remember this." She slowed, nearly stopped, but the mobi bumped into her calves from behind and Theo reached back and caught hold of her hand to get her moving again. "I remember Grandfather talking about this. He was arguing with someone..." A chill ran through her belly. "Grandfather argued that all the accidents that people use as ammunition to argue that God does not exist, or that He doesn't care, as you said... those were perhaps the best signs of all that God has His hands on us at all times. That those horrid things were actually blessings, because God stopped something far worse from happening."

"Exactly. Better and wiser to accept the world as a gift from the Creator's hands, than to try to remake it. If Job, who had God's favor, was scolded to put him in his place and remind him that he knew nothing about the foundations of the world... well, who are fallible human beings who doubt God's existence to dictate what should be?" He squeezed her hand. "We wait here."

They had reached the other side of the cluster of trees. Open sky stretched out ahead of them, and open land, other than the dark smear of railroad tracks on its raised hump of ground.

"Why is it impossible to change history? I'm not clear on that," she said, after they stood there in silence for several long moments. Long enough for her pulse and breathing to return to normal. She assumed the *Golden Nile* was coming, or else some of the Society's soldiers he had mentioned, but Ess decided it would be wise to stop assuming anything when it came to the Originators.

"Imagine you are standing on top of a tall cliff. You don't like the way the cliff face looks. So you climb down the side of the cliff, hanging on a rope attached to a spire of rock at the top of the cliff. You start digging and dynamiting to change things."

"If you dig deep enough, you shear off part of the cliff face. Maybe the part you're anchored to," she offered, guessing where this was going.

"Exactly."

"But what kind of machine can let you reach back and change history?" She inhaled sharply, as her mind made one of those leaps her Grandfather had always praised. But then Granny would always sit her down and make her work out with books and drawings why something worked the way it did. This time, Ess was sure she didn't have to prove anything. "The Great Machine you're trying to find the pieces for. That's what it does—it's supposed to change history. So you're gathering up the pieces to keep the Revisionists from having it."

"Hmm, not exactly."

A hot surge of pique shot through her, hearing the amusement in his voice.

"Explain something to me. Why, in all those old myths, when someone gets a prophecy that a child born that day is going to cause someone's downfall, or if an evil magician who is locked in the cave by a magic spell ever escapes, he will destroy the civilization, why do they perform the magic spell in the first place? Why do they put the child out on the hillside to die of exposure and then walk away, instead of doing the sensible thing and killing him? Killing both of them?"

"What does that have to do with what we're talking about?" Laughter made Theo's voice richer. She was glad she couldn't see his face clearly.

For a moment, Ess thought about using the mobi as a seat. Just to give back to him some of the irritation he poured on her now. She reconsidered that immediately. What if the mobi didn't like it, and shot her with acid? She reached back for a convenient tree trunk and leaned against it.

"Why did you disassemble the Great Machine and hide the pieces inside clay and wood and metal? Why not just destroy the machine?"

"Because it doesn't take people through time."

"Well then what's the problem? Why talk about the threat of time travel at all? Do the Revisionists have a machine that does it? Or does the Society have such a machine, and they're afraid of the Revisionists getting hold of it? Which takes us back to the question I—"

Ess froze, with Theo's hand suddenly flat against her mouth. For two seconds she considered biting him. Then she heard the low *hum-thud*, more felt in her bones than heard with her ears. It felt familiar. A good kind of familiar. She waited, and didn't speak immediately when he removed his hand. She listened, until a dark shape seemed to enter the edge of the sky, far to the right, blocking some of the stars.

"*Golden Nile*?" she whispered.

"Probably another twenty minutes away. They're trying to stay as quiet as possible. No one ever looks up at night. Odd, isn't it?"

"Extremely." There was something about the undercurrent of amusement in most of the things he said that made her want to strike out at him. Or at the very least kick. She should have bitten his hand.

They waited in semi-companionable silence, watching as the dark smear against the sky grew larger, swallowing up more stars every minute. Ess cast aside one topic of conversation after another, most of them because she suspected Theo would be cryptic in everything he said, or he would be amused. Either way, she wouldn't learn anything. She needed something to break the silence and throw him off balance. Something useful to her.

Then she found it, and briefly considered banging her own head against the tree behind her, for letting the subject drop before.

"You mentioned my brother."

"Ulysses, yes." Theo stepped out from the shadows of the trees, his attention focused on the approaching airship. Now it was close enough, a faint hint of solidity and some details giving it shape grew visible.

"Did you know him? Or do you know him now?"

"Uly is a valuable soldier for the Society. He has an incredible talent for doing the impossible. That's why he gets sent on rescue missions for people who are presumed dead. But not for your grandparents, if that was what you were going to ask next."

"I wasn't." She bit her tongue, realizing how immature she sounded with that response.

"We've worked together a few times. I like him. So I wasn't quite disparaging you, when I compared you to him."

"Not *quite* disparaging?" She flinched when the mobi brushed past her and moved up next to Theo. The top third lifted up again and tilted back like a big lid.

He didn't answer, being too busy digging in the storage area inside the mobi and pulling out the metal box that held what she had assumed was a compass. He flipped it open, and this time did something to a series of crystals embedded in the metal. They lit as his fingers brushed over them. Ess felt a tickling inside her skull, in the bones under her eyes and the roots of her teeth. She held her breath, mostly because she feared she would hiss, and she didn't want to attract his attention. Not yet, anyway. When she got answers for these odd things that she kept sensing, ever since the Society came into her life, she wanted them to be on her terms. Privately, so she could do what she wanted with the information instead of always being at someone's mercy.

A dark rectangle opened in the belly of the *Golden Nile*, now that the airship was close enough to give it color, somewhere between dull brass and chocolate, distinguished against the black and diamond dust of the sky. Ess had never been on an airship until the *Golden Nile*, and she had never been close enough to one to see it being brought in to dock, but she was very sure that this wasn't the usual docking procedure, even if it wasn't "usual" to dock without something high to tie up to.

"What are—" She stopped, feeling that chill of warning up her back. Ess turned, pulling the Zeus gun from her belt before she realized she was doing it.

Maybe she unconsciously copied Theo, because he had done the same.

Footsteps crashed and crackled through the forest behind them. Ess glanced over her shoulder at the open field and the approaching airship. There was too much open space, and too much light from the stars, even streaks of moonlight from the crescent climbing up from the horizon. As soon as they stepped from the shelter of the trees, they would be visible and easy targets. No matter how fast they moved, bullets were faster.

Theo tucked the Zeus gun under his armpit, tapped some sparkles of light from the crystals, then slid the metal box back inside the mobi. It closed up and turned, and the next moment darted into the forest.

"The Revisionists?" she whispered. She hoped if their pursuers were the Revisionists, they were just as immune to the tranquilizer gas as she had been, so the mobi would have to use acid or some other means of attack on them. Ess wasn't repentant for her fierce thoughts at all.

"Either that, or very persistent street thieves." Theo looked over his shoulder, probably gauging the arrival of the *Golden Nile*. "They know we're under attack."

"How?" Then she thought of the resonance in the bones of her skull and the lights in the crystal. "Morse code, but with lights?"

"Careful." He bared his teeth at her in a fierce grin. "Be too clever, they'll lock you up in the Sanctuary and never let you out."

"You'll tell me what Sanctuary is later?" she guessed. He nodded.

A howl of mortal agony erupted, maybe fifty yards away from them. Followed by gunshots. Ess strained her eyes for the blue-white lightning bursts of Zeus guns, but they never appeared. Hopefully, that meant the enemy didn't have such weapons. She had little if any understanding of what electricity did or the scientific laws that governed it, but she knew that tall objects and metal objects attracted it. Metal objects, as in guns. In theory, she wouldn't have to be dead-on accurate with the Zeus guns like she would be with her derringer. She mentally added another item to her incredibly long list of things she needed to learn.

Chapter Sixteen

The gunshots stopped soon, but the snarls and cries of pain didn't. She hoped that didn't mean the mobi had been shot and disabled.

"Ess." Theo grasped her arm, tugging to turn her.

Behind them, something with squared edges descended from the opening in the belly of the *Golden Nile*. It wasn't going to land. She swallowed hard, remembering the basket she had seen lowering Theo and his men to the ground in Washington. It was one thing to let people disembark by basket in daylight, another to pick up people in the dark of night, when the airship wasn't tied up at a dock.

"They're almost here. Go meet them."

"What about you?" She reached to grab hold of his arm when he shoved her out into the open, but Theo evaded her.

"You're the bait. I'm the ambush." He went to his knees, better hidden in the shadows and underbrush.

Ess somehow didn't believe him. Not entirely. The crystal dust, which felt incredibly heavy now in the pouch on her hip, was the highest priority. She had to get it up to Athena, no matter what. So she ran.

The incoming airship seemed to be miles away. Ess hunched her shoulders, urging her legs to move faster. How wide was this field? It seemed to stretch to eternity. She tried to keep her mind off the image of how she would be drawn up into the belly of the airship. Why was it, something that would normally be exciting to experience had to be ruined by needing it to save her life?

Behind her, more gunfire erupted. She felt the sting of electricity in the air, heard the *buzz-zap* of the Zeus gun. A horse screamed, and she looked back, to see a pale horse erupt from the darkness of the trees. She stopped. Better to face the enemy coming at her than to make them chase her down.

At least, that was the theory. She would face the rider, not keep looking over her shoulder, or worse, feel the horse ready to race up her back. Or a bullet lodge in her spine. More horses shrieked and the sound of large bodies crashing through the forest reached her on the too-still night air.

The *Golden Nile* seemed to be mired in midnight-black molasses, just hanging there in the sky, too far out of reach to do her any good.

The oncoming rider fired. Fired again. She braced, but felt no bullets. Not even the hot whizzing of one streaking by her face. Still the man kept coming, and firing. Incredibly, she realized he pointed up, not at her. For all she knew, he didn't see her. He was trying to shoot the ship out of the sky.

Ess braced herself, arms outstretched, both hands gripping the Zeus gun, and aimed slightly above the target as Theo had told her. Now the rider was close enough to make out his brown jacket and battered gray hat and his iron-colored whiskers. He pulled out another gun and shot with both. She pulled the trigger and nearly shrieked as the air tightened all around her. Time slowed, letting her watch the blue-white, jagged arc of electricity from the Zeus gun streak upward, then down, hitting the barrels of the rider's guns, first the right hand, then the left. Arms like spider webbing streaked out and caught the three bullets escaping the guns. They exploded, sharp retorts almost simultaneous with the blue-white electricity that expanded to wrap around the horseman. The horse screamed, rearing, and the man bellowed, his voice rising to soprano before he tumbled backwards from the saddle.

She inhaled on a gasp, feeling as if she hadn't been able to breathe for that eternal moment of the lightning strike.

Two more horses raced out of the black blot of the trees, more gunfire coming from them. She dropped. A bullet scorched past her cheek. She rolled, but the messenger bag full of crystal dust stopped her. Expelling a growling sigh, she got on her hands and knees. Her back felt entirely naked. The grass of this open meadow didn't stand nearly high enough.

The buzzing of a Zeus gun answered the gunshots, and from the corner of her eye she saw the blue-white bursts. Theo was nearby. She raised her head, looking back toward the trees, and saw a third horse racing across the open ground, seeming to shoot lightning bolts from its mouth. Theo was coming, riding a horse wrested from one of their attackers. Ess hoped he got in a couple good punches for her.

Fire caught her shoulder, turning her over, slamming her into the ground on her back. Ess gasped from the impact, breathless. Then a heartbeat later the pain tore through her flesh and she smelled blood and burned cloth and brimstone.

"Should have shot my gun hand," she growled, and pushed herself upright.

More bullets whizzed past her head as the two horses galloped up, then split apart, circling her. She hunched her shoulders, waiting for the killing strike, and muffled a pained gasp as the movement ratcheted up the pain. Her hand tightened around the grip of the Zeus gun, and without thinking she pulled the trigger, whipping the weapon around, trying to catch both circling riders in the sweep of lightning. She caught one, but not the other. His horse spooked and fought him, trying to race away. Fighting back sobs that choked her, Ess got to her feet, aiming her stumbling legs toward the descending basket.

Theo shouted, but the lone rider ignored him. He got control of his horse again and brought it back around, aiming straight for her.

Black movement in the sky yanked Ess's gaze upward, just as a dark shape arrowed down, straight at the rider. It resolved into a man, who hit the rider hard, tumbling him out of the saddle. The two went down, rolling. Ess stared at the sight of eight men, coming down head-first, trailing black lines behind them. They turned somersaults at perhaps ten feet up, landing on their feet and going to their knees, the nearest ones grunting from the impact. Each held a Zeus gun in his hand, the dark glass barrels glowing and churning with leashed lightning.

Theo reined his horse to a stop and vaulted to the ground.

"Ess?" He dropped to one knee next to her, his face crinkling in dismay as his gaze focused on her arm. Not a good sign.

She cursed him in three different languages and let go of the semi-conscious effort to hold back the pain. Tears burned her eyes and she fought not to sob. She had been shot before. It had never hurt like this. What kind of bullets did the Revisionists use?

Every movement sent new, blinding pain through her, so she could barely see what happened. The warriors disconnected from the black lines and scattered. Some headed back to the trees, following Theo's gestures. The rest gathered up the three men who had been shooting at her and the *Golden Nile*. Blinking away the tears, fighting to breathe without sobbing, Ess watched that dark shape coming down from the airship resolve into a basket big enough to hold ten people. Without asking her leave, Theo swept her up in his arms and over the side of the basket while three of the four men inside it climbed out.

"Yes, yes, I know," he said, as she cursed him and fought to see through the fireworks of pain from the sudden movement. "You can give me a black eye later. Get her to Sylvia first, then fetch Athena. She has at least five pounds of crystal dust."

"Dust?" the man remaining in the basket said, his voice threatening to crack with incredulity. He reached out and caught hold of Ess's good arm and danced back a moment later when she raised the Zeus gun.

"The battle's over," Theo said, and neatly yanked it from her trembling grip. "Get her up there fast. She's semi-immune, so most of our painkillers won't work."

"Ouch," the man said. He took a tighter grip on Ess's arm. "Hold on, lass. It'll take your breath away, but we'll get you to the doctor faster than you can spit 'Yankee Doodle Dandy.'"

"Who'd want to?" she growled, and reached with her good arm to grab the side of the basket. Immediately, the ground dropped away from her, making her stomach lurch. Unfortunately, not enough to fight the throbs of fire stabbing to the bone. "Theo!" She leaned over the side of the basket. "Thank you!" Oddly, she felt as if the basket were spinning and bucking around her, but her eyes disagreed.

He saluted her, just before the basket got too high up to see any details. Ess closed her eyes, swallowed hard, and gripped the basket harder with her good arm. Her ears felt odd, as if the pressure inside and out didn't want to cooperate. That sent another surge of nausea through her belly. She leaned over the side of the basket again in case she needed to spew.

If she was lucky, it would land on the man who shot her.

The jolt of the basket landing on the interior deck of the *Golden Nile* ripped a choked cry out of her. She bit her lip and breathed hard through her nose, and didn't mind at all when the man in the basket with her put his arm around her. Ess opened her eyes, and through her tears and the weird red-tinted lighting, she saw people scurrying around to fasten the basket down. Someone brought a folding ladder-stepstool arrangement that went over the side of the basket, allowing her to climb out rather than be tossed like a sack of grain. She felt dizzy, but at least the pain was receding.

"Odessa." Sylvia's familiar face appeared out of the flurry of activity. "Come on, young lady. You're just as bad as your brother. When he sees what you've done to your arm..." She sighed, then offered her a green glass tumbler half-filled with a dark liquid. "Drink this down, every last drop, so you can survive the walk to my infirmary."

It tasted bitter and cloying and rotten all at the same time, and startled her by fizzing across her tongue, but Ess drank down the entire contents. Even if it did make her gag at the end of the large dose. The woman's words penetrated the drumming of her pulse in her ears.

"My — is Uly here?"

Maybe she was delirious from the pain?

"Well, he was." Sylvia tucked the tumbler into one of the many pockets of her long coat, then hooked her arm through Ess's good arm. "He was part of the rescue team. I'm sure he'll laugh when he learns how the two of you passed each other."

"When can I... oh." Ess wobbled. Her knees and ankles seemed to have turned into jelly. She tried raising her arm to press her hand to her head. The resulting pain from the unwise movement seemed to come from a long distance, rolling over her like a wave of hot molasses studded with roofing nails. They poked and stabbed but didn't make much of an impact on her. "That's... incre... credi... double... shtuff." She sighed and stopped fighting to keep her eyes open. They felt as if weights were tied to each lash.

"Indeed it is, and I see I gave you far too strong a dose. Well, you'll probably grow immune to it, just like Ulysses. You Fremonts have the most obstinate, resistant blood chemistry, when it comes to medical science." Sylvia patted her hand and guided her through a door and away from the red-tinted light.

"Wuzz 'at mean?" Ess felt a giggle churning in her belly, a pleasant change from the pain and nausea, but she was too sleepy to let it out.

"The same gifts in your blood that let you heal quickly also fight against any kind of medicine we might give you for pain or illnesses. The same thing that lets you fight the tranquilizers. And here we are. Amos, we have a bullet wound, high in the shoulder, lots of tearing. Knowing the Revisionists, lots of fragments, and the bullets coated in that nasty toxin they've started using. That's where most of your pain is coming from. We need to rinse the flesh thoroughly and apply the antidote, then sew her up before the soporific wears off."

"Sop-riff-icky," Ess mumbled. The giggle felt a little closer to coming out. She managed to pry one eye open, just as Sylvia guided her onto the examination table.

"Be a good girl, and help me get you out of this jacket, all right?"

Ess watched from a distance, not really feeling her body cooperate as Sylvia removed her jacket. Her tongue tangled, but she thought she explained clearly enough when the woman tried to slide the messenger back off her shoulder. Sylvia let her hold the bag on her lap, gripping it hard with her good hand. She wanted to remark that it was good she wore her bindings garment to flatten her breasts, because it preserved her modesty when Sylvia removed her shirt, but she couldn't seem to wrap her tongue around the right words. She smiled muzzily at the young man with the fascinating blue, Asian-shaped eyes and golden-red hair, and sat at a slight angle while the doctor and her assistant cleaned and stitched her torn shoulder. Ess tried to watch what they were doing, especially when the antidote paste made the toxin clinging to her torn flesh bubble and hiss. Her head swam when she turned it too far, so she looked straight ahead and focused on the anatomical diagrams posted on the wall on the other side of the long room. She thought perhaps the words were in Arabic script, but couldn't focus her eyes enough to be sure.

"Odessa?" Athena's voice cut through the pleasant ringing hum building up in the back of her head that helped muffle the discussion between Sylvia and Amos.

Ess thought maybe she didn't really want to understand what they were saying as they worked on her shoulder.

"H'lo," she said, and realized her eyes had closed at some point. She couldn't be sure. It was an effort to get them open again, and when she did, they didn't want to focus right away. "'thena?"

"Yes, it's me." A crooked little smile pulled on the woman's mouth, when Ess could finally see her features clearly. "I see you've had your first dose of loopy-loo."

"Zat iss name?" The giggle came a little higher up her throat. Ess couldn't quite remember why she didn't want to giggle. Something to do with her stomach trying to empty.

"That's what we call it. Do you have something for me?"

"Dust." Ess sat up a little straighter, causing an odd tugging sensation in the shoulder Sylvia was working on.

"Sit still, girl," the doctor snapped, and gripped her right where neck merged into shoulder.

"Sorry..." She blinked a few times, wondering why Athena was there. Then she remembered. "Cry... crystal dust," she pronounced, puzzled by the thickness of her tongue. She raised her hand off the messenger bag in her lap. "Canopic jar full o' it," she said with exaggerated care for clarity. "Funny ol' geezer brought it an' I tapped the rod an' it... it jus' sang. Like a choir. Revisionists heard — heard th' song. Careless, huh?"

"Oh, my dear child." Athena cupped her cheek for a moment. "Not at all. You haven't been trained."

"Gotta train, huh?" Ess blinked rapidly a few times. She felt stuck halfway between clarity and a thick, cloudy, sticky sensation that tried to suck her back down into it.

"Indeed you shall." She reached down and took the bag from her lap. "When you're patched up and you've got your head straight on your shoulders, we need to have a long talk."

"Can't. Gotta go back. Promised Allistair. Job," she added, feeling rather proud to have spoken so coherently. Her tongue didn't feel quite so stiff and heavy now.

"Yes, your job. One more stop after Kansas City." Athena sighed, cradling the messenger bag of crystal dust against her chest. "The most important one. Sylvia?"

"Maybe five more minutes. Girl's lucky she only got it through the fleshy part of the shoulder. Though I'm sure she won't feel so lucky when the medicine wears off. She could have chipped or even fractured bone."

"Ouch," Ess murmured.

By the time they had finished bandaging her shoulder, helped her put on a fresh shirt, then bound her arm to her side to keep it still and keep the weight off her shoulder, clarity had returned to her head. It brought a medium-level sensation of heat, and not so much a throbbing of pain as a feeling of rising and falling on a sea of aching. Ess told herself to be grateful she wasn't the sort to get seasick. At least, not yet.

"Vivian's daughter, eh?" a rumbling male voice said, when Ess followed Athena into the conference room. The big, black-haired man turned away from what looked like an elevation map hung down the length of one wall. He watched her settle down gingerly at the table.

"You're practically the first to say that," she said. Her voice sounded as bruised and tired as she felt, and she would have smiled, but even the muscles of her face felt stiff-sore-exhausted. "Everybody else says 'Matilda's granddaughter' or 'Ernest's granddaughter.' Since I've met you people, it's like my parents didn't exist."

"Yes, well, it depends on who you're meeting," he said, coming over to the seat opposite her, letting Athena take the seat at the head of the table. "I'll wager once you meet people who actually worked with your parents, they'll refer to Vivian and Edward. Most people so far knew your grandparents. That's all."

"That's all," she echoed. She decided she rather liked him, with his common sense explanation for something she hadn't even realized bothered her until just now. An amazing combination, pain and medications. They opened up doors in her mind and made connections she would have missed otherwise.

"Pleased to meet you, Miss Fremont. I am Fordyce Chamberlain. My claim to fame is that I finally persuaded our Athena to agree to marry me."

"You finally got up the courage to ask me outright, instead of hinting outrageously," Athena said.

To Ess's amazement, the woman blushed faintly. She didn't have time to marvel over it. Athena asked Fordyce to bring an enormous wooden bowl to the table from the cabinets that filled the far wall of the room. While he did that, she unwrapped the outer layers of the makeshift bag holding the crystal dust, finishing the job after putting the dress silk-wrapped layer in the bowl. Then she left the dust to sit there, while she had Ess go through the entire sequence of events that took her from Mr. Stephenson bringing the canopic jar into the museum, until she sat down in Sylvia's infirmary with her bullet-torn shoulder. Interestingly, Fordyce took notes and interrupted with questions while Athena said very little.

"What can we do with it?" Ess asked, after watching Athena carefully, slowly, slide the square of silk out of the pile of crystal dust.

A faintly shimmering layer of it clung to the cloth until Athena brought out the crystal rod hanging from a chain around her neck. She struck it, softly, and the last layer of dust leaped off, as if violently shaken.

"We won't know until we present it to the lotus," Fordyce muttered, staring at the pile of dust through half-lidded eyes. "It could be the most vital part of the Great Machine turned to dust, just to make sure the Revisionists didn't get it. Without the lotus, who could ever remake it?"

"What lotus?" She grinned, a bubble of mirth pressing against the heavy exhaustion, when Fordyce gave her a wide-eyed look, then hunched his shoulders and glanced at Athena. He made her think of a little boy caught in some mischief when he should have been in bed.

"That is part of your education," Athena said. "Suffice to say, the lotus is the keystone to reassembling the Great Machine. And it is the reason for our name, of course."

"Suffice." She yawned, when she would have said more. The dizziness blurred the words she had meant to say, the questions she wanted to ask.

"The girl isn't going anywhere," Fordyce said. "She needs a good, solid twelve hours."

"*The girl* is only going to get about six," Ess said, blinking hard to try to uncross her eyes. "If I'm not back at the hotel in the morning, like I promised, Allistair will probably cancel the opening gala and send for more Pinkertons to look for me."

"Well, if he's half as intelligent as I thought when we met in

Washington," Athena said, getting to her feet again, "he will learn the *Golden Nile* is here in Kansas City. Besides, Theo said you left a note. However, we should not make him come here. Come with me."

"You aren't going to dress me up like a French gift doll again, are you?" Ess had to try three times before she could get her feet under herself and stand upright.

"Not quite, though I do enjoy it. Costumes are so much fun." She looped her arm through Ess's. Fordyce came around her other side and put his arm around her waist, without pressing against her wounded shoulder. "No, it's straight to bed for you. Then we must have a war council before depositing you back among your teammates."

"Costumes?"

"Costumes are just as vital a weapon in our war as our Zeus guns and mobis." Athena nodded for punctuation. "Women always have the advantage, because society is trained to consider us naïve and uneducated, and either unable or unwilling to defend ourselves. The more frilly and delicate you appear, the more they underestimate you."

"Oh. Good." Ess wanted to close her eyes as they stepped out of the conference room and headed down the passageway, but that made her dizzy and threatened to wake her up. Right now, she wanted sleep as much and as soon as possible.

~~~~~

Athena let Ford do the talking over a very early breakfast. She silently scolded herself for not realizing that the lack of any sort of mention of Ess's parents might trouble the young woman. The truth of the matter was that Matilda and Ernest were such brightly shining stars among the Originators, brilliance bordering on insanity, that Vivian and Edward — intelligent, hard-working, honorable and much-loved in their own right — rather faded away into the background. So Athena sat back and let her betrothed talk about adventures he and Edward had enjoyed when they were Ess's age. He ended with a string of outrageous stories about how Vivian had been so enrapt with her studies that she hadn't realized that three-quarters of her male patients came with self-inflicted wounds, just for an excuse to spend time with the lovely young doctor.
~~~~~

Chapter Seventeen

"In the end, we realized that was entirely the wrong battle strategy," he said, getting up to fetch the coffee pot to refill all their cups. "Vivian admired Edward because he *wasn't* a clumsy clod, constantly using up her supplies. I know a good dozen men who volunteered for hazardous duty, cutting their way through dense jungles, following obscure clues, just to work out their grief, the day your parents married."

"I remember Mama saying..." Ess shook her head and bowed it over her cup, watching the streaks as she stirred cream into the inky depths.

"Saying what?" Athena reached to brush the backs of her knuckles against the girl's cheek. Ess had managed five hours of sleep, and she did look better, but Athena feared fever setting in. Her skin did feel a little warm, but not too dry or too damp.

"Papa teased her that she married him to experiment on him. Only he couldn't decide if it was her attempts at cooking, or her medical studies. Because he healed so quickly." She cracked a crooked grin. "He healed quicker from bullet wounds, he said, than he did bad cooking. Mama would just laugh, and then she would say his rapid healing did fascinate her, but she liked a man who could read poetry without stopping every other line to look up words in a dictionary."

Ford let out a bark of laughter and leaned back. "That sounds just like them. Never saw a pair so in love and having so much fun bickering. Edward confessed he riled up your mother just because it was so much fun making up." He instantly turned bright red. "Sorry. Probably not what a young lady like—"

"This young lady stayed alive for years disguised as a boy. I'm sure she has heard more salacious talk than that," Athena said, keeping her expression and tone cool and even, when she wanted to laugh. Only Fordyce could be so earthy, and yet so prickly about what was "proper" for a young lady to hear.

"Hmm, sounds interesting." Fordyce grinned at Ess. "Gotta admit, the more I think about Vivian and Edward, the more that sounds like fun. What do you say, my love? Shall we try bickering and making up for the first ten years or so?"

"If you live that long." She held her expression for a good five-count, until Ess lost the battle with her grin. Athena nearly sputtered as she gave in to her mirth, and soon the three of them were laughing together.

He shook his head. "Wonder where that scapegrace brother of yours is.

Should have heard by now you were on board. I spent some of our trip back to civilization telling him all sorts of tall tales about your father, by the by, so you can probably get them from him."

"Was Uly—no." Ess shook her head. She winced when she reached for the butter dish with her wounded arm.

"Was he what?" Then Athena thought she knew. "No, he wasn't on board the last time we met up. He was part of the team that went out to rescue Fordyce and his team from Antarctica."

"I'll have you know, my love, that we had just about rescued ourselves." He winked at Ess. "The problem was getting from where we rescued ourselves to, to back home."

"What was in Antarctica?" Ess asked. "More crystal?"

"Unfortunately, no." Fordyce gave a melodramatic sigh and his entire body slumped in grief and defeat. That earned a grin from Ess.

Athena decided that if she didn't already love the frustrating man, she might have fallen in love there, just for his clowning. Ess needed some foolery in her life. To be deprived of her parents at a young age, so she only had a few memories of them, and then to lose her brother through his own idiotic need for adventure and risk, and then be abandoned by her grandparents in their pursuit of answers to the many riddles the ancestors left them—it was a wonder the girl wasn't trapped in opium or belladonna or other odd and dangerous medicines that would let her forget her woes for a little while. She was of the same solid mental and physical stock as her parents and grandparents.

Then again, the elder Fremonts were somewhat eccentric, even among the Originators, and their son and his bride had been a little too adventurous, and careless of their safety. Ess might not be that stable, though she certainly seemed to be the most solid and commonsense of the entire family.

Fordyce had only begun to regale Ess with stories of her brother's exploits when they had to dress up for disembarking. Dawn was just starting to streak across the plains, stretching out golden arms toward Kansas City.

"Where is Uly?" Ess asked, when she emerged from the costuming room with her hat tucked under her arm, working on the buttons at her wrist. "Dr. Sylvia said he was part of the rescue effort."

"Yes, and that's why he isn't back yet. He led the team backtracking the ones who hunted you and Theo. He will be there at the gala, if he doesn't come to you at the hotel this afternoon." Athena caught hold of her hand. "I promise."

The docks where the *Golden Nile* tied up were only two blocks away from the Grand Hotel where the Pinkertons were quartered. Fordyce, Athena, and Ess walked instead of trying to find a cab available at such an early hour. Athena found it rather bracing, not just the chill in the air and the increasing traffic, but the visible progress of the shadows shortening as the daylight grew brighter, just in the short time they walked.

"Charles," Ess murmured, and gestured with a tip of her chin to a shoeshine stand where a man sat reading a paper with his foot propped up, but no boy working on blacking his boots.

Athena looked without turning her head, and saw the Pinkerton observing them over the top of his paper. He watched them walk by without moving. She thought she heard the crinkle of newspaper once they put the shoeshine stand behind them.

"Following," Fordyce said.

"Do we find out now, or when we reach the hotel?" she mused.

"The fewer witnesses, the better," Ess said. She pulled her shoulders back, winced, and turned to face their shadow as she stopped. "Hello, Charles. Was there a big mess in my room?"

"Mess?" Charles jammed his fists into his hips. "The hotel was ready to call out the police and declare you either kidnapped or murdered." He grinned and raised a hand to tip his hat to Athena. "Ma'am. It's good to see you again."

"And you, Detective. May I introduce my associate, Dr. Fordyce Chamberlain."

"Medical doctor, I hope." His eyes narrowed as he looked Ess over, focusing on her arm and the makeshift sling Sylvia had fashioned to go with the dress and the little cape built into her coat.

"Archeology and history," Fordyce said, extending his hand to shake. "Can we assume the rest of your associates are somewhere out on the street, waiting for us to arrive?"

"Waiting for Odessa, and whoever is out to hurt her."

"What exactly did those men do to her room?" Athena asked.

"What were they looking for?" Allistair said, stepping up onto the curb behind them. "It strikes me as a little suspicious that you were there when Odessa was involved in a robbery and vanished, and now you show up again. After someone tore her room apart, looking for something."

"Odessa intercepted coded communication between several cells of Resurrectionists," Fordyce said. "She learned what we were working on, the last time she was on board the *Golden Nile*, and—foolishly, I might add— decided to get involved and keep the message until we were set to rendezvous here in Kansas City. Their agents confronted her in the museum, but they were unable to do more than slip her a threatening note. When she left last night, it was to meet us. Time was of the essence, because these men are desperate to keep their identities and activities hidden."

Athena slid her arm through his, amused at her combined pride and dismay at how easily he came up with lies. Very clever, believable lies, as there were always pockets of Southerners who wanted to re-fight the war, but lies all the same.

"And you are involved in this how?" Allistair didn't cross his arms and give them a skeptical look, but it was all there in his tone of voice.

"How better to infiltrate all levels of society, investigate the unusual and the ancient, than under the guise of archeologists?" Athena said.

They retired to the team's suite, where the Pinkertons ordered a massive breakfast. Athena was amused to watched Ess and Fordyce dig in as if they hadn't eaten two hours earlier. Fordyce didn't surprise her. The man still ate as if he were a growing boy. Of course, he could be making up for months of privation on the arduous journey back from Antarctica. Ess, however, seemed out of character with her hearty appetite. Perhaps part of it came from rising so early. Or perhaps Ess took refuge from too many questions by keeping her mouth filled, albeit with small bites that she took an inordinately long time chewing. That was something Ernest was more likely to do, Athena reflected. Matilda had enjoyed the verbal tussles. She loved playing with words like other people would play with scraps of metal and glass, harnessing steam, creating new devices.

The mess in Ess's room had been cleaned up. "Earthquake and tornado, on a biblical scale," Briscoe had called it. The furniture had been turned over, the smaller pieces smashed, the larger pieces hacked into with large, sharp implements. Her clothes had been ripped to shreds along all the seams.

"Searching for that communication, no doubt," Allistair said.

"My books?" Ess turned to Athena, losing some of her color. With the background pain she had to deal with, she had little color to spare. "Were any of my books left?"

"Everything torn apart. Like a snowstorm," Roger said.

"Even the books Miss Latymer gave me? The Egyptology books?"

"Ah." Allistair's dour expression lightened a little, as if a great mystery had been explained. "We gathered up everything that we thought was yours, including all the papers, so you could sort through them. Sorry, Odessa, but I really think they're all a complete loss."

"Well, as long as all the pieces are there." She tried to smile, meeting Athena's eyes. "I'd much rather my books destroyed than to think of them in the hands of those Rebels."

"We can replace those books with no problem," Athena assured her.

"The printed books, I know we can. But my journal. With all my study notes. I was re-learning all the Egyptian lore and alphabets and such my grandparents taught me, and I used that lovely journal you gave me to keep my notes."

Athena thought she understood. If the Revisionists had taken the time to look through Ess's personal items that they had torn apart, they might have picked up enough information to realize that the book was written by their age-old enemies, to train the next generation of searchers and warriors and scholars. They would deduce that Ess was in training to work with the Originators.

It warmed Athena's heart to know Ess had good friends among her teammates. She wondered, however, about the way Allistair glowered at the girl, and the way his expression softened when all attention at the table was elsewhere. As the discussion turned to Egyptology and what the Pinkerton men had learned during the long assignment of escorting and protecting the exhibition, she let her thoughts roam. Could it be, perhaps, that Allistair had warmer feelings for Ess? On a more personal level than simply being a good leader, taking responsibility for a member of his team? That put Ess's few remarks about Allistair's attitude toward her in an entirely different light. The man perhaps felt caught between duty and personal interest, and it made him somewhat cranky to have to put duty first. Athena amused herself with images of what the young man might do and say, once this assignment was over and the artifacts were safely on their way back to Britain, under someone else's care. Would he ambush Ess with a courtship she couldn't have predicted? Or would he be wise and simply let a cordial working friendship turn into something warmer? Some men didn't have much patience when it came to matters of the heart. They thought that time was fleeting. The more oblivious of them excused it as concern for their young lady's dreams and hopes and wishes, assuming she wanted above all things to become a mother.

Athena thought of Vivian's dismay when confronted with the interests of the young men around her. She wanted to put medicine and her studies ahead of everything else, and protested that she had no use for men in her life, except as co-workers and someone to dig the truly hard, stubborn soil when she was at an excavation. After all, she had no problem killing rodents and insects, hunting her own food, doctoring her own wounds, defending herself and navigating from one section of jungle to another. What did she need a man for? Chances were good, an independent, self-reliant girl like Ess shared her mother's opinions about romance and courtship.

~~~~~

Allistair was fair on his way to earning a black eye. Ess felt the weight of his gaze on her no matter where she went. Granted, the main room of the team's suite wasn't that large, but there were other people in the room. Couldn't he watch them? Talk to some of them? Couldn't he at least do her the courtesy of letting her examine and sort through her possessions in a little privacy? She wondered how he would react if she shook out the shreds of her petticoats or bloomers, so there was no mistake what they had been. Would he be embarrassed for at least a few seconds and look away?

Instead of following through on that grumbling thought, she tossed the torn garments into the bag the hotel had provided for disposal, and reached for the next item. Her teammates had loaded all her possessions, or what remained of them, into two crates and brought them into the suite for her to sort through. She was grateful that they would give her the choice of keeping or disposing of the items. Some people would have just gathered
~~~~~

up everything and consigned it to the trash without considering her.

Ess tossed her brand new, unraveled stockings into the bag and picked up the wad of soft blue that had been her favorite shirt. It had black, tarry footprints all over it.

"I don't suppose anyone followed up on where this tar might have come from?" she asked, only halfway glancing over her shoulder.

"We asked." Roger came over and squatted by her chair. "Too many places, too many things use tar around here."

"At least you tried." She stiffened, seeing a dark blue corner sticking out from under her fancy shoes. She reached with both hands, and muffled a snarl as the unwise movement aggravated her shoulder.

"Careful now." He reached for the blue corner and pulled out her journal. "This what you were going for?"

"Yes. Thanks."

"Somebody would think you need a bodyguard, Odessa," he said with a wink.

"You should see what happened to the ones who did this to me."

"Ouch." He grinned at her as he stood up and walked away.

He stepped out of the direct line of sight with Allistair, who certainly seemed to be scowling at either Roger or her. As soon as their gazes met, he looked away. Ess sighed and flipped open her book.

More tarry footprints, but not as bad as on her shirt. Probably her shirt took the brunt of the filth. Although why the men who ransacked her room couldn't have walked off all that tar before coming into her room, she couldn't imagine. Unless ...

"Was there tar on the roof?"

On the other side of the room, Athena looked up from the small pocket journal she wrote in. Her gaze met Ess's, and she nodded slightly. Fordyce glanced at her, then stood up and came over to look over her shoulder.

"Ah. Footprints on your book. Of course. If they were on the roof before they came down here and punished your room... yes, that would make sense," he said.

"It doesn't help us much, though." Ess tried not to sigh as she flipped through the pages. Some were bent over, some with boot prints, some torn. But as far as she could tell, no one had ripped out any pages. She would have to, or else leave the ruined pages in her book and write around them.

"Every little bit you can learn about your enemy is a little bit closer to security," he said, patting her good shoulder.

"Enemies of the exhibition, or the British Museum, or some enemies you haven't discussed yet?" Allistair said.

Ess snapped her book closed, though she doubted he could have made sense of anything in her journal. If she did say so herself, she had the worst handwriting imaginable. It was almost a cipher unto itself.

"Enemies in general. In this case, the Resurrectionists," Fordyce said with a genteel nod for emphasis. "Since they didn't find what they were looking for in Miss Odessa's hotel room, they must assume she has it on her person, meaning they will be back to try again. I fear with every year that passes since their defeat, the Southerners' determination to restart the war only grows, along with their viciousness. We had discussed this eventuality on board the *Golden Nile*, but came to no decision because she is, after all, under your authority as a Pinkerton. However, Miss Latymer and I agree that it would be safer for all concerned if Miss Odessa spent her nights on board our airship with us. She cannot stay in this suite with you four men, after all."

"No, that's true." Allistair looked like he had swallowed back several unpleasant or at least argumentative responses. He glowered down at Ess, more like his normal self, and gnawed on his bottom lip for a few seconds.

She dared to look away and dig through the crates again. She felt much lighter inside, having her journal with all her notes back in her possession, and not in the Revisionists' possession.

Several handfuls of papers turned out to be pages of books, torn out completely at the spine. She played with the idea of asking someone to repair the books. Maybe there was someone on board the *Golden Nile* who had the materials? Glue, leather to patch the binding, maybe gut and a needle for sewing the binding and pages together again? She did a rough sorting job, trying to tell the books apart by the different typeface on the pages. Over her head, Allistair asked questions about tracking down and capturing the Resurrectionists, which Fordyce answered quite glibly. Or at least, his answers sounded glib to Ess, who knew the crew of the *Golden Nile* was doing no such thing. She concentrated on her task, silently commanding them both to go away.

To her frustration, both men continued their discussion, changing it gradually to a general comparison of dealing with criminal elements and searching for stolen valuables. Meanwhile, they picked up handfuls of pages and helped her sort. Ess couldn't fault them for that, or complain, but she wished Allistair would go away. She was sitting, while the two men stood directly behind her. She sorted on the table next to her and her lap and the floor around her, while they dragged another table over. It was irritating to have them take over so much of her task. Even more irritating when she could not legitimately complain.

Maybe she was just irritable from the ache in her arm? Sylvia had warned her that when the soporific wore off entirely, she would be bad-tempered and her head would hurt abominably, unless she drank large quantities of water and plain, strong black tea.

Another dark blue book cover caught her attention. She tossed aside the handful of pages she had just picked up. Ess ignored the ache in her shoulder as she reached with her bad arm and yanked the book out from under her slashed valise and her good traveling shoes. Tears filled her eyes, only partly from physical ache, as she ran her fingers over the slashed cover of the Blue Lotus Society manual.

"Athena?" She blinked away the tears and held up the book.

Allistair and Fordyce gave way as Athena came over to look through the book with her. Fordyce brought her a chair, and the two of them leaned in close over the book, shoulders touching, as they flipped through it one page at a time.

There were pages missing, but they had been halfway torn out, and the pieces turned up among all the pages retrieved from the wreckage of her room. It looked to Ess more and more like the Revisionists had simply indulged in temper tantrums. They didn't look at what they destroyed. As long as it didn't have any chance of holding crystal, they didn't examine it.

"Perhaps it is a good thing you didn't jump immediately into your studies," Athena murmured, when the men had finished sorting through the last of the pages and they finally wandered over to the other side of the room. "If you take after your mother, I would have expected you to write in the margins and make notes all over the pages."

"The border decorations are messages, aren't they?"

"Of course." A tiny bubble of laughter escaped the woman, so soft, Ess thought no one else in the room heard it. "Were you that irritated with us, that you refused to take the bait?"

"I felt... herded. Pushed in a direction I wasn't certain I wanted to go."

"Perhaps you have been too long on your own. Even working with these fine detectives, you have been your own person. We of the Society must be ready to always put the good of the many ahead of our own. That is what your brother had the hardest time accepting, and his rebellion nearly cost him, as well as the Society."

"Rebellion against what, exactly? What does the Great Machine do?" Ess muffled a snarl deep in her throat that she feared would emerge as a shriek. "What do I have to do to prove you can trust me?"

"It's not a matter of trust, child. Not entirely." Athena patted her hands, which clutched her book. "It's a matter of education. There are some things you cannot be taught until you have proven mastery of simpler, more elemental, foundational things."

"Read the book, then ask you for more?" She felt weary with an ache that was more in her soul than her body.

Chapter Eighteen

Simon Witherspoon, curator of the Kansas City Museum of Antiquities, was one of those rare men who adored all things Egyptian, and yet did not style himself an Egyptologist. As he told Ess, when they were introduced shortly after lunch that afternoon, no one had the right to call himself an Egyptologist until he had spent at least four seasons in Egypt itself, so the dust got into his skin and the past permeated his blood. He had some of her grandparents' books sitting on the shelf in his office, and when he saw her looking at them, eagerly pulled them down to show to her.

"I met the great lady and her husband just once, nigh on thirty years ago," he said. "Fascinating people. So knowledgeable, yet so... dear me, 'humble' isn't quite the right word, but they were so very generous with their knowledge, so willing to listen and consider other people's theories and conclusions. None of this rude contradiction and interruption you find nowadays in academic circles. Ah, here they are."

He tenderly withdrew an envelope of oilcloth from the back of the book where it was anchored in a pocket attached to the back cover. From the envelope he withdrew a flat package wrapped in tissue, which he unfolded to reveal a tintype of Matilda and Ernest Fremont.

"Miss Peabody? Miss Peabody, are you quite all right?" He gently patted her on the shoulder. Fortunately her good one.

"Hmm?" Ess blinked, and realized to her mortification that her eyes were heavy with tears. "I'm sorry. It's been so long since..."

She wished she could shed her false identity as easily as she planned to shed her lavender-sprigged muslin dress at the end of the day. Maintaining the lies she had to tell suddenly seemed the most onerous task she had ever taken on. Looking into Mr. Witherspoon's eyes, she hesitated to trust her judgment. After all, she had made some foolish choices lately. Yet she trusted him. She liked him. He admired her grandparents, showed off their books and the letters they had written to him, discussing an academic matter long ago, as if they were his most precious possessions.

"Mr. Witherspoon, I can trust you with a very precious secret, can't I?"

So what if Allistair scolded her until her ears rang for this? Ess wanted to sit for just half an hour and talk to someone who remembered her grandparents. Admired them. Saw them the same as she had seen them as a child: amazing, intelligent people with an overbearing fascination for all things Egyptian, not people involved in some bizarre secret society that clashed with enemy agents and devised amazing technology and mind-altering medicines in the pursuit of some goal they had yet to reveal. The Fremont family had never been ordinary, even without the secrets of the Originators hanging on their coattails, but she would willingly risk this mission for just a taste of what she had always thought of as "normal."

"Of course you can, Miss Peabody." He settled down at the desk where her grandparents' books and letters had been spread out.

"First of all, Evangeline Peabody is a nom de guerre for the sake of this mission. I am as much a Pinkerton agent as the men I work with, escorting and guarding the exhibition."

"Fascinating," he breathed, and leaned a little closer. His feathery whiskers trembled with visible excitement.

"My real name is Odessa Fremont. And I have not seen or heard from my grandparents in nearly eight years."

Mr. Witherspoon's eyes widened slightly and his smile faded. He sat back in his chair and studied her face. Several times he glanced back and forth between the tintype and her face. At last he reached out and took hold of her hand.

"Yes, I can see the resemblance. But one thing puzzles me, Miss Pea — Miss Fremont."

She inhaled slowly, trying not to stiffen. She certainly couldn't explain where her grandparents had vanished to, what they were looking for, and when she expected them back.

"Why, with Egypt so strong in your family's blood, didn't they give you an Egyptian name? Odessa sounds rather Greek."

"Yes, well, my brother's name is Ulysses. Maybe they wanted us to go into Greek archeology, or concentrate on the Greek rulers of Egypt." She shrugged, and winced when the movement pulled on her shoulder. "You do believe me, Mr. Witherspoon?"

"Absolutely." He patted her hand. "And your secret is most assuredly safe with me. I'm flattered that you entrusted it to me."

"It's been so long since I've been able to talk with someone who knew them. I wasn't even sure if their books were available anywhere. All the museums we've stopped at along this journey, none had their books. I was quite thinking that perhaps I imagined my grandparents' expertise and all the books they published."

"Hardly." That delighted little boy brilliance returned to his eyes as he leaned forward and whispered loudly, "It just goes to show you that our museum here is of higher, finer quality than all those others. We know who the masters of Egyptology are." Then he chuckled.

They had a delightful afternoon, setting up the exhibit in the echoing rooms of marble and oak with vaulted ceilings. The museum had been closed to prepare for the opening of the exhibition. For once, Ess didn't have to work around people who thought the rules didn't apply to them, and they could wander in and out among the tables and display stands and crates, picking up artifacts and handling them while Ess and the museum's staff set up the exhibit. Not this time. She welcomed the reprieve and the common sense of Mr. Witherspoon. The semi-privacy allowed them to speak of her grandparents' writings, their exploits and adventures. She felt quite safe sharing with him some things she remembered from her childhood, discussions she overheard her grandparents have with various archeologists and explorers. She was quite disappointed when all their work was done and Charles came to escort her to the hotel for dinner, and then to dress up for the evening.

Her mood plummeted as she lay at an awkward angle in the big brass tub, keeping her shoulder and bandages out of the water. She couldn't turn her head enough to see, but Ess was positive the bandages were dark stained with infection seepage or even blood. What other explanation was there for the ache and the faint, hot throbbing? Especially her mood? Granted, she hadn't been drinking plain, strong tea or cold water as often during the day as Sylvia had ordered, but honestly, how much could one person take in before she sprung leaks? Her petticoats and corset and bloomers made it difficult to use the women's facilities every half hour. Ess thought about her boy clothes, dirty and streaked with blood and torn by the bullet, and she missed them with a hungry longing. How soon until she could change back into her boy façade and relax?

From there, her inner grumbling turned to her grandparents. Yes, she had enjoyed discussing them and their theories with Mr. Witherspoon, but after all this time guarding those silly, faded trinkets from a vanished civilization, Ess was tired of the entire subject. There was more to archeology than Egyptology, after all.

Why, she wondered, not for the first time, didn't people get excited about the mythology and artifacts and remnants of civilization of the people groups who once inhabited the United States? True, the grossly inaccurate mental image of all Indian tribes was of people living in skin teepees that they moved from one place to another. But surely the general population, or at least, those who took the time to think about it, realized that even the nomadic tribes had special locations where they built monuments or reminders about special events in their history? What about the pueblos in the southern part of the country, the mound builders in the Ohio River Valley, and other tribal groups that had permanent homes and settled territories? The archeological remnants of those ancient civilizations were waiting to be discovered.

That was what she had thought about doing someday, when she was old enough to strike out and choose her specialty. Why go to a foreign country, spend exorbitant amounts of money for supplies and hiring workers, and deal with foreign governments? Why not stay in the United States and learn what happened to the original inhabitants, what the people were like, what they believed, how they worshipped? Her grandparents thought it was a reasonable argument, hadn't they? They had encouraged her to expand her studies to the native peoples of the United States.

Yet, hadn't they been lost on an expedition to South America? If they had listened to her and followed her reasoning, wouldn't they be alive and with her right this moment?

"Stop," she told herself.

Yet she couldn't tear her mind away from the path her thoughts raced down. If everyone in the Blue Lotus Society was seeking pieces of the machine, then it stood to reason, her grandparents had theorized pieces were hidden among the ancient ruins of South America. The pyramids and other structures of the Incan, Aztec, Toltec, and Mayan civilizations.

Wouldn't it make sense that if those civilizations were hiding places for crystal, then some of that had been hidden further north in the same land mass? Could some pieces of the Great Machine even now be waiting in some ruined pueblo, or in a cave complex that the ancient Indian races had turned into an underground city? Would she be the one to discover those last few missing pieces, hidden in a place nobody thought worth exploring?

What exactly did the Great Machine do?

That thought nagged at her, while the hired maid came in to help her dress and arrange her hair and paint her face so the rigors of the last twenty-four hours wouldn't show. Ess stared at her reflection, and caught the reflections of the other three mirrors in the room. Their reflections fed into each other, bouncing back and forth and creating multiple images of themselves within them. She wondered what it would be like if someone could somehow step through the surface of the mirror and fall backwards forever into the multiple reflections of the mirrors inside themselves.

Something like time travel, perhaps?

That brought back Theo's words. Maybe she was just tired from a long day of thinking and fighting the pain, and she was indulging in flights of fancy. But what if... what if her grandparents hadn't been hunting *crystal* in South America's jungles? What if they were looking for a time traveling device that the Revisionists had built? What if they went down there to stop it, before people changed time, as Theo had mentioned, and they were caught up in the device, instead of stopping it?

Where would they go? Were they still down in South America, but they just hadn't arrived at the "when" since the "where" wasn't going to change?

It had to be time travel into the future, she reasoned, because time travel into the past was impossible. How could anyone travel into the past? Traveling backward in time would in essence have to change time in some fashion, and time couldn't be changed because once something had happened, it couldn't be changed. A page written in ink couldn't have the ink removed from it, so it could be written again. Anyone with any sense knew that.

So, conceivably, could her grandparents return to her after many years, but to them hardly any time at all had passed?

Ess absently thanked the maid when the girl finished arranging her hair and dusting her nose with powder, while her mind ran through the theory repeatedly.

Was it possible?

The only way to find out was to sit down with Athena and learn everything the woman could teach her, so they could finally discuss the things she wanted, needed to know. Were her grandparents time traveling? If so, could they be contacted so they could stop traveling?

Ess judged the resolution and plan of action settled. Now, she needed to clear her mind to let her concentrate on tonight's opening gala. After all, she was on duty. She had to be alert to protect the artifacts from the common thieves who threatened it. The Egyptology craze had spilled over into the rest of the world. The upper crust wanted to own pieces of Ancient Egypt and be able to brag about it. They were willing to pay exorbitant prices for small treasures. Then there were the private collectors, the art collectors and rare coin collectors, the people who didn't care if they bought through legitimate or illegitimate channels, because they didn't care about bragging to others and lording it over them with their treasures. What mattered was owning, not being seen to own. Those people made it possible for thieves to make a very good living, fulfilling the desires of the secretive and rich.

That, Ess reminded herself, was what she had been hired to prevent. Falling into the hunt for crystal between the Originators and the Revisionists had not been part of the plan. She had a job to do, and she vowed to do it to the best of her ability. No matter how repetitive and boring the evening. No matter how inane the comments from the new rich or the pretenders to intellectual understanding.

~~~~~

When he arrived at the museum that night, Mr. Stephenson relieved some of the boredom by the simple expedient of throwing around his money and influence. He had a chair to sit in and one of the hired waiters dancing attendance on him, bringing him wine and then whiskey and some of the fruit-flavored ices the museum had decided to indulge in. Because Mr. Stephenson camped near the spot where Ess had to stand all night, answering questions and keeping watch, he kept her supplied in fruit ices. He also kept her on the verge of laughter with his comments about all the upper crust people attending the gala. Ess couldn't decide if he was good friends with everyone in the city, and therefore knew all their dirty, embarrassing secrets, which he gleefully related to her, or the man simply loathed everyone among his social peers, and he made up the stories in the hopes of embarrassing them. He kept her amused enough she could ignore the aching in her shoulder.

Then Ulysses stepped into the room.

She knew him instantly, even though his hair was longer, nearly to his
~~~~~

shoulders, with deep lines around his eyes. That scar across his left cheek created a white notch in his beard. He hadn't even begun his first beard before he left home. Now it neatly trimmed his jawline, outlined his full mouth, gracefully swooped down from his thick sideburns to his moustache. He looked elegant, but in the sense of a finely etched sword blade, with blood embedded among the jewels crusting the hilt.

He wore the sleek, silver-gray and deep royal blue uniform of the U.S. Air Corps.

"Well, that's a fine howdy-do," Mr. Stephenson muttered, when he turned to follow the direction of Ess's gaze. He scowled. "Since when do the military-types show any interest in culture?"

To her amusement, Briscoe focused on Uly and followed him as he crossed the room toward her. Ess wanted so much to tell her teammate that this man, out of everyone in the room, posed the least threat to her. As long as he didn't resort to the childhood teasing that sometimes resulted in week-long feuds, each one setting up traps and stealing treasures and fighting to make life as inconvenient as possible for the other, stopping just short of bringing Granny Matilda's wrath down on them.

"Miss Peabody, I presume?" Uly swept off his neat billed cap and bowed low. "Sir, I hope I'm not interrupting too badly. I've been waiting quite some time to meet this fascinating lady."

"Interrupting is interrupting," Mr. Stephenson said with a loud harrumph. "Sir, I know the niceties aren't what they used to be, but shouldn't you introduce yourself?"

"Thank you for reminding me, sir." Uly tucked his cap into his wide belt and offered his white-gloved hand. "Miss Peabody, I am Captain Ulysses Edwards of the Fifth Fleet, Exploration Division. It is my distinct pleasure and honor to meet you. I've heard so very much about you and this exhibition you are entrusted with escorting across this country." He glanced briefly over his shoulder, likely sensing Briscoe coming up behind him. One eyebrow cocked, daring her, he offered his bent arm. "Ma'am, would you do me the honor of a promenade around the room and a private lecture on the wonders of Ancient Egypt?"

"Miss Peabody—"

"Oh, don't worry, Mr. Stephenson. I'm not about to let a uniform and dashing manners sweep me off my feet. I assure you, this gentleman is the very last one in this room I'd ever consider marrying. Your grandson is still at the top of my list of suitors." Ess slid her hand into the crook of Uly's elbow and winked at Briscoe as the two of them moved out of the doorway.

Briscoe, per agreement, had to step into her place and guard the doorway. Ess wondered if he would make her pay for that later, or he would just scold for letting a uniform sweep her off her feet.

"Marriage, is it?" Uly muttered. "What sort of trouble have you been getting into, baby sister?"

"Not as much as you have. Athena hasn't told me much, but enough to let me read between the lines." She swallowed hard and blinked harder, fighting a totally unreasonable longing to weep.

"I missed you."

"When you could remember me."

"Ah. They told you that part, did they?"

"What have you been doing? And what sort of trouble, exactly, did you get into that Athena and her friends had to sweep you away and make you vanish?"

"That is something best not discussed in mixed company." He gestured at the first display, a scale model of the ritual city of Hamunaptra.

"Then why would you talk about it in front of me?" She slid her arm free of his and stepped around to the other side of the table, moving her hands as if pointing out various features of the model.

"Originators, possible Revisionists, and everyone else. That's mixed company."

"I'm not quite an Originator, yet."

"You were born an Originator, baby sister."

"I'm not a baby anymore." She fought to keep her expression neutral, when she wanted to laugh at him.

"True. I found the four detectives you're working with — my congratulations, by the way, for getting that sort of work — but it's the other men watching you with eagle eyes that worry me. Now I hear you assuring that old man you're not considering marrying me, because there are others higher on your list. My heart is broken, by the way."

"You're an idiot."

Ess gestured away from the scale model, toward the slanted tray displaying various faience beads and bangles. When Uly caught hold of her hand again, sliding it back into place in the crook of his elbow, she squeezed his hand. "Don't you ever vanish on me again, do you hear me?"

"Someone would think you actually missed me."

"Painfully." She smiled, tipping her head back to gaze up at him.

"I'm sorry, Ess. It won't happen again. The things I've done the last few years... I might just have grown up. Finally."

"I'll believe that when I actually see it," she said.

Uly tipped his head back and laughed, so the sound rang off the vaulted ceiling.

Too soon, other patrons of the gala invaded their allegedly private lecture, and Ess had to prove her knowledge of Egyptology. Uly drifted to the back of the group, offering bits and pieces of knowledge every once in a while, earning the admiring smiles of all the ladies with his humor and impeccable manners. He managed to dilute the scowls of some of the men. Mr. Stephenson seemed to approve of him. Maybe it was because Uly contradicted self-important Mr. Godfrey's entirely false statements, always using solid facts that Ess was glad to confirm.

Allistair, Roger, Charles, and Briscoe, however, didn't trust him at all. Ess could understand their reasoning. Uly didn't belong in Kansas City. He was an outsider, coming in and displaying more knowledge than all the rich, influential, highly educated people in the room. They weren't prepared for him, they hadn't researched him, read reports on him weeks before coming into town. His knowledge about the artifacts made him a prime suspect, if any trouble occurred tonight. After all, who was more likely to try to steal these artifacts? Someone who knew enough about these bits and pieces of a vanished civilization to value them, to want them. It was a given that all the robberies of private collections were instigated by highly educated people who had the time to research Egyptology to know what was truly valuable and worthwhile, and the money to obtain pieces.

At the end of the lecture, which took up nearly an hour, walking slowly around the exhibition hall, Ess returned to her position at the door. Uly let the young ladies, and some of their mothers and grannies, sweep him away to a corner where they could talk. He did most of the talking, they did most of the sighing and giggling. Ess wondered if her brother felt sickened with all the sweetness and froth, or if he was flattered. She turned her attention back to the old men and scholarly women, and monitoring every person who entered the exhibition hall.

Finally, the clock struck eleven. A civilized hour, allowing the upper crust folk to go on to a dinner party or ball or some other social event. Ess bade farewell to every man and woman, idly wondering if all those men who insisted on kissing her hand had ever thought about the illnesses that could be spread by such casual contact. She nearly giggled when an image filled her mind for a moment, of turning away to wash with soap and water after every old man with damp whiskers slobbered on the back of her hand.

Uly was among the first to leave.

"Tomorrow morning, Miss Peabody. Bright and early. I insist you and I shall go for a leisurely ride and a breakfast picnic." He bowed over her hand but didn't kiss it.

Ess laughed at him, neither agreeing nor refusing. She choked down a sudden need to weep. What she wanted, had wanted since he walked in the door hours ago, was to fling her arms around him and hug him. Walking arm-in-arm with her brother wasn't enough to assure herself he truly was alive, solid and real and healthy and *there* with her.

She certainly didn't want to wait until morning to be alone with him and talk. Plus take a few punches at him, to pay him back for leaving her alone and worried about him for so long.

Chapter Nineteen

"Good riddance to bad rubbish," Roger muttered, coming up behind Ess, as Uly sauntered away, making his bows to several mother-daughter groupings near the door. They giggled and blushed and waved, and Ess wondered which ones imagined they were in love and halfway to the altar, just because he smiled at them.

Uly was a charmer. She had forgotten that. Fortunately, she was immune to that charm.

Her head ached, and during the ebb tide of the throbbing, she could trace the heating thread of discomfort in a straight line to her shoulder. Ess fought to ignore it and silently cursed herself for not drinking as much water as Sylvia had insisted on. What she wanted was another dose of loopy-loo, as Athena had called it. She was clear-headed enough to know that taking the soporific to ease the discomfort of the last dose wearing off would, in essence, merely start the clock running again.

So this is how men become addicted to opium and whisky, she mused. A moment later, she mustered up a meaningless smile for another man who had made erroneous statements about the artifacts all night.

A shimmer of non-sound crept down her bones. Ess continued shaking hands and murmuring non-committal responses. Where had that come from? She couldn't be sure, having only experienced the silent song of crystal a few times. Or was that the sound of the testing rod? Maybe she sensed someone trying to identify crystal in the artifacts, rather than an artifact reacting?

She muffled a snarl at her own stupidity. Who else would be testing the artifacts here, but the Revisionists? No one belonging to the Society would be testing, because they knew she had done it already.

Of course, Uly was long gone. Theo had stopped in and left already. Athena and Fordyce had come, gathered up a string of fawning admirers, and left. Would they return to take her to the *Golden Nile* for the night, in time to catch the hopeful thieves?

Thinking over what she would do, Ess had to decide no, whoever was out there, trying to find crystal, would not linger. How many times would she tap the testing rod, listening for crystal resonance, before she concluded there was none nearby and she could therefore leave?

"Unless they did hear a response," she mused aloud. She smiled and turned to a charming older couple who walked arm-in-arm, matching canes in their free hands, in perfect rhythm. They looked nothing like her grandparents, and yet they made her think of Matilda and Ernest, simply because they were so perfectly in tune with each other.

The last few people in the exhibition hall lingered with Mr. Witherspoon in front of a display of pieces on loan from local benefactors, including Mr. Stephenson. Ess glanced around and made sure no one was headed in her direction, then she hurried as quickly and quietly as she could from the doorway, down the access hallway, to the workroom. It was the quickest exit route she could think of. Besides, where else would she hide if she were trying to get close to the artifacts to test them without stepping foot inside the museum? She caught up a piece of wood used to elevate artifacts requiring some repairs, and left it in the doorway to hold the door open, then stepped out into the wide alleyway used for deliveries.

Her most vulnerable moment was right there in the doorway with the light behind her, casting a long shadow into the alley. Ess crouched low and stepped into the shadows before reaching into the clever pocket sewn into her sash, where she had stashed the testing rod against just such a need. She listened with her ears and her bones for another try of the stranger's crystal rod, or whatever they used to test for crystal. Common sense told her to try several times, and make allowances for the thickness of the bricks of the building, the numbers of people still inside, the noise they made. She would try at least three times; five or even eight would be sensible, just to make sure that as the conditions changed, she wasn't overlooking something.

There. Another humming sensation, stronger, almost audible. She clenched her teeth against the itching sensation in their roots, and thumped the testing rod against the back of her hand, then bent over it, using her body to muffle what audible sound it created. The sound seemed to move through her bones and settle some of the ache in her shoulder. She waited.

Silence.

She counted to twenty, and decided she would count to twenty again. If there was no response, she would go inside. Then she would drink the biggest cup of water she could obtain, even if it was warm.

A groan escaped her lips as another shimmer of silent song trickled along her bones. This time it felt louder. Did that mean it was closer?

Why hadn't she insisted on holding onto the Zeus gun Theo gave her?

Ess felt cold and alone and exposed, here in the darkness of the alley. Why did she act without thinking? Or rather, thinking only so far, but not far enough to consider the possibilities?

Movement at the far end of the alley caught her attention. Holding her breath, she dropped back as far as she could without running into anything. Bowing her head, she attempted to hide her paler skin with the dark sleeve of her gown and her dark hair. What she wouldn't give to be dressed as a boy right now. She could dirty her face and no one would think twice if they saw her later. It was highly inconvenient, she decided, to be womanly at all times. Perhaps men dictated fashions and standards of propriety simply to keep women hobbled?

Two men strode down the alley. One of them raised his hand, revealing a glowing rod with a red-tinged light. So the Revisionists had unusual technology too. Ess shrank back, watching the edges of that light, imagining it reaching out for her. Any moment now, it would touch her, set her on fire, reveal her to the enemy.

"Door's open," one man murmured.

"He's an idiot. We told him midnight," the other man said with a chuckle that sounded almost fond.

"He's a problem and a danger. What good is it having a man on the inside if he can't obey simple orders?"

The man who didn't hold the red light reached into his pocket as they approached the door. He held a squarish rod as long as his hand. Ess couldn't tell what sort of metal it was in the reflected light, but it gleamed, and gave off a long, low note when the man struck it against the doorframe.

The crystal rod tucked into her sash sang softly in response. Ess flinched, then froze. *Please, please, don't let them have the sensitivity to follow the echoes.*

"Something isn't right," the first man said. He stepped over the threshold into the museum workroom.

Now would be a good time for one of her teammates to come looking for her. Ess wished they would be just as overbearingly concerned about her now as they had been this morning.

"Where is he?" The other man struck the rod against the doorframe even harder, so the sound turned sour as it rang against the brick walls.

The crystal rod buzzed through the layers of her clothes. Ess tried to muffle the sound between her hands.

"Who's there?" the man with the rod snapped. He snatched the red light from his companion and swung his arm out, stepping toward her. The light touched her, and Ess hoped she only imagined the heat penetrating her clothes. Especially when the man laughed.

"So he sent you to run his errands?" the first said.

Now she could make out details, more than just their overcoats and hard-sole boots, short-trimmed hair and lack of beards. She had seen both of them at the exhibition, wandering the room, watching everyone. She hadn't paid them much attention because they seemed so much more intent on being seen with the glittery upper class of Kansas City, rather than the artifacts spread around them.

Now she understood. They had come to contact their inside man.

"Should have guessed that was what he was after, flirting with you this whole time," he continued, giving Ess that smirking, assessing look she wanted to punch off most men's faces. "Well, hand it over."

"Hand what over? I'm out here to meet..." Ess edged to the right, testing. Neither man moved. "Please, don't tell anyone?" The plan creeping into the back of her mind was nebulous at best, but she remembered her grandfather declaring that those of criminal minds expected everyone to have the same thoughts and goals.

"Tell them what?" He looked her over again.

"Well, it's a lot of money, isn't it? And of course it's the most important piece. He wanted me to give it to him tonight, but they'll notice it's missing, won't they?"

"He's taking a lot on himself," the man with the rod said. He stepped back and looked through the door into the museum workshop again. "He doesn't have the rod, so how can he test?"

"Maybe we have somebody else after a different prize," his partner said.

"Then why did we hear it sing out here?" He tapped the rod against his elbow and held it up so it could chime unimpeded.

The testing rod sang softly at Ess's waist. She couldn't press her hand against it to silence the song, or risk giving away its location.

Where were Allistair and Roger and Charles and Briscoe? Why wasn't Mr. Witherspoon looking for her, to lock up for the night?

He struck the rod again, harder, and pointed it directly at her. The crystal rod sang audibly, and warbled when the man waved the rod around in a figure eight in the air.

Did Athena know it could do that?

"Might not need our inside man after all," he said with a chuckle, and lunged at her, his hand moving with a rattler's speed.

Ess swallowed a curse and dodged aside, spinning and kicking hard, as Briscoe had taught her during long, sleepless nights on board the train, when they had the car to themselves. The man cursed and drew back his arm, tucking his hand under his other arm. His associate raised the red light and pointed it at her like a gun.

For all she knew, it could shoot lightning like the Zeus gun. What did red lightning feel like?

"She's not spun sugar, is she?" he mused. "We thought you were just window dressing, parroting all the ballyhoo lines they fed you. But you've got a bite, don't you?" He gestured at her sash. "Hand it over."

"I don't think so," a man said from the darkness at the street end of the alley.

Blue lightning spat and sizzled. Ess bit back a yelp as the feathery edges of it snapped at her and made her fingers and nose tingle. She thought she smelled her hair scorch, and stumbled backward, tripping over a crate. Men spilled into the alley and more Zeus guns spat lightning at the two men. They curled into fetal balls on the packed dirt and brick walkway of the alley. Ess stayed still as the men gathered up the two fallen men. She wasn't sure if she should hope they would ignore her, or if she should be angry that no one seemed ready to offer an explanation.

"You shot too soon." Theo struck a match against the brick wall.

Warm, normal yellow light spilled through the alley as he lit one of the oil lamps hanging on either side of the doorway.

"He was going to manhandle her," the first man said as he stepped into the light. He kept his head turned, watching the other four men haul her two attackers out like so much limp, heavy bags of refuse. Then he finally faced her and grinned. "Can't let them do that to my little sister."

"Uly." Ess felt a churning ball in her belly. Either tears or fury. Neither one would do her much good. "It took you long enough to show up," she said instead.

"We didn't hear them identify their contact," Theo said.

"Yes, they did," Ess retorted. "Someone who flirted with me."

"Everything in trousers flirted with you." He kept his voice and face sour, but she thought most of that was from fighting not to laugh.

"We know there's someone on the inside now. Can't Doctor Sylvia give them something to make them answer questions? Give them a double dose of the loopy-loo, and they'll tell you everything that passes through their minds."

"True. Well, it's a good night's work. Two more Revisionists off our tails. Don't be late, Uly." Theo snapped off a salute to her and headed into the darkness where the others had vanished.

"Are you all right?" Uly said, crossing the alley to her side.

Of course he protected her pride, not offering to help her, and she was grateful, even as part of her snarled at men who always did the opposite of what she wanted or needed. This was the last straw, as far as her injured shoulder was concerned. Ess gasped, feeling as if something had torn in her arm, and subsided, sliding forward onto her knees instead of standing up.

"Ess..." Uly groaned as he bent and picked her up with his big hands around her waist, just like he used to do when she was little. She had forgotten how strong he was. "Here, what's wrong? Is your arm worse? I told them they shouldn't have let you off the ship," he finished on a snarl as he led her back to the light by the door. "Here." He pulled an enormous white handkerchief from his pocket.

She realized her eyes swam with tears. Gasping, fighting down sobs that made absolutely no sense to her, she blotted at her face. Among the smears of makeup that came off, she noticed the embroidery on the handkerchief. UJF, his initials—Ulysses Joshua Fremont—along with the U.S. Air Corps emblem of a small dirigible against crossed cutlasses.

"Uly, are you really a captain?"

"Oh, please, Ess," he groaned again. "Don't I even get a hug from my baby sister? Especially when I just pulled your bacon from the fire?"

"Pulled my bacon," she fumed and shoved the handkerchief back into his coat pocket, then finished the movement by flinging her arms around him. More tears came, and she didn't care. Even knowing makeup would mar the pristine beauty of his coat.

He was still taller than her, so her head barely reached his shoulder. He even smelled the same, of sun-hot hay at harvest time, and leather. She welcomed the fierceness of his arms around her, the way he swayed back and forth, rocking them both, the pressure of his face against her hair. So what if it was a horrendous mess now? She didn't need to pass society's inspection for the rest of the night.

"Don't you ever do that to me again," he mumbled against her hair.

"Do what?"

"Scare me like you did. I came down the alley, intending to sneak in and spirit you away, and found you facing down those two scoundrels. Fortunately, Theo and the rest were right behind me. They seem to think you need guarding."

"Scare you? You're the one who gets into trouble all the time." Ess pushed free with one arm, just enough to look up at him. She felt some satisfaction to see tears in his eyes to match hers.

"I want to throw you over my shoulder and carry you away and never let you come back to solid ground again. That's the only way to keep you safe—keep you up in the air." He drew her back into his arms, not quite as fierce a grip this time. "Don't make me paddle your bottom like I had to when we were little."

"Paddle my—?" She huffed and tried to push free, but he held onto her too securely. Besides, it was far too pleasant to rest against him, warm and safe in his arms, to hold onto him and reassure herself he was indeed real. The only thing more pleasant, she supposed, would be to punch him in the gut, maybe bruise his jaw. A black eye wouldn't be out of order, in repayment for what he had put her through since he vanished. "You're the one Grandfather had to punish, not me."

"All right, I won't argue with you. This time. And only because I love you so painfully much." Uly sighed. "You never know how important it is to tell someone you love her until you can't do it. Say you love me, Ess. I'm not really sure of anything right now."

"You're an idiot." She sighed, feeling her breath go ragged. "Yes, of course. How can I help loving you?"

"Excuse me." Allistair's voice held all the cold primness he had ever inflicted on Ess. He stood a good ten feet back inside the building, near the door into the museum's workshop. "You are still on company time, Miss Fremont. When you were put on my team, I was assured that you would never let your emotions distract you, like other women. You can pursue your petty romances on your own time, not company time."

"Petty?" Ess pushed hard on Uly, and this time he let her go. She stomped into the workshop as Allistair turned to leave, and caught hold of his sleeve. With her bad arm. That just fueled her fury. "I was assured you were the rare man who didn't jump to false conclusions! I suppose they were wrong, weren't they?"

"False?" He turned around so fast, she thought he would keep turning. His eyes flared and ice dripped from his voice. "What sort of false conclusions could anyone jump to? It would take a deaf man not to hear the protestations of love between you."

"I was not hugging my sweetheart, you overbearing prig! This is my brother, who until recently, I feared was dead. Forgive me for indulging in some celebration, to see him alive!"

"You must be Allistair Fitch," Uly said, stepping up beside her and holding out his hand. "Ess, let the nice man go. You're frightening me."

She swallowed down a stream of choice words that would likely shatter half the precious, ancient items in the museum, with the strength of her vehemence, but she let go of Allistair's sleeve. It galled her to see the two men shaking hands, but she did find some satisfaction in seeing Allistair's cold fury thaw into something that might just become embarrassment. Uly, of course, was being his thoroughly charming self.

"Thank you for watching over my sister, sir," Uly continued. "We have some mutual friends among the crew of the *Golden Nile*, and when they learned she had finally surfaced, well, they had to bring us together. That is what has kept them so busy the last few months, since the robbery in Washington. Now we are back together. Or we will be, once Ess's assignment with your fine organization has ended."

"Who says I'm leaving the Pinkertons?" she blurted, stepping away from him.

"I don't suppose exerting my authority as your elder will do any good, will it?"

"I am afraid not," Allistair said with a flicker of a smile. Now Ess wanted to punch him. "She is an invaluable member of the team, of course. But if you disapprove of her activities, well, we must defer."

"It sounds as if you wish to rid yourself of her services." He winked at Ess. "Dueling isn't quite out of style yet. Shall I defend your honor, baby sister?"

"Ask me if I care if the two of you pump lead into each other." Try as she might, Ess couldn't hold onto her scowl. Even Allistair relaxed enough to allow a short chuckle.

Uly slid his free arm around her shoulders, careful of her wound. "Now that's all settled, I do need to get my baby sister to the safety of the *Golden Nile*." He snickered at her exasperated sigh. How was she going to break him of the habit of calling her *baby sister*? "It's a hard battle we fight, putting down the Resurrectionists, but a worthwhile one. I do regret, however, that Odessa has been caught in the crossfire."

"Crossfire. That's a good word for it," Allistair muttered. He finally met Ess's gaze again. He looked suitably repentant. "Are you sure you're all right, Odessa?"

She bit her lip against remarking that he became extremely formal when he was enraged. That would mean admitting that he had become enraged, and she didn't want to explore that particular trail of thought.

"Yes, I'm fine. But I do need to fetch my possessions, what little survived, before I go on board. Uly, you need to meet with Theo and the others. Will you meet me outside the hotel in... say two hours, by the time we finish up here, then ride back to the hotel, and give me time to change my clothes. Will that suit?"

"Doesn't matter if it suits or not." Her brother flashed that charming grin that made her want to both laugh and shriek in frustration. "We must do as her majesty decrees." With a smirk clearly aimed at Allistair, he leaned forward and planted a peck kiss on her cheek. "Two hours from now, Ess. Don't be late. Mr. Fitch, it was an honor meeting you, sir." He tipped his cap to them both and strode out into the alley and the darkness.

"Brother, eh?"

"Allistair..." Ess didn't want to get into an argument with him. She was too tired, her shoulder throbbed, and she wanted to get out of these borrowed fancy clothes and into some trousers and a loose shirt. That would have to wait until they performed their final check of the museum's security for the evening.

"I can understand why you ran away from home," he said, as they crossed the workshop to head back to the exhibition hall.

"I did not, and you know that."

"Yes, but still, it's understandable why you prefer being on your own."

"My brother is not a horrid person, nor is he a scoundrel." She silently admitted Uly might have changed considerably in the intervening years.

"I didn't say he was. Merely exasperating." Allistair crooked his arm, offering her his elbow. As if she needed help walking. "Shall we attend to business, Miss Fremont?"

"Yes, we shall, Mr. Fitch." She delicately rested her hand in the crook of his arm. Mostly to let him know she didn't need to lean on him for support. Although, with anyone else, she wouldn't be too proud to accept some help. Why did it always have to be Allistair at the worst possible time?

Chapter Twenty

As they finished up the security check and Allistair related to the other three men what had happened, Ess wondered what Horace would say. What advice would he give her? How could she ask anyone for advice if she couldn't tell them all the things she had to consider?

Go with the Society, work with Athena, possibly with Uly? Or stay with the Pinkertons? She could do the Originators much good, using the detective agency as extra eyes and ears, but how much could she tell the leadership of the agency, to get their cooperation in her assignments? How easily could she communicate with the Blue Lotus Society, to pass on that information? How much investigative work could the Pinkertons do for the Society without raising piles of dangerous, hard-to-answer questions? The detective agency wasn't composed of oblivious fools or men who would take "Not for you to know," as an answer.

"I hope that doctor is still awake at this hour," Allistair commented as he walked her, Roger, and Charles out to the carriage that would take them from the museum to their hotel. He and Briscoe had the first watch shift, working with the museum's guards. He tipped his head toward her bad shoulder. "When you get back to the airship. You're very adept at hiding your pain, but the lateness of the hour makes you vulnerable."

"Perhaps I feel somewhat safe in my present company," she offered, and bit back an urge to tell him her pain was none of his business.

Allistair was only being a conscientious team leader, watchful of them all. When Roger had injured his foot more than a month ago, stepping on a nail long enough to pierce his boot, Allistair had scolded him on more than one occasion when the young detective insisted on staying on his feet. Allistair was simply doing his job.

"Something to take the edge off?" Roger offered, holding out a flask, when the carriage had left the museum two left turns behind them.

"I would love some, but he's right, Doctor Sylvia will be awake, ready to scold me when I come aboard." Ess closed her eyes and leaned back, sitting crookedly so her shoulder wouldn't rub against the side of the carriage.

"What does that have to do with taking something now?"

"A cousin of mine is a physician," Charles said. "He doesn't like mixing alcohol with some of the newer medicines. Odessa is wise to wait. Though I'll wager you're not too happy about it, are you?"

"Since when does anyone care if I'm happy or not?" Ess retorted. That earned chuckles from her companions and she smiled, grateful to have them as her friends as well as teammates.

They were why she hesitated and felt a pang when Uly talked so glibly about her leaving the Pinkertons. Horace had given her the first sense of family, of belonging, in years. By the time he died, she had made a place for herself among the Pinkertons. The knowledge she belonged, that she had useful and necessary skills, more than made up for the sense that no one truly cared about her, about Ess, the little girl she had left behind for the sake of survival.

This late at night, traffic was practically nonexistent, and the brass cage of the hotel's lift was empty, so they didn't have to climb the stairs to their suite. Ess changed her clothes and packed up the remnants of her belongings and had nearly an hour to wait until Uly arrived.

She gave in to the ache in her arm and rigged a sling with the sash from her dress. It was dark enough it didn't clash and look out of place with her boy clothes. Especially when she slung her coat on over the sling and let the sleeve hang empty. The hotel kitchen was open for service at all hours, so she used up some time asking for a fried egg sandwich and a mug of hot tea. Both soothed part of her ache, so she attributed it to weariness. Now she was more awake, and restless. She left her bag with the desk clerk on duty, who was obviously too tired to question why a young lad was awake so late at night or to ask for her room number. Then, with another half hour to wait, she wandered out the front door and across the street to the nice little park. The trees were straggly, more limbs than leaves, but the bushes were tall and lush and provided cool shadows among the puddles of moonlight and gas streetlights. Ess wandered through the darkness, letting her mind wander as well, but always keeping the hotel front door in her sights. It wouldn't do to have Uly arrive and throw the entire hotel into a panic when he couldn't find her immediately.

She felt as if she hadn't had a chance to really sit and think about the situation she was in, the possibilities she had inherited from her grandparents, and the mysteries waiting ahead of her. Ess wanted answers. She wanted confirmation for the things she sensed and guessed and theorized. So much education had been stolen from her, when her grandparents vanished. She might even now be assigned to an airship like the *Golden Nile*. She would know all the unspoken things Theo had hinted at when he talked about the ability to travel through time. She wouldn't feel like an outsider, looking through the window at a home and family that should have been hers by all rights.

The question that lingered behind all the others was the one of belonging. These people wanted her because of her family, her heritage. How long would she have to study and work and prove herself before she understood the inside jokes, the cryptic comments, the traditions and goals?

"There you are," Charles said, stepping into the moonlight on the other side of the clearing. Beyond him, the hotel was an island of lights and warmth. "Exciting evening, eh?"

"That depends on your definition of exciting, I suppose."

"Having your brother returned to you." He looked up at the moon, then crossed to the bench sitting in the clearing ahead of her. "Allistair didn't tell me everything, but from the sparks shooting between the two of you..." He chuckled.

"What?" Ess stepped into the moonlight and settled down on the bench with a few feet between them. She sat crookedly, resting her good arm along the back of the bench. "What sparks?"

"Irritation from you, I'd say. Allistair..." He whistled. "We were starting to speculate that he might have tender feelings for you."

"Me?" Her voice cracked and squeaked. "Never."

"He tried to make a joke of finding you in the arms of a stranger."

"Uly was no stranger to any of you. He was at the exhibition. You all saw him."

"Yes, the dashing Air Corps captain, catching the attention and the hearts of all the fair maidens and the envy of all the young men. And the ire of the older men and mamas who wanted you matched up with one of their sons. I saw it happen in the other cities—"

"You did not." Ess reached to punch him in the arm, but she had settled too far away. The attempted movement irritated her shoulder and she subsided back into her place with a scowl and a muffled hiss.

"Yes, we did, but you were too busy being the good little detective to notice. You're a pretty girl when you dress as a girl, Odessa. Very intelligent, very common-sensical."

"That's not a word," she muttered. That earned a bark of laughter.

"You're a fascinating combination, linked with something as exotic as Egyptian artifacts. Of course the high society folks are going to think what a good match you would be, even without a dowry or a family name. False family name," Charles added with a wink. "Back to what I was saying. Allistair has feelings for you."

"I don't think so."

"I've never seen him so icy and fighting so hard not to show it. What did he say when he caught you two together?"

It took several moments to recall the words and situation, but she managed perfect mimicry that earned chuckles from Charles.

"He has never exploded at anyone like that."

"That was an explosion?" Ess sniffed, mimicking the disdainful accents of a woman who had come to the exhibition in St. Louis. Despite her disdain for every piece, expressed in long diatribes, she spent an entire day at the exhibition, ruining the enjoyment of everyone else. Mimicking and mocking her had provided the team with hours of laughter on the long train ride to their next stop.

"For Allistair, yes."

"Well, then I must be careful in the future not to excite his fury again. Who knows what damage he might cause?"

"Odessa..." Charles sighed and reached out to clasp her hand momentarily. "I hope you don't plan on leaving us any time soon. Even if we didn't like you enormously, it would be highly entertaining to see Allistair stumble through his paces as a lovestruck swain."

She giggled, and didn't even care that the movement hurt her shoulder. The idea of efficient, sensible, somewhat aloof Allistair Fitch acting lovestruck about anyone was so ridiculous as to be nearly sublime.

"Have some mercy on the man, would you?"

"Charles, I really think you've had too much of Roger's whiskey this evening. Go back to the suite and sleep it off."

"I haven't had more than two swallows, and that was after we talked about it."

"We? You and Roger? Or did you have a discussion with Allistair about his supposed feelings for me?"

"Roger and I. Just a short time ago. He thought it might be wise for me to talk to you about it before you left with your brother."

"The coward." She couldn't dredge up enough energy for scorn or irritation.

"Hmm. Maybe. Maybe he knows I have more influence with you."

"Only because I feel sorry for you, because I beat you at poker so often."

"We let you win. It isn't gentlemanly to humiliate a lady."

"I'm no lady." She gestured down at her trousers.

"That depends on your definition of a lady. We are all quite fond of you, Odessa. As a friend, a little sister, a co-worker. This assignment of ours, as exhausting as it is, has been enjoyable because of the fellowship. We wouldn't mind keeping the team together."

"Oh, yes, and to do that, of course you must defend my honor and marry me off to someone, is that it?"

"No." Charles grinned as he got to his feet. "You're right, of course. I need to get some sleep, but I won't sleep off the idea. I'm sure Briscoe will agree with us, in the morning."

"Well, unfortunately for you, I will not be around for you to bully into accepting the idea."

"It just gives us more time and privacy to come up with ways to convince you." He tipped an imaginary hat to her and turned to stride across the cleaning. "Sleep well, Odessa. Pleasant dreams."

"I wish you nightmares!" she shot back, and slouched against the park bench, chuckling. Charles' laughter drifted back to her as he vanished through the last ring of bushes, then appeared again in the puddles of gaslight in front of the hotel.

"He's right, you know," Uly said from the darkness behind her.

Ess barely managed to hold back a yelp. She turned, looking for him, as he stepped out into the moonlight.

"I am far too tired to think about such ridiculous things."

"You'll have to deal with it eventually. If you stay with the Pinkertons."

"If?" She flinched at the emphasis he had put on the word.

"Ford says some of the leadership will want you safely ensconced at the Sanctuary, cramming ten years of education into three or four."

"And then what?" She responded to the hand he held out to her, and let him draw her to her feet.

"Well, they hope you have Granny and Grandfather's flair for archeology. Since you inherited their crystal sensitivity, the leadership hopes you inherited the rest of the package."

"Go off on digs to Egypt and Africa? What about South America? What about going after Granny and Grandfather?"

"Other teams are working on it. I worked on it for a while. The thing is, Ess, we have to plan and work as if they aren't ever coming back. We have to fill in the huge hole blasted into our plan by their absence. We need your expertise, the things they taught you before they vanished." Uly stepped around behind her so he could put his arm around her and not press against her bad arm.

They walked out the other side of the park. For a few seconds, they said nothing as he hurried them across the street, down an alley between buildings, and then out the other side.

"From what I hear, you used quite a few of Granny's inventions to escape that penal colony of a boarding school." He shook her a little, until the renewed throbbing in her shoulder made her scowl. "You are so incredibly devious, baby sister."

"If you don't want to be seriously injured, stop—"

"My adored younger sibling," he said with such glib ease, Ess knew he had the words ready. "You are brilliant. Have I told you lately I adore you?"

"No. Tell me."

Uly's rumbling laughter assured her more than anything else that they were safe. He might have been reckless when the Originators snatched him away years ago, to protect him, but Ess sensed the change in him. He had learned caution and discretion through harsh lessons. She saw evidence of it in the scar on his cheek, felt it in the tight muscles of his arm wrapped around her and the lean strength of his body.

"If the Society sends me out on archeological work, I want to follow up on Granny's theory about American Indian artifacts and culture," she said, when they stepped past the last building into an open field. It was on the opposite side of the city from the place where she and Theo had taken their stand against the Revisionists. She saw the dark bulk of the *Golden Nile* hanging in the air above the dock towers with their large lift systems.

"Which theory was that?"

"She proposed a link between some of the Indian cultures, mostly the southern ones, extending into Mexico, and Egyptian culture and legends."

"Ah, that one. Of course."

"You knew about it?" She wanted to dig him in the ribs with her elbow for that. When she was a child, she was sure Uly couldn't have given two figs for their grandparents' archeological theories.

"From what I gather, some in the leadership pushed Granny and Grandfather into that last trip, because the theory promised we would find... well, we would find important things."

"More pieces of the Great Machine?"

"Exactly."

He said it so quickly, she knew there was far more to the theory and their grandparents' quest than simply finding more crystal.

"What are you looking for? What do you think the machine will do, when you finally assemble it and get it to work?"

"Who knows?" he said softly. "I'm certainly not in the know." Uly chuckled, but she detected a false note. Even discounting some of it as her weary imagination, that hurt. Her brother had to hide things from her.

Well, then, she just had to buckle down and study hard and earn the trust of the leadership. When she had access to all the information they kept from her now, she would work miracles, and they would regret leaving her in the dark, no matter how short a time it was.

~~~~~

"I fear the Revisionists are employing biology to attack us now," Sylvia said, coming into the conference room the next morning in place of Ess.

"Biology?" Athena traded glances with Fordyce and Theo, her partners in this first breakfast meeting with Ess.

The girl had years of education to make up for in a short amount of time. Uly had relayed to her the questions his sister had asked on the short journey from the hotel to the docks. He looked visibly uncomfortable as he confided that he thought Ess was disgruntled about something. That was the rub, Athena knew. It hinted what transpired in her incredible survivor's mind.

Ess was used to taking care of herself, not depending on anyone. She was used to finding out what she needed to know for survival. She had to be uncomfortable and most likely lost some of her trust in Athena and the Society every day she was kept in the dark. Her choice to study Egyptian alphabets and symbols before tackling the messages hidden in the margin art of the Society manual was evidence of that.

"Biology," Fordyce echoed. Then he pointedly glanced beyond Sylvia to the doorway. "The girl is sick?"

"They added something new to the toxin on that bullet that tore up her arm. All that parading around in public yesterday didn't do her any good. She should have been sitting down with her arm propped up, plastered
~~~~~

with a strong extraction and purification poultice. She irritated it and impeded the healing." Sylvia shook her head, frowning at an unseen point in the air as she came over to the table and sat down. "Regardless of that, she should only be sore today. Something is not only impeding her healing, but digging roots in and sending her backwards, if you will."

"Some disease, impregnated in the lead?" Theo offered.

"Warfare with bacteria and viruses." Athena picked up her cup of coffee and sat back in her chair, sipping slowly as she gnawed on the mental imagery those simple words engendered. "Well, the ancient civilizations did it. Anthrax to guard their tombs and penalize thieves. Poisoned darts set up in the ruins along the Amazon and Yucatan. I don't suppose you have any clue what sort of disease they gave Ess?"

"Let us hope it was a very weak strain and not the airborne, contagious variety," Sylvia said. "Has she been coughing at all? Runny nose? Any sort of excretions, even sweat, that could be used to pass along the illness?"

"Blessed Lord, protect us," she murmured, thinking of all those people Ess had shook hands with and simply spoken with all evening.

What an ingenious and yet vicious method of decimating the elite of a growing city. Somehow, though, Athena couldn't accept that as the goal. How were the Revisionists to know that Ess would guess they were imposters with the flute signal song, and she would not only flee but have help in doing so? How could they know they wouldn't be dead accurate shots when they fired at her, and she wouldn't die of her bullet wounds? How could they be sure that the boy who fled them was in actuality the scholarly Evangeline Peabody, who hosted the exhibition? No, the bullets had been meant to kill, and the substance impregnated in the lead had been as a backup method, to kill over time if death was not instantaneous.

"The best one to ask about her health last night is Ulysses," Theo said. "We were on the periphery throughout the night, while he spent nearly an hour at her side."

Ulysses was with his sister in the infirmary. He had sensed something was wrong when he escorted her to her new quarters last night, and came back an hour later just to make sure she was asleep. He heard her muttering, and entered to find her sitting on the floor, dizzy and feverish and thirsty, and unable to get to the pitcher of water, because the floor kept tipping underneath her. He had been with her all night, once Amos examined her shoulder and gave her a concoction to treat the symptoms.

"Whatever it is eating away at her," Sylvia reported, as the four of them traveled the corridors of the *Golden Nile* to the infirmary, "Amos had the right idea. He immediately dosed her for infection, with an injection as well as treating the wound itself. The wound looks better than when he worked on it last night, but not as good as it did when I bandaged her up yesterday morning."

Ess looked like a sodden, angry little kitten, slumped to one side in the infirmary bed. The Society manual lay open and pages-down on the rumpled blankets, Athena was pleased to note. The girl had sense enough to know she wasn't going to get much sleep, with the way she was feeling, and tried to use her time wisely. Although, looking at the unpleasant flush in her cheeks and the glassy gleam in her eyes, Athena wondered just how much Ess actually absorbed and would remember of what she read.

"No, I was quite comfortable at the museum," Ess said, after Sylvia asked about her condition the night before. "No sweating. Just a headache that came and went, and the throbbing in my shoulder. I wore gloves, so even if I did sweat, it wouldn't have been passed on to anyone by skin contact. No sneezing or coughing, and no vile dripping down the back of my throat. Granny always insisted we had to report it the moment we had the slightest sign of..." She managed a crooked grin, just for a moment. "Condensation, do you remember, Uly? Granny always used the most unlikely words, and yet they always fit, when you thought about it."

"Yes, Matilda liked to expand the minds of everyone around her," Fordyce offered. "By force, if necessary."

"So unless she spat on someone or bit them," Sylvia mused, earning a chuckle from Uly, "she wasn't contagious."

"I haven't needed to bite anyone since Uly and I last fought." Ess managed to mirror the momentary grins the others shared, then tipped her head back against the sweaty pillow supporting her upright in bed. "It feels like someone is stabbing a dull stick into my shoulder. I don't suppose you have something like that loopy-loo, but not with the end effects? My head hurt yesterday, when the more pleasant effects finally wore off."

"Most people wouldn't complain about the pleasant effects," Sylvia murmured, and stepped away from the curtain-hung cubicle.

"Yes, well, I'm not most people, am I?"

"Survival skills." Fordyce rested a hand on Athena's shoulder, edging up a little closer to Ess's bed. "You'd rather be uncomfortable than go under, lose some control. It might have been an amusement park carousel the other night, your first dose, but when you got your feet back under you, you decided it wasn't worth the risk, eh?"

"Something like that," she said, nodding slowly, her gaze locked with his.

Athena blinked hard, fighting tears. Her best friend's daughter, her mentor's granddaughter, shouldn't have to worry about surviving, about being able to defend herself at a moment's notice. Especially among the people who had wondered about her for years, afraid she was dead.

Chapter Twenty-One

Yet, she realized, relaxing that caution, settling in and allowing others to be concerned about her welfare once in a while, would change Ess in some small, significant way. The tough, independent, wary young woman sitting in the bed was just the sort of person the Society needed to be at the forefront as they stepped into the twentieth century. Someone who might be able to figure out how to activate and operate the Great Machine when it was finally fully assembled. Or more importantly, how to destroy it.

No, she wouldn't change Odessa Fremont in the slightest, erase one single part of her past, even as she ached for the bright, inquisitive, laughing child she had glimpsed in letters from Vivian and Matilda.

~~~~~

The sensation of a smoldering stick poking her shoulder grew more insistent as the day progressed. Ess tried to read, but her eyes kept crossing and the pounding inside her skull pressed at her temples and her sinuses, making her nauseous. Uly went to let Allistair know she was too ill to handle her duties, and returned with flowers and a bag of horehound drops from her teammates. The horehound soothed her throat, but the colors of the flowers were too bright for her eyes.

That bit of news worried Sylvia, so she insisted that Ess recline and give up reading. Moments later the doctor reappeared with a band of absorbent cloth that held a rubber tube full of cold water, to hold in place over her eyes. It turned out to be rather soothing, so Ess didn't mind the tiny trickle of condensation that always seemed to find a channel directly to her ears. She couldn't sleep, she couldn't read, and voices in the infirmary soon grew too loud. All she could do was lie among all her pillows, which grew hard and hot far too quickly after they were fluffed, suck on horehound until her mouth felt raw, and think.

And remember. Strange, how easy it was to remember scenes from her childhood. People and events. Insignificant. She wondered how she remembered them at all.

When the memories came one after another, faster, changing in mid-stream, she wondered if they *were* memories. Especially when her parents appeared in some of them, walking in on classrooms full of students from the boarding school, getting into arguments with her teachers. Her father shouted and swung his fists, and Edward had never been like that. At least, not in her memory. Hadn't she heard stories of him getting in almost as much trouble as Uly, when he was young?
~~~~~

"Yes, indeed, Edward was rather a scoundrel. But he learned his lessons quickly enough. Love taught him self-control," Athena said.

Ess inhaled. Her lungs actually hurt from the effort. She felt as if she had been pressed flat, with an entire train of cars resting on her chest.

"Can you hear me now?" Athena asked.

"Hmm?" Ess tried to open her eyes. They felt as if they had been glued shut. "Athena?"

"Welcome back." A cool, dry hand cupped her cheek, making Ess aware of just how hot and sweaty she was.

"Back?" Her voice cracked. Her eyes grudgingly opened and she winced at the brightness.

"Thirsty?"

"Yes." Her throat felt like it held as much sand as her eyes.

Amos was suddenly there, and Ess feared she had momentarily lost consciousness. Did that explain her odd memories? They were fever dreams, delusions, pieced together from fragments of things she had thought about, wondered about, feared in the last few months? Between Amos and Athena, they got her sitting upright with only a few surges of nausea and a new outbreak of sweating. The cup they put up to her lips held cool, sour juice. Ess started to gulp, then common sense awoke and she held the juice in her mouth, letting a little at a time trickle down her throat while the liquid soaked into the tissues.

She was exhausted by the time one of Sylvia's assistants helped her wash up and change her sweat-soaked nightgown. Then they moved her to a new cubicle and bed so they could change the sheets on the one she had been lying in. Sitting upright seemed to clear her mind.

"How long have I been delirious?" she asked, when it was just her and Athena again, with the older woman sitting on the foot of her bed.

"Four days."

"The exhibition is over. What did they do without me?"

"I filled in for you. It seemed to go over well."

"But if the Revisionists know... my head hurts too much to think, but whatever comes from this, it can't be good."

"Your fellow Pinkertons think your life is endangered because you are helping in the fight against the Resurrectionists. Your brother is helping to make that theory believable. We passed along the story that you were attacked by someone trying to steal artifacts, after the opening gala. There are quite a few sympathy cards and presents and enough bouquets from admirers to start your own florist shop." Athena's eyes sparkled with mischief, and Ess decided that was a good sign. The woman wouldn't be quite so relaxed if the situation were as bad as she imagined.

"What made me so sick?"

"The bullet." She raised a hand to silence Ess when she opened her mouth to ask more questions. "The material shattered, leaving fragments in your flesh that Sylvia didn't find. Small enough to require a microscope to find them. The metal was poisoned, to put it simply. It incited an infection, which I am inclined to believe was the intention. If they couldn't kill their intended targets, then they wanted a second chance. Spoilsport mentality, as Fordyce puts it."

"How did you get it out?"

"That will be your first lesson, and your next treatment."

"Treatment." Ess swallowed hard. Maybe she was still a little delirious, but it seemed to her that the words meant Athena had been handling part of her care. Or was she wrong to think the phrasing implied her treatment combined with her education? Then her thoughts jumped the track somehow, focusing on her strange, twisting dreams, and how Athena had responded to her thoughts. Meaning she hadn't been just thinking them. "Was I very... noisy?"

"Hmm, somewhat. Don't worry, we kept you isolated. Your brother spent most of his free time here. I think you embarrassed him a little, some of the things you said. He was quite a rascal, wasn't he?"

"Rascal." Her face actually hurt to smile. "So I'm saved from humiliation?"

"That would be one way of putting it." Athena patted her knee and stood. "I believe Sylvia is going to try to get some nourishment in you. I don't care to be here if you respond... negatively."

"Thank you ever so much." Ess wished she could have the lung power to laugh.

Sylvia gave her broth, lukewarm so it wouldn't jar her system, and cautioned her to sip it slowly. When that didn't come up, she allowed Ess a cup of coffee with extra sweetening and rich cream.

"If you're still awake in an hour, we'll give you another dose," Sylvia said with a pat on her shoulder. She took the mug and seemed to have a little bounce in her step as she walked around the curtain.

Ess thought she must have fallen asleep almost immediately, because she blinked and looked around, and found herself tipping sideways. Her mouth felt dry and tasted of the inside of dirty boots.

A humming like crystal, but with more harmonics and multiple scales, sang in her bones. As she shifted herself upright, the ache in the back of her head faded, trickling away, like a sack of beans deflating as they slipped out a hole. Or maybe she was hallucinating again, because the light had turned pale blue. No, it seemed to be coming from outside the cubicle. How peculiar.

Athena stepped into the little room, and brought the blue glow with her. It surrounded her in a corona. She held her arms crossed in front of her, cradling a bundle of cloth against her chest.

"Am I still hallucinating?" A bubble of laughter escaped Ess, making her chest hurt. "Of course, if I am, and you say no, it won't do me any good, will it?"

"You are not hallucinating." Athena stepped around the bed to sit down at the end by Ess's feet, exactly where she had sat before. "This is your treatment, and your first lesson."

She unfolded the cloth, and the blue glow brightened, spilling out of an object that seemed to be made of glass. Ess shaded her eyes, even as she couldn't take her gaze off it.

"What is it?" she whispered.

"This is the blue lotus. It is the keystone, if you will, of the Great Machine." Athena tipped her head to one side and considered Ess for a few moments. "You are so sensitive to the song of the crystal, perhaps... well, that can wait until you are healed completely."

"This can heal me?" Ess stared into the slowly pulsing shimmer of blue light and had that feeling she sometimes experienced, that if she just pushed a little harder, read a little further, listened a little more closely... the answer would come. Full understanding. The vital thing she needed to know would finally shift from nebulous to solid, and fall into her hands.

"It is healing you. The lotus found the fragments of poisoned metal and pulled them from your flesh. It is adding to your body's ability to heal itself, strengthening it."

Something in Athena's eyes, a flicker of darkness, of sadness averted, made Ess ask, "How bad off would I be if you hadn't used it on me?"

"It is hard to know for certain. Everyone responds differently to the lotus. You have responded amazingly well, incredibly fast."

"If I feel so terrible, then I must have been fairly close to death." She had tried to make it a joke, but the words fell flat in the room. That darkness flickered in Athena's eyes again.

"As I said, it is hard to know for certain. You are healing now, and you have the journey to San Francisco to rest and recuperate fully. We offered to take the Pinkerton team, to save them time and help protect the artifacts, but when Mr. Fitch telegrammed his superiors for permission, they declined."

"That doesn't make sense. It can't possibly be that they don't trust you, or the Society." Ess frowned, sensing a new idea on the verge of slipping away. A troubling idea.

"What is it?" Athena asked.

"I just have this... this sense that something is wrong with the higher-ups." She snapped her fingers, and even the movement felt soggy. "That's it. Someone specifically chose me for this job because they knew about my background."

"Why would that be wrong?"

"Horace and a few others knew about Granny and Grandfather, but they promised to keep my identity, my connection with the search, secret and separate. Mostly it was because if the higher-ups knew my whole story, they would feel duty-bound to turn me over to the lawyers."

"Ah, yes, and if you had confided in your grandparents' good friends, you would have begun your education as an Originator seven years ago. Endicott, Lewis, and MacDonald are part of our organization." Athena shook her head, her smile turning rueful.

"I did the best I could. Everyone was keeping secrets from me!" She moaned, the momentary rise in her volume making her head ache.

"Hindsight is always so much clearer."

"Yes, but how did someone find out that information Horace promised to keep secret? Maybe he had it written down somewhere and someone found it when they went through his records after he died. But... Oh, my head. It hurts to think."

"I know this won't make sense." Athena rested a hand over hers, stopping Ess from pressing her fists into her temples. "But try not to think. Just let the ideas come as they will."

"They *shouldn't* know, at the main office. Yet someone does." She pounded her fist once into her thigh. "I knew I should have asked before this, but Horace always said to keep quiet and do my job and save questions for later."

"Hmm, yes, well, we shall start an investigation of our own." Athena's eyes narrowed. "Coincidences rarely are. Someone is manipulating events behind the scenes. If we are blessed, we will discover the Lord is doing so. However..."

"However," she said, nodding. "Athena—"

"Let us start investigating." She patted her hand. "We have vast resources to help us learn what we need to know."

"All right." She sighed, knowing Athena was right and wanting to protest anyway. "Well, what do I do?" she said instead, and flicked her fingers at the lotus.

"Simply lie there. You didn't have to do anything to help the lotus while you were unconscious, did you?"

Ess shook her head, and winced when the injudicious movement made the bed seem to sway underneath her. She gladly closed her eyes and slid down in the bed when Athena instructed her to do so.

Blue light seeped under her eyelids. She held her breath, waiting for something, maybe a spill of electricity through her veins, along her nerves, perhaps on the order of a Zeus gun shooting her. Athena told her to breathe normally. The bed swayed underneath her. She tried to grip the sides of the bed, but her fingers seemed to go boneless and wouldn't burrow into the blankets. She exhaled, and the sound echoed forever in her ears. Blue filled her blood, her lungs, her marrow. She tasted blue, soothing, thick, rich and cool, and gladly drowned in it until she sank down and down to sleep.

~~~~~

Athena dealt with necessary duties after she put the lotus away;
~~~~~

checking reports, giving permission for training exercises during the voyage, acknowledging weather predictions and Captain Astrid's proposed route. She appreciated the lighter burden of chores while the *Golden Nile* was in flight. Until technology changed enough that communication could take place between the air and ground, she didn't have to deal with dispatches and requests for information. Especially, she didn't have to worry about whatever newspapers were saying about poor, injured, Miss Evangeline Peabody, and the sudden assistance of the Blue Lotus Society while the lady was indisposed.

Finally, when she had answered every question and made every decision, and before anyone realized she was back in her office, she fled back to the infirmary. She wanted to watch over Ess while she slept. The girl was responding much more quickly to the blue lotus' healing energy than they had anticipated. There was no predicting how soon she would awaken from this latest treatment.

Uly sat astride a folding wooden chair, facing backwards, his crossed arms resting on the back of the chair, watching his sister. He looked like he hadn't slept much. Athena rather liked this development in his character. Maybe with Ess to watch out for, he would be a little more careful, a little less daring and willing to risk his life. The dark smears under his eyes, the fine new lines dug by care around his mouth, gave him some badly needed maturity.

"How is she?" Athena murmured, stopping at the foot of the bed and bracing herself with her arms against the raised footboard.

"Tired of being tired," Ess said, and let out a jaw-cracking yawn. She managed a somewhat sheepish smile as she opened her eyes. "Time for my lesson?"

"As long as you can stay awake."

"Well, since you're in good hands, I will see what Dr. Chamberlain has for me to do." Uly stood, swinging his leg around and off the chair. He executed a bow to them both. "Do me a favor, baby sister?"

"If you stop calling me 'baby sister.' Maybe," she added quickly.

"Try not to get hurt any time in the near future, please. I've just found you again. I don't want to lose you before I've gotten to know the woman you've become."

"Well, I shall certainly try. It all depends on what sort of work the Society will give me when I'm on my feet." Ess met Athena's gaze as she finished speaking.

"Something on the ground, please, Miss Latymer? Preferably underground, keeping her so busy she doesn't realize that years are passing." Uly winked at her and sauntered out of the room.

"Underground?"

"The Sanctuary has quite extensive chambers and passageways underground." Athena settled down on the end of the bed. "Well, you do look better. Your color is back, and your eyes aren't quite so sunken. How is your dizziness?"

"I'd prefer not to test it. Even if my stomach is empty, I don't want to take the risk."

"Ah. Hunger. A very good sign of healing." She scooted around a little more on the bed, to put her back against the fanciful metal framing of the footboard.

"What are we?" Ess asked.

"Well, that is a good question. Please define what you mean."

"I don't know if it's my fever, the bizarre dreams I've been having, but it strikes me that what I've seen you do... it tends toward magic. If magic is possible."

"Hmm... yes. That *is* a very good question to start your first lesson. Consider this: our current technology would seem like magic, high sorcery, to people of only three or four hundred years ago. So in a sense, it is safe to say that what seems like magic now, could very well turn out to be very basic, very boring technology in another hundred years."

Athena watched Ess think over those statements. She swallowed hard against an aching tightness rising in her chest. How delighted Vivian would be with her daughter. It was the height of injustice that she had been denied the chance to raise her children, train them, and watch their minds unfold.

"All right, we simply have better, more advanced technology than most people. *What* are we?"

"*Who* we are is, essentially, the ancient gods of Egypt, Britannia, the various scattered tribes of South America... the list goes on." She laughed when Ess just gave her a skeptical, wide-eyed, compressed lips look of disbelief. "The Revisionists' ancestors tried to set themselves up as the gods of many different cultures, using their technology, which at the time could indeed be considered god-like, magical. They failed because they erred grossly in their masquerades, and... well, *our* ancestors devoted their lives to stopping such arrogant behavior."

"Why would—how could they even try? How could they have technology so long ago when people believed in other gods?" Ess pushed herself upright, most likely not even paying attention to what she was doing. Her face reddened and sweat beaded her forehead.

"The technology was not devised long ago, but rather far in the future." Athena got up and adjusted the pillows behind Ess while she still struggled to get upright.

"The future?"

"Theo said he briefly discussed time travel with you."

"But it's impossible. Grandfather taught me that things cannot be two places at the same time. For someone to travel backward in time, no matter how far he travels, the substance of his physical being already exists elsewhere, so it cannot be in its original form at that time, and in his body, both at the same time."

"Correct." She muffled a chuckle when the girl gave her another frowning look of confusion. "That rule of reality, of physical being, led our ancestors to believe the Revisionists could not possibly succeed in their quest to travel backward in time. If they managed to get their machine to work, to manipulate the fabric of space and time, they would simply destroy themselves when they tried to enter an earlier time stream."

"But they were wrong?" Ess swallowed hard. "How far back in time did they travel?"

"That is another lesson. We are starting with the basics. In a sense," Athena admitted. "Yes, our ancestors realized almost too late that they were wrong. The Revisionists succeeded in their journey. Fortunately, our ancestors were humble enough to admit they could be wrong. They kept careful watch on what the Revisionists were doing over the generations to build the machine. Our ancestors were able to duplicate the technology and enter the time stream to go after them. They never expected to come out in this world." She sighed. "No, certainly they could not have expected it. Ever since then, we have been in a battle against the Revisionists."

"To keep them from traveling back to their own time?"

"Oh, no, to keep them from doing the damage they set out to do when they traveled backward along the time stream."

"Couldn't you just go further back and be waiting when they arrived, and, well, stop them?" She looked away, as if she were ashamed of something, just for a moment.

"Destroy them, you mean? No. That would be too much interference. The ancestors chose to stay here and do all they could to keep the Revisionists from changing the flow of this particular time stream. Even though, to all intents and purposes, our very presence has changed this Earth from what it should have been."

"*This* Earth?"

Chapter Twenty-Two

"Have you ever heard the theory of cascades?" She waited until Ess thought, then shook her head. Athena was pleased when she showed no ill effects from that movement. "The theory of cascades essentially postulates that whenever you make a choice—whether a major choice, such as refraining from killing a man who threatened your life, or what field of study you will pursue in college, or a minor choice such as what you will eat for dinner or wear to worship, or even whether or not to swat a mosquito—reality diverges at that point. So by the time you have reached adulthood, your choices have created hundreds if not thousands of possible, alternative worlds."

"How do you know that's real or true?"

"Ah, that is why it is called a *theory*," Athena said. "There is no way of proving it true or false. No technology is able to accomplish that. At this point in time, at least. The theory our ancestors devised is that we are in a parallel world, in the distant history of a world parallel to the one where our ancestors originated. The same power that keeps the Revisionists from interfering with key events in history most likely deflected them and our ancestors to this world."

"So..." Ess sat forward, rested her elbows on her thighs and her chin on her fists, frowning as she visibly digested the theories presented to her. "So I'm a copy of the real me, who lives in another world just like this one?"

"You are you. In each world, you are you, the original you, making your own choices. Just as I am the original, central me, making my own choices. No matter what world this is, because you are here, because I am here, this is the central, the original world."

"But you just said that the ancestors were deflected..." She sighed and raised her hands to press her knuckles into her temples. "I must be feverish, because it seems to make sense. Even if I can't exactly put it into words. But how can it?"

"Just because something seems impossible or illogical doesn't mean it is. After all, how can someone die as brutally as the Savior died under the hands of the Romans, and yet come back to life?"

"Because..."

Something clutched at Athena's heart at the hesitation and frown. When she was the girl's age, she had glibly responded to the same question with, "Because God said so." She wished Ess still had the simple, childlike faith that Vivian had been so proud to relate in letters. All the trials and struggles the girl had endured to find her freedom, to survive, had dented or perhaps dimmed her faith.

"I know it's so," Ess finally said. "It's recorded as being so, despite what so many strange people with their even stranger revisions of the scriptures say about it. Or the people who say it never happened. I *know* it did. But when you think about it too long, it does seem impossible, doesn't it?"

"Indeed. I fear in the months to come, as you catch up with all your lessons, you will be asked to not only believe and accept, but base your actions upon many seemingly impossible, illogical things. We have so very little of the knowledge the ancestors brought with them when they chased the Revisionists to this Earth. What we have managed to preserve or retrieve is in fragments. We have many scientific principles and rules, but we do not have the technology or the underlying principles to help us understand. We of the *Golden Nile* are the ones who travel the world, gathering up the fragments that the ancestors of both sides scattered everywhere to hide it, or preserve it, depending on whose history you believe." She offered a smile, which Ess returned hesitantly. "But there are five times as many people among the Originators who spend their time piecing together the lost knowledge. Backtracking what we are taught. Finding the proofs. Creating new technology, such as the mobis and the Zeus guns."

"What does Mr. Chamberlain do? And Uly? They don't seem scholarly."

"They are our warriors, our explorers, the ones who face the dangers for us and blaze the trails and pull civilization into uncivilized places so the rest of us can travel there in safety." Athena sighed. "But the situation is changing, I'm afraid. It is no longer a matter of wading through jungles full of poisonous plants and man-eating animals. This craze for archeology sweeping the world, this lust to learn about and excavate all the ancient cultures, this isn't just an explosive expansion in academic pursuits. I am convinced it is part of the Revisionists' plan. It is far easier, and safer, to drum up enthusiasm and send others in to face the dangers and do the hard work, and then rob them when they return with the spoils."

"Which is why you came to check out my artifacts. To keep the Revisionists from taking anything that someone else dug up."

"You see, it isn't just the one Great Machine that was disassembled. Our ancestors, the Originators, deemed it prudent to disassemble all machines. They nearly destroyed all our records, all our technology that we needed merely to protect ourselves. They felt it better that we all fall into barbarism rather than risk polluting and warping the pace and the path of development, in civilization, technology, the arts, literature, that should have happened in this alternative world they landed in."

"But what guarantee could they have that the Revisionists didn't still have some technology and their own records? If they held onto just one history book, they could still have the right information to make changes to suit their plan."

"Exactly." Athena grasped Ess's uninjured shoulder, gazing into the young woman's face.

Vivian, you would be so proud of her. Forgive me, for not finding her sooner. For letting her face danger all alone. For not educating her sooner.

"We are in a race with the Revisionists to find the pieces that were hidden and forgotten. To regain enough technology and knowledge to stop them, and also to keep them from finding it and using it for their own profit." She released Ess and sat back. "I will not ask you now. You have the right to learn more before making your decision, but someday, soon, I will remind you of all we have discussed, and ask—"

"I'm in." Ess reached out and grasped Athena's hand. "I think I know enough already to know this is where I need to be. Where Granny and Grandfather, and my parents, would want me to be."

~~~~~

Allistair looked the most sour that Ess had ever seen him, when he met her at the airship docks in San Francisco. There were many reasons for the way he glowered at her as she came down the long caged walkway from the *Golden Nile* to the docking platform a dizzying two hundred feet up in the air. Most of the reasons were ridiculous and she discarded them. The only one that made any sense to her was that Allistair didn't like having her out of his sight. She was a member of his team and he was responsible for her: misdeeds, duties, and her physical welfare. Uly confided in her that Allistair had discussed canceling the remainder of the exhibition and hauling everyone back to Washington. After she had time to recover in the Kansas City hospital. However, the fact that she was already on board the *Golden Nile*, securely in Dr. Sylvia's care, helped everyone overrule whatever he wanted to do.

"And there's your lovelorn swain now," Uly murmured, resting his hands on her shoulders as he came down the walkway behind her.

"You hush." She refrained from jabbing backwards with her elbow only because this prim suit Sylvia and Athena had dressed her in hampered such movement.

"I wonder how miserable he made the others during that hot, dirty train ride from Kansas."

"He wasn't that worried about me. Or angry that I left the team and didn't do my part."

"Oh, really? You know how he thinks?"

"If he didn't trust Athena to look after me, and Doctor Sylvia to bring me back to full health, and if he didn't think the four of them could handle the escort duties without me, then he would have resisted everything Athena decided to do. At the very least he would have sent for more agents to take over my work. He could very well have complained to the Air Corps and someone would have caught up with the *Golden Nile* and forcibly
~~~~~

removed me. He did nothing because he wasn't worried."

"Hmm. Perhaps."

"Perhaps?" She glanced over her shoulder at him, just as they reached the dock platform. Ess sighed, exasperated by the teasing light sparkling in his eyes, so they looked positively green, his mouth flattened into an *almost* believable expression of somberness. She considered risking the seams of her new jacket and elbowing him, but Allistair was crossing the long platform to meet them and there were appearances to keep up. Her older brother was assigned to be her guard, and continue her lessons for the last stop of the exhibition. Would anyone believe he was responsible for her if she scolded and glowered and he was a mischief-maker?

"Well, Miss Fremont. Captain Fremont." Allistair nodded to them both. His expression softened into something warm. His eyes took on a pleasant sparkle. She was hard-pressed to keep her jaw from dropping. Especially with Uly's teasing still ringing in her ears. "It's good to see you back to your normal self. Are you ready to get back to work?" He turned, offering his bent arm to her, and gestured at the lift car, which stood open and waiting.

"More than ready." She turned her head so she couldn't see her brother's face, and curved her fingers around his arm, to let him escort her.

"Do I detect some eagerness?" His smile looked relaxed and genuine, this close up. "A boring convalescence?"

"Oh, I had more than enough to occupy my mind, but I was uneasy the whole time, because I left a job unfinished."

She thought about the hours of study she crammed in every day, devouring the history of the Originators. She had maintained an exhausting schedule, limited only by the weakness of her body as she recovered. She had read until she couldn't see straight, and then when she was able to get up on her feet, she was introduced to Digory, a quiet little man of an indeterminate age who taught her exotic methods of fighting, brought from lands in the far east. Then there were lessons with Dr. Sylvia, doctoring and diagnosing herself, and creating her own medicines when she couldn't quite trust those around her.

"There has been some speculation that you will leave us, now that you are reunited with your brother." He nodded again to Uly as they stepped into the lift car. "I hope that is a false fear."

"Who speculated?" She glanced at Uly, who shrugged.

"Mr. Judson said there was some question among the leadership in the home office, but he thought he could quell the rumors, once he had spent time with you." Allistair pulled the gate closed and signaled the operator on the ground that they were ready to descend.

"Mr. Judson? I don't know that name."

"That's odd, since he chose you for this assignment."

Allistair didn't react to the doubly tense alertness that shot through her at that bit of information. Ess was proud she didn't grip his arm.

"I believe he was promoted," he continued, "a short time after Mr. Winslow died. He's been mostly in the southern states, and specializing in diplomatic relations with South American countries."

"South America? That's interesting," Uly said in a bland tone. He put out a hand to steady Ess when the car shuddered a little as it started downward.

"What sort of authority does this Mr. Judson have?" Ess didn't like it that someone had come all the way to San Francisco to talk with her. Horace had always told her that as long as the heads of the agency seemed to be ignoring her, she was doing her job well. When they paid attention to her, then she should worry. They were either getting ready to sack her for some flaws, or promote her to a sedentary position in the agency.

"He's here to make sure everything is documented, that we turn over the artifacts to the British authorities with every piece intact and all questions, all threats and problems dealt with. Once it's in their care, we are free and clear of all responsibility, and the Pinkerton reputation still unblemished."

"Is that all that matters?"

"Hmm? Oh, our reputation." A stronger smile momentarily quirked up the corners of his lips. "It does seem like that sometimes, doesn't it? I wouldn't worry about that, if I were you. You're in very good odor with our superiors."

Ess glanced up to Uly, who met her gaze and shook his head just slightly. He didn't believe that, which confirmed the uneasy shiver that worked through her gut. Perhaps Allistair believed all was well, that Mr. Judson's visit would have no impact on her career, but she sensed otherwise. She had learned long ago to ignore what people said when her gut told her otherwise.

"If I may ask, why aren't you in uniform?" Allistair continued, as the lift car slowed to a soft landing on the ground.

"We decided the less attention we drew, the better. We couldn't be sure if my presence in uniform would discourage the Resurrectionists or goad them into acting," Uly said. "I am officially on leave, to spend time with my sister. If I happen to be on hand to apprehend an enemy of the Union, well, so be it," he added with a careless shrug.

"Have you considered going into civilian work?"

Uly laughed as the operator stepped up to unlock the gate across the open side of the lift car. "Are you asking in an attempt to make sure my sister remains with your agency?"

"Which answer would be more likely to have you seriously consider the idea?"

"Did this Mr. Judson tell you to ask?" Ess asked.

"Mr. Judson doesn't know about your brother." Allistair's smug little expression cracked into a full-fledged grin, with a touch of mischief, when

Ess could only stare at him.

She let him take her arm and escort her out of the lift, with Uly close behind. She waited until they had walked to one of the steam-driven cars that plied the tracks running up and down the hills of San Francisco, and secured one all to themselves.

"Why would you risk your career by holding back that sort of information?" she said, pitching her voice low.

"I didn't. I merely categorized it under 'personal friends of Miss Fremont,' and stated that their names were being withheld to protect their reputations and safety. Because they are in service to the United States, we cannot interfere with their security."

"Impressive," Uly said.

"Why are you risking—" Ess began.

"Teamwork relies on trust," Allistair said. "Until we are sure of your situation, Ess, we are going to rely on your history with us, and protect your future."

"Thank you." She felt as if her heart were rising up in her throat.

"Definitely besotted with you," her brother whispered, during the ear-splitting clang of the bell at one of the crossing points.

Ess did manage to elbow him this time, and didn't strain the seams of her coat.

~~~~~

Briscoe offered her a lovely little pistol and a clever harness to hold it low against her side. Roger had a vest with tiny metal crescents sewn all over it, overlapping, in a kind of flexible armor. Charles bought her a new suit of convincingly worn boy clothes, much like her suit that had been bloodied and torn in the flight to the *Golden Nile*. Ess couldn't come up with the words to thank her teammates. She hadn't really thought that they would miss her so much that they would give her gifts. True, they all got along well, but she thought of it as merely being friendly.

She had almost too much to think about, as she settled into her position for her share of the watch that evening, to guard the crates of the exhibition artifacts before the museum staff set everything in place tomorrow. Being distracted wasn't wise, so she put her emotional turmoil and all the questions out of her mind until this final part of her assignment was successfully completed. Tonight, the crates were stored in the museum. Briscoe was stationed outside the door to the museum's receiving room. Ess found a perch on top of a massive cabinet where she could be unseen and yet had a good, clear shot at anyone who might try to get into or even take the crates. She reflected that being able to avoid another overhead perch in the rafters was a benefit.

Unless, of course, she might borrow the aid of the mobis to stand guard. That thought amused her enough to set her imagination running, until she realized she spent so much time there, she didn't attend to her
~~~~~

duty.

The night passed quietly and uneventfully enough, even with Uly coming back in his self-appointed rounds to check on her. He walked all the halls and rooms of the museum, multiple times. Each time he came back, he had a humorous remark to make about one exhibit or another. Ess wondered if he regretted going from the academic life their grandparents had been training him for, to pursue military work. It was in the service of the Originators, true, but he wasn't making use of all his knowledge of ancient artifacts and cultures. As evidenced by his disparaging remarks about the inaccuracies in some of the exhibits.

When her shift was up, she waited until Charles came to relieve her, then Uly walked her to the curator's quarters, where cots had been set up for the team. Ess was amused to note that there were three cots, and two had obviously been slept in, leaving one pristine and untouched, and tucked behind a bookshelf for good measure. In so many ways, her colleagues accepted her as one of them, with no consideration for her being female. Yet in other ways, amusing ones most of the time, they were almost prudish and endearingly careful of her. She didn't have the heart to tell them that she didn't worry about her modesty, but about the rattling snores that emanated from Briscoe almost the moment he lay down to sleep. A bookshelf didn't do anything to muffle it.

Allistair had no shift, per se, but he slept for an hour, then got up and walked the halls of the museum, checked in with the agents on duty, then went back to sleep for another hour. Ess couldn't understand how he could do that, and yet look rested and comfortable in the morning. When she tried such a schedule on a watch duty more than two years ago, she was headachy and had a sour stomach in the morning, and there was little that could remedy it. Not even Horace's concoction of honey, lemon juice, pepper, and whiskey.

When morning came, Uly returned to the *Golden Nile* to report to Athena, and assure Sylvia that Ess had behaved herself and hadn't done anything to aggravate her still-tender shoulder. The team turned over security to the museum staff and the local police and Mr. Thomas Schultz, the San Francisco Pinkerton agent. They retired to their hotel for breakfast, a strategy session, and sleep. Ess left the suite after the strategy session to go home, still dressed as a boy, with Mrs. Schultz. She insisted Ess call her Betty, her middle name, because she had refused to use her first name of Victoria ever since Britain supported the South in the war. Betty thought it highly amusing and clever to have a woman not only acting as an agent for the Pinkertons, but to masquerade as a boy. She put Ess to bed in the spare bedroom, and took great delight filling her in on the gossip of the upper class and middle class of San Francisco when she awoke just before lunch.

The story given out was that because of the injuries she had suffered during an attempted robbery in Kansas City, Miss Evangeline Peabody was in somewhat delicate health and required special attention. Betty proudly drove her around the city all afternoon in her one-horse gig, introducing her as her new Egyptologist friend and commenting on her near brush with death and need for medical supervision. That necessitated a visit to the offices of Dr. Filpot, in the busiest part of the city, where anyone who cared to look could see Ess arrive. The doctor was an ally of the Pinkertons, and more importantly a good friend of the Schultzes, and found just as much amusement as Betty in carrying off the deception. No one wondered when Miss Peabody declined social invitations and retired to the Schultz home to rest before the opening of the exhibition. Even better, nobody would wonder when the exhibition closed at a conservative ten in the evening, instead of staying open until midnight, as previously planned.

The hope was that whoever intended to steal artifacts would take advantage of the early closing and the organized chaos of the opening night. The people roaming the country stealing from private collections had yet to be caught. Ess hoped they would show up here, and not only make foolishly arrogant mistakes to get caught, but would turn out to be ordinary thieves, not Revisionists. She supposed Athena and Fordyce would disagree with her, but if Revisionists weren't stealing artifacts in San Francisco, then that meant they had given up on the British Museum's artifacts and wouldn't attempt one last robbery of the airship that would take them home again.

Ess laughed when she returned to the Schultz home that afternoon, to discover she really was tired. Socializing had never been one of her favorite activities. In boarding school, she had preferred sitting on the fringes of chatting groups. Observing and wondering what went on behind people's polite social masks was much more fun. When she wasn't reading, of course.

Her laughter died immediately when she noticed an unfamiliar hat hanging on the rack by the front door. There was a scent of bay rum in the foyer, and Thomas Schultz did not wear bay rum. Ess loathed the smell, associating it with arguments she overheard between her grandparents and strangers who came to their house at all hours, sometimes uninvited.

When she heard male voices in conversation, and only recognized Allistair and Thomas's, she guessed Mr. Judson had come to speak with her.

Chapter Twenty-Three

"Oh, dear," Betty murmured, pausing in the long hallway to the dining room. It was the only room in the house with enough chairs for a meeting of any kind. The parlor had a horsehair sofa and two footstools and most of the room was taken up with Edison's musical cylinders and their player. "Guests already? I really do think you need a nap, just to refresh yourself."

"I can take a nap after the meeting. It should be short." Ess crossed her fingers, something she hadn't done since childhood. Why were so many childhood memories and habits returning? It wasn't like crossing her fingers would ensure success or counteract a lie or protect her from the consequences of telling one.

Then they stepped into the room, where Thomas, Allistair and the presumed Mr. Judson sat at the far end of the table. Coffee was strong in the air, coming from the kitchen on the other side of the hall, and Ess guessed it was still brewing. The cups and the sugar bowl were still neatly arranged in one spot on the table, meaning no one had been served yet. That was a good sign. Mr. Judson had only recently arrived, and no one had talked long enough to make decisions about her and for her without her input.

"Miss Fremont." Mr. Judson smiled slowly, reminding her of a particularly sly, lazy cat at the boarding school. He stood and executed a half-bow and gestured at the three chairs remaining empty at the long table. "Your timing is impeccable. Please, do join us."

Ess decided she loathed anyone who couched a command as an invitation. Starting with Headmistress Van Hastings. She hoped Mr. Judson wouldn't prove to be worse.

Allistair got up quickly and pulled out the chair next to his for her, relieving her of having to choose where to sit. Betty would want to sit next to her husband. If Ess chose the middle seat, that might insult Allistair, if he were romantically interested in her, and would put her directly opposite Mr. Judson, who took the head of the table.

Her head hurt, just from trying to analyze the implications of something as simple as taking a seat, all in the space of the few seconds it took to walk from the doorway. She thanked Allistair softly and sat down. At least she wore her prim, slightly fussy Miss Peabody dress. It forced her to sit up straight and hold her shoulders back and felt like armor. Mr. Judson could draw whatever conclusions he wanted from her clothes, but they would be wrong. She could use that to her advantage.

Something is wrong if I'm thinking war tactics.

Ess was pleased that once again her gut protected her. Now if she could just remember to listen to it, to stay out of trouble.

Mr. Judson was a rather non-descript man. He could have been a shopkeeper, a butcher, a doctor, or a policeman. Browned by time outdoors, but not too brown. That was his main color: brown eyes, brown hair, wearing a dark brown suit. Not lean, not fleshy. Clean-shaven, curly hair trimmed short and glistening. Probably the source of the bay rum smell.

"How are you feeling now, Miss Fremont?"

"Very well, thank you, sir. May I assume you are here to analyze my past actions and determine where I went wrong?" Ess folded her hands before her on the table and tried not to let the combination of coffee aromas mixing with bay rum make her sneeze.

"Very good. Horace's notes said you waste no time with niceties."

"Social niceties are to keep people from going for each other's throats in the struggle for dominance."

"Ah, of course. I hear your grandfather's teaching." He chuckled and leaned back in his chair, folding his hands in his lap.

He wanted her to relax and consider him a friend, since he had spoken of her grandfather. Ess decided to do the exact opposite. How much more obvious could the man be, in his attempted manipulation of her emotions and reactions? She refused to ask where he had met her grandfather, because that would give him another avenue for getting closer to her, gaining her confidence.

Hang it all, the man shouldn't know who she was in relation to Ernest Fremont!

For nearly an hour they went back and forth, politeness wearing thin in places. Mr. Judson walked her through every stop along the path of the traveling exhibition, asking nearly the same questions with each one. Ess was grateful that all during her convalescence, she had worked on her cover story for each encounter with the Society and the Revisionists, and the totally fictitious encounters with the Resurrectionists. She wondered if Mr. Judson grew irritated with her when he couldn't seem to shake her with his questions. She knew better than to anticipate what he would ask for next. That was a trick Horace had taught her: ease the suspect into a repetitive pattern, and then break the pattern so he would say or do something revealing or open himself up for capture. It applied in boxing, in chess, and questioning suspects.

At the end of the hour, Betty insisted that Ess be allowed to rest. She needed to bathe and curl her hair and prepare for the opening night gala. Somehow, without scowling, without raising her voice, she visibly intimidated Allistair and Mr. Judson. Thomas seemed rather smug, even as he verbally demurred to his wife's instructions.

Upstairs, Ess opened the window of the spare room for some fresh air. The odors of coffee and bay rum had permeated her clothes, her hair. She wished she had to wear a wig as Evangeline Peabody, so she could remove the smell without washing her hair. Inhaling deeply, she rested her elbows on the windowsill and gazed out over the steeply rolling landscape of San Francisco. She admired the steam-powered trolley cars and wondered how fast they could travel. What would happen if the steam brakes failed on the downward plunge along a street? Maybe she could convince Uly or maybe Charles to adventure out with her tomorrow, early in the morning, in disguise, pretending to be ordinary folks going off to a day of work along the wharfs or the shops or the factories.

Movement off to her left caught her attention. She frowned, sensing a problem even before she recognized Roger coming up the wooden plank sidewalk. He stopped at the waist-high fence that separated the Schultzes' yard from their neighbors' and stepped back into the shade of an overgrown clump of bushes that seemed to be pushing the fence over.

Mr. Judson came out of the door of the neighbors' house. Ess didn't move, didn't breathe, and strained her ears. Roger handed Mr. Judson a sheaf of papers. A report. That nail-studded lump of nausea returned to her stomach at the suspicion that the report was about her. How could Roger do that to her?

"No such thing as friends in this business," she whispered, repeating what Horace had told her numerous times. Ess had thought her mentor had never needed to warn her not to trust too much in others, because she had been on her own for so long.

Obviously, she had been wrong. She had softened enough that she considered her fellow agents her friends.

"What are you going to do if my report doesn't match what Odessa told you?" Roger said, as Mr. Judson folded the papers and put them in his inner coat pocket.

"Well, first I'll have to figure out who is lying. Then determine why. That should tell me what I should do." Mr. Judson's pleasant expression never changed, nor his even, confident tone.

"Sir, I have been honest in everything I wrote in that report. I'll stake my reputation, my position with the agency, on it."

"That's why I chose you, and not your associates." He reached out and clasped Roger's shoulder. "You are absolutely trustworthy."

"So is Odessa. I've worked with her before this job. She would never betray us."

"I'm not accusing her. However, there are circumstances that could be putting pressure on her. People who may try to use her for their profit. Everyone has a weak spot. I fear that people who know who her grandparents were might find a way to force her to act against the Agency's mission. Against the healing diplomatic relations with Britain and Egypt."

Mr. Judson thought someone would try to use her? Someone who knew who her grandparents were? Did anyone at headquarters stop to ask how Mr. Judson knew? Matilda and Ernest Fremont had not published anything noteworthy in the last fifteen years. They had made no new archeological or scientific discoveries of note. Outside of academics, no one really knew them.

Except for the Originators she had met, who seemed to worship the memory of the elder Fremonts.

"Revisionist, or Originator?" Ess murmured.

"Everything Odessa has done, the people she has talked to, from the beginning, from the day you gave me this assignment. I just don't know even now what you had me looking for." Roger took a step back. "Sir? If you don't mind my asking—"

"What is so special about her grandparents that I would think they could be used against her? Besides them being Egyptologists before it was fashionable? That was what made her valuable to us in this assignment." Mr. Judson patted his chest where the papers rested. "I hope, for her sake and ours, I find absolutely nothing. You've done a good job. The entire Pinkerton organization thanks you."

~~~~~

"Excuse me?" Allistair looked up from the coffee he had been about to pour. He put the pot back on the tray on the table and sat back in his chair in the parlor of the team's hotel suite. "Why do you want to know now?"

"I've been considering writing my own memoirs of the assignment." Ess said a silent prayer of thanks that Fordyce had considered the need for a whole host of lies and cover stories, and had worked on them with her. The lack of hesitation alone made a lie much easier to believe. "Mr. Pinkerton is writing up the case files. Perhaps someday people would be interested in hearing about our cases from the perspective of a woman who was there at the time."

"If they aren't scandalized by the idea of a woman doing a man's work, taking a man's risks." Allistair gave her one of his full-strength grins, holding up a hand to silence her.

Ess hadn't been about to say anything. She was too concerned with answering questions and putting together the enormous puzzle churning through her mind.

"You and the other ladies in the agency have proven yourselves a dozen times over," Allistair continued. "But you must be honest and agree that the world at large will always see women as less in terms of courage and fortitude, strength, and cleverness. As for your question... Mr. Judson chose you before anyone else on the team."

"Why?"

"Ask him."

"I'd rather not, thank you." Ess wrapped her arms around herself, fighting off a sudden chill. She needed to talk with Athena. How, without rousing suspicion? Especially since she now knew she was being watched,
~~~~~

her every move and encounter recorded and reported. "I find it odd that he asked for me, when it certainly seems that he doesn't trust me."

"Truly? How could you tell?" Allistair's mouth flattened and that grim, determined light filled his eyes for a moment before he looked away and reached for the coffee pot again. "He is a man burdened with ten times the responsibility of agents at our level. He can't afford to trust anyone." He frowned at the stream of steaming black liquid spilling into his cup.

"There comes a time when you're so cautious you paralyze yourself and everyone around you." She gathered up her heavy, dark emerald skirts in preparation for leaving. "I can't help thinking that he had some personal reason, outside the Agency, for including me. And now for questioning me."

"Do you?" He held her gaze while he picked up his cup and sipped. "To be honest, I agree with your... hunch. But we are, neither of us, in any position to be asking questions of a superior in the agency. At least, not in the middle of an assignment."

"Perhaps when you return to Washington or Philadelphia?"

"Oh, most definitely. You can count on it."

~~~~~

Uly arrived at the start of the reception with a false beard, moustache, and wig, all in iron gray and reminiscent of Custer in his heyday. Ess watched him stroll through the long exhibition hall in his old-fashioned frock coat, hands clasped behind his back, peering at the hustle and bustle through yellow-tinted spectacles, and she envied him. Despite the danger, despite the hope that they would set a trap for the Revisionists and deal them a harsh blow, her brother was having fun. She could tell by the energy and whole-hearted attention he devoted to the masquerade. When he finally reached her position by the door into the exhibition hall and bowed over her hand, she was sorely tempted to yank on his beard, just to see how securely it was fastened. It looked so real.

Then again, with the wonders the blue lotus performed, healing her, perhaps it contained the power to grow hair and change its color, for the sake of deception.

She tucked a note into his hand, and accepted his praise for "the wonders being hereunto displayed for the edification of the populace," declaimed with a thick Southern drawl. The frustrating man wandered among the displays for nearly twenty minutes before excusing himself and sauntering out of the room and down a hallway, where she hoped he read the note immediately. Yes, absolutely, Uly was having far too much fun.

Her brother did not return for the rest of the evening, and that worried her. That increased when Athena and Fordyce didn't show up as planned. She saw several men and women she recognized from her stay on board the *Golden Nile*, but they were dressed as middle and lower class people and didn't come through the reception line to "press the flesh," as her grandfather always put it. Ess knew something had gone wrong.
~~~~~

Her note asked Uly to go to the gallery above the exhibition hall, where he could look down on the throngs, and watch for Mr. Judson when he came in with the Schultzes. Ess didn't like how the man had kept pressing her for the names and descriptions and even the words of the people who had helped her when she was injured. As if she could disobey direct orders from the military of the United States. That was her cover story, that she had been caught between members of the Secret Service and the Army and Air Corps, seeking Resurrectionists who were financing their activities by stealing artifacts. The story was more than believable, because Ess had indeed worked with the Secret Service before she joined the Pinkertons. By necessity, Ess had been ordered by her government not to speak of what had happened during this alleged investigation. Obviously, Mr. Judson didn't think the rules applied to him, or perhaps he simply maintained that the leadership of the Pinkerton Agency lay beyond the authority and the silences imposed by the United States government.

The fact that he kept pushing, even when Allistair backed up her refusal to divulge the information, and the reasons why, made her wonder if he had other reasons for wanting that information.

She had written as much as she could in as few words as possible and folded the note on itself three times to hide where she had written on both sides of the paper. She wondered just how long Uly had taken to read the note, and then how promptly he had acted.

Ess endured the rest of the reception, grateful for the change in plans. Despite all the visiting Betty Schultz had put her through that morning, the numbers weren't as high and the room wasn't as thronged with people as they had hoped. Obviously in cosmopolitan, modern San Francisco, with so many other amusements offered, Egyptology wasn't a fascinating topic that drew the attention of the entire city, as it did at the other stops along the way. On a positive note, one pleasant difference between San Francisco and other cities was that no one felt inclined to play matchmaker with the scholarly young woman escorting the exhibit.

Perhaps, if tonight was so quiet, compared to other opening nights, the exhibition might close early?

A crash of wood and metal and a voice raised in a bull bellow made Ess flinch. It almost felt like a response to her wondering hope.

"Just a newspaper photographer," Briscoe reported, coming back from the outer room of the exhibition hall, where he had gone in search of the source of the noise.

"Not 'just,'" Charles said, catching up with him almost on his heels. "He's using those new-fangled flash photography methods, where they set off a near-cousin of gunpowder. Scared a bunch of high society dowagers. He's getting pictures of everyone. From the way he's sliding those plates in and out, trying to catch every face, it's an expensive night for him, and a waste of time. The newspaper got the pictures of all the important people at the very beginning."

"That's the main paper in town. This troublemaker works for the rival paper."

"Troublemaker is a very kind word indeed," Mr. Judson said, stepping through the doorway into the exhibition hall. He tugged his coat straight and ran his finger along his collar and smoothed his hair. "He set off his flash nearly in my face. Could have blinded me. I wouldn't be surprised if my eyebrows were scorched off."

"I would have, if I had thought it would have helped us," Uly said, three hours later. He guided Ess down the street, in her boy garb again, heading back to the *Golden Nile*.

"I'm guessing you flashed him so he couldn't see you?" she said.

"He's why Athena and Ford and the other higher-ups didn't come tonight. Among the Originators, his name is August Stryker. As far as Athena and Fordyce know, he isn't a Pinkerton. Or rather, he isn't *supposed* to be." He wrapped his arm around her shoulders and pulled her against him in a sideways hug. "I'm proud of you, baby sister. You might have saved a good number of lives tonight."

"Including my own?" She wished she could snap at him to stop calling her "baby," but nausea with sharp prongs had settled into her belly again.

"Athena theorizes that he knew who you were the moment your mentor brought you into the Pinkertons."

"Meaning he knows why the Blue Lotus Society has been involved. But why is he pushing me for names and details, when he knows about Athena?"

"That's just it. He doesn't. At the most, he might suspect. He needs proof. You see, we're very careful about our security, about keeping the Revisionists from guessing what we're doing, where we are, and how strong and numerous we are. Only the highest levels know all the different faces we wear, how many important people in academia and science and the military are ours. Or the locations of our research and development centers. Very few among the Originators know that our particular division runs the Blue Lotus Society, and that the *Golden Nile* is equipped with Originator technology. Which is why Athena and Fordyce didn't come. They couldn't afford him seeing them, recognizing them, and making the connection. And betraying us all."

"Then they believe he is a Revisionist?"

"The chances are very good." Uly stopped them at an intersection, before they stepped out from the shadows of the buildings into the pool of gaslight. He looked in all directions, including up. Ess found that interesting, and saved the observation for later. "The game would have been up, even with my disguise, if we had come face-to-face," he continued, once they had crossed the intersection and stepped into shadows again. "Stryker was supposedly a friend of our parents. He ran with Athena and Fordyce,

Mama and Father when they were younger. *He* sent Ford on his expedition to Antarctica. Which is another grim tale that should have made someone suspicious of him years ago. Then, he sent me to look for Ford. I was convinced long before this that he gave me the wrong information. If Ford and his men hadn't already managed to fight halfway home, my team and I would have landed several hundred miles off their route. We would have wandered the Antarctic wastes for months."

"And been lost?" she hazarded, reading the lines forming around his mouth, visible even in the shadows and the thickness of his false beard. The thoughtful grimness in his voice told her volumes.

"Thank the good Lord we were both pushed off course by unseasonable storms. Essentially, we got through into the same harbor." He huffed an attempt at laughter. "When I was young, I dreamed about places like this unnamed, unmapped harbor. I thought pirates and adventurers were incredible, admirable men. Not so, when you meet them face-to-face. I think our two groups found each other by simply seeking the company of others who didn't spend their days drinking and brawling, and their nights drinking and whoring."

Ess knew Uly was distracted by his thoughts and probably a thousand images he didn't want to share with her, when he didn't trip over such words. After all, she was his baby sister. Even if she was a Pinkerton and could shoot and box and pick locks, she needed to be sheltered.

"Stryker or Judson or whatever you want to call him, is a liar. It doesn't matter who he's allied with, he can't be trusted." He glanced down at her. "I suppose having you vanish at this point in the game would just arouse his suspicions."

"Or confirm them."

Chapter Twenty-Four

"I always wondered if Stryker didn't have multiple motives, when I set off for Antarctica," Fordyce said, looking around the conference table on the *Golden Nile*. He waggled his eyebrows at Athena, and barked laughter when Ess frowned at him.

"What he wants me to confess," Athena said, "is that Stryker was a suitor, and used the Antarctica mission to get him out of the way. I'm more inclined to think if he is a traitor and a Revisionist, he was maneuvering to get strong leadership and loud voices out of the way. Perhaps suspicious minds, too." She glanced at Ess.

Something in the woman's eyes, a flicker of apprehension and dark thoughts, set Ess to wondering. She inhaled sharply as an idea came to her. The worst part was that it was something that had been hovering and slowly unfolding at the back of her thoughts for some time now.

"How powerful were our parents and grandparents?" she asked, slowly putting down her mug of strong, black coffee, heavy on sugar. "A threat to someone who was on the inside and planning to splinter or just weaken the Originators?"

"Stryker proclaimed himself Edward's good friend. I thought sometimes he saw me as a rival, as if someone could only be friends, good friends, with one person at a time," Fordyce said, his voice softening to a thoughtful rumble. "The sad fact is that for the right price, men will betray those they love the most."

"Because they love themselves and their own profit the most," Athena offered. "Stryker has been absent from the Sanctuary every time I have visited over the last four years. In fact, ever since Fordyce went missing."

"Playing hard to get," the older man muttered, and winked at Ess. "Absence makes the heart grow fonder, and all that rot."

"There has to be some fondness there for the heart to grow fonder," she retorted with a faintly amused calm that Ess admired. "The point is that Stryker has been busy elsewhere every time I and my people have returned to the Sanctuary. I will have to check with others around the world, to see how often he has been present at the regular gatherings. That is an aspect of being an Originator, Ess. If you are near to one of our sanctums, our repositories of resources and information, you are expected to report in at specified intervals. Just to make sure everyone is still alive and functioning. The theory is that eventually, though certainly not quickly enough to make a large difference, patterns of movements will emerge and we will realize that someone has been silent and invisible for too long. If we move quickly enough, we can backtrack where he or she has last been, and hopefully pull them out of trouble, or pick up the pieces and discern what hurt or delayed or even killed them."

"If Stryker has been avoiding reporting in," Uly said, "maybe we can backtrack his pattern enough to figure out when and where he turned against us."

"It was long before any pattern appeared, you can be sure. But I can hazard a guess when and why." She sighed and leaned back in her chair, closing her eyes and rubbing her temples for a few moments. "Shortly after Fordyce left for Antarctica, Stryker built up pressure to be allowed to not only be tested by the lotus, but to become a guardian. He maintained that he had proved himself. I wonder now if that was the entire point of everything he did, including courting me. To gain access to the lotus."

"Tested by it?" Ess asked.

"There is something born into our blood and bones, our brains, that makes us more sensitive to the energy given off by the lotus. The first test is being able to hear when crystal responds to the crystal rods. But then," she said with a deprecating smile and a shrug, "the mobis are built to be able to respond. Part of their command structure is made of metal that vibrates in the same frequency. That is why they are our advance scouts in situations such as the warehouse where we found you. The sensitivity increases, to the point that a very few are able to actually touch the lotus, and... well, I suppose you would call it being able to communicate with it. To focus the mind to create images that touch the memories stored inside it. I am one of the few who are able to use the lotus to test retrieved crystal and activate the resonance that makes the disparate pieces of the Great Machine come back together."

"I'll wager you, young Odessa, are among that elite group," Fordyce said, saluting her with his coffee mug.

"Was Granny? And Mama?" Something tightened in Ess's chest when Athena nodded. "All right, so Mr. Judson—or Stryker—was trying to get possession of the lotus. Since being male automatically disqualifies him for some duties, for what purpose would he use it? If he could use it at all."

"I can theorize only one direction," Athena said. "The Revisionists have gathered up enough pieces of crystal, they want to try to start re-assembling their own version of the Great Machine."

"Uly said that Stryker can't know you're here, even if he has read in the paper that representatives of the Blue Lotus Society are here on board the *Golden Nile*. Even if he doesn't know Originators run the Society, I don't understand. Isn't the name like throwing a torch into the armory? Everyone has to at least guess."

"Poe, my dear girl," Fordyce said with a bad British accent. "Of course, we thought of the concept long before he wrote his fascinating little story about the purloined letter. It's the concept of hiding in plain sight. Only a fool would advertise that he has what everyone is looking for, so therefore, someone wearing the name of the Blue Lotus could not possibly be someone who knows what the blue lotus is to the Originators. Do you follow?"

"It is very shaky logic," she said.

"Very few among the Originators know that the *Golden Nile* belongs to us, and that I am in charge," Athena said. "Very few know who the proven guardians of the lotus are. Stryker has moved so far out of the circles of power and information among us, it would be very hard for him to know that I have the lotus with me. After all, only a fool would send the greatest treasure in the world out of the safety of the Sanctuary."

"So that's why they did it?" Ess guessed. "Because the Sanctuary is the prime spot for the Revisionists to attack in their effort to possess the lotus?"

"You caught on to that faster than I did," Uly said, and leaned back in his chair with a shrug and a grin.

"The Originators have been splintering ourselves into tiny groups, connected by nebulous strands finer than a spider's silk, for generations now," Athena said. "It isn't a matter of the right hand not knowing what the left hand is doing, but some fingers of the right hand not knowing what the other fingers are doing. We had planned to take you to the Sanctuary after the exhibition is finished here in San Francisco, but we would have gone by land, leaving the *Golden Nile* far behind, just so anyone who encountered us in the Sanctuary could not make the connection between us and our ship. We wear many names and play many roles out in the ordinary world, to foul the trail so no one can follow us back and endanger others."

"Then isn't it possible that Stryker really is following the orders and the agenda of the Originators, but it's a lack of communication that is getting in the way of knowing what he's doing?" Ess asked.

"Oh, we have considered it. But our personal experience with him makes us suspicious. If he was acting honestly, he should have reported to our leadership the moment he learned you joined the Pinkertons. At the very least, he should have investigated that you were indeed our Odessa, daughter of Vivian and Edward. Athena and your brother and I would have been contacted immediately, because we have the closest ties to you, of blood and friendship." Fordyce shook his head, his normally cheerful expression darkly grim. "The fact that he kept the news secret and put you in this position... I have to wonder what prize he is after. And if you aren't part of it."

"Such as?" She considered trying to drown the prickly nausea with a long draught of scalding hot coffee. "Oh. Of course. I inherited Granny's sensitivity to crystal. They could use me. They want to recruit me for the Revisionists." Ess sat back and glanced at Uly. He caught hold of her hand under the table. It wasn't enough. She wished she were small enough again to curl up in his lap and hide her face against his chest.

"I would wager they will make their move after the exhibition has run to its end, to avoid attracting any more attention. Mr. Judson, an authority among the Pinkertons, will give you a new assignment. Perhaps make you his assistant on an important job that must be done quickly, and secretly. No one will realize anything is wrong until weeks or months later, when either both of you have vanished, or he returns with a terrible story of your death, such that there is no body to bury."

"Then what can we do? After Kansas City, he has to suspect that I've made contact with someone among the Originators. Even if the Revisionists didn't learn about the crystal I found, as a supervisor among the Pinkertons, he has to be suspicious. Yes, I used to work for the Secret Service, and it would only make sense to retain my friendships and connections, but we can't explain away every odd incident as another encounter with Southern rebels. How do we find out who he works for or with, and how do we cut the snake's head off before he does any more damage?"

"We set a trap," Uly said, leaning over to slide his arm across her shoulders.

"With me as the bait." Ess offered them as confident a smile as she could manage.

Ironically, the nausea faded away and the sharp knobs jabbing her stomach dulled to a heavy sensation that made her feel old and tired.

"There is another problem to deal with," Athena said, her tone soft and weary, so that Ford reached to catch hold of her hand. "As I said, we had planned to take you, Ess, to Sanctuary. For training, and to let the rest of your family's friends know you have been found. That could be dangerous now. Just the access you have to your family's vault, by virtue of the crystal lock coded to you... If Stryker is a traitor, he could be one of many. The access that Revisionists could have even now, to the forbidden history books, to the secret records identifying all our divisions and leaders. The danger is incalculable. Something must be done to deal with the poisoned wound at the heart of our effort."

"One step at a time, my dear," Fordyce said, enveloping her hand with both of his.

~~~~~

Just like in Kansas City, collectors temporarily loaned their treasures to the exhibition. Mr. Judson, aka Stryker, had no way of knowing that Athena had already checked the new items in the exhibit. He could hear when the crystal testing rods were struck, but he could not hear the response of what was tested, so unless he had someone with him who could hear, he could not know if crystal had been found. The men who had chased Ess in Kansas City had been captured or killed. The survivors were unsure if their dead associates had sent a report to their superiors, stating that Evangeline Peabody was testing artifacts for crystal. Nothing would be certain until they could get answers from Stryker.
~~~~~

It was a given that he would try to be alone with Ess at some point, to either pry decisive information from her, or overpower her. As long as he thought she was still weak and recovering, he could underestimate her. He hadn't been happy to learn alleged friends in the military protected her from the Resurrectionists, which reinforced the theory that he wanted to get her alone. Ess had the duty of making him susceptible to questioning. Sylvia had given her an atomizer loaded with the soporific, loopy-loo, to spray in his face when he confronted her, somewhere solitary. The best place was near the water, where damp in the air would keep him from realizing he had been sprayed until after he lost control of his tongue. Uly and Fordyce would be there, with their soldiers, to witness Stryker's confession and take him prisoner.

The second night of the exhibition, Ess made a point of discussing plans for the next day with Betty Schultz, where Stryker could hear them and learn she was staying overnight with the Schultzes. In the last half hour of the evening, she excused herself and made sure Stryker saw her going down the hall to the workroom. Then she pulled out the testing rod and struck it. Five times, unevenly spaced. He could read that any way he wanted. Hopefully, he would see it as a sign that she had found several artifacts. Ess hoped it drove him mad, wondering which among the many small, sometimes strange, temporary donations was the container or disguise for crystal.

As soon as she and the Schultzes reached their home that evening, Ess hurried upstairs and changed into her boy clothes, with Betty's chuckling help. Her new friend didn't ask what she was up to. It was enough that the Schultzes could be trusted to keep silent and not report to Stryker simply because she asked them. Ess waited until she saw movement in the shadows of the neighbors' house, then slid down the gutter pipe from her window. Once she heard footsteps behind her in the darkness, she picked up her pace, heading for the shore. She planned her route to give her several options for the confrontation. Now if only Stryker would cooperate before he realized that others followed both of them.

The infamous San Francisco fog courteously filled the air. Ess imagined it warped all sounds. She had a few anxious moments when she couldn't be sure if she had lost her pursuer. Then several more, when she wondered if Uly and Fordyce and their men had lost her trail.

I will trust them, she scolded herself.

That spun her thoughts off along a new tangent. Athena had spoken to her during her convalescence about her faith, or rather lack thereof. Ess wished she could fully believe and rely on Jehovah God as Athena and Fordyce and Sylvia believed and trusted. She had been on her own too long. She had too many clear, strong memories of childhood tears, of crying out for help, and no one came. Of being mentally battered by the teachers at the boarding school. She had been forced to make her own help, her own escape. Athena had not argued with her as Ess expected, countering that her intelligence and resilience and talents had been the tools God gave her to effect her escape. She hadn't compared Ess's lack of faith in the people who should have been listening for the flute signal song to her lack of faith in God. That was wise, because after all, God was there all the time, whereas her grandparents' and parents' friends among the Originators couldn't be everywhere at once. Athena had merely said that just like various prophets and kings in the Old Testament had been seemingly left alone in silence to test them and make them strong, perhaps that was Ess's testing time. After all, even Christ had cried out, asking why God had abandoned Him.

"Idiot," she muttered, realizing that she had indeed gone off on a tangent. The best time for her enemy to attack was when she was distracted.

She listened, and the footsteps were still behind her, echoing in the fog. The water slapped against the massive broken rocks of the shore, sending up spray and splatters of larger drops of brine. The first possible stopping point was just up ahead.

Please, Lord God, could You make him –

"Odessa Fremont," Stryker called out behind her.

Ess flinched, and then nearly laughed at herself. At least she didn't have to pretend to be surprised. She glanced ahead and saw the rocks were just about thirty, forty feet away, glistening dully in the few blots of moonlight penetrating the fog. She ran.

"Stop!" The man had the gall to laugh. "It's Seth Judson. I'm a friend."

Liar.

Ess stopped when the packed soil and sparse grass gave way to rocks. She could maneuver him closer to the water if necessary.

Turning her back to the water, she waited for Stryker to catch up with her. Wind came in off the water, brushing the back of her bared neck. She shivered and nearly took a few steps forward before she caught herself. Ess didn't like the thought of the wind shredding the sheltering fog. She glanced over her shoulder and saw clouds seeping in across the sky, stretching misty fingers across the moon to replace the fog. Rain might just be better.

"How long have you been following me?" she challenged, and took a few more steps back, until the ground completely surrendered to the rough rocks along the shore. "It would have to be since the Schultzes' house, for you to even know it was me in these clothes."

"I wanted to talk to you about tonight's showing, and saw you sliding down just as I arrived. I'm surprised you didn't hear my carriage."

"The fog muffles sound." She crossed her arms, hugging herself and glanced around.

"There's no need for fear, Odessa."

"Mr. Judson, I may be dressed as a boy, out alone late at night, and I may be under your authority as a Pinkerton, but there is no call for such familiarity."

"True. If that were all we were to each other." He took a step closer. She took two steps back and he held up his hands in surrender. "This is part of why I need to speak with you. It's about the crystal."

"The crystal? I'm not sure—"

"You were testing the artifacts this evening. I heard you."

"Testing them?" Ess jammed her hands into her coat pockets, and prayed for the wind to pick up. Either rain or a strong wave to spatter them, that was all she asked for. Her fingers closed around the atomizer.

"To see if they held crystal." He tipped his head to one side, his smile widening. It looked sinister to her in the shifting shadows of clouds streaking the moon.

"They didn't. Or at least, if the crystal was in them, I've yet to hear the song. Whenever I'm around artifacts, I test them, like my grandmother taught me. Just in case—" She caught her breath, stunned and amused by the new tactic that popped into her brain.

"In case what?" The aggravating man didn't step closer, though she had certainly given him a good opening.

"In case there was someone who could hear the crystal sing. I've never heard it sing. Granny could, and she taught me to test, and told me I would grow into it. I thought if I met up with someone who could hear it sing, then maybe they would know what happened to my grandparents, because they would be friends of theirs." She shrugged, keeping her hands in her pockets. "At least, that is my theory."

"A very good one." His voice sounded tight for a moment. She couldn't read him with his face momentarily shrouded in shadows. "So you have never heard the crystal sing? So when you fled those people in Kansas City... who were you fleeing?"

"Oh, just like I said. Resurrectionists. I've been helping the Secret Service since I fled boarding school. You won't tell Mr. Pinkerton and the others on the board, will you?"

"Tell them what?" He took a step closer, his smile unveiled as the wind pushed the clouds away from the face of the moon. That smile sent chills up her back with little hobnail boots.

"I'm supposed to be entirely committed to the Pinkertons, but I can't say no when my friends ask for my help, can I? Then things got messy. I hope my contacts show up soon and tell me everyone has been captured, so I can stop looking over my shoulder all the time."

"Is that what you're out here for? To meet your military contacts?" Stryker looked around. "What happens if they aren't successful? If the Resurrectionists who have seen you aren't captured?"

"They'll have to whisk me away without a moment of warning, and hide me somewhere, then help me become someone new. I've had to do it before, working with them. It's only fun the first time."

"We can't let that happen, Odessa. Your talents are needed elsewhere."

He smiled wider and held out his hand to her. "I'm going to ask you to trust me completely."

"And I am going to remind you not to speak so familiarly to me." She backed up as she withdrew the atomizer and palmed it, hiding it from his view. Her foot skidded on dampness covering the rocks, and she prayed for a large wave with some spray.

"But we are old friends. I knew your parents."

"Why didn't you say so before?" She flinched when her foot struck a large rock, stopping her backward movement. Ess glanced over her shoulder and it seemed the water was only a step away.

It wouldn't take much for Stryker to send her tumbling backwards, hit her head on those rocks, and be stunned long enough to drown.

"There are some personal details the leadership of the Agency doesn't need to know. I wanted to make sure you really were the daughter of Vivian and Edward Fremont before I spoke up." He sighed, sounding weary. "I had hoped you inherited your mother's talents. Among them, hearing the crystal sing."

"Why doesn't everyone hear it?"

"A gift of the gods, I suppose," he said with a shrug and a chuckle.

The gods? You think you're a god.

"What good does it do to hear the crystal sing? What makes that particular crystal special?"

"My dear girl, that is what I wish to teach you. But you must trust me implicitly. Keep no secrets from me. Entrust your life into my care. I can offer you the riches and the wisdom of the universe, but I must first make sure you are worthy."

Ess sensed the large wave before it struck. She hunched her shoulders and hissed as water spattered her, and staggered forward, pretending shock. Stryker turned his head as spray washed over them both. She sprayed his face, and prayed the water didn't wash away the soporific before it could act.

"Perhaps we should find another place to talk," he said, withdrawing a handkerchief. It seemed to glow in the spotty moonlight, white against his dark suit. He made to mop his face, then handed it to her before he did so.

"What is there for me to know?" She stepped sideways, turning to hide the action of soaking the handkerchief with the atomizer before putting it back in her pocket.

Chapter Twenty-Five

"Oh, there is a great deal you need to know. But because this is a matter of utmost secrecy, well, you will just have to trust me and take a rather large step of faith." He chuckled and wiped at his face, wincing a moment later and frowning at the damp cloth.

Her heart leaped when he put his hand to the side of his head and swayed, just enough to be visible in the shadows. Stryker lowered his hand and shook his head, resulting in another sway.

Thank you, Dr. Sylvia. You are a genius.

"Did my parents take a step of faith, when you sent them on that archeological dig?" She stepped sideways again, so she now faced the rocks and Stryker turned automatically, putting his back to them.

"Eh? What?"

"My parents. You were one of their supervisors, meeting them and gathering up their reports. You were one of the last to see them alive. Nobody knows what you told them."

"Silly child, it's in the report I made." He chuckled.

"Did you tell the whole truth in that report?"

"Of course not." He frowned, his eyes darting to the right and left.

"Why did you want them dead?"

"Not Vivian. Just Edward. Too smart for his own good. With Vivian, I could have all the crystal I wanted. Women are so easy to manipulate. I could get hold of her heart while she was grieving him, and convince her the old men were wrong and she should listen to my new friends and..." Stryker pressed both hands to his head and staggered back two steps before he caught his balance. "That's not what I wanted to say."

"What you want doesn't really matter anymore," Uly said, stepping out of the darkness.

"It's about time you got here." Ess grinned up at him as he put an arm around her shoulders.

"You? You're—you're supposed to be dead." Stryker shook his head and moaned, closing his eyes, as his ankles wobbled.

"Am I supposed to be dead?" Fordyce asked, coming into the spotty moonlight from further down the shore.

"You? How?"

"Well, you sent me out to find Mr. Chamberlain and his men, didn't you?" Uly said, his eyes wide with false innocence. "So I did. I always do what I set out to do. Even if I'm given directions and warnings that send me *into* danger instead of away from it."

"Let's clear up something before we take you into custody," Fordyce said. "Did you send me away to clear the field to win Athena? Or were you after something bigger? Although, personally, I can't imagine what could be more important than that woman." He winked at Ess. "You'll be sure to tell her I said that, won't you?"

"Tell her yourself," she retorted, voice cracking, caught between exasperation with his foolery at such a time, and amusement.

"You killed my parents," Uly said. "I say custody is too good for you. But more powerful people have decided you can give us some helpful information about the Revisionists. Maybe later they'll let me pound you into a bloody, whimpering pulp."

"I won't tell you anything!" Stryker reached into his coat pocket.

"Gun!" Ess shouted.

Gunfire burst out of the darkness, proving the Society's soldiers were close at hand, and able to see quite well, despite the shadows. Stryker howled and spun sideways, clutching at his shoulder. He dropped into a half-crouch, gasping, blood seeping through his fingers.

"I won't tell you," he growled.

"Yes, you will. Right now, if we want," Fordyce said, advancing on him. "Ess, dear, how much more of Sylvia's amazing concoction do you have left?"

"Oh..." She withdrew the atomizer from her pocket and shook it. "Less than half the bottle, I think. Not enough to knock him unconscious before he tells us so much more."

Horror warped Stryker's face, partially hidden by the shadows creeping across the moon. The wind picked up, as if taking its cue from the man's emotions, and another wave splashed up, spraying them so Ess could feel it on her face even ten feet away from the water's edge.

"How many Revisionists are there in San Francisco, working with you?" Fordyce said. "How close are they?"

"They're waiting—they don't know—I have to contact—I don't want to tell you!" His face crumpled in nausea and he gagged.

"They don't know you're even here, is that it?" Ess speculated that trying to resist the drug caused illness. That would be something to keep in mind for the future.

"Yes." He glared at her.

"You're trying to get one over on everyone. You didn't believe that cock and bull story I spun, did you?"

"I'll kill you. Lying little whore!"

Uly leaped, crossing the last few feet between them in two steps. He caught Stryker by his shoulders and twisted, throwing the man down to the rocks to land on his wounded shoulder. Stryker let out a howl that ended in a cracked sob of agony.

"Nobody talks about my sister like that," Uly snarled.

"I'm guessing there's a massive power struggle going on among the Revisionists," Fordyce said, stepping up on Stryker's other side. He gestured out at the darkness, and a dozen men with pistols and rifles at the ready stepped into the fading moonlight. "I'll wager he thought he had hit the mother lode when you joined the Pinkertons, Ess, and he's been trying to maneuver you into position to test and recruit you. He didn't tell anyone, keeping you as his ace in the hole. I'm guessing when you ran into trouble, he panicked, thinking someone had stolen the march on him. Imagine how much power he would have among the Revisionists if he had an obedient little servant who could hear the crystal sing. Especially if she was of Matilda Fremont's blood, with the potential to speak to the blue lotus."

"He must not have read all of Horace's report on me." Ess was quite content to keep some distance between him and her. "He'd know I'm quite stubborn and only obey when it suits me."

"Ho there," a man called in the distance. A faint yellow light bobbed, appearing on the horizon where Ess guessed the dip in the road sloped up again before dropping to the shore. "What's going on here? Halt!" he shouted, as some of the soldiers stepped back into the darkness. The light grew closer. "This is the police. Stay right where you are."

Just at the point when the man became visible in the light of the lantern he held, Stryker got to his knees and grabbed onto Uly, pulling himself to his feet. Her brother cursed and twisted, trying to get free.

"Knife!" Fordyce leaped at the two struggling men.

Ess stepped back, the flicker of weak moonlight on a knife blade trapping her gaze. She felt as if she were mired in molasses, unable to help her brother. Stryker slashed down as Fordyce hit him from the side. Uly cursed and Fordyce shouted words she didn't recognize. The three men staggered and fell over the jumble of rocks. Uly hit first, and Stryker and Fordyce seemed to roll right over him, his body providing a ramp. He yelped in pain, and then the tangle of bodies broke apart. He stayed sprawled on his back, while the other two men vanished into the darkness and water.

Dropping to her knees beside Uly, Ess searched for wounds. The policeman raced up next to her, setting the lantern down on the highest point of the rocks, and braced himself to look over the edge.

"Ho there! Come up now, no funny business." He glanced sideways at Ess. "How's that man, lad?"

"Please tell me you still have some of Sylvia's potion," Uly groaned, as he pushed aside Ess's hands and levered his arms under himself, to sit up under his own power.

"He's cut." She showed the officer her hands, streaked with blood from the back of her brother's head. The blood was black in the shadows and moonlight, garish red in the lantern light, hot on her skin.

"Someone help me with this filthy—" Fordyce sounded like he was choking.

Four soldiers from the *Golden Nile* climbed down the rocks to help him, while the police officer looked on, holding the lantern high with one hand and his pistol at ready in the other. Ess tore the bottom of her shirt off and dampened it in the puddles of splashed up seawater and got to work on the gashes on the back of Uly's head. Most of the bleeding had stopped by the time they hauled Fordyce and an unconscious Stryker back onto dry land.

Stryker had smashed his head badly on the rocks. Ess's stomach tightened as she saw the torn flesh and bone peeking through on the side of his head, above his ear and stretching across his forehead.

"All right now, before we haul this one off to a doctor, I want to know what you lot were doing down here," the policeman said. He glanced up the way he had come. "Filthy fog. Any other decent town, I'd have a crowd by now and a half dozen officers come running to assist."

"It's actually providential that we don't have a crowd," Allistair said, stepping into the weak pool of light from the lantern. He bent and struck a match on a nearby rock, and lit the lantern hanging on his belt. "Officer, I am Allistair Fitch of the Pinkerton Agency. This young lady here—" He paused, his mouth flickering up in a smile, when the officer startled and leaned closer to give Ess another look. "This young lady here is one of our agents. And unfortunately, that wounded gentleman is a supervisor who has recently come under suspicion of underhanded dealings. We set up a trap, to lure him into revealing his treachery. Obviously, he was in deeper than we anticipated, and he resorted to violence to make his escape."

"Pinkerton, eh?" The policeman narrowed his eyes and gnawed on his bottom lip. "Don't suppose you got any identification on you?"

He seemed at first irritated, then mollified, when Allistair pulled his badge and identification folder from his pocket. Then he chuckled when Allistair pointed out that Ess, of course, couldn't carry her identification on her in her current costume. If he and his superiors cared to come to their hotel in the morning, they could look over her credentials in more comfortable surroundings.

Stryker never regained consciousness. He let out a few rattles and gasps and gagging sounds when they bundled him up and hauled him up the streets to the nearest lit intersection. There, the policeman blew his whistle and got the attention of nearby officers, someone found a wagon, and the entire company went to the nearest stationhouse. By the time a doctor arrived to examine Stryker, he had quietly expired.

Ess wondered if anyone would mourn him, other than the loss of information they could have obtained from him about the Revisionists, their activities, and how many Originators had turned traitor with him.

~~~~~

"Blame the Resurrectionists, of course," Allistair said.
~~~~~

He had been unusually quiet from the moment he stepped on board the *Golden Nile*. Athena had kept him under observation, seated on the far side of the conference room, drinking coffee and writing up his report for the Pinkertons and the police, while Fordyce and Uly and Theo filled her in on what had happened in the fog and darkness. Ess had excused herself to change her clothes, which Athena found interesting, and wondered just what it indicated about the young woman's state of mind. Ordinarily, she would have expected her new protégé to stay in boy clothes as long as possible. That musing ended with a tiny snort of laughter, when Ess had returned a short time later with a tray of food for them all, accompanied by Sylvia and her seemingly never-ending bottle of whiskey — and still wearing trousers. Her hair was freed of her cap and pins, hanging in two neat braids, she had washed her face and changed into one of the knee-length, loose shirts that Athena herself preferred for shipboard comfort. Ess had served Allistair and sat down with him, talking softly for nearly twenty minutes before Athena called the meeting officially to order, first by asking Allistair what he would tell his superiors.

"The seeds are already planted," the Pinkerton man continued, and offered Fordyce the report he had been working on.

Athena breathed a little easier, seeing this gesture of cooperation.

"Besides," Ess said, "he can't quite explain some of the things he saw and heard down at the water's edge."

"I know when I'm over my head, and when it's wiser to trust people to be honorable. Some secrets shouldn't be shared." Allistair picked up the coffee cup a few inches. "This is one secret I wouldn't mind hearing, though. I've never tasted coffee like this on board an airship."

"He hopes Doctor Sylvia will share the soporific. Strictly for police work," Ess added.

"I think that can be arranged," Athena said slowly. "Am I to understand you are willing to lie to the police, your superiors... in exchange for what?"

"Someday when you think it's safe, you'll tell me the whole story, that's all." Allistair glanced at Ess, making Athena wonder if Uly's teasing about the agent's feelings might just have some solid foundation. "The less fuss and mess for us to clean up on our side, the better. Since you know Judson by another name, I'd hazard a guess he had other identities, and has been playing games at several different tables. Unraveling the tangled web will take some time. Better to start small and quietly."

"Indeed."

"We might have need of the Pinkertons in the future," Fordyce said. "Shall we say an alliance?"

"That would suit us all very well," Allistair said.

A wave of weariness swept over Athena that had nothing to do with the lateness of the hour. "For now, we need to do some intensive housecleaning. Stryker cannot possibly be the only traitor."

~~~~~

"What are you going to do first?" Ess asked.

She stood with Athena on the observation deck of the *Golden Nile*, looking out over San Francisco on one side and the ocean on the other.

"As I told your Mr. Fitch, we are going to clean house." Athena smiled at the tiny snort and shrug Ess gave in response to "your Mr. Fitch." "We are obviously not protected enough by splintering and separating the many divisions of the Originators. It is only by the grace of God that the *Golden Nile* and the Blue Lotus Society have been shielded as well as they have. Perhaps keeping one hand from knowing what the other is doing has worked against us. We need to regroup. Close ranks. We will stay here until Stryker's life as Seth Judson, Pinkerton agent, has been thoroughly excavated and we have some idea of the depths of his treachery." She gripped the rail and leaned more weight into it, and looked down over the countryside, the waves creating frothy white lines along the coast. "Then we go to the Sanctuary."

"To do what?"

"Enroll you in lessons, of course, to catch up on all that schooling you missed."

"But...don't you think that's dangerous? If the Revisionists have spies and traitors among us, won't they be at the Sanctuary?"

"Most definitely. You, my dear, are our best bet to infiltrate and listen and observe, because you are an unknown quantity."

"Won't that make me your weakest link? I don't know anything."

"That will be your protection. No preconceived notions, no sense of how things should be, clouding your judgment. You will question everything you see, and you will see what those of us who are familiar with the Sanctuary and the operations and rules of the Originators could miss."

"You can't take me to Sanctuary. If the treachery is there like you fear, we can't let the traitors know you are head of the Blue Lotus Society. The people who know you can hear and use the lotus will make the connection. It will be like blowing a trumpet or hiring a carnival barker to tell the world you are the custodian. Plus, we need to keep the existence of the *Nile* a secret, our ace in the hole."

"True." Athena fought not to smile, especially when Ess's eyes narrowed and her expression turned to a scowl.

"You already thought of that problem, didn't you?"

"We did. I'm glad to see we are on the same page."

"The problem is figuring out who else is available to turn me over to higher authorities. Who has the power to..."

Athena caught her breath as Ess's smile turned sly, and just for a moment, Matilda Fremont looked out through her granddaughter's eyes.

"All we need is a good excuse for running to them," Ess murmured, and turned to look out over the ocean again. "Some reason for a self-reliant,
~~~~~

independent young woman to suddenly need advice and shelter and go running to the other side of the country."

"To whom?"

"To the family lawyers. Endicott, Lewis and MacDonald. Someone did say they were all three Originators, or was I mistaken?"

"You were most certainly not mistaken." Athena rested a hand on Ess's shoulder. "Yes, quite logical. Who else but lawyers entrusted with delicate Originator business would be expected to take you under their wing and set you back on the track of claiming your heritage?" She sighed, satisfied at having another niggling, troublesome detail dealt with. "Yes, our enemies will never suspect a thing when you turn up and settle in for some long-overdue schooling."

"There's so much I need to learn. Like an enormous gaping hole was cut out of my life." Ess glanced back at her. "You never said. What were the first Revisionists trying to stop or change in history?"

There were so many answers she could give, all of them at least partly true, pieces in a great puzzle. So many theories of what prompted the beginning of the Revisionists' efforts.

"They were trying to erase Bethlehem and Golgotha. Although they failed, and their descendants have failed in changing other pivotal moments in history... well, we think they hope to try again."

Ess met her gaze, unblinking, not breathing, for what felt like many minutes. Slowly, she nodded, expression solemn, and looked out at the horizon.

THE END

About the Author

On the road to publication, Michelle fell into fandom in college and has 40+ stories in various SF and fantasy universes. She has a bunch of useless degrees in theater, English, film/communication, and writing. Even worse, she has over 100 books and novellas with multiple small presses, in science fiction and fantasy, YA, suspense, women's fiction, and sub-genres of romance.

Her official launch into publishing came with winning first place in the Writers of the Future contest in 1990. She was a finalist in the EPIC Awards competition multiple times, winning with *Lorien* in 2006 and *The Meruk Episodes, I-V,* in 2010, and was a finalist in the Realm Awards competition, in conjunction with the Realm Makers convention.

Her training includes the Institute for Children's Literature; proofreading at an advertising agency; and working at a community newspaper. She is a tea snob and freelance edits for a living (MichelleLevigne@gmail.com for info/rates), but only enough to give her time to write. Her newest crime against the literary world is to be co-managing editor at Mt. Zion Ridge Press and launching the publishing co-op, Ye Olde Dragon Books. Be afraid … be very afraid.

And please check out her newest venture: Ye Olde Dragon's Library, the storytelling podcast. Each week, listeners are invited to join Michelle on her blog to ask questions and give feedback and suggestions. Interspersed between the chapters will be interviews with authors of fantastical fiction. Listen to the podcast on your favorite podcast app or listen on the website: www.YeOldeDragonBooks.com, and click on the Ye Olde Dragon's Library link. Then go to her blog to interact: www.MichelleLevigne.blogspot.com

www.Mlevigne.com
www.MichelleLevigne.blogspot.com
www.YeOldeDragonBooks.com
www.MtZionRidgePress.com

Look for Michelle's Goodreads groups:
Guardians of Neighborlee

Voyages of the AFV Defender

NEWSLETTER:
Want to learn about upcoming books, book launch parties, inside
information, and cover reveals?
Go to Michelle's website or blog to sign up.

Thanks for reading!
**If you enjoyed this book, would you help Michelle by posting a review
on Goodreads?**

**Are you a member of Book Bub? If so, please follow Michelle on Book
Bub, and you'll get alerts when new books are coming out.**

**As a way of saying thanks, Michelle invites you to the Goodies page on
her website. It will change regularly, offering you a free short story, a
sample audiobook chapter, sneak peeks at new cover art, inside
information on discounts and new release dates, etc.**

Please go to: Mlevigne.com/good-stuff.html

Also by Michelle L. Levigne

Guardians of the Time Stream: 4-book Steampunk series
The Match Girls: Humorous inspirational romance series starting with **A
Match (Not) Made in Heaven**
Sarai's Journey: A 2-book biblical fiction series
Tabor Heights: 18-book inspirational small town romance series.
Quarry Hall: 11-book women's fiction/suspense series
For Sale: Wedding Dress. Never Used: inspirational romance
Crooked Creek: Fun Fables About Critters and Kids: Children's short
stories.
Do Yourself a Favor: Tips and Quips on the Writing Life. A book of
writing advice.
To Eternity (and beyond): *Writing Spec Fic Good for Your Soul.* A book
defending speculative fiction.
Killing His Alter-Ego: contemporary romance/suspense, taking place in
fandom.
The Commonwealth Universe: SF series, 25 books and growing
The Hunt: 5-book YA fantasy series
Faxinor: Fantasy series, 4 books and growing
Wildvine: Fantasy series, 14 books when all released
Neighborlee: Humorous fantasy series

Zygradon: 5-book Arthurian fantasy series
AFV Defender: SF adventure series
Young Defenders: Middle Grade SF series, spin-off of *AFV Defender*
Magic to Spare: Fantasy series
Book & Mug Mysteries: cozy mystery series
Quest for the Crescent Moon: fantasy series starting in 2023
Steward's World: fantasy series reboot and expansion
The Enchanted Castle Archives: fantasy series, Liars' Quest, 1st book in the Ye Olde Dragon's Library podcast